LIGHT FROM HEAVEN

LIGHT FROM HEAVEN

By

CHRISTMAS CAROL KAUFFMAN

MOODY PRESS

CHICAGO

Moody Diamond Edition, 1965

ISBN 0-8024-3814-8

29 30 31 32 Printing/LC/Year 92 91 90 89

Moody Press, a ministry of the Moody Bible Institute, is
designed for education, evangelization and edification.
If we may assist you in knowing more about Christ and
the Christian life, please write us without obligation to:
Moody Press, c/o MLM, Chicago, Illinois 60610.

DEDICATION

To every boy
and
To every young man
Who has, or has had,
A Praying Mother
This book is dedicated
with
Christian Love

PREFACE

A number of years ago when my husband held a Sunday afternoon jail service, his group sang for the inmates, "If I Could Only Hear My Mother Pray Again." One young man stepped close to the bars, and said indignantly, "Don't ever sing that song in here again! I never heard my mother pray. Maybe you did, but I didn't. All I've heard from her was cursings. If she'd prayed for me, I might not be here."

About that same time the evangelist who preached on the night Joseph Armstrong, the hero of LIGHT FROM HEAVEN, gave his heart to God, became one of my close friends. After learning about the tragic story of this boy and the tremendous influence his praying mother had on his life, it gripped my soul. Having two boys of my own, I was deeply touched. I immediately asked God to make it possible for this story to be published so that other young men and boys who have, or have the memory of, a mother's prayers will appreciate what a blessing is theirs. No other force on earth is equal to their power.

I was quite taken aback when someone asked if the motive for writing this story was to reveal hypocrites. That would be my last motive. To depict adequately the misery and the soul struggles this boy went through, it was impossible to do other than reveal in part, the character of his father Bennet, who would have ruined his life had not his mother, so characteristic of true Christian motherhood, held him continually before the Lord.

It is surprising the number of letters of confidence which have come to my desk since this story started as a serial in *The Youth's Christian Companion*, telling of other Bennet Armstrongs still living. To every Joseph

—to every Annie—to every Lowell and Virginia, my heart goes out in true concern and sympathy. May this sad but true story somehow give you a little comfort and courage.

It seems fitting that I should here express, in part, my gratitude for the many letters of appreciation for this serial. Two are most priceless. One came from an eleven-year-old boy, the other from a bishop past eighty, but who is still young in heart.

A young mother of five boys who was not a little disappointed when her sixth child was a son, looked wistfully at another young mother holding a small baby girl in her arms.

"So you have another boy?" the second mother asked, a hurtful little tinge of unmeant pity in her voice because the infant was not a girl.

"Yes," answered the first mother, softly, looking lovingly at her own baby, caressing him, and smiling bravely, "But little boys can be sweet, too."

It is my sincere prayer that the sweetness of the life of this boy Joseph will inspire every other boy and young man, who has a praying mother, to cherish those prayers and to love and respect her as Joseph Armstrong respected his mother; that he will choose for himself the kind of wife who will make a praying mother for his children; that he will not quench the voice of the Spirit when He calls; and that he will learn how to live a victorious, winsome, fruitful, beautiful life in spite of any or great difficulties—this alone was my motive for writing LIGHT FROM HEAVEN.

C. C. K.

INTRODUCTION

It is a privilege to introduce LIGHT FROM HEAVEN by Christmas Carol Kauffman, the author of *Lucy Winchester,* which has been so widely read. Indeed, an introduction to this volume is hardly necessary because of the extensive publicizing of this splendid work through the pages of *The Youth's Christian Companion* and its thousands of readers. The fact that many of them have inquired about securing this story in book form is an evidence of the great amount of interest created by the writer.

That truth is stranger than fiction is once again proved by this remarkable story, depicting the events in the lives of characters who actually lived and made their contribution to their homes, their church, and to society in the communities in which they lived. These characters portray devoted spiritual living on the one hand and extremely selfish and self-righteous living on the other. The author brings to the reader in most conspicuous contrast these two types of lives.

There is extant today literature of all kinds and types, but little is found of the true-story kind which teaches forcibly great and noble lessons from life. So-called true stories are either written in popular romance style to gratify the passion of readers, or in the form of biography or narrative. It is very exceptional to find a true story of the noble type, such as is LIGHT FROM HEAVEN, written in romance style! Christmas Carol Kauffman is found to be at her best in this story.

The reader will find the thread of interest running through every chapter that will motivate his reading the book uninterruptedly until finished. The lessons in life to be learned will prove valuable helps in Christian living; and when one has finished reading, he will be satisfied that his time was well spent. I count it a privilege to recommend to the public this book for wholesome Christian reading which is entertaining, as well as profitable.

C. F. YAKE, Editor
The Youth's Christian Companion

CHAPTER I

She loved that baby! Not as some mothers love their first-born, not as many mothers do, but like few, for she had longed and prayed and waited for years for his coming. She had prayed and longed alone, for Bennet had said from the beginning he did *not* like babies. They cost too much for one thing; then they squalled at night when a hard-working man needed his sleep, and you never could take them anywhere without getting lint all over yourself—even if you tried not to get near the blankets. Bennet had watched how it went with Lois and Riley Doane with two babies in three years; one for each of them to lug along to town and to church, and besides them, a funny-looking brown bag (that Lois herself had made out of some upholstering material) full of bottles and other baby things. But before Bennet saw how it went with Lois and Riley he had said emphatically he did not want a baby, let alone two or three. And how Lois and Riley Doane could act so proud of those two youngsters was beyond Bennet Armstrong.

"You can't make me believe in a thousand years," said Bennet to Annie on the way home from church one warm Sunday in July, "that Lois and Riley really wanted those babies."

"I can't believe anything else, Bennet," returned Annie, drawing a long deep breath and looking out over the top of the hedge fence. The sad, hurt look on her young face grew more sorrowful, and her slender hand stroked gently the small Bible on her lap. "I know Lois too well for that. Why, her whole life is wrapped up in those two darling children."

"Dar-ling?" shouted Bennet, and the word was cut in two by a dry cough that wasn't natural.

"They are adorable, Bennet," came Annie's half-suppressed answer. "Everybody else thinks so. The little girl looks just like Lois, and the baby is Riley all over. And I know they were welcome—both of them—and I can hardly keep my eyes off of them, and—"

"I see you were holding the baby in your class."

"Well?"

"Well, could you hold that baby and listen to your teacher too?"

"Certainly." Annie almost whispered her answer. Her long, dark lashes swept her soft cheeks, and her lower lip quivered.

"And I suppose your best dress is covered with blanket fuzz."

"It will brush off."

They drove on past the old Ballington place where Jessica had jumped into the well one night and ended it all.

"You know what she did," reminded Bennet, not for the first time.

Poor little Jessica Ballington hadn't jumped into the well because she had had three little ones who still couldn't talk plain and two others in school. That wasn't the reason, but what was the use for Annie to refute Bennet's arguments. She had tried it a time or two, and it never changed him. His concluding remarks had always been, "I'll bet anything those five children drove Erie crazy, and she saw herself going that way too, so she did it."

So Annie Armstrong just looked with feeling at the well as they drove past, and said nothing. He turned and looked down over her with an expression of simple severity, and although Annie did not look up, she felt his glance, and her body trembled. He noticed it and he blinked his large blue eyes twice before he spoke.

"You think it will brush off?" he asked.

"Of course." She answered as in a dream.

"Well, Lois and Riley could have their new hen house built and paid for if it hadn't been for those babies."

Annie didn't answer. Bennet waited. They drove past the Tiffney place, where two knee-panted boys were quarreling over a rope swing, and another was sicking the dog on the cat which reached the acorn tree just in time.

"Look at those Tiffney youngsters." This Bennet said, pointing them out with his large Roman nose. "Maybe some would say, or did say, they were adorable, or darling babies at one time, but they don't act adorable now. Their father should put them to work."

"But this is Sunday, Bennet."

"Sunday is right, and they are desecrating it by such conduct right in the front yard. I presume Mrs. Tiffney is busy in the house rocking little Sally Mae, or whatever her name is, to sleep so she can get the dinner in peace, and the rest of the children run wild. Children are expensive and make lots of bother, and they are not worth it any way you figure."

"Is that what your mother said about you?"

Bennet was sure it was coming. Annie had asked him that same question once before—months before. It had made him quite angry that time. With indignation that made his blue eyes fiery, he reached for the whip and gave the horse a stinging crack across her back.

*   *   *

Annie Stokes Armstrong loved that baby like few babies have been loved. Bennet's ill-feeling and displeasure over the child's birth amounted to actual resentment. He told Annie to name him. He wasted no time in bending over his crib or fondling him evenings after supper.

J. Bennet Armstrong was a father at twenty-three, but he was not proud of the fact. He looked in the green-framed mirror hanging beside the kitchen door and combed his thick black hair carefully. He was not a bad-looking young man. In fact, Annie Stokes had been envied by a dozen pretty girls when she announced her engagement to the handsome, ambitious son of Grant Armstrong, who promised each of his five children a thousand dollars and a team of horses when they got married. Just why Bennet chose Annie Stokes several girls never could figure out, namely Becky Cornelius and Adelaide Heathman. Both thought they were more strikingly beautiful than plain, modest Annie Stokes, although no one could actually find fault with Annie. She did have a pretty face. Everyone agreed to that. She came from a good family, and her father was a bishop over a large congregation in Wickville. Although he was not wealthy in comparison to some of his parishioners, he was far from being a poor man. J. Bennet Armstrong married well, but some said Annie wasn't built to be a farmer's wife. Her slender form measured scarcely over five feet, and her delicate fine features seemed to demand not too hard a life. Annie was a refined, cultured girl, devoted to her family and her father's church. Her loyalty was wholehearted and pure, and Bennet saw all this. He saw too that even though Annie Stokes wasn't a robust sturdy-looking girl like Sara Botts, who could carry two pails of milk up a steep hill from the barn and shock wheat as fast as any man, she was nimble and quick, and more than that, she was not extravagant. That appealed to Bennet almost as much, if not equally as much, as Annie's sweet face. Her soft hair and eyes were both brown.

*   *   *

The moment she looked down into his tiny face she called him Joseph.

"At last I have you," she whispered, touching his soft, soft cheek with her finger tips. "I want you even though your father does not. You will soon be so sweet and dear, he can't help loving you like I do. Joseph, oh, you dear little Joseph," and Annie Armstrong buried her face in her arm. The love that the young mother lavished on her little one was what Bennet called unreasonable.

"I believe you love that baby more than you do me," he remarked with a note of irritability in his voice one evening. "I expect supper to be ready when I come in. I've had to wait the last three nights."

"I know it, Bennet, and I'm sorry," sighed Annie, turning the potatoes, "but Joseph has a fever again, and—"

"That's it; babies get sick so easy. Next thing it will be a doctor bill."

Annie shuddered. She had fully intended on suggesting to Bennet at the supper table that they take him to town in the morning. There were at least twelve dozen eggs to take to market, and the rent was paid in advance —and—but—moreover—well—Annie was stuck! When Riley's baby got sick they took him to Dr. Lindquist and he knew exactly what to prescribe, and the baby was definitely better in ten hours. Bennet did not look worried in the least. He did not rush to the bedroom or ask any questions like most fathers would. Instead he fretted during the supper because one of the cows acted sick, and Michael Hunter, who had borrowed his crosscut saw, had not returned it as he had promised to do.

* * *

Little Joseph got no better. As the days went on, several hard inflamed spots appeared on his stomach, and by morning there were similar spots on his little arms, his back, and face.

"Bennet," cried Annie one evening while hot tears streamed down both cheeks. She walked toward her husband with the suffering baby on a pillow, his tiny helpless form a pitiful picture of misery and suffering. "Please have Dr. Lindquist come out to see this baby. These spots seem to have pus in them, and I've counted over forty places. It's about to get me down."

"Annie." He looked at her for a long moment and without another word put on his hat and went to the barn. In a short time she heard the horse going down the road on a trot.

He came that night, Dr. Hudson Lindquist, the noted physician. "Why didn't you call me sooner?"

Annie brushed away her tears. She couldn't answer with Bennet right there.

"Every one of those spots will have to be lanced."

"Oh!" Annie covered her face with both hands and turned away.

"There's nothing else to do now, Mrs. Armstrong," he said in a kind deep voice. He opened his satchel with his big hands and pulled out a knife. It was sharp on the end.

"You'll have to hold him for me, J. B.," said the doctor without looking up at Bennet. "Over here by the light, I mean."

Annie sank into a chair and with each feeble outcry from her little son, she thought her own heart would stop beating altogether.

Dr. Lindquist came back in several days and lanced new eruptions, and repeated the operation on most of the old ones. The little one was so weak he could scarcely cry, but a whine that was ghastly pitiful escaped his parched lips now and then.

"I'm sorry," said the doctor, walking slowly toward the door. He hesitated when he looked again at Annie's troubled face, "but—you surely realize," he added, "that your child can't possibly live many hours."

CHAPTER II

For nearly two weeks Annie had lived in almost constant fear that her little son could never get well. She had watched him growing weaker every day, and yet her fear was always accompanied by the hope that Doctor Lindquist could be used of God in some way to diagnose this strange disease and know a remedy. She prayed with almost every breath she drew that his little life would be spared.

Annie Stokes Armstrong had been confident that the love and affection Bennet displayed to her before and on their wedding day was of the fadeless kind. But after less than sixty days of married life she knew what it was to be craving tender words and a husband's love and fellowship. Now after these years she found her only satisfying comfort in caressing her little one. Though he was not old enough yet to talk, he definitely recognized her with his gentle blue eyes that seemed to speak, and she could tell in more ways than one that he loved her.

Annie wanted to be loved, and many people did love her. All the neighbors loved Annie Armstrong. She had the love and respect of every one in the church where she attended. More than one unmarried woman her age envied the pretty wife of J. Bennet Armstrong, the ambitious young farmer who was bound to get ahead financially. Despite all this, Annie wanted the love of some one her very own, that some one whose name was Bennet. Little did her neighbors and friends realize the aching void in her young heart. Annie would die before she'd tell anyone she had been disappointed. But mental suffering will eat a person's life away unless he can confide to a human being. So Annie whispered it to her tiny son now and then when she held him close, and she found genuine comfort in imagining he answered back, "Yes, Mother, we'll be pals as long as we live."

And now! What was this terrible affliction—these awful sores on his little body? Why must he suffer so? Could it be (and Annie shuddered at the thought of it), could it be that it was because his father didn't want him? Annie had asked God in tears again and again, but no answer was given.

Little Joseph lay on his pillow on the kitchen table, and the lamp on the shelf above him flickered. Annie looked at Bennet and he looked at her. Neither spoke. She didn't because she couldn't, but she wondered why he didn't. Annie felt numb and cold. The silence was awful. Wasn't he going to cry? Wasn't he going to come across the room and take her in his arms and say something? Wasn't he even going to look sad, or ashamed, or—

Bennet cleared his throat, put on his cap, and left the house. Annie stood where she was until she saw the lantern moving toward the barn; then she took the baby into the bedroom and closed the door behind her. For some reason she did not burst into tears, but while a deep groan escaped her lips, she laid the pillow on the bed and fell on both knees beside him. Placing one hand on his hot little head she prayed in an audible voice, "Dear Lord in Heaven,"—she felt his uneven breathing on her forehead—"I thought I could not give him up—I love him so, but You know best. I told You long before he was born that if You gave me a child I would give him back to You, and I meant it. I still mean it. I long to see this child grow up to love and serve You, but if You want to take him now, I won't insist that he stay here, even though I feel I need him. If I have done wrong in asking for him when Bennet didn't want him, please forgive me—O God." The child made a helpless, pitiful cry, and Annie's eyes filled with sudden tears. "Oh, you poor, poor child! God have mercy on him. Take him tonight if you want to, Lord; I think I can't stand it to see him suffer any longer. I want to be willing to give him up, and if I know my own heart I am willing, Lord, if You'll grant me just one request." Annie held her breath and waited. She was thinking fast. She remembered how one morning, at least eight months before, her baby had laughed out loud for the first time. She had just finished giving him a bath, and his little plump body smelled of talcum power. The shirt which at first was much too big was now fitting him much better. It crossed in front and was pinned in the back. Just when she turned him over, Joseph looked up and laughed out loud. Annie thought she had never heard anything so sweet in her life. She marked it down on a little piece of paper that afternoon and tucked it away in the bottom of her handkerchief box. "Lord Jesus," cried Annie with tears now streaming down both cheeks, "I'll give him up, but please, oh, please, dear Lord, let me hear him laugh just once more. It's been weeks and weeks since he's even smiled at me, and I fear now he's too near gone even to recognize me again. Maybe I shouldn't ask it, but, dear Jesus, it would make me so happy; I'd never forget it if I could hear my baby laugh once more."

The blind at the south window was up, and the light from the moon shone in across the bed. Annie heard Bennet turn the knob on the kitchen door, and she got up from her knees. The baby stretched and put both hands up above his head. "Are—you—dying, darling!" whispered Annie, bending over his little form. She pulled back the white blanket and caught one hand in hers. He opened both eyes and looked up at his mother—the muscles in his face relaxed, his lips parted until she saw his eight tiny teeth, and he laughed out loud twice. He drew one long breath and fell into a peaceful sleep.

Awe struck Annie to her heart's depths. She had prayed and asked, but she was overcome with this sudden answer. The awe that came over her was not a fear or dread of God Almighty, but a reverence and solemn wonder, as though God Himself had stepped into the room.

Annie opened the door. Bennet was hanging the lantern on the lantern's hook where he always hung it.

"This chimney needs to be washed, Annie," he said. Without turning around, he saw her in the mirror.

"All right," she answered.

He could see her teary eyes and wasn't surprised. Annie was too emotional, he thought. He'd much rather see her brace up and take it. This ought to teach her a lesson to never beg for another baby. And it would be better to bury him now than feed and clothe him for five or ten years, then bury him just about the time he could be handling a team and helping to milk.

"Aren't you about ready to go to bed?" he asked, sitting on the first chair he came to and untying his one shoe.

"Yes." Annie's voice sounded like an echo in a large cave.

"I suppose he's sleeping," he added. Bennet meant he hoped so. He'd rather talk about lantern chimneys, or the woodpile, or the corn, or anything else than Joseph. That any person so small and helpless should cause so much trouble and anxiety, and bring forth so many tears seemed absurd to Bennet and almost disgusting.

"Yes, he's sleeping," answered Annie strangely, for she was still overwhelmed with that impressive baby laugh a few moments before.

"Thank God," Bennet said.

"Yes, thank God," added Annie sweetly. They agreed with their lips, yet how utterly different were their hearts' thanks to God.

In the morning Joseph was decidedly better. His temperature was normal on through the evening, and for the first time in weeks there was no new appearance whatever of any eruptions on his body. In fact, in less than twenty-four hours several spots showed definite signs of healing.

Annie was so happy that for days she lived as in a dream. Each time she looked at her baby he was better, brighter, stronger.

"Well," said Bennet one evening, "that Dr. Lindquist doesn't know what he's talking about or he just talked like he did so we'd think he's a wonderful doctor."

"I think, Bennet," came Annie's gentle voice as she tied the baby in the high chair with a white towel, "that the Lord touched his body."

"The Lord?" Bennet looked at Annie and combed and combed his black hair.

"How could it have been anything else, Bennet? I prayed. Didn't you?"

The comb in Bennet's hand fell to the floor, and Joseph looked quickly in that direction and laughed. He might have thought his father dropped it on purpose to make him laugh.

J. Bennet Armstrong went to church every Sunday, not only in the morning but in the evening whenever there were services. Since Joseph came, Annie had not been to church often, so Bennet went by horse. It saved the buggy and the harness as well. Most people judged Bennet's Christian character by his faithful church attendance. He was never late. He appeared to be a righteous, God-fearing young man, and the elders of the church took for granted that he read his Bible as faithfully as he attended church, and that he also conducted daily worship in the home long before the family numbered three. He joined heartily in the song service and could offer a commendable prayer when called upon. How much he prayed in private no one knew, not even his wife. He never knelt beside her at night, and at meal-time he bowed his head in a moment of silence. Annie often wondered if Bennet prayed for little Joseph. In view of the fact that he wasn't wanted, how would he pray? The child's serious and prolonged illness had not seemed to develop any degree of fondness in him. He barely returned the smile the little one gave him, and yet the child looked up and smiled again.

Little Joseph got well enough that Annie could take him to church.

"What a sweet little boy you have," cooed plump Mrs. Irons, while a dozen other women clustered around her. "What beautiful eyes—such expression in them—and how fair his skin is after such a time as he had. Poor little dear, how proud his father must be of him," and she patted him under the chin. Annie only smiled and said, "The Lord has been so good to us, I can't thank Him enough."

"He's not walking yet?"

"Not yet," answered Annie.

And Joseph didn't walk until he was two. Although he was an exceptionally brilliant child, his early sickness had retarded his walking.

When Joseph was three his Grandfather Armstrong died. That meant that his father inherited $27,000.

"I'm going to buy a farm, Annie."

"What farm?"

"The one I've had my eye on," and Bennet made a significant wink with his large blue eyes.

CHAPTER III

Michael Hunter straightened up from the cabbage plants over which he had been bending and pulled out a large bandanna handkerchief that was hanging halfway out of his right hip overalls pocket. He wiped his face and neck, and spoke to the man on the wagon seat.

"Armstrong," he called out in a high-pitched feminine voice that was characteristic only of Michael Hunter.

Bennet pulled on the reins, but all the while hoped sincerely Michael didn't want to borrow his crosscut saw again.

"Movin', eh?"

Bennet nodded; a smile of peculiar satisfaction played around his stern lips.

"I hear ye bought the DeVenter place." Michael Hunter walked toward the picket fence and leaned on his hoe handle.

"Yes."

"Pretty big place fer a young feller like you to handle, ain't it?"

"I guess not," answered Bennet, chagrin in his answer. "I've got me a hired man."

"A hired man? Who?"

"Well, it's Earnie Eloy."

"Do tell. Well, he's a worker, I hear," squeaked Michael Hunter, and Bennet was certain it was jealousy that made Michael's voice squeak so funny that time. Bennet wanted to laugh.

"I couldn't do it alone," said Bennet, telling his horses to "ged-ep."

"Spec not," agreed Michael, tilting his hat back past his bald spot and scratching his head. "An yer wife'll need a hired girl too in that eight-room house."

"Big place," he said, half under his breath. "Nice place." This he said three-fourths under his breath.

Bennet told the horses to "ged-ep" harder and they did. Annie and little Joseph were on the wagon seat beside him. Annie looked back over the load of furniture and saw Michael Hunter walking slowly back to his cabbage plants. She looked back at him with a kindly expression on her sweet face which had a touch of sadness on it. She hadn't seen the place yet. Mr. Hunter probably was right when he said she may need a hired girl to help keep an eight-room house clean. Bennet had said the rooms were large. There were but Bennet, and she, and little Joseph who still slept in their room in his iron baby bed. He was small for his age. Annie looked back kindly to that funny-voiced Michael Hunter, but she knew she'd never be permitted to have a hired girl. It would cost too much. Bennet Armstrong was as close with figures as any man in the Deep River valley. Some men get that way after several sad experiences of financial loss, but Bennet had been that way from his wedding day. The sum he fell heir to at the age of twenty-six was enough to buy the hundred-acre DeVenter place and pay his hired man thirty-five years in advance if he wanted to. Of course Bennet didn't want to. He would buy some new implements, some hogs, some good horses, or perhaps the small Dowdy place down the road a mile. He could invest in a sawmill, a mint distillery, a cheese factory, or a cannery. Bennet had all kinds of ideas, but he kept them to himself. Annie saw him scratching figures on paper many times, but she knew not why or for what.

Annie caught her breath at the largeness of the house. There were so many windows! It was yellow. That was her first impression. It was the same shade of yellow as the old Stokes home in Wickville. That gave her a sort of homey, friendly feeling at once. A cement walk cut in two the beautiful lawn from the iron gate to the front porch steps. Lilac bushes in early bud were clustered around a large bay window to the south. As they followed the bend in the road Annie could see another longer cement walk stretching from the side gate to the low back porch. Everything from the outside showed careful upkeep and pride.

"Why did the DeVenters sell this nice place, Bennet?" asked Annie looking up wistfully into his ruddy face.

"Well, DeVenter's youngest son got married and old Reuben is too old to handle this alone. He wants to retire and live in the city now."

"And you'll do that too some day when we're old?"

Bennet laughed as he jumped from the wagon. Annie didn't think it was a happy laugh exactly. Maybe she shouldn't have asked such a question. It usually seemed that Bennet resented her questions, such questions at least. But the kind he thought a wife should ask were, "How shall I spend this dime, Bennet?" or, "What more can I do, Bennet, to help you outside?" or "Bennet, shall I close up the front room to save fuel?"

Having both south and west windows, the large kitchen and dining-room combined was a most delightful and pleasant room. The living room faced east and the bedroom north. The wallpaper was neither faded nor soiled in any of the downstairs rooms. The woodwork was stained oak.

"Bennet," said Annie, thoughtfully, "our furniture won't nearly fill this house."

"Of course not," he answered curtly. "Who thought it would? There are stoves in town, and I'd hate for anyone to think I was so silly as to buy an eight-room house and live in it for years before I could furnish it. I'm going to buy me a roll-top desk for one thing, and a safe, and a new bookcase, one of those sectional ones, maybe two, and I'll need a new lawn mower."

"I'd love to have a sewing machine," said Annie longingly.

"Oh, yeh."

"I can't make little boy's pants and coats very nice by hand, Bennet."

He seemed not to hear.

"Here comes Earnie Eloy now." Bennet saw him through the south bay window. "He's on time, too," he added, looking at his gold watch. "I told him to be here by ten. We'll begin unloading at once. And Annie, you go on upstairs and pick out the smallest room and that will be his. He's come now to stay."

Earnie Eloy, the hired man, was a tall, lanky, dark-complexioned man with a long black mustache. He came in a two-wheeled wooden cart drawn by a white horse. In the cart was an old-fashioned round-topped trunk covered with varnished tin or sheet metal. He tied his horse to the fence and met Bennet half-way up the walk.

"Don't tie your horse to the fence, Earnie," were Bennet's first words. He looked at the man nineteen years his senior with a commanding superior expression, and his voice fitted his look. "Over there is a hitching post." He pointed to the right.

"I didn't notice it, sir," answered the man, looking back over his left shoulder.

"Change it," said Bennet, somewhat like an officer in charge of an army.

Earnie Eloy changed it.

There were four rooms upstairs. If one was smaller than the other three, Annie could hardly tell without a yardstick, but she finally decided the north room to the east would be the one for the hired man.

She didn't like his black mustache. That and his high leather boots made her think of a picture she had seen once of a criminal. And this is the man Bennet hired to work for him—and he'd stay in their upstairs? Annie shivered. Where did Bennet meet this Earnie Eloy and how much would he pay him for . . . ?

They were at the foot of the stairs now—both men carrying the old-fashioned trunk. "Which is the room, Annie?" called Bennet. He was at the bottom end and Earnie was on the third step already.

"Come up and I'll show you."

Joseph clung to his mother's dress and cried as though something had frightened him.

"What is it, sweetheart?" Annie stroked his pretty little head.

"I—I," he sobbed in her dress, "I don't like that—man."

"Sh," whispered his mother patting his cheek, "Don't let Pa see you crying."

"Do you like him, Mama?"

"Sh," she whispered, bending over him, "I don't know yet."

The trunk was heavy. "Whew," Bennet whistled and ran his hands back through his thick, black hair. "What on earth have you got in there?"

The man pulled a key out of his pocket and unlocked the trunk. "Am I obliged to show you what's in here?" he asked, hesitating a little. One large hand rested on the curved lid.

"Well," answered Bennet, placing a hand on each hip and standing up very straight, "guess I've got a right to see what comes under my roof, don't I?"

"Reckon so." Earnie Eloy wet his lips carefully, and brushed his mustache, then he lifted the lid of the trunk slowly.

Annie's face turned white, and her arm around Joseph tightened. There were knives of different kinds and sizes; guns, several of them; pistols; and a revolver in a leather belt; shells and boxes of various descriptions. Some had locks on them.

Bennet's eyes opened wider and his lower jaw dropped suddenly. "What's the idea of all that?"

"Oh," laughed Earnie Eloy, "it's just my hobby."

"Hobby?"

"That's all."

"You'll keep it locked when you're out of this room?"

"Bet your boots," answered Earnie, looking at Joseph standing wide-eyed beside his mother.

"And what's in the bottom?"

Bennet tried to make his voice sound commanding, and he could too.

"You mean under this here tray?"

"Yes,"

"Why, my clothes." Earnie Eloy closed the trunk and locked it.

"Let's get to work now." Bennet looked at his watch again. "Annie, we'll set up the cookstove as soon as we can, then you'd better start the dinner a while."

"Where is the kindling?" she asked.

"Joseph, you come out and carry some in."

"Oh, Bennet!" objected Annie with compassion for her son; "he's so little to work like that. I'll carry it in."

"Too little, nothin'," snapped Bennet impatiently. "Don't talk like that in front of him again. He's my son, and he's going to learn to work, and he might as well begin today. Come on out to the wagon, Joseph. Maybe if I teach you to work, you won't be so puny."

CHAPTER IV

Joseph fell asleep at the dinner table. He fell asleep holding a piece of butter bread in one hand. Although he was a frail child and small for his age, he was not in the habit of beginning his afternoon nap at the table, but today dinner was a little later than usual, and Joseph was at the point of exhaustion by the time he had half filled the woodbox. Joseph was only three, and he could not carry more than three sticks of wood at a time, sticks about the size of his mother's forearm. Once Joseph sat down on the bottom porch step to rest, and his father said with an austere voice as he bent over him and twisted the little boy's ear, "You'd better get busy here or I'll send for old Fonzo to come and get you."

Joseph looked up in surprise and stared at his father in dumb amazement.

"You don't know who I mean, do you?" demanded his father sternly.

Joseph shook his head.

"Well, he's a big black nigger who lives on the other side of that hill over yonder, and he drives Squire Mc-Cracken's six-horse team, and if I tell him to he'll come over here and get you," and Bennet Armstrong rolled his big blue eyes over to yonder hill and back.

Terrible terror struck Joseph to his heart. Only once had he seen a black-faced man, and that was when he was in town with his parents. Like any normal child he had asked his mother many questions about him and she had tried her best to put his puzzled heart at rest. She had told him (while Bennet was in the harness shop) that God loved the black-skinned people as well as the white, and that he should not be afraid of that man, and that it wasn't nice to call such people "niggers" as some folks

did. And now his own father knew a big black man who
was a nigger and came to get little boys who didn't work!

Sickening terror sent a tremor through Joseph's little
body. He tried to get up, and it seemed his pants' seat
was glued to the porch. Roughly his father helped him
up and half pushed him down the two steps, and to one
side, to make way for Earnie Eloy who was coming with
a rocking chair. Annie was busy peeling potatoes and did
not hear what Bennet had said, for he had closed the
door as he went out.

"Mama," Joseph dropped the wood in the box beside
the stove, and Annie saw tears quivering in both eyes
when he looked up. "Mama," and he looked anxiously
toward the door, "will Zo-zo come get me?"

"What?"

"Zo-zo get me?"

"What?" asked his mother the second time.

Just then Bennet came through the door with a box
full of dishes and skillets.

"Zo-zo," repeated his mother. "What are you talking
about?"

"Pa said—if I—didn't," his childish voice quivered.

Bennet put the box on the floor, and turning, laughed
banteringly down into Joseph's face.

"And don't call me Pa any more either," he said
harshly. "Call me Father. Do you hear that, Annie?
I want you to teach that boy to call me Father. Just
because you called your father Pa isn't saying that's
what I'll be called."

"Yes, Bennet," answered Annie somewhat stunned.

Joseph ran to his mother and burying his face in her
blue apron clung to her tenaciously. "Don't—don't let
him come an' get me, Mama," he sobbed.

"Joseph, sweetheart, what's wrong? Nothing is going

to get my little boy. Why, your heart is simply pounding.
What has Pa—Father—been telling you?"

"Zo-zo—big—black—"

"No. Surely not, Joseph. I don't know anything black
that would get you. Did he say a dog?"

"No," cried Joseph in fresh terror, "a—a nigger
man."

"No!"

Annie was wounded and ashamed of Bennet Armstrong. She knew he did not want Joseph; she knew he
had very little affection for him, but she hardly thought
he'd stoop to threatening his son by any such a story.
She knew of no one by the name of Zo-zo, but there was a
Negro by the name of Fonzo Bullet who drove a six-
horse team for Squire McCracken. He was well known
by everyone within a radius of ten miles from the Mc-
Cracken mansion, but he was known only as a kind-
hearted, obedient servant who was once a slave to the
Squire's father.

"Did your father say Fonzo, Joseph?" Annie Armstrong stroked the little one's head tenderly. The potato
water ran down both sides of the kettle, and she reached
over and lifted the lid. "I'm going to ask him what he
said," and there was consternation in her voice.

Annie kissed him twice on the forehead when she laid
him on the settee. The bed wasn't made up yet.

*   *   *

Bennet was sitting at his desk, his open Bible and
Sunday-school book before him. He was studying the
Sunday-school lesson, which he did religiously every Saturday night. He did not study for the spiritual help he
felt he needed or craved, but it would have been too hard
on his pride to be asked a question he could not answer.
In fact, Bennet Armstrong took great satisfaction in

being able to answer a question no other man in the class could. The teacher of the younger married men's class was Eli Mattson, a talented retired schoolmaster and real Bible student of his day. He enjoyed teaching this class of young men, most of whom were fathers, and he banked on at least two men in his class coming with well-studied lessons. The discussion usually ended somewhat like a spelldown toward the close of the class period, and the two still answering or discussing were Scudder Madox and Bennet Armstrong. Almost invariably Bennet had the last word. Eli Mattson thought he was wonderful. The way Bennet could turn to Scriptures and apply them to the lesson showed remarkable skill, not only skill but spiritual interest. Bennet might make a preacher some day. And he could sing a splendid bass.

Bennet was studying his lesson, and Joseph was playing on the floor with the cat just inside the kitchen door.

"Don't be so noisy," called his father out of the right corner of his mouth. He did not take his eyes off his Bible. In a short while Joseph forgot himself. This time Bennet stood up and stamped his foot on the floor until the oil lamp on the desk shook and the flame flickered.

"You bad, disobedient boy, shall I have old Fonzo Bullet come and get you tonight? He's got a big horse whip on his wagon."

"Come to me, Joseph dear," called his mother from the bedroom. "Let the kitty go and come to Mother at once."

Heavy footsteps were heard on the stairway, and Earnie Eloy appeared at the door. He held a key in his one hand.

"I have something to tell you, Mr. Armstrong," he said with an important air, brushing his black mustache.

"What is it?" asked Bennet, the palm of his left hand resting on his open Bible.

"Someone has been into my trunk."

"Someone has, you say? And how do you know?"

"Because my knives have been moved. I can tell because I always keep them just exactly in a certain place."

"I thought you said you keep your trunk locked whenever you are not in your room."

"I do, but this once I forgot it."

"Well, and who do you think that someone was?"

"I think it was no one but that little boy of yours," answered Earnie, looking toward the bedroom door through which he had seen Joseph disappear.

"Joseph," called Bennet roughly, "come here at once."

Both mother and son appeared in the living room. Annie held Joseph by one hand, her Sunday-school help in the other, for she too had been reading her lesson conscientiously and in true Christian sincerity.

"Did you open Mr. Eloy's trunk, Joseph?" he demanded.

Joseph nodded.

"Why did you do it?"

Silence filled the room. Joseph's heart came up into his throat, and he trembled from head to foot.

"Answer me," commanded Bennet gruffly, taking a step toward him and glaring at him fiercely. "Don't act like a baby. If you were meddling in that trunk you ought to know why. Answer me, I tell you."

Tears streamed down Joseph's pale cheeks, and brokenly he answered thus, "I—I—don't know, Pa."

"Yes, you do, and I told you to call me Father. Did you pick up a knife?"

Joseph nodded. His mother put her arm around his shoulder and her hand trembled. She could feel his little body shaking.

"More than one?"

Joseph nodded.

"Can't you talk?"

Joseph shook his head. His tongue was paralyzed with fright. There stood his frenzied father, and there stood Earnie Eloy looking down at him under those shaggy eyebrows. He seemed to be thoroughly enjoying the whole thing.

"Shall I whip him, Earnie?" asked Bennet.

"I think that's what he needs, Mr. Armstrong. Spare the rod and spoil the child is a good old saying, and I believe in it."

Bennet stalked to the bedroom and returned with his leather belt. Joseph almost danced now with fear and dread.

"Oh, Pa, Oh, Pa — I — I mean Father, Oh, I'll never—"

Bennet jerked his son away from Annie and gave him six cracks across his back and legs.

"Bennet," cried Annie, wringing her hands. Tears blinded her eyes. "Bennet, have mercy! He's so little and didn't know any better—Oh, Bennet!" She wanted to scream. Annie would have fainted if Bennet would have given that child another crack. The whole thing seemed cruel and unjust. Joseph was only three years and nine months old now, but she was sure he'd never forget this as long as he lived, for he was a very precocious child and already knew his father only as a person to be feared and obeyed. His mother too seemed often to fear him, so they had something in common.

"When I'm correcting this child I want you to keep still," said Bennet, dropping the belt and turning to his wife. "He's old enough to know he's to stay out of other people's property, and the best way to teach him this is to give him something he'll remember. Now go to your mother, Joseph, and stop that crying immediately. Do you hear? And go straight to bed where a boy your age belongs at this time of night. And Annie, let me tell you something." The child was clinging to her arm and gasping between broken sobs. "I think it's your duty as a mother to keep that boy downstairs with you. He has no business prowling around upstairs."

Annie could have explained that Joseph had been with her upstairs that afternoon while she was washing windows, and that he had walked through all the rooms by her permission, but what was the use. Bennet was angry to the point of near frenzy, and she had concluded once before that it was almost a disease with him, a disease of the mind, and any agitation of the slightest kind only made him more excited. True enough, she should have called Joseph when he stayed in Earnie Eloy's room so long, but what boy wouldn't have wanted to peek in that strange-looking trunk?

The next morning while Bennet was sitting in the Sunday-school class helping, calmly and as one with experience, to discuss "The Beauties and Benefits of the Temperate Life," Annie was at home holding Joseph on her lap, and she was telling him something. He sat with open eyes and mouth.

CHAPTER V

The yellow cat was sitting in the sun between two blooming begonia plants on the wide window sill in the living room. The big bay window made possible a full view of the spacious lawn between the front porch and the gate. From the rocking chair on which Annie was sitting she could see quite a distance down the road in the direction toward the church where she had been a member for six years, and Bennet a little longer, for he had been received with a class of applicants a month or two before their marriage. Joseph's hand was resting on her left shoulder and one little hand held that part of her apron that fitted up over her right shoulder. Every now and then as she talked, her head went over and her warm cheek touched his hand. His wide open eyes looked through the window at nothing in particular.

"Then what, Mama?" Joseph came back to earth and saw the cat again.

"That's all of that story, dear. You like stories. don't you?"

Joseph nodded.

"I'm so glad you do. It helps to make me happy when I can make you happy. I hope next Sunday we will both feel like going along to Sunday school. You like to go to Sunday school, don't you?"

Joseph nodded.

"And what is your teacher's name? Can you say it?"

"Lottie."

"That's right. Lottie Woods. She's a nice teacher, isn't she? Yes, and she loves little children like you."

"An'—an' Father don't?" Joseph's voice held the hurt and disappointment. His left hand tightened on his mother's apron strap.

"Well, Joseph," patted his mother. She rocked gently and looked out the bay window. "I love you. Some things are hard to understand now, but maybe someday we will. You are 'most too little to understand what I'm going to tell you, but I'll tell it anyway. I was very, very lonesome for a long time after I got on the train and came way out here with your father."

"Train?" Joseph sat up and looked into his mother's face. "Choo choo train?"

"You know what a train is, don't you?"

"In town?" He pointed down the road.

"That's right, you've seen a train several times. Well, long ago, almost seven years ago, I said good-by to my mother and father and came way out here with your father to a country I had never seen before."

"Good-by?"

"Yes, we kissed each other good-by, and I got on the train with your father, and—"

"And me too?"

"No, not you."

"Why not, Mama?"

"Well, dear, you weren't born yet."

"Where—was I?"

"You were still up in Heaven."

"Up there? Way up there, Mama?" Joseph pointed and looked up.

"Yes, sweetheart, I'm sure you were up in Heaven yet. And I came way out here and didn't know anyone. But all the people in the church were nice and friendly to me. We were invited out often for Sunday dinner, but whenever we came home I was so lonesome I'd feed the chickens and the cat, and help milk the cows, but I was very lonesome because I had no little boy like you."

"What did you do, Mama? Did you cry for me to come?"

"Yes, dear, I often had to cry."

"Like we did last night when Pa—Father whipped me?"

"Call him Father, dear. Let's not say Pa any more. Maybe he will be kinder if you call him Father. No, dear, not like we did last night, but real softly all to myself at night when nobody knew it; I often had to cry because I wanted you very much."

"What did you do? I'd-a come if you would-a called me."

"Well, I told Jesus all about it, how lonely I was and I wanted someone to talk to, for Father never had much to say. He was always busy working or reading, so I would talk to God when I fed the chickens and worked in the garden, and I prayed every night down on my knees beside the bed like we do together. We know how to pray, don't we?"

Joseph nodded. "Then what?"

"Well, one day Jesus sent you to me and you were the dearest, sweetest little baby with a cute, tiny, pink nose, and I was so happy I felt like singing a song."

"Did you?"

"Not that day, dear, because you slept a lot, so I just let you rest, but I sang sometimes when I rocked you on my lap."

"Like this?" and Joseph laid his head again on his mother's shoulder.

"Yes, like this, only I had a nice warm blanket around you and little blue booties on your feet that I made myself, and one day when you were just able to be propped up with pillows before you were big enough to walk, well—one day I got awful sick. I couldn't get up and get the breakfast that day, so your father got a neighbor girl to come here to do the work."

"Who?"

"Well, her name was Eola Griggs. You'll never remember her name and I wouldn't want you to. This Eola was busy in the kitchen ironing your father's Sunday shirt, when you took a crying spell and I was too sick to go to you, so she took you to the kitchen with her. She tried this and that and she could not comfort you. You just cried and cried, and of course that worried me, and she couldn't get her work done. Your father came in and he didn't like it because you were keeping Eola from her work, so he told her to tie you in that little rocking chair over there." She pointed to it in the corner of the room.

"Did he?"

"When your father went outside again, Eola tied you in the rocking chair, but you cried all the harder. I think you were afraid of her, for you had never seen her before, and you couldn't understand why I didn't come and get you. All at once I heard a strange noise in the kitchen."

"What?" Joseph sat up straight.

"I couldn't imagine what it was. I thought the ironing board fell down, and I heard you cry as if you had been terribly frightened."

"Was I?"

"You must have been. In just a little while the girl brought you into the bedroom and put you into your little bed. You sobbed a while and then fell asleep, and you slept all forenoon, but you made such a strange noise in your throat, and every now and then you would cry out in your sleep. When your father came in I told him about it, but he didn't think it was anything to worry about. When you woke up I told Eola to fix your bottle, and she did, but you didn't want it. Then I asked her what that strange noise was in the kitchen. 'What noise?' she said. 'Well,' I said, 'it sounded as if the ironing board fell down.' 'Oh, no,' she said, 'that was the baby. He bent forward too far and the rocking chair tipped forward.' 'Did it hurt the baby?' I asked. 'I guess not,' she said. 'Bring him over here to me,' I said, so she did, and right away saw that your little face was all black and blue right here," and she put her fingers on the spot. "I took hold of your little chin like this, and it felt funny and loose and you flinched when I did it. I believed right then that your little jaw was broken. I told Eola so, but she said 'Surely not. He didn't fall that hard.' 'What did he strike when he fell?' I asked. 'I don't know,' she said 'maybe it was the stove, and maybe it wasn't for it happened so quick when I wasn't looking.' Well, anyway you acted as if something hurt you, and you wouldn't take your bottle for three days. I told your father to call the doctor, but he thought it wasn't necessary, so there I lay and there you lay. I was very glad when I could get up and do my work again and take care of you, for you cried every time Eola came near you. When I got up and took you in my arms to the window, I opened your mouth and looked in it, and there was pus in there."

"What's that?"

"That means there was infection in your mouth, Joseph. I took you into the bedroom and prayed to Jesus that He would heal you and take that pus away, and heal your broken jaw."

"Did He?"

"Joseph, that's what I want to tell you. You have been such a dear child to me. God heard my prayers, and your jaw was soon better so that you could take your bottle, but in a few months you broke out all over your body with terrible sores like boils. You were very sick again for a long time, and I had to carry you around on a soft pillow so I wouldn't hurt you. The doctor from town came and told me you were going to die and go back to Heaven."

"And did I, Mama?"

"Oh, no, dear. I prayed again. I told God (that's Jesus' Father, you know)."

"Is He like my father?"

"No, Joseph."

"Does He whip Jesus?"

"No, Joseph. God is very kind."

"I wish God was my father."

"He is, Joseph, you dear child. He is."

"He never comes to see us."

"Yes, He does, dear. He sees us all the time. He's here with us today."

"Where?"

"Right here in this room."

"Where, Mama? Call Him."

"I don't need to call Him, Joseph. He's here beside us; He can see us, but we can't see Him."

"Well, why not, Mama? Huh? Will I someday, Mama?"

"Yes, dear, someday we both will if we love Him and obey Him. Even now if we can't see Him, we can see the things He does. He makes the trees and grass and the clouds. He makes the flowers and the birds, and the light that comes down from Heaven."

"And me?"

"Yes, and you, dear. Surely God made you."

"And you, too?"

"Yes,"

"And—and Father?" Joseph sat up very straight and looked his mother full in the face.

"Yes, dear, when your father was a little boy I suppose he was sweet, for he is a nice-looking man, and—"

"Not when he scolds me." Joseph shook his head from one side to the other.

"Well, anyway, Joseph, listen to Mama. I promised God when you were a tiny baby and when you were so sick, that if He'd let you stay here with me to help make me happy—"

"Do I, Mama?" He reached up and patted his mother's soft cheek.

"Yes, darling. I'd be so sad if it were not for you. And if you grow up to be a good man, I'll be so happy!"

"Happy again?"

"Yes, Joseph, happy again and again. Whenever we cannot go to church on Sunday, I'm going to spend the time with you telling you stories from the Bible that will help you love Jesus and want to serve Him. I know God has spared your life for a purpose, although you can't understand it now. I have a story to tell you, but I believe I'll wait until you are that old," and Annie held up Joseph's hand and bent down the thumb. "Soon now you'll be four years old, and I'll tell you the story about — Oh, Joseph, there comes Father already. Church must be out, and I've been talking when I should be getting the dinner on."

"Will he whip us for that, or tell Zo-zo to come get us?" A look of extreme fear crossed Joseph's childish face.

CHAPTER VI

"Church must have let out earlier than usual." Annie tried to speak as kindly and as agreeably as possible.

"Why?" Bennet looked at the clock, the stove, and the table in one sweep.

"We seldom get home at this hour."

"Well, did you want me to stay and shake hands with everyone and explain why you two didn't go today?"

"No," answered Annie feebly, "but," she hastened to add before he had a chance to ask, "I was telling Joseph stories, and that's why the dinner isn't ready. I'm sorry, Bennet."

"Stories, you say? I suppose he understands them." Bennet's voice was chilly with sarcasm.

"He understands remarkably well for a child his age, Bennet. Why," she added quickly, "is that unusual with the father he has?"

Bennet hadn't expected this. In spite of his early sickness Joseph was far from being a tardy child mentally. And Joseph was his child. Of course Joseph was a smart child.

"Well," and Bennet made his voice sound fatherly, "I hope you waste no time telling that boy fairy tales and crazy old legends that have no truth to them."

"No, Bennet," came Annie's soft answer. She opened a can of corn. "I was telling him a Bible story."

"All about my father," said Joseph clasping his little hands over his breast.

"Your father?" inquired Bennet crossing his hands behind him and taking a step backwards. Consternation and displeasure crossed his face.

"My father—my good father that comes every day to see me an' I can't see."

33

"He means God, Bennet," said Annie with tender affection.

Bennet put his denim work jacket on over his Sunday suit and without saying a word walked swiftly to the barn.

The table was set, the ham fried, the potatoes mashed, the water poured, the cake cut, and Annie waited. The clock struck one-thirty.

"I wish Father would come in. Joseph, do you want to walk out to the gate and call him. Say, 'Father, dinner is ready now.'"

Joseph opened the door. He hesitated, then closed it very softly and tiptoed to his mother.

"Father," he whispered, taking her one hand in both of his little ones, "is sitting out there crying, Mama."

"Crying? Are you sure, Joseph?"

Only once had Annie seen Bennet shed tears, and that was the first year they were married when the potato crop did not pay for the seed. Annie would never forget how shocked she was when he angrily dug into the ground with the fork only to find a few scabby potatoes the size of walnuts, and how at the end of the second row he leaned on the fork handle and cried. It didn't exactly appeal to her to cry that time, and Bennet had chided her for manifesting such an unsympathetic attitude.

"It's not that I'm not sympathetic, Bennet," she had said in reply to his accusation, "but I believe if God had thought we needed and deserved potatoes He'd have helped them grow." "Deserved?" Bennet had shouted. Annie could never forget how he looked at her through his tears and cried out so loud and vehemently just as Michael Hunter was passing. "If a hard working man like me don't deserve a good potato crop, tell me who does. Tell me, Annie Armstrong!"

"Well, I believe all things work together for good, somehow, Bennet, even when it's impossible to see how.

We still have plenty of green beans that I canned, and we can eat mush or sell a calf and buy some shipped-in potatoes, maybe."

"Sell a calf? Not so long as the prices are down to what they are today."

That was the only time Annie had seen Bennet cry. Trembling with wonder and dread she opened the kitchen door. Joseph was right. Bennet was sitting on the second step with his handkerchief over his face. Perhaps he had heard something in the Sunday-school class or the morning sermon that had touched him. Maybe he was ashamed and sorry he had so mercilessly punished his little son. Or maybe he really wanted to take Joseph on his knee and tell him a story from the Bible about God, the good Father—maybe he longed to but didn't know just how. Trembling now with wonder and hope, Annie bent over and touched her husband on the shoulder.

"You're not hurt or sick are you, Bennet?"

He did not answer.

"What is wrong, dear?" Annie hadn't called Bennet dear for years. Not that she didn't long to, but she never felt like it. Her own heart pounded when she said it.

"Pete died," he choked.

Pete? The only Pete Annie knew was Pete Lehenbaur, Lois Doane's half brother and father of a large family.

"Oh, Bennet, how awful!" said Annie sitting down beside him and putting her arm across his shoulder. "Did you hear it in church?"

"In church?" he looked over at her and blew his nose. "No, I just found it out since I'm home."

"Who told you?"

"I found it out myself."

"How?"

"How!" he shouted, tears streaming down both checks. "How do you suppose? I went out and found him."

"Found him where, Bennet?"

"Why in the barn, of course."

Pete. Annie had forgotten for the moment that Bennet had a fine black horse he called Pete. Annie Armstrong was struck again with disappointment and humiliation over her husband's display of "novel" grief because of a personal loss. If he had ever showed any signs of distress or sympathy when she or Joseph were in trouble this would not have smote her as it did. The words in her mouth froze there, and it was hard for her to swallow them. She got to her feet and watched Bennet trying to gather himself together.

"I—I thought you meant Pete Lehenbaur," she said, reaching for the door knob. "Come, dinner is on the table."

"I don't want any dinner."

"Yes," she hesitated; she turned the knob, "come, Bennet. Eat with us. Joseph is hungry."

"Maybe he is, but I'm not. Neither of you knows the value of a good horse. What hurts me is that I had a chance to sell him just last week to Mr. Hightower for $100.00, and I was getting him ready to sell for $125.00 before Christmas, and now he had to die; I noticed this morning something was wrong, and I had a notion to stay home from church, and I wish now I would have." Bennet's large Roman nose was red.

"Let's eat, please. You'll sit out here and take cold yet."

Very reluctantly he got to his feet. He sat at the table but refused to eat. He only sipped from a cup of coffee now and then.

"Bennet," said Annie meekly. She looked sadly at him across the table. The wind was chasing some fallen leaves across the lawn and one clapped against the windowpane and clung there.

"Yes."

"I want to ask you a question."

"Go ahead." He put the coffee cup on the saucer. "Women can ask more questions than any man can answer, but try me out and see."

"Why did you marry me, Bennet?"

The man's sensitivity at this moment provoked him now to the point of nausea. He looked at her for a moment across the dishes of half warm food he refused to eat, and he bit his lower lip.

"Because I wanted a wife," he said at length, and Annie thought she heard disgust in his voice. "Why did you marry me?"

"Because I loved you," came her ready answer.

"That's fine," he said dryly.

"Didn't you marry me because you loved me?" Her brown eyes looked into his blue ones hungrily.

"Didn't I say so before all who were present?"

"Yes, you did," she agreed, "but you haven't told me so more than once since."

"Well, is it necessary to say it every day?"

"No," answered Annie cheerlessly, and there was a strain of pathos in her voice, "but I like to tell the Lord every day that I love Him."

"Sometimes," remarked Bennet rising, "I think you are ninety-five per cent emotion."

* * *

Earnie Eloy was seldom at the Armstrong place on Sundays. He and a bachelor friend of his usually spent that day of the week hunting or fishing or smoking by the fire in Alex Burns's log house. Alex never married and neither did Earnie, and both declared they were stronger and wiser living a single life.

"Peers ter me," drawled out Alex putting his feet up on the old cookstove and tilting back in his chair while the smoke from his corncob pipe curled above him, "Earnie, you're puttin' on some weight since ye're workin' fer Armstrong. The missus must be a right smart cook."

"A right smart cook she is all right. Can't be beat in that line, an' fer workin', too. She ain't nothin' fer size, but how she can dash an' scurry roun'! Puts out more work in a day than Sallie Handcock ever did. Like it better there too, only Bennet Armstrong is orful stern at times. No loafin' on the job when he's aroun'. Man, I'm tellin' you that thar little kid o' hisn has ter step the chalk, too. Why, he's not more'n four, an' this las' week he had that young'un out helpin' plant trees. Yeh. Made him carry water, too, till I thought 'twas near a shame. I believe in teachin' 'em ter work—an' work young, too —but that kid'll have a weak back or a bad heart next thing. Whips him, too, when he don't mind. I've seen him get the lickin's fer nothin' he done. Once he got one, an' I tole on him that time. He was in my trunk messin' roun' 'mong my stuff an' I got my Dutch up, but somehow I sorta like that little chap ever since. I won't tell on him no more.

"Bennet's got money, but do you think he'd buy that thar little tyke a stick o' candy now an' then? Nope. All that boy hears is, 'Git ter work now, an' hurry up, an' mind you now or ole Fonzo Bullet'll come an' get you.' That thar makes me mad whenever he says that. Why, one day that poor little kid o' hisn ran ter the house screamin' like all get out when Fonzo came down the road. Jes' as he passed the place he reached over fer the whip an' rolled his eyes over ter Joseph—whew—poor kid, his pa has him all in a stew 'bout that thar nigger comin' after him every time he don't do jes' thus an' so. Gets me all woolly under the skin. Don't min' teasin' a kid in fun sometimes, but that's wrong, an' I'm no Christian either. Armstrong, he goes off ter church every

Sunday o' the year an' studies in his Bible every Saturday night sure as the calendar says Saturday, but if I know anything he's got a long way ter go to live out what he pretends he is ter them church members. But one thing I know, his wife is what I call a Christian."

"Well," said Alex in his low-toned voice, "I never got much acquainted with Armstrong. He's a rich man, I reckon, an' I'm a poor man, an' he don't need my help, an' I hope I never need his. I heard he has a sister, Hepsi, too."

"Who?" Earnie Eloy bent forward and tapped the ashes out of his pipe.

CHAPTER VII

Annie made Joseph a warm topcoat out of one she wore when she went to school. It was a remarkable piece of work for having been put together by hand. But a good flat iron, a wet cloth, and plenty of pressure did wonders. All the while Annie was making it she wondered if she would have had a sewing machine had Pete not died. Regardless of that loss, Bennet came home from town the following week with a new suit of clothes and a fine new black felt hat.

With a lump in her throat Annie admired his choice of material and told him it was a beautiful fit.

"I'd love to have a new dress," she said, looking timidly at the floor.

"You had enough clothes when you got married to last another five years," he replied, with emphasis on the last two words.

"Five years?"

Bennet hung his suit in the closet between his brown serge and gray tweed. It was a handsome suit.

"Joseph," he said, changing his shoes, "you run out and close those barn doors to the west. It looks like Earnie forgot them. I've told him twice those doors should be closed this kind of weather. If he forgets again I'm going to dock him when I pay him."

"Go do it," whispered Annie, reaching for Joseph's coat.

He went.

That evening while at the supper table a sudden wind storm came up and Bennet looked at Joseph sharply and said, "You closed those barn doors, didn't you?"

"Yes, Father," he replied.

An hour later when Bennet came in he was furious.

"Come to me at once, Joseph Armstrong; you're going to have a whipping before you go to bed."

Joseph could not think of anything he had done that day that required a whipping. He was now a little past four and capable of recalling clearly the activities of a day. He faced his father with a most pitiful look on his face.

"Why, Father? Why do I need a whipping?"

"For lying to me."

"Lying?"

"Yes, lying."

"When did I tell a lie—Father?"

His father was near him now, and Joseph could feel his breath fan his hair. "You lied to me at the supper table. You said you closed those barn doors and you did *not*."

"I did."

"Don't contradict your father." And Joseph got a slap on the mouth.

"I—I," he stammered weakly, and tears blinded both eyes. His father's strong hand had hold of his arm.

"I'll not have you lie to me like this. You did not close those barn doors. I just came from there and the floor is all wet from this rain. If you had closed them, why would the floor be wet? Stand up here and take what's coming to you," and Joseph got a beating like he never had before, and he had had many.

Annie shook with anguish, and with every blow her own body suffered torture with his. "Bennet, I put his coat on him, and I know he did go out to close those doors."

"Maybe he did go out, but he never shut them," and Joseph's teeth chattered as he finished the beating with a severe shaking.

Earnie Eloy stepped into the kitchen. He stroked his black mustache and stood in the doorway.

"Mr. Armstrong," he said, "I happen ter know your boy did close them doors, an' it was the wind that tore them open."

Bennet was angrier than ever now. He glared at Earnie in his sore displeasure. No apologies were offered. No remarks were made. J. Bennet Armstrong swallowed twice, cleared his throat, and hurried from the house.

"Come on up ter my room, sonny," and Earnie Eloy took Joseph very gently by the arm. "Come on up an' I'll show you my knives an' things in my trunk."

Several months after this incident occurred, another sad experience came into Joseph's young life which made a lasting impression on him. His mother had buttoned his nightgown as usual and helped him say his prayer.

"And now, Joseph," she said with feeling, "I guess you'll have to go to bed upstairs tonight because we're getting company."

"Company?"

"Yes, dear."

"Who, Mother?"

"You'll find out in the morning when you come down."

"But Mama, let the company sleep upstairs. It's dark up there."

"I know dear, but you're four and a half years old now, and I'll go up with you and tuck you in."

"Oh, but Mama, I like it best down here near you. Don't you know that?"

"Yes, I know, Joseph, but you must go up tonight. Earnie will be right across the hall. Come now, I'll take you up."

Joseph tried hard to keep back the tears, but they would come. His lips quivered and soon he was crying out loud.

"And what's all this commotion in here?" Joseph's father walked heavily across the room.

"He's afraid to go upstairs, Bennet."

"Afraid of what? Come up with me and show me what there is to be afraid of." And Joseph was marched upstairs by his father. "Now you stop that crying and go to sleep," and with that Joseph was left alone in the big dark room. The bed felt damp, and his little legs shook with both cold and fear. It was Saturday night and Earnie Eloy had gone to town and would return, maybe late. In his childish way Joseph asked God to help him not be afraid, and to bring sleep to his eyes. Just when he dropped off to sleep, no one ever knew, but by daylight he was standing beside his mother's bed with his hand against her warm neck.

"I didn't like it up there, Mama."

"You didn't?"

"No, I didn't! And I don't want to go up there any more—ever!"

"But Joseph, go over there and see what's in your little bed in the corner."

"What is it, Mama?"

"A little sister came last night to live with us, Joseph. Now you'll have a playmate."

"I don't want her. I want my little bed. I don't like to go upstairs unless you do."

"You poor child!" Annie drew him close to her and held him there.

How vividly Annie remembered that at the age of seven she did not like to go upstairs at night even with her sister. Her mother heart went out to her son in genuine sympathy.

"Now, Joseph, you'll have to let your Aunt Hepsi dress you this morning, or maybe you can dress yourself. You're four and a half now. Nice big boy. Try it, dear.

Your Aunt Hepsi has come to help us for a couple of weeks, and if you can do all but tie your shoes, that will be fine."

Joseph had seen his Aunt Hepsi on several occasions and he decided at once he'd rather learn to dress himself than have her do it for him. While he was getting himself into his blue flannel shirt she made her appearance in the doorway. Yes, there was no mistake. Joseph had seen this aunt before, and she had made an indelible impression on his mind, for she was utterly unlike any other woman he had seen. She was tall and skinny, and her streaked gray hair was drawn tightly back from her forehead and ended in a small knot on the top of her head. And the thing that Joseph looked for in particular was still there—that wart like a ripe huckleberry nestled closely to the right side of her peaked nose. Her full gathered skirts hung below the tops of her black laced shoes, and around her shoulders was pinned a small dark gray shawl, and some of its fringe was missing as her teeth. She looked at Joseph with her snappy gray eyes that shone green across the room. She held up a bony finger at him and made her initial announcement in a voice that was anything but musical.

"Joseph," she said, "it's a good thing you're dressing yourself, for I won't have time while I'm here. And Joseph, I want to tell you another thing. My name is Hepsi Myrtle Armstrong. But just why my parents ever named me Hepsi is more than I can tell. I've asked your father repeatedly to please call me Myrtle, but he claims he can't call me anything but Hepsi. I want you to call me Aunt Myrtle while I'm here; do you understand?"

Joseph looked at that long bony finger and for a moment forgot he was trying to button his shirt, forgot where he was, and that he had gone upstairs the night before this morning. Joseph didn't exactly know whether to nod or shake his head, or what to do or answer.

"Say, 'Yes, Aunt Myrtle, I'll try to do that'," helpfully suggested his mother.

"Ye—yes, Aunt Myrtle," repeated Joseph feebly, blinking his eyes.

So this was the company that came during the night. The infant in the bed made a baby's wee cry, and for a second Joseph shifted his gaze from Aunt Hepsi to the corner.

"Mama," he whispered, burying his face in the pillow beside her, "I don't like it that you got it."

"You mean your little sister?"

"I don't like it." His voice quivered. "I want my bed. I don't like to go upstairs in the dark, and I—I don't like that woman. I won't let her tie my shoes."

"Now, Joseph," came his mother's soft answer, and her arm circled his half-dressed body, "she's gone to the kitchen. Put on your shoes and hold each foot up here to me. I'll tie them for you. Just be a good boy and talk nicely to her. She won't be here many days. She's your father's oldest sister, Joseph, and we must respect her as much as possible. Your father asked her to come, so that's that. She will fix you an egg and some porridge, and before you eat, bow your head and say your thanks and be sure to say please and thank you. If she asks you anything you don't know how to answer, come in here and ask me. And now put on your overalls, Joseph, and I'll buckle them for you. And your little sister, Joseph, will help make you happy, I'm sure. Her name is Virginia."

"I'm going to be sad all day long, Mama."

"Why?"

"I want my own bed. That bed upstairs is too big and cold, and I can't see you when I wake up."

"But, Joseph, remember, God sees you all the time."

"Even in the dark, Mama?"

"Yes, even in the dark, sweetheart."

"Does He bring a light along down with Him?"

Joseph had one foot in his overalls now.

"You'll understand it better some day, you dear child. God Himself is light, and in Him is no darkness at all."

CHAPTER VIII

Aunt Hepsi came into Bennet Armstrong's home because he insisted, not because she wanted a job. The meager wage he offered her was not sufficient, she thought, for the amount of work that would be required of her. But he reminded her that a young girl probably could not bake bread fit to eat, and that it was her religious duty as his sister to come even if he couldn't pay her more than forty cents a day, so she said she would come; but she would not help to milk.

"Bennet," she said, "if I have to get out and milk, I won't come for as much as sixty cents a day. I've been having the neuralgia in my right arm and shoulder for near five weeks now. Maybe it's neuritis; I can't tell, but it's one of them two, and I've got to keep myself in the warm. Will you have plenty of fuel on hand if I come?"

"I'll have all any woman needs," he assured her, "but my hired man—he don't like the kitchen too hot at meal time. He's a warm-blooded man."

"Well," answered Hepsi in a sharp, edgy voice, "your hired man and me aren't making this agreement. If I come, be it understood, Bennet, that I need it good and warm in the house, and good and warm it will be."

"Very well, Hepsi. Put on three or four skirts, your high buckled arctics and your big woolen shawl."

"You mean I'm to go along back with you now?"

"Yes, now."

So Hepsi was a little tired, a little cross, a little nervous, and quite a little at a loss to know where everything was to be found that first morning in her brother's kitchen. There were two things at the start that were much to her disfavor: the tall gangly, black-mustached hired man and the yellow cat. Hepsi Armstrong had a decided aversion to cats, and yellow cats in particular,

47

and she had as great a repugnance for a man with a mustache. Earnie Eloy's mustache hung in his coffee cup. Hepsi affirmed in her soul before that first breakfast was half over that she'd not only have to wash but also scald his dishes separately. Furthermore she marked his cup with a piece of red store string on the handle to make sure she'd never drink out of that cup. She kept it in the corner of the cupboard.

Earnie Eloy was at the Armstrong place on business and business only. He was a man of no religion, but he and Bennet got along tolerably well. Out of respect he hesitated before each meal while his employer bowed his head in silent prayer. He did what he was told to do and asked very few questions. But the first time Earnie Eloy met Bennet Armstrong's sister Hepsi, he formed as strong an antipathy for her as she did for him. The feeling was mutual. Neither told the other. It was felt. Hepsi kept her head bowed twice as long as Bennet did, and the men could hardly start to eat until she gave the signal. Earnie heard Bennet draw a deep breath, and Bennet heart Earnie draw a deeper one. There was a most unpleasant tension during the entire meal, for no one of the three knew what to talk about. Earnie ate his oatmeal with a blank expression, and Bennet seemed to have a deep, dark secret on his mind. Hepsi looked cross, but then that was her ordinary look. Had she looked any other way, folks surely would have thought that at last some man had chosen her as his ideal woman. Since that hadn't yet happened, she retained her natural expression.

Earnie Eloy wiped perspiration from his forehead before he cut his pancakes, and Hepsi pinned her gray shawl closer to her neck. She was certain he did it just to plague her, for how could anyone think it was warm in the kitchen? Hepsi hurried and scurried and fumed around all day.

A sad little boy went upstairs again that night. The minute he raised an objection he was severely whipped and forced to go up unaccompanied. His mother pitied him, so she could not keep from shedding a few silent tears when she heard his little bare feet plodding up those wooden steps above her.

"Dear Lord," she prayed, "shine down on him tonight and give him sweet rest and take away all fear."

"Say, boy," whispered Earnie Eloy. He heard the child's stifled sobs and tiptoed across the hall. He put his face down close to the tiny hump under the covers. "Do you want ter come over an' sleep with me ter night?"

"Is that you, Earnie?"

"Bet yer life it's me, an' I know yer cold over here all alone. Want ter cuddle up ter me an' get warmed up?"

Joseph said "yes" real, real softly, and before he knew it he was in Earnie's strong arms and was being transferred to the room across the hall.

The twenty days Aunt Hepsi Armstrong managed the housework for her brother were no longer days than we live today, but for Joseph they seemed everlasting. Almost everything he did was the wrong thing. He heard "don't do this" and "don't do that" so much that at night when he knelt to say his prayers he almost thought he heard a voice say "don't pray that way." On only one occasion did Joseph succeed in making his aunt smile, and she smiled out loud. Joseph was so overtaken with surprise that he ran to his mother and said, "She smiled like this, Mama," and he made a funny little chuckle in his throat. "Really, Mama, I saw her do it right out there by the window."

"Tell me about it, Joseph."

"Well, you know Tabby was on the rug by the stove sleeping, and making that funny noice in his head."

"You mean purring?"

"Yes, and she said she couldn't stand that noise. So I got the oil can out and put some oil in his ears."

"You did? Why Joseph, did you really?"

"Yes, I oiled him in this ear and this one, then she asked me what I was doing, and I told her maybe that would make him quit it and he'd run quieter, you know. Then she looked real cross for a little, and all at once she smiled out loud and said, "You can try that on your baby sister when she gets to screechin'.""

"But—but you really won't do that, will you, Joseph?"

"No, Mama; not if you tell me not to. Shall I?"

"No, indeed," and Annie had to smile a little too.

"Anyway our baby don't screech, does she, Mama?"

"Not exactly—no, and you like her by this time?"

"Yes."

"And you're not afraid to go upstairs any more?"

"No, I'm not afraid any more because you said God can see me with His light, and Earnie comes over every night pretty near and tells me things or holds my hand till I fall asleep."

"He does?"

"Yes, and I tell him things too."

"Things like what, Joseph?"

"Oh, about—about my good Father an' how He loves me an' never whips me for not closing barn doors when I do, an' how He can see us all the time."

"You do?"

"Yes, and he says he don't know whether all that is true or not."

"He does say that?"

"Yes, but he says I should always believe everything you tell me because he said you are a good woman."

"Earnie said that, Joseph?"

"Yes."

*   *   *

The day came when Aunt Hepsi (who insisted she be called by her second name, Myrtle) was buggied back six miles to her own home. She was pinned snugly in four skirts, two shawls, and a heavy lap robe. She held tightly her black handbag which contained the sum of $8.00, her earnings of the past twenty days.

"There's one thing, Bennet," she began when they had driven possibly a mile down the road, "that I'm terribly disappointed in."

"What's that?"

"It's that you insist on calling me Hepsi when I requested you call me Myrtle."

"Well, it's like this, Hepsi," he answered, "you put your request in too late. You've been Hepsi for forty years now and I can't call you anything else. You were always Hepsi at home. I can't understand why you want to change it now. I've been calling you that since I could talk."

"And Joseph never called me Aunt Myrtle a dozen times all the while I was there! He just called me she or her. I think if you would have insisted he call me Myrtle, he would have."

"Maybe so, Hepsi, but there's one time I didn't feel like it."

* * *

A group of women were clustered around Annie Armstrong in the vestibule of the church, each wanting a peek at her new baby. Plump Mrs. Irons, one of the most talkative of the group, was stroking Joseph on the head affectionately.

"Annie, you have a very nice baby," she said.

"Do you think so?" smiled Annie, warm circles running around her heart.

"I mean every word of it. I can't make an ado over a child and not be sincere. And Joseph is a handsome little boy. Such a lovely shaped head, and those expressive eyes! I don't know when I've seen a child his age who looks so intelligent. Doesn't it just thrill you when you remember how sick he was once?"

"I thank God for him every day, Mrs. Irons."

"He's small for his age, isn't he?"

The woman was still stroking Joseph's head fondly.

"Quite small, yes."

"Is he well?"

"Real well, I think. Of course he's not as robust as most boys his age."

Annie didn't care to add that her little son had to work as hard as other boys twice his age. She didn't care to tell that he was a child who got many cruel whippings from his father until his eyes sparkled at anyone who treated him kindly. She didn't want to tell that she herself was so hungry for love that she alone lavished all her affection on him. Annie Armstrong wasn't a woman to tell such things to anyone, and so no one knew. Not one of the women clustered around her suspected that these two lovely children were not welcomed by their father. Why should she tell these things?

"Well, Annie," said Mrs. Irons with a twinkle in her eye, "any time you want to give this little boy away you let me know. I could take him home with me this very minute. How old are you, Joseph?"

"I'll be five my next birthday." He looked up at the woman and smiled, and a sudden light that was almost heavenly lit up his innocent face.

"God bless your life, little man," she said.

CHAPTER IX

Virginia was a light-complexioned, fine-featured baby with soft blue eyes like two forget-me-nots. Lois and Riley Doane were waiting just outside the church door beside Bennet.

"Hurry up!" laughed Lois, unconsciously making a deep dimple in each cheek. "We want a look at your baby, too. Now isn't she sweet? She's going to look like you, Annie. I can see it already. Can't you, Bennet?" Lois beamed all over him, and the warmth of her smile brought forth a pleasant answer.

"She does right now," laughed Bennet, showing both sets of fine even teeth. How handsome he looked in his new suit and black felt hat.

"And so proud you had to celebrate." Riley slapped Bennet on the shoulder.

"Celebrate?" exclaimed Bennet in surprise.

"What's all this new suit for? That's all right, that's all right, Bennet," and here Riley Doane added two more slaps. "I know just how you feel. There's nothing in life like being a father, is there? Well, you've all got our best wishes. Annie, the children want to see the baby yet, then we must be going. We're invited to the Bauchmans for dinner."

"And we'd like to have you folks come to our house next Sunday," concluded Lois, buttoning her coat at the throat.

Annie looked at Bennet for the acceptance of this invitation, which he gave with a slight bow. She watched with deep reverence the happy couple as they walked toward their carriage and wondered if she would ever live to see Joseph and Virginia skipping along beside Bennet holding to his hands as Riley's children did. Just why Bennet didn't look and wonder the same thing is hard to say, but he very likely was wondering how much Riley gave for his horse or how both Lois and Riley could seem so happy-go-lucky when they made so little headway financially.

Next, Lottie Woods came dashing around the corner of the church, her gloved hands clasping her Bible and purse. "Wait just a minute, Annie." Everyone in the congregation, both young and old, called Annie Armstrong by her first name. "I want to see Joseph's little sister too. He told me all about her in the class this morning, didn't you, Joseph?" she smiled at him fondly. "He's a most delightful child to have in a Sunday-school class, Annie. I'm just thrilled over his ability to think things through and give answers. And I can tell that you folks teach him at home too. I really miss him when he can't come. He told me how he didn't like to go upstairs alone at first, and—"

"We must be going, Annie," cut in Bennet. He seemed a little nervous and impatient.

"Oh, I beg your pardon, Mr. Armstrong," said Lottie Woods. "I shouldn't be keeping you folks. Maybe the baby will catch cold. You have a nice little one there, Mr. Armstrong. And I want you both to know that I think Joseph is a wonderful child."

"Thank you," said Annie modestly. "We want him to grow up to be a good man."

"Well, he's a little man already."

Bennet motioned for Joseph to come, and he himself started toward the horse shed.

"Folks act as if they never saw a new baby before," grumbled Bennet before they had driven out of the churchyard. "We could have been home half an hour ago. And I don't see why you have to tell every one how you didn't like to go upstairs alone, Joseph. I'd be ashamed to tell it if I were you—the way you cried and carried on."

Annie located Joseph's little hand under the blanket and pressed it meaningfully. He made no answer but snuggled closer to his mother's side.

There are experiences in every child's life that stay with him as long as he lives. Joseph had more than one. In the months following the coming of Virginia, Bennet Armstrong heaped more and more work upon his young son. Whenever he grew slack in any way his father would say in mocking tones, "Well, he's a little man already, isn't he? That's what Miss Lottie calls you, so stand up and be one. Show me what you can do. She said we teach you at home, so now let me teach you how to work. Those stories your mother is forever telling you aren't what make bone and muscle. Come now, and I'll have you harrow today."

Joseph was tossed upon old Dick and given orders to stay there until he was lifted off. Of course once he was on, there was no way of getting off unless he fell off. While Earnie was working in a distant field, Joseph, not quite seven, was left alone to harrow from eight until dinnertime.

"What if I get thirsty, Father?"

"Just forget it. You can wait till you get to the house. And don't you let me hear you calling to your mother to bring you out a drink. She's got no time for that."

Joseph went back and forth from one end of the cornfield to the other, and he got thirsty. The sun was sickeningly hot.

The next morning when his father threw him up on old Dick, he looked down at him and said pleadingly, "Father, if you'd only fix me a strap here, I could get up by myself."

"Nothin' doin'! I know what you have in your mind. If you could get up yourself, you'd get down too."

"I could put a little bucket of water here under the trees, Father, and then—"

"Then nothin'. You'd get off and take a nap or fool around. I'm fixing no such strap. You'll stay on Dick till I come and take you off. And I want you to get more done than you did yesterday."

Joseph's lips trembled.

"None of that now. You straighten up or I'll sure tell old Fonzo Bullet to come and get you."

Somehow Joseph didn't care a lot this time. His mother had said Fonzo was a kind old man and wouldn't hurt him.

"Well," he said to himself after his father had walked away, "if I get so hot and thirsty I die—I—I—hope Mama dies too, because I don't want to go to Heaven without her." Tears fell on his shirt. He looked back. His father was gone.

Every morning from the day Joseph was seven he was compelled to get up at five o'clock and go to the barn and milk three cows. He was not allowed to carry a lantern, for fear he'd set the barn on fire. No matter how sleepy he was, he was punished without mercy if he didn't jump out of bed the moment he was called. No matter how dark or cold it was, Joseph had to go to the barn and milk. As a rule Earnie hung a lantern up high for Joseph's benefit. After breakfast he had the chickens to feed. He carried heavy buckets of scalded bran and meat scraps to the hen house. His back and arms ached much of the time. Joseph was always tired—always.

The day came when he was to start to school. Annie packed his lunch in a small tin bucket. She followed him to the gate and kissed him good-by.

"Joseph," she whispered, "be a good boy in school. Be honest and true and do your best. Tell your teacher your name and tell him you were seven last month."

Joseph was tired before he started. It was seven

o'clock and just turning daylight. He had a mile and a half to walk. Trembling with anticipation and timidity, he approached the schoolhouse. The teacher met him at the door. He was a middle-aged man who had five children of his own in the school. His name was Amos Pennewell. His head came within a few inches of the top of the door. He looked down at Joseph in a kindly manner and took his mittened hand in his own large one. He pressed it.

"Good morning," he said smiling. And from his large person came a voice so tender, so soothing, and so elegant that Joseph's soul cried out within him for joy. What? When had he ever heard a voice like that? He thought at once it must be something like the voice of God.

"Good morning," answered Joseph. "My mother said to tell you my name is Joseph Armstrong, and I was seven last month."

"Fine, Joseph. Come inside and hang your cap over here." He led the way into the cloak-room. "This will be your hook right here. Put your mittens in your coat pocket. You may set your dinner pail on the rack above it like this." The teacher placed it there for him. "I'll show you where to sit, and we'll soon get acquainted."

Joseph looked all around, and several of the biggest girls smiled at him. It made him tingle strangely all over. The teacher opened the school by saying "We now have thirty-six pupils in our room since Joseph Armstrong has been enrolled. Let us all be kind to this new pupil, for we want him to enjoy coming to school. All of you who feel that way raise your hands." Every hand went up.

"Let us bow our heads in prayer."

In unison the children repeated the Lord's Prayer. Joseph found himself joining in, for his mother had already taught it to him.

"Mama," said Joseph that evening before he had time to remove his coat, "I liked it. Mr. Pennewell is nice to me. I like him, Mama. I like him. I wish it was tomorrow."

It was almost impossible for Joseph to keep his eyes open at the table that night. He was completely exhausted from the excitement of the day and the long tramp home, and his hands trembled when he took the potato dish.

"Sit up there and watch what you're doing," scolded his father. "If going to school makes you lazy, I'll keep you out now and then."

After such a threat, Joseph sprang out of bed when he heard his father call in the morning. He hurried to the barn through the dark and milked the three cows with enthusiasm, in view of sitting another day under the sound of that kind-voiced teacher, Amos Pennewell. The buckets of warm bran were not quite so heavy as the morning before, nor the road quite so long and tiresome, for inside that schoolhouse were rows of smiling children; there was singing and praying, and best of all, a big, kind-faced man who spoke in a low gentle voice to both boys and girls, the youngest and the oldest ones alike.

His little legs could hardly take him fast enough. He'd try never to act tired at the supper table any more. He loved school.

* * *

Annie coughed again. She'd been coughing for weeks now, and it annoyed Bennet terribly.

"If you can't get over this," he announced one evening after supper, "I'm going to take you away somewhere."

Joseph stood up very straight, and a new pain flew into his aching legs.

"Where, Father?"

CHAPTER X

Joseph could scarcely wait until he had a chance to be alone with his mother so he could ask her.

"Where are you going, Mama?" he whispered. He held her hand in both of his and looked up into her face. Bewilderment and distress were written there.

"I don't know," she answered.

"What did Father mean?"

"I have no idea, Joseph."

"Well—well—Mama—will I go along too?"

"Joseph, I have no idea what Father had in mind when he said that. He doesn't like to hear me cough, I know, and I try my best not to—but he never gets me any cough syrup or anything, and he never—oh, well, Joseph, I shouldn't be saying this. Please don't worry about it. Maybe he was just talking."

Maybe his father was just talking, but nevertheless Joseph had a hard time dropping off to sleep that night. Where would Father take Mother—where—where? Little minds can imagine big things. Toward morning Joseph fell into a troubled sleep.

Every time his mother coughed he looked at his father with both fear and uneasiness.

Cold weather came to stay a while. Joseph left home while it was yet dark in order to get to school on time, and waded snow above his knees. Amos Pennewell took off his stockings and hung them on a wire behind the stove, and wrapped Joseph in his own overcoat until the stockings were dry enough to put on again. One evening it looked very much like a blizzard outside. Joseph Armstrong was the only pupil in school whose father did not come for him. Everyone else had gone but the teacher and his own five children. He was ready to lock up, and still no one had come through the storm for this littlest pupil.

"Do you think your father will come yet?" he asked, looking anxiously down the road.

"I don't suppose so," answered Joseph sadly.

"Then I'll take you home myself. No child your age ought to go home alone in a storm like this."

Annie met Joseph at the door. "Thank you many, many times," she called out to Mr. Pennewell.

When Bennet heard that the teacher brought Joseph home in his buggy, this is what he said: "He gets eighty-five dollars a month and he ought to when he thinks it's necessary. I can't remember that anyone ever ran after me and toted me home from school when it snowed or rained."

And Bennet never did go after Joseph. Never once. Not when a sudden rain storm impelled all the other parents to go after their children. Joseph was always the only one who had to walk home. So his mother kept him at home when the weather was severe. Much as Joseph loved school and hated to miss, he obeyed when his mother said, "You'd better not go today, dear, you'll be wet through and through till you get there."

About a month before school closed in the spring, Annie's older brother Timothy, who was married and had four children, moved on a farm three-quarters of a mile east of the schoolhouse. One afternoon Agnes, Freddie, Maryanna, and Dennis Stokes introduced themselves to the teacher, and said they'd like to visit the school they would all be attending the next fall.

"You say your name is Stokes?"

"Yes, sir," answered Agnes, the oldest of the four. "Joseph Armstrong is our cousin. That's him right over there." All four smiled across the room and of course Joseph's face beamed. He was anxious to get better acquainted with these cousins he had met but once or twice before.

"And you're living on the first place east here?"

"Yes, sir," answered Agnes still smiling at Joseph. "We used to live over by Callcott. We just came a week ago."

"Isn't he cute?" She whispered this to Freddie and pulled his coat sleeve when she said it. Freddie smiled from ear to ear, and Joseph smiled back at Freddie across the room.

"Come and take these seats, children." Amos Pennewell placed four chairs in a row along the east blackboard.

"Now tell me your names again, and your ages, and we can see about where you'll fit in next year."

"Well, my name is Agnes Stokes," began Agnes, standing up straight, for she had been taught at the Callcott school always to stand while reciting. She spoke in a clear voice that was noticeably rich for a girl her age. "And I'm eleven, going on twelve. I'll be twelve on the twenty-first of July. Maryanna is ten. Freddie is eight —you're eight, aren't you, Freddie? Yes, just before we moved he had a birthday, and Dennis is six. But he's never started yet."

She sat down and folded her hands in her lap. She had on a blue and white plaid gingham dress with a white collar and white sash. Joseph sat spellbound. Not a girl in the schoolroom was as pretty as Agnes Stokes, and to think she was his own cousin. And Freddie was too, and he was eight years old, just a little older than himself! A tingling for new joy made Joseph's heart beat faster. He'd been sad so much that it felt queer to be happy once. His eyes sparkled and color came into his cheeks.

* * *

"Father," said Joseph, trembling with excitement, "Freddie is eight years old."

"Yes, what of it?"

"We're almost alike then, aren't we?"

"I don't know yet. Time will tell."

"We'll, Father—we'll, we'll—"

"Well, say it."

"They'll all come over here sometimes, won't they—and we'll all go over there sometimes?"

"Sometimes, of course. But not all the time. Cousins can be a blessing, I suppose, and maybe a curse too. Getting together too often wouldn't be good."

*   *   *

Annie continued to cough. It wasn't exactly like a cold cough.

"I'm going to take you away next week." Bennet stood in front of the green-framed mirror on the wall beside the kitchen door and combed and combed his black hair.

"Next week?" Annie caught her breath. She would have fallen had she not been close enough to the table to catch herself. "Where—are you going—to—to take me—Bennet?"

"I'm going north on a business trip and I'm going to take you along with me and see if you can't get over this. We'll leave Joseph here to take care of the chickens."

Joseph's mouth dropped open and a lump came into his throat that he could not swallow. His hands and arms got numb, and his legs felt like frozen pipes ready to burst.

"Virginia can go along," added Bennet before either had a chance to speak. "We can take her for nothing, but it would cost too much to take Joseph along, and he must take care of the chickens."

"What kind of a business trip—" Before Annie had finished her question she knew she had started the wrong one by the way Bennet drew in his lips.

"Come now, let's eat supper," said Bennet. "This is Saturday night and I want to study my Sunday-school lesson." He looked at the clock.

"No, this is Friday night," said Joseph, and while he spoke his voice broke, and two big tears started rolling down his cheeks.

"Well, are you crying because it isn't Saturday night, or what's gone wrong now?"

Joseph couldn't answer. He wanted to throw his arms around his mother's neck and keep them there. Where was he going to take her and why couldn't he go along too? He'd never had a train ride. And would he and Earnie stay alone? The door opened and Earnie Eloy stepped in. He usually knew when to come in for supper. Not too soon or Bennet would think he wanted to get out of a few minutes' work.

"How you been today, Joseph?" asked Earnie, stroking his black mustache as he always did just before he sat down to the table.

"All right," came the boy's feeble answer.

Earnie looked at Joseph across the table of steaming food, but just as he had learned when to come in for supper, so he had learned when not to ask that boy questions in the presence of his father.

Joseph seemed to have a certain expression that withheld Earnie, and there was a certain and distinctive pressure or something in the air at times that made Earnie know it was best to keep still. Tonight Annie looked sad and troubled again. She took scarcely anything on her plate, and she seemed more pale than usual. He noticed her hands were shaking too. Little Virginia, now almost three, sat between her mother and Joseph, the picture of both health and contentment. She would soon be old enough to notice it when her mother couldn't eat, and wonder why. Virginia was a beautiful child and far from

stupid. She was much more of a chatterbox than Joseph
was at that age, and yet in spite of the cunning ways she
had of saying and doing things, Bennet showed only a
little more affection for her than he did for Joseph. It
was Earnie who talked to her at the table. It was Earnie
and Joseph who played with her on the floor after supper.
It was Earnie and Joseph who noticed the new words
she could say, not Bennet. Joseph dearly loved little
Virginia.

*   *   *

"Alex," said Earnie Sunday morning, "Stir up that
thar fire a little. Sorta chilly in here."

Alex stirred up the fire.

"Wish we had a mess of frog legs fer dinner."

"Well, wishin' won't make 'em come round."

"No, if wishin' brought things in I'd make a wish, so
I would."

"What'd you wish now, Earnie?" Alex leaned back in
his chair and snapped his suspenders. "Wish fer a
woman, eh?"

"Yes, that's it, Alex. I'd wish fer a woman."

"What?" Alex's feet came down.

"Don't take me wrong now, Alex. I'd do some wishin'
fer a woman—fer a woman's good, I mean. Don't know
when I ever felt so sorry fer anyone as I do fer that thar
Annie Armstrong."

"What now? Seems every time you come over here
you're feelin' sorry fer that thar woman of Armstrong's."

"Alex," said Earnie, getting up and looking out the
window, "if I was a married man, I'd rather live in a
shack like this than live in a fine, big house like Bennet's
if I couldn't treat a woman better'n he does his'n."

"Now what? You're not sayin' what you aim to, are
you, Earnie?" Alex blew his nose.

"Work an' money is all Bennet Armstrong thinks 'bout. His wife is jes' dyin' under his nose, an' he can't see as how he's killin' her inch by inch. She slaves an' works fer him from mornin' till night an' seldom gets a kind word fer it. If I was a member o' that thar church I'd just tell the preacher what kind of a man Bennet is 'round home. Yes, I would."

"Bet you would."

"I'd show him up in some way or other. Beats all how he can study his Bible an' be so mean ter that thar kid o' his'n, an' now he's a plannin' on goin' somewheres on business, he says, an' Joseph is ter stay home with me an' milk an' tend the chickens. Poor kid knows nothin' 'cep' work, an' Annie, poor soul's been goin' downhill ever since I been ther'. He's a takin' her 'long on this trip; wonder if he's goin' ter buy another farm. An' listen ter this. That Hepsi is acomin' ter do the cookin'. If it wasn't fer Joseph I wouldn't stay. I told Bennet without a raise I won't stay no how."

"Are you goin' ter get it?"

"I won't stay if I don't."

CHAPTER XI

Sunday evening found J. Bennet Armstrong sitting in church under the sound of the Gospel. His rich bass voice rolled out above the voices of all the other men sitting in the left wing.

Virginia was asleep and tucked in by seven. The wind whistled around the corner of the house, and Tabby took her place behind the cookstove.

"Joseph."

The boy stood closer to his mother. She was sitting on the armless rocker and Joseph's left arm was around her shoulder. When he stood beside her his head was about even with hers. Her soft brown hair touched his cheek and he could smell the sweetness of her body and the starch in her white apron.

"It breaks my heart to think of leaving you, but perhaps if I go with Father he will learn to love me more. I'll pray for you every day I'm gone, Joseph. Many times. And I'll write to you if I can. Surely Father will get me the stamps so I can. And I've thought of something else that will help you. I'm going to try to see Uncle Timothy and ask him if he won't let Freddie come up here every Saturday evening before dark—"

"Oh, Mama!"

"Yes, and stay with you so you will have someone to sleep with on Saturday nights when Earnie goes to town."

"Mama."

"Then he can help you hitch up the buggy on Sunday morning and ride along to church with you and Aunt Hepsi."

Joseph hadn't thought of that yet. How strange it would seem to go to church alone with Aunt Hepsi.

"And maybe sometimes you can go along home with

Freddie for Sunday dinner if Aunt Hepsi don't care. Of course you can't leave her alone too often."

"But Mama, how long are you going to be gone?"

"Maybe several weeks, the way Father talks. He says he has some relatives he wants to visit. I do not know who they are, but I am sure I must go along this time." Annie coughed. She pressed her hand on her chest.

"Joseph, I'll try to bring you a present when I come back."

"For me?"

"Yes, dear, if I possibly can. What would you like me to bring you?"

Joseph thought.

"I know, Mama. A picture of God holding His light."

"What do you mean, Joseph?"

"You know, Mama. Like on that little card Miss Lottie gave me once long ago. Don't you know? God holding His light so He can see in the dark."

"Precious child," answered Annie drawing him closer to her. "That was a picture of Christ knocking at the door; and you're right, in one hand He had a lantern, didn't He? Well, if that is what you'd like me to bring you, I'll pray that somewhere I can find you a picture like that. You mean a picture to hang up on the wall?"

"Yes. Mama?"

"Yes."

"Tell me that story about Joseph."

"Again?"

"Yes; I like it."

"But I've told it to you so often you know what's coming next."

"I don't care, Mama. Please tell it. I like it best."

"Why do you like it best, Joseph; can you tell me?"

"Well," Joseph shifted from one foot to the other and

twisted the button on his shirt, "maybe someday Father might make me a coat of many colors like Joseph had, because one night I dreamed he did—and he loved me like Joseph's father did, and I was so happy, and when I woke up Father was calling me to get up and milk, so I knew it was only a dream. But almost every night I like to think about how happy I was, and wish I could dream that again. Why did you name me Joseph, Mama?"

"Because I couldn't think of a sweeter name to call you, dear. I knew before you came you weren't—" Annie caught the word before it came out. "I thought perhaps," she went on rapidly, stroking his hand, "that maybe you'd have trials in your life like Joseph had."

"You mean, Mama, someone might throw me in a deep, dark pit some day?" Annie could feel Joseph's heart pounding against her body, and his breath came in bunches.

"Oh, no, I didn't mean that, Joseph. But maybe some day when you get older you'll have to work out among strangers, maybe, or you may be misunderstood or—or—"

"Or would—would"—Joseph looked horrified now—"would Father sell me to Fonzo Bullet or throw me away, or—"

"Joseph, dear, let's not think of such things now. Let me tell you why I named you Joseph. Because when I was a child my grandfather came to visit us once, and he told me that story in such a beautiful way I never forgot it. I can see him yet as I sat on a little wooden box by his knee and Timothy standing beside him as you are beside me now, and little Rachel who died the next winter sat on his knee looking up into his kind face as he talked. He had a long white beard that hung almost to his waist, and Rachel would stroke it while he talked to us. He had such a kind way of speaking."

"I know, Mama. Like Mr. Pennewell talks?"

"I don't know, Joseph. Oh, yes—yes, as Amos Pennewell talks, I'm almost sure. When Grandfather got through telling us that beautiful story of that boy who was true to God, I said to myself then, if I ever have a little boy of my own I want to call him Joseph, and I hope he'll grow up to be a good man like Grandfather Stokes. I've told you the story of Joseph several times but each time I tell it, it becomes more beautiful to me, and it makes me very happy to know you love the story too. I hope it will stay with you and especially while we are gone. If anything sad or disappointing comes your way, if you are ever misunderstood or blamed for something you know you are not guilty of, remember how Joseph did. What did he always do, Joseph?"

"You said he always trusted God even in the dark."

"That's right, Joseph, for he knew—"

"He knew God could see him in the dark."

"That's right, dear. When we are gone you may be lonesome sometimes, but remember God sees you, He loves you, He knows all that will happen to us in the future, as He did in Joseph's life. When he was down in that dark pit, God saw him there, and I like to think as Grandfather said, that maybe after all his brothers had gone away and no one else saw, maybe a light from Heaven shone down on him and gave him courage to be true before he started on that long journey into a strange country."

"Start at the beginning and tell it all to me, Mama." Joseph's hand touched his mother's throat.

*   *   *

Bennet went after Hepsi right after breakfast. Then it was soon time to leave. Earnie would drive them to town and bring back a few groceries. Annie clasped

Joseph to her breast and kissed him on the forehead and lips. Tears blinded her.

"Darling," she whispered, "you'll never know how much I love you. It hurts me so to leave you here, but I must go."

Joseph cried. Of course he did. What child could have kept from it?

The first few hours were terrible! He sat by the gate and cried. He walked back and forth in the garden. He sat on an old bench in the woodshed and buried his face in his hands.

"I feel almost like Joseph," he said to himself at length, and maybe there was a tinge of self-pity in that thought, but Joseph was only seven.

"Joseph!" He heard Aunt Hepsi's shrill voice from the kitchen door.

"Yes." He made his appearance at the woodshed door.

"What are you doing out there?"

"Nothing."

"Well, your father said you're to keep busy in the potato patch."

"What doing?" Joseph came closer.

"Didn't your father tell you?"

"He didn't say anything about the potato patch."

"Now, Joseph Armstrong. Don't try to lie out of work like that the first day they're gone. Your father gave me orders to see to it that you pick potato bugs. You're to go over the entire patch every day, so you'd better get busy at it."

"But—but," stammered Joseph feebly, "they aren't big enough yet to have any bugs on them."

"Tut—tut—now, Joseph. You're to pick potato bugs, for your father told me so, and milk twice a day, and feed the chickens and give them fresh water at noon. Did you do that?"

"I'm going to right now." Yes, it was true in his sore distress he had forgotten to do it.

"See there, now, and your father isn't gone mor'n a few hours. I'm to give a full report of your behavior when he gets back, so you'd better just go water those chickens this minute and get your pail out with the coal oil in it, and go over the potato patch as you're supposed to."

Joseph watered the chickens and found a gallon pail and put some coal oil in it. He went over the entire potato patch—fifteen rows across the end of the garden —and found not one bug.

"Joseph, guess you an I'll have ter run this here farm fer a while, won't we?" Earnie spoke to Joseph in the barn. He was feeding the horses, and Joseph had just started to milk the first cow.

"I guess so," answered Joseph.

"Well, when it comes mealtime, Joseph, you talk ter me an I'll talk ter you, fer I'm not talking to Miss Hepsi. 'Spose she'll make you wipe dishes fer her?"

"I don't know, Earnie. She made me pick potato bugs this afternoon and there weren't any yet."

"Huh! She's rushin' the season a little, ain't she? Them bugs won't show up fer a week or ten days yet. Say, want ter go 'long with me Sunday ter Alex Burns's shack an' see how two old bachelors get a meal an' do?"

"I couldn't do that, Earnie," came Joseph's ready answer. "I go to church on Sunday, and Miss Lottie wouldn't like me to miss. Anyway, Mama said I can have Freddie come over and sleep with me Saturday night and go along to church with us."

"Oh, well, oh, well, good fer you. That'll be fine. I was jes' wonderin' how you'd like ter be alone with Hepsi, drivin' them three miles ter church an' back."

"Freddie will be with me." And Joseph smiled when he said it.

"An' who planned that all out fer you? Your father?"
Earnie Eloy threw his voice across the mangers between
them. His heart, though cold and stony toward God,
had a tender spot in it for this small son of Bennet Armstrong.

"My mother did that," answered Joseph.

"Ain't you got a peach of a mother, now? I can't even
remember mine, fer she died afore I could walk."

CHAPTER XII

Time, nor space, nor words could tell all that happened to poor little Joseph during the twelve weeks his parents were away. Hard as he tried to be good and obedient to Aunt Hepsi, few were the kind words he received from her lips. She nagged at him about one thing or many from the time he came downstairs in the morning until he went upstairs at night. It was "Don't do that," or "Hasn't your mother taught you this?" or "Take that cat out of the house," or "Get busy on those potato bugs" until Joseph's head was in a whirl. Wherever he went her greenish-gray eyes followed him, only to criticize. Her look was always severe and stern. She would pussyfoot through the house and pounce upon Joseph at some unexpected moment, only to chide him for just sitting around, or shake her bony finger at him and scold until the little wart beside her nose would tremble. If Joseph was at the farthest end of the garden she could send her shrill high-pitched voice across to him, and order him to come at once and chase the chickens out of the lettuce bed. He soiled too many clothes and ate too much bread. He talked too much to the hired man at the table one day, and the next was scolded for being a dreamer. If it had not been for Earnie and Freddie, the twelve weeks would have been unbearable. Cousin Freddie helped a lot. Joseph became greatly attached to him that summer.

And Joseph got several letters from his mother that were priceless. But the thing that nearly tore his heart out was that Aunt Myrtle, as she insisted on being called, demanded the privilege of reading them to him. Of course Annie supposed she would.

"Dear Joseph," one read, "I had no idea your father had so many relatives to visit. He enjoys it more than

I do, because it makes me very tired. I am so anxious to come home to my little son. I know before I get there that you've been a good boy and made Aunt Hepsi no trouble. I pray for you every hour of the day and when I go to bed at night. Don't forget how much I love you. I am still looking for that picture you want. I haven't seen any yet. Unless Father changes his mind we'll start home the 12th. My cough is no better.

"Most lovingly,
"Your Mother."

"Such a letter!" scoffed Hepsi, folding it with her long bony fingers. She almost hissed the words through her sparsely scattered teeth. "Such a letter!" she repeated, sticking it behind the clock. "Your mother thinks you're 'punkins' no matter what you do. Pride goeth before destruction the Bible says, an' she's what I call teetotally proud of you."

*　　*　　*

There was one preacher who always shook hands with all the boys after the benediction. He was tall and broad-shouldered, and his flowing whiskers were fast turning white. His name was Grissley Steward, one of the nine or ten ordained men who sat on the bench behind the pulpit every Lord's Day. His eyes twinkled when he spoke, and his voice always came from smiling lips. From his earliest recollections, for some reason, Joseph held a special fondness and reverence in his heart for this man. Joseph never slept in church, though many children did. The first Sunday his parents were gone he sat beside Freddie and Uncle Timothy on the men's side, close to the front. After the singing of three hymns the door to the council room opened and out filed ten devout men, each with a Bible under his arm. Joseph shuddered at this holy sight, and a feeling of deep awe took hold of him. He sat spellbound while Brother Grissley Steward took the floor and opened his Bible before all the people.

He read as one who understood, and so clearly that
Joseph could understand. The thing that thrilled Joseph
was that he said that day some of the very things
his own mother had told him. When he realized that
his own mother and this great man of God believed alike,
his little soul burned within him. His gaze never shifted
from that preacher all during his sermon. The next
thing he knew, Brother Grissley Steward was holding
his hand and asking him questions, personal questions.

"You're a brave little boy to stay at home like this,"
he was saying, and Joseph felt a tender but strong hand
on his shoulder. "God bless you, Joseph," he heard
again, "and help you grow up to be a real man for God."

The next afternoon Joseph found a place beside a pile
of old lumber out behind the barn, and there he knelt and
said his first audible prayer alone. He had prayed often
when his mother helped him. Yes, and he prayed, "Now
I lay me down to sleep," every night before he crept
into bed. And in his childish way he breathed or whispered many a prayer to God, but that day Joseph started
his own private devotion of his own desire. He was only
a child, and some might be tempted to doubt his sincerity, but sometimes the sincerity of a child will put to
shame that of an adult. Joseph Armstrong was not yet
eight years old when his parents went away and stayed
for three months, and during that time his association
with cousin Freddie, the impressions he received from
Brother Grissley Steward, and his prayers beside the
woodpile, all melted together to make a stone in the
foundation of his character. This stone was swathed
in the beauty and warmth of his mother's love.

*   *   *

At last the day came when Earnie drove to town to
get them. Bennet, Annie, and Virginia all smiled when
they met him. Bennet had gained in weight, but Annie

looked more frail than ever. Virginia had developed as any normal child would in three months' time.

"Joseph!" He ran to the gate and buried his face in her dress. It was his mother.

"Hi, Joseph," is all Bennet said.

"I have it in the suitcase, Joseph." They walked toward the house hand in hand, while Virginia ran on ahead, her blond hair bobbing in the sunshine. "It is a gift from your great aunt Matilda. I saw it hanging in her bedroom and told her how you wanted one like it —so she took it down and said I could bring it home for you. You'll like it, I know."

Annie coughed. Hepsi, stiff and skinny, stood at the open door.

"It's so good to be home again," smiled Annie. Her voice sounded tired. Hepsi held the screen door back and Annie passed inside. The linoleum on the floor seemed to come up to meet her. Linoleums have a way of doing that after one's been gone a long time. The cat somehow followed Annie inside and rubbed his back on her leg. It felt like home. Poor, lonesome Tabby!

"Yes, Joseph, the picture." She read his anxious, waiting face. "I'll get it out for you as soon as Father brings the suitcase in."

He loved it. It was what he wanted. "We'll hang it beside your bed."

* * *

September soon came. "I'm going to drive to town this morning," said Joseph's mother after breakfast, "and I want you to go with me. Father is too busy to take me, so you'll go with me."

She let Virginia off at Uncle Timothy's place. Aunt Sara was a motherly aunt.

"What are you going to town for, Mama?"

"I'm going to see Dr. Lindquist, Joseph. I cannot quit coughing, no matter how hard I try. Your father seems quite put out about it. He was certain our long visit in another climate would help me, but it only made me feel worse. This is why we stayed away so long, and then, too, Father said he needed a vacation. His Aunt Martha wanted him to take me to a specialist, but he didn't want to. Joseph, I'll have you stay in the buggy while I go in."

Dr. Hudson Lindquist's office was not hard to find. Annie tied the horse, and walked slowly up the stone steps to the portico where the doctor's name hung on a chain in a glass frame. It was fully forty minutes before she returned.

When they had gone half a mile out of town, Annie stopped the horse under a big maple tree and, turning to Joseph, she said softly, "Son, I must tell you something you ought to know. It is hard for me—to—tell you, Joseph, but I—know I must. You are only eight years old now, but I have confidence in you that I can tell you things I couldn't tell anyone else." She hesitated. Joseph was waiting, his eyes open wide. "I suppose you're old enough, Joseph, to realize that I've had a very unhappy life with your father." His eyes told her he understood, so she went on. "I hate to say it, Joseph, but your father has never made me happy since our wedding day. I did not know him when I promised to be his wife. I thought I was marrying a real Christian, and although it was hard for me to leave my home and come way out here among strangers, I was not afraid—because I loved him, and I thought he was going to be good to me.

"I have often wondered why my life has been so sad. I was not a wicked girl when I was young; I tried to be obedient as far back as I can remember. I was a sinner, of course, and confessed my sins to Christ when I asked to be baptized, but I never went out into the sins of the world. Why I've been so deceived and disappointed I may never know. Joseph," she reached over and took his hand in hers, "if I didn't trust you I wouldn't tell you all this. For over eleven years now I've been living with a broken heart. I've been living mostly for you." Her lips quivered and sudden tears welled up in both eyes. "Your father has been very unkind to me in many ways. He is not a poor man, Joseph, and yet I've been deprived of some necessities of life. You know how many suits Father has, but for years I've had only one suit of underwear to my name."

"Mama!"

"It's true, Joseph. You wouldn't know it unless I tell you, that every Saturday night after you go to bed and Earnie is gone to town, I have to wash out my underwear and dry it behind the kitchen stove over night so I can go to church clean on Sunday. God knows this is true. I've been doing it for years. I've not had one new dress since we're married, and you know how I've made your pants and coats out of old things I brought from home. Thank God I brought them. Your father inherited $27,000 when his father died, but you and I do not get to enjoy any of it except that we live in a nice, big house. My mother never knew before she died what I went through. None of my friends know all this unless they'll soon wonder why I always wear the same old dresses. I've mended and darned and patched until I can't any more."

"Well, Mama, I'll get you a new dress somehow."

"How would you get me a dress, Joseph? I'll not need another dress now." Her voice faltered and she pressed his little hand still harder. "The doctor told me this cough I have is caused by my heart. I've been afraid of it for some time. He asked me what I was grieving over, and I told him. He said he guessed that when you were so sick when you were a baby. Now he said I've waited too long and my days—are—numbered."

"What did he—he mean, Mama?"

"He meant—I haven't many days to live—Joseph."

CHAPTER XIII

When Joseph realized what his mother had said he burst into tears, and his entire body shook with sobs that choked him.

"Oh, Mama! Oh, Mama!" he cried, "don't die; oh, please! Where would I go? What would I—I do without—you? I can't stand it if you—die."

"Joseph," spoke his mother at length, "if my time has come to go, I'll have to go. I think I must live for your sake and Virginia's—but if God thinks I've finished my work here below—I'm ready to go. I've tried to teach you about God, Joseph, and for a boy your age I think you understand as well as can be expected. If I should die—"

"Oh, Mama, don't!" Joseph almost screamed now. He could not control his emotions.

"Go to Amos Pennewell when you want to know something. He's a good Christian man and understands boys. He's a kind father to his children and I believe he'd try to help you. And then Brother Grissley Steward is a real man of God and loves children. He would help you, I'm sure. If I have a chance on Sunday I may speak to him. If your own father took an interest in you I wouldn't need to talk this way. It grieves me so, but it's true.

"And Joseph, I'll say this yet, too. I want you to love and respect your father as much as possible, for he still is your father. You've noticed what fine clothes he wears and how nice he can act out in public. If—after I'm gone —he falls in love with another woman—and you know it before they marry, please go to her with a message from me. Maybe she won't believe you, but tell her just how your father has treated me and give her a fair warning.

I wouldn't want another woman to be fooled as I was. I feel it's my duty to give her this message."

"Mama, I couldn't do that. She wouldn't hear me, and Father would beat me for it."

"That's right, Joseph. I'm afraid he would. Well, let's pray about this." Annie coughed and her lips turned blue. Joseph could see her neck quiver.

"Well, Mama," choked Joseph, wiping his tears, "I made me a secret place out behind the barn by that old pile of wood—where—I go to pray every day. I went out there almost every day—while you—were gone. If Earnie was near the barn I went out beside the apple tree."

"Joseph, you dear boy! What made you do that?"

"Oh, I just felt like it after you left. Then Brother Grissley Steward shook hands with me and said he hoped I'd grow up to be a man for God, and—when I thought of the Bible Joseph and all you told me before you left, I just—just wanted to, Mama." He laid his head on her shoulder.

"God bless you, my son. Keep it up. If I must leave—you, surely—oh, surely God will look down on you in mercy."

"But," sobbed Joseph anew, "if—you die, I—want to, too."

"I've prayed so long now that Father's heart would be softened toward us and he's still the same. Sometimes I think it will kill me, Joseph. Lois and Riley seem so happy, and I know Uncle Timothy is good to his children. I think it can't be Father talks so cruel to you at times, but maybe if we both pray, things will be different someday. Maybe we'd better go home now. I'm afraid Father will see we've been crying."

"I don't—care," sobbed Joseph. "Are you sure that doctor knows you can't live long?"

Annie sat in silence. She looked out over the stubble fields in the distance and a faint smile lit up her sweet sad face.

"Once—once—he was wrong when you were a baby."

Joseph drew a long, deep breath.

*　　*　　*

He was sitting beside his father on the fifth bench from the front. The chorister, a middle-aged man in a black suit, had started the second verse when something wet and shiny started trickling down Joseph's sad face.

> "Does Jesus care when my way is dark
> With a nameless dread and fear?
> As the daylight fades
> Into deep night shades,
> Does He care enough to be near?"

Bennet noticed Joseph's tears and sniffed nervously. He closed and opened his hymnbook.

> "Oh, yes, He cares, I know He cares!
> His heart is touched with my grief."

Bennet cleared his throat. What ailed Joseph all of a sudden? Bennet was embarrassed. He sincerely hoped no one else noticed.

*　　*　　*

Annie didn't tell Bennet all the doctor had said. In fact, she told him very little because he inquired but little.

Until the weather would no longer permit it, Joseph went daily to his secret place of prayer behind the barn. The angels still bow their heads when they pass that hallowed spot where a grief-stricken lad, full of nameless dread and fear, knelt and poured out his soul to God.

Do you suppose God could treat lightly that cry? Do you suppose the great heart of the good Father was touched when little Joseph Armstrong knelt there beside that woodpile and begged Him to spare the life of the dearest person on earth to him? There is a place similar to that spot by the woodpile for every soul who wants a place near to the heart of God.

From that hour in September when Annie Armstrong stopped under a certain tree on the way home from town and confided in her young son, the bond of love between them grew stronger each day. How could it have been otherwise? It was stronger than any written agreement or certificate ever issued by a government. Before Annie was married she had read in her own Testament how the love between husband and wife is likened unto the love between Christ and the Church. She anticipated realizing this joy. When her heart was crushed under the disappointments and sore trials, she naturally lavished that love on Joseph, not as some foolish mothers waste their affection on a disobedient or naughty child who does not return it, but because she could do nothing else and be honest. She loved that child with a godly and jealous love. Her highest desire was to teach him how to love and fear the God who had given him to her, and saved his life from that tiny grave. Together they worked and planned and prayed. She told him all her secrets and he told her his. Every night when Joseph ascended those stairs to his room above he wondered if he'd have a mother in the morning. It was an aging experience for a lad. What comfort it would have been had his father shared with him this soul distress! If Bennet really cared that Annie was suffering from a heart condition, he kept his feelings hidden.

* * *

Joseph and Annie prayed that God would increase the egg yield. With the extra eggs Joseph brought in, Annie made noodles in secret and hid them. By careful managing she saved enough cream to make an extra pound of butter. She made some extra doughnuts on Saturday morning, and to her happy surprise Bennet said it would be all right if she and Joseph would take the eggs to town. With a strangely pounding heart, yet with new spirits, Annie knocked at several doors in the better residential district in town and, smiling genially, displayed her products. They were not hard to sell. Her pleasant voice and sincere personality were irresistible. What joy, what satisfaction enveloped the mother's saddened heart to place in Joseph's hand a nickel's worth of candy!

"You must not tell Father," reminded Annie cautiously. "We will do this again next week. If God gives me the strength I can get some new underwear the next time. You and I will both have new stockings now for Sunday."

"And Mama," said Joseph confidentially, "maybe you can get a new dress too. You are not going to die yet. Something tells me so. Aren't you getting better?"

"Sometimes I think I am and sometimes I think I'm not. I know this, Joseph, that God hears your prayers, and I know I believe in my own. I feel the Lord's presence with me all the time, and if He wants me to live He'll give me the strength from day to day to keep going. If I should be taken suddenly, remember what I've been telling you. There will never come to you any experience so dark but that God's light will pierce through."

All through the month of October Annie figured and studied and prayed for a way and ways to earn a little pin money. She made a delicious minute pudding that brought a ready sale. She made cottage cheese and boiled mush that city folks liked to slice and fry. Virginia looked forward to staying at Aunt Sara's house while Mama and Joseph drove to town. A tired, but happier Annie drove home to the Armstrong place. Joseph helped peddle. It was not long until patrons waited at their doors, anxious to sample any new goods this pleasant-faced country woman had to sell.

How could she do this and Bennet not find it out? It was one of those extraordinary things that few women have tried and that no one but the good Father could have helped her perform. It was almost miraculous how she could make something good out of so little. Bennet's wife was a wonder, and he did not know it.

*   *   *

There was corn to be husked. Joseph Armstrong was the only boy in the school district who could not start to school when the term opened. Bennet could easily have hired a man, but Joseph was compelled to stay at home and help until after Thanksgiving. Because Amos Pennewell was a true-hearted Christian and loved this boy, he took special pains to help Joseph make up what he had missed. He seemed to understand Joseph's unspoken words. The lad did not fret or complain or grumble because of his father's perverse reasoning. It was not hard for Joseph to make up his back work. Amos Pennewell was astounded at the boy's ability to advance, especially in the arithmetic. In fact, by Christmas Joseph was two grades ahead of the class.

Joseph learned to laugh. What fun they had at recess playing Hide-e-hoo, Andy Over, and Throw a Chunk. The teacher played with the children. Imagine J. Bennet Armstrong playing with his boy!

Rosie Magee smiled at Joseph. She sat across the aisle from him, her plump face resting in two dimpled hands. Her cheeks were pink like ripening peaches, and flaxen curls hung over both shoulders. Rosie Magee winked at Joseph. Although he was too dumbfounded to respond,

t sent funny happy prickles all around his heart—that
kind of prickles Joseph hadn't felt very many times in
his life.

"I like you," whispered Rosie Magee one day before
Christmas.

"I like you too," whispered Joseph, smiling shyly.

Joseph was the only pupil that had to walk home
through the snow. Rosie Magee felt sorry for him.

One day she passed him a note: "If you lived down
my way, you could ride in our sleigh."

*   *   *

Joseph was milking. He turned and looked behind
him. No one was there, but he was sure someone had
called him by name. It sounded like the voice of Grissley
Steward. So sure was Joseph that someone had called
him that he walked to the stable door and looked out. He
opened it and stepped outside. He looked to the right
and to the left. No one was in sight.

"Brownie, did you bark?" Joseph's little dog came
bounding. "Who called me, Brownie?"

When Joseph finished milking that evening and while
the long gray shadows deepened into night, there crept
over him the consciousness that it had been the voice of
God.

"Mama," whispered Joseph that evening, "tonight,"
and a serious expression crossed his face, "tonight in
the barn I believe I heard God speak to me."

"And what did He say, Joseph?"

"Just my name; that's all."

"Was it—Joseph, was it around five o'clock?"

"I think—about."

"At that time I was reading in my Bible, Joseph, in
Genesis, words something like these: 'Joseph is a fruitful

bough, even a fruitful bough by a well,' and as I rea
those words, Joseph, a strange feeling passed throug
me that it was for you."

"What do you mean, Mama?"

"Someday I believe it will be revealed to you."

CHAPTER XIV

Lottie Woods stood before her class of boys, and the morning sunbeams glittered through the windowpane on her gray hair. Her pleasingly plump face beamed on the children as the sun did on her. She wore a green challis dress full of fine, fine checks of brown and other colors that blended perfectly with the green.

"We are going to have something special today." Her voice sounded like chimes. "I know you will all be delighted, for someone is going to speak to all the children this morning." She smiled, and the gold beside the eyetooth glittered in the sun. "You may all sit over there now on the benches with the other children. Joseph, you go first."

Joseph led the way and sat on the end of the first bench. About forty children were soon in a happy cluster waiting for the surprise.

"How many of you children," asked Lottie, "know who Uncle Tom is?"

Every hand went up.

"Of course you do. Everyone who comes to this church knows who Uncle Tom is. We seldom hear anyone call him Mr. Bradly, do we? What is it, Freddie? You want to sit beside Joseph? All right. Move over, Charlie. That's a boy. Now is everybody fixed? Freddie and Joseph seem to be big friends, don't they? Well that's all right—I don't blame you, Freddie. If I were a boy your age I'd like to sit beside my cousin too. Well, Uncle Tom has consented to give a little talk to you children this morning. He said he wasn't a speech maker, but we all believe he is, don't we? Anyway I told him it's not like getting up in church just to make a speech to a small group like this, so he finally consented. Here he comes now!"

Every head turned when the classroom door opened. In stepped Uncle Tom Bradly (who really wasn't anybody's real uncle, and no one knows who started calling him that), rubbing his large muscular hands a little nervously. His bronze-colored face had a wind-blown, reddish hue, and his deep-set hazel eyes twinkled when he smiled at the children. How strong he looked! Tom Bradly was not a large man in height, but he was chunky and husky-looking. Every boy admired him. He made a quiet little chuckle in his throat and wet his lips.

"Well," he said, trying to get started. "Miss Lottie has a-asked me to-a come in here and make you children a speech. Now-a, if I had some of you boys out by the buggy shed in a corner, maybe I could make a real stump speech, but bein's as I'm one of the trustees I reckon Miss Lottie thought I'd do for this sort of thing. Now," he wet his lips again and went on slowly, trying to choose the words. If Miss Lottie and Mrs. Christopher, and Mrs. Brooks, the deacon's wife, hadn't been in the room, he could have gone faster and with greater ease. Strange that a strong man like Tom Bradly should get embarrassed when a few women were listening! He cleared his throat and ran his finger in his collar to make it feel a little looser.

"You children have-a all heard about the missionaries way over in India who are-a working hard to win souls for Christ. Well, those missionaries have children just as we have over here. Nice children like you children. Nice children who get hungry and-a—like to eat and-a —read good books—and-a—they have to have shoes and other things to wear same as you do—and-a some of us trustees and ministers got together the other week and talked this over with Brother Grissley, and we thought it would be a nice idea to-a have our Sunday-school children give money to support at least one of those missionaries' children, a—child—I mean, well, whichever way you'd say it, you know what I mean. One boy—one little boy maybe—a—like this one right here —like little Joseph Armstrong just about ready to start to school. I guess you're about six, aren't you, Joseph?"

"I'm eight," answered Joseph, squeezing his hands between his knees. Joseph's cheeks got pink. All the children looked at him and some smiled.

"Well, pardon me, Joseph," Uncle Tom remarked, rubbing his brawny hands. "You're older than I thought you were. Well, anyway a little boy maybe as nice-looking as Joseph here lives way over there in India and needs some help from America. Or maybe a little girl like Susie there. Now if every one of you children here today could bring a penny each Sunday and put them all in a box, how many pennies would we have? How many are there here today, forty?"

"Forty-three," answered Miss Lottie.

"Then we would have forty-three cents, wouldn't we? And there are fifty-two Sundays in a year—let me see now, that would be around twenty-two dollars a year, maybe twenty-three without figuring to the cent. Who could bring a penny each Sunday?"

Most of the hands went up. Joseph's hand went up over half way, then all the way. He remembered his mother saying she had another idea—making popcorn balls to sell in town.

"Now look at that! And maybe some of you could bring two or three pennies. Who could?"

A few hands went up.

"Well," continued Uncle Tom, "maybe some of you who say 'no' right now will change your minds after you think it over. Once there was a young man who came home from town with a pair of new trousers and they were too long, so he asked his wife to shorten them for him, about an inch and a half. 'No,' she said, 'I haven't time.' So he asked his sister to do it for him. 'No, I haven't time either,' she said. Then he asked his mother to do it for him. She said, 'Get your wife to do that.'

"While the man was out working hard his wife thought to herself, 'Guess I was pretty selfish; I'll go do it and surprise him.' So she cut an inch and a half off the trousers and pressed them nicely and hung them in the closet. She went out to feed the chickens.

"Then the sister thought about how selfish and mean she was and she repented in her heart and slipped in the room and cut an inch and a half off the trousers and pressed them up nicely and hung them back where they were. She went out to milk, feeling much better in her heart.

"After a while the man's mother said to herself, 'I'm sorry I said, "no," to my son. If his wife won't fix those trousers, I will. I'll surprise him.' So she went and cut off an inch and a half, pressed them nicely, and hung them in the closet where they were.

"Now when the man put on his trousers that evening, do you think he was surprised? He certainly was. His trousers were three times as short as he intended they should be, and who was disappointed? He was, and so was his wife, his sister, and his mother. Now we know it wouldn't go that way with us. It would be the opposite kind of a surprise. If those of you who say you can't bring three cents a Sunday change your minds and do it, think how much we'll get together. We'd have three times as much as we thought at first and no one would be disappointed, but everyone would be glad. Maybe some could even bring more than three cents. Now this was a very crude illustration, I know, boys and girls, and I'm sure you'll not ask me to make a speech soon again.

"When we decided one of us-a should make this speech, everyone was willing but not all in the right way. I had to think of old Bill and Ned. Those two horses were both willing. Bill was willing to work, and Ned was willing to let him. I was willing to have a speech be made, but I was willing that Brother Grissley or one of the preachers should make it. Then Miss Lottie said, 'we want Uncle Tom.' " His eyes sort of twinkled and he shifted from one foot to the other and went on.

"I'd-a rather reached down in my own pocket and given the money for you than make this speech, but then you children would miss the blessing of giving. It's one of the grandest things in the Christian life to share with others. Leastways, it makes me happy to give. That's part of my religion. How many would like to start this missionary fund idea next Sunday?"

Every hand went up. Not one stayed down. Even Miss Lottie's hand went up. So did Mrs. Brooks' and Mrs. Christopher's. Uncle Tom Bradly wet his lips and stepped toward the door.

"Who thinks Uncle Tom can't make a speech?" asked Lottie Woods.

One little girl's hand went up, than down with a jerk.

"How many say he can?"

Forty-three hands went high.

"Thank you, Uncle Tom," chimed Miss Lottie, "and now that the ice has been broken we may call on you again some day. We all liked your talk."

Uncle Tom loosened his shirt collar with his forefinger and walked out of the room.

Joseph looked at the door through which Tom Bradly had passed and another hero was added to his list. There was Amos Pennewell, Grissley Steward, and now, Uncle Tom Bradly. In front of him stood dear Miss Lottie, beside him sat his favorite cousin Freddie, and beyond that closed door was his mother somewhere in the congregation of several hundred worshipers.

* * *

In the years to come Joseph learned in school what a supplement to his history was. He learned also when he started to school late, what it was to receive supplementary instructions from the teacher. But little did he realize that Sunday morning as he sat there wrapped in thought what it would mean to him in the future—the near future—to have such characters impress him early in life. Those boyhood heroes added to his life what his home lacked. He needed this supplement. The Christian religion holds up high ideals, but children read those ideals not on pages or on stone, but in flesh and blood. Bennet Armstrong had flesh and blood. The religion he held portrayed daily to his son such cruel, disappointing behavior that Joseph could have been crushed to the earth. Joseph was an intelligent child. In several respects he was remarkably brilliant for his age. He had a fanciful imagination about heavenly things. He had a supreme desire to please his mother. He had an extraordinary craving to learn.

"Father," said Joseph at the table that day, "do missionaries always go to school first?"

"Why?"

"Well — I'd — I'd like to — to be one someday — Father." His fingers fumbled with the corner of the tablecloth.

"You mean"—shouted Bennet contemptuously. "You mean, you've got it into your head now to go to college? Not with my consent. That would give you a straight ticket to hell." And Bennet's fist came down on the corner of the table.

CHAPTER XV

Improbable or impossible as it may seem, Bennet Armstrong gave Joseph permission to go to Freddie's house to stay overnight, Saturday night. How those two boys loved each other! Freddie Stokes was a little larger than Joseph and stronger physically. His hair was lighter, but his skin was darker. They did not look alike at all. But those two boys had a good many common likes and dislikes. They talked about little things, and discussed big things, as boys do when they like each other.

Several times a year the Stokes and Armstrongs got together on Sundays, and indeed those were happy times for Joseph. Bennet acted remarkably congenial and sometimes even jovial in a crowd. For this Annie was grateful, even though in her heart there came a sickening taste that verged on disgust, for he never displayed these traits of character at home. The longer she lived with him the less she understood him, but what woman could have understood him as well, and been willing to endure what she did without complaining?

Bennet was a most remarkable character—remarkably puzzling. Annie was a most remarkable character, too—unusual in her devotion to God, unequaled in her patience, and unique in the respect in which she was held by the entire congregation. Little did Bennet recognize the esteem and high regard the household of faith had for his wife. Annie Armstrong was remarkable in yet another way, and that was her endurance of pain and physical weakness. But it must be accepted without dispute that her power to stand up and go on working as she did came from the Almighty One.

Yes, Doctor Hudson Lindquist was seldom wrong. He had told her to her face, frankly and honestly, that with such a heart as she had her days on earth were numbered.

She knew by the seriousness in his voice and eyes he was not trifling with her emotions. But there was a Maker and Ruler of the world and all beings in it who looked down with compassion on Annie and her son that day on the roadside, remembering the love He Himself had for His own mother, Mary. The Father's pity expressed to mortals is one of the most beautiful and touching dramas ever exhibited in all history.

Annie acknowledged her daily dependence on God for bodily strength to carry on. Joseph, too, understood that his mother relied on superhuman power to keep going, for hadn't he found solace by the woodpile, and hadn't he prayed in faith? The trust of a child is not only surprising but sometimes stupendous. As Joseph watched his mother month after month, is it any wonder his confidence in God deepened? And when he put his own mother and the Christian ideals she upheld in the same catalog with Amos Pennewell, Uncle Tom, Miss Lottie Woods, and Brother Grissley Steward, is it any wonder his own ideals of life were held high? It had an aging effect on so young a lad to live in constant fear that his mother might pass away suddenly: but dread was changed to trust that gave him a peaceful feeling of security. It had a refining and disciplining effect on Joseph, too, for whenever he was tempted to do wrong he would hear those words: "My days are numbered." God has mysterious ways His wonders to perform, and it could even be that this was one chastening rod He used on little Joseph Armstrong to keep him from yielding to the common sins of youth.

On one occasion Joseph helped another schoolboy write with chalk a silly little rhyme on Michael Hunter's lane gate. Bennet Armstrong himself happened to notice it one day, and upon inquiring of Michael, learned his own son had taken part in it. It is to be expected Joseph received his just dues and more. He was not only severely strapped but made to go to Mr. Hunter and ask forgiveness. Joseph learned his lesson. Many were his whippings. A few he deserved, but countless more were laid on him unjustly.

"Bennet," said Annie one evening, "did you transact that business when we went North?"

"What business?" mumbled Bennet.

"When we went North?"

"Well, when did we go North?"

"A year ago."

"What business are you talking about?" asked Bennet somewhat peevishly.

"I don't know, Bennet," answered Annie. "I was just wondering if you transacted it."

"Well, who said I was going to transact any business on that trip?" he scowled.

"I thought you told Earnie you were going North on business."

"Maybe I did," came his sarcastic answer.

"Well, I was only wondering," came Annie's subdued voice.

Silence.

"I went on business." He tried to make the words sound casual.

"I only wondered," she said.

"But it was a useless trip," he added with resentment.

"Tell me, Bennet."

"You know how it went as well as I," he retorted.

"How do you mean, Bennet?"

"You didn't quit coughing after I kept you away three months."

"Oh! That was—the business trip?" Annie's voice sounded strangely far away.

"Did you think I went to buy a farm?"

"I didn't know, Bennet. You—you never said."

These things are anything but pleasant to relate, but in order that the characters of this story be understood, they are given. J. Bennet Armstrong never took his wife into his confidence. He never asked her advice about any purchase, any plan, any project.

"You are to keep your fingers out of my desk," he told her once, and once was enough. He kept his desk locked, and no one but Bennet knew where he kept the key.

There was one commendable thing about Bennet besides his faithful church attendance, and that was that he did provide Annie with things with which to make a meal. He knew she couldn't make a steak dinner without steak. He knew it took flour to make good bread, and Bennet liked Annie's bread. Once in a while he was on the verge of asking Earnie Eloy to hold back when he tilted the cream pitcher, but when he viewed again those sinewy arms, he decided each time to let it pass. Earnie was a worker.

*   *   *

Rosie Magee winked at Joseph. He was standing at the blackboard with the fifth-grade arithmetic class. She was next to him working the same problem in long division. Joseph had his answer first and was watching Rosie scratch at the bottom of the board, 97 x 6.

"Help me," whispered Rosie softly.

Joseph made a tiny 7 and rubbed it out with his fist. Then Rosie looked over and winked. That evening on the way home from school Joseph found a piece of paper in his overcoat pocket. He unfolded it and read, "I like you best of anyone in this school. R. M." Joseph carried it in his hand until he got to the front yard gate, then tore it into bits and dropped it in the tall weeds.

*   *   *

In the late fall Lowell was born. He was fair-complexioned like Virginia, and had blue eyes like Joseph. Now there were two children to carry on the family name. On Sunday evenings when Annie stayed at home, she would sit in her armless rocking chair; Virginia and Joseph sat at her feet, or stood beside her, an arm on each shoulder, while she read to them from her Bible or told them in her own words the fascinating stories therein. Bennet always went to church. Sometimes the three would sing hymns and songs of praise to God. Charles E. Little has written a beautiful little song which runs:

"When Father took the Bible down at night,
  And from its sacred pages read us with delight,
  Then we would sing so sweet and low
  The dear old hymn we all loved so:
  'Nearer, my God, to Thee, nearer to Thee';
  When Father took the Bible down at night."

But in this case it was mother who took the Bible down. Invariably on those evenings Joseph would hear again that voice by the barn. It sent terror through his body. Father had said an education would give him a straight ticket to hell—but that voice that had called him by name came back again and again, calling him to service.

Joseph and Annie peddled berries in berry season. There were dewberries, wild blackberries, elderberries, and God seemed to bless their yield. Annie bought two new dresses and cut her old ones down to fit Virginia. Then there was oyster plant to spare, and the chickens must have known Joseph wanted three cents to take to Sunday school, for they did their best. Annie Armstrong became well known along the best streets in her home town. Her pleasant and gentle manner made her, like few others, a very welcome peddler. Joseph didn't have to go any Sunday without his three cents for the missionary child support fund. What joy and satisfaction enveloped his soul when he walked to the front and dropped them in! Of course Miss Lottie Woods took for granted it came straight from his father's pocket.

*   *   *

Joseph proved to be quite prominent in school activities, especially when it came to reciting poetry or playing the rôle of an important character in a dialogue. Amos Pennewell had Joseph and Freddie act the part of two colored friends who met on the road.

Part of the story read as follows:

Freddie: "Hello der, Zeek, ole chum, where you's been dis week back?"

Joseph: "I'se been no whar, an I neber had no weak back. I feel strong. I feel strong as a lion. I feel like a lion dis blessed minut."

Freddie: "Wal, did you eber see a lion?"

Joseph: "Course I did. You should a seen de long ears ob de critter, an heard him roar."

At this point Joseph made a noise like a donkey braying, and the school laughed in one loud roar.

Amos Pennewell laughed until his face was red.

"Now children," he said at length, "let us quiet down again. It was very well given. Rosie, you may come forward and recite your poem."

Rosie Magee smoothed her dress down with both hands and pushed her flaxen curls back. She stood up very straight and looked intently at the stove in the rear of the room.

"He is only a boy whom you see every day.
    With a smile do you greet him, my friend?
  Or do you pass by as you meet on the way,
    Never thinking it pays in the end

To give to a boy what is rightly his own—
    Recognition by you when you can?
Though only a boy his heart is not stone.
    You can help him to be a good man."

Rosie swallowed twice and went on:

"He is only a boy, but deep in his soul
    Lie slumbering thoughts full of joy,
That will thrill this old world while the years onward
        roll—
    Thoughts born in the heart of a boy.
Then friend, just give to the boy what you should
    And help him whenever you can,
For when you are helping a boy to be good
    You are helping to build a good man."

Joseph looked straight ahead even after Rosie had taken her seat.

"Yours was the best," he whispered as she passed him in the schoolyard.

CHAPTER XVI

It was remarkable how well the three Armstrong children got along with one another. Not one of them displayed the fiery temper of their father. They were normal children, and it is to be expected there were occasional scraps, but nothing ever proved to be serious. Virginia and Lowell both loved Joseph. In fact, they adored him. He was kind and gentle to them and often acted as a mediator when Lowell and Virginia could not agree. The little mother and her three children stood together. In the evenings after all the work was done, they'd sit around the kitchen stove and Annie would tell stories of how she lived and what she did when she was young.

"Oh, Mama!" said Lowell one time, "why can't we play and have fun like that sometimes? Father always makes us—"

"Sh, Lowell. Here he comes."

Annie was more lenient with her children than Bennet. She thought they deserved at least fifteen minutes a day for recreation and play, and a rest right after dinner on hot days would be altogether reasonable, but Bennet said, "No."

Virginia had to walk to school too. Rain or stormy weather, if she got there she had to tramp through the cold and mud. If it had not been for Annie's energetic disposition and her thrift, poor Virginia would have had to appear in school the shabbiest of any pupil.

The morning Annie put on her new dress to go to church, Bennet was just in the act of lacing one shoe. He looked up in surprise and his lower jaw dropped.

"Well," he said, "and where did you get all that?"

"I bought it in town, Bennet," answered Annie, adjusting the belt. "Do you like it?"

"Like it!" he shouted. "Tell me what you paid for it and then I'll say whether or not I like it."

"It didn't cost so much, Bennet," sighed Annie wearily. "It was only thirty-nine cents a yard, and it's real silk poplin, too."

"Silk!" shouted Bennet with fury and indignation. "Why must it be silk? Isn't cotton good enough for you?"

"I'm glad for anything new once, Bennet. This is my first new dress since we're married. I made Virginia two dresses out of two of mine that were past wearing. The skirts were the only parts that weren't almost in shreds. You don't"—Annie coughed—"you don't care that I got this, do you, Bennet?"

"Well, how could you do that and still get the chicken feed? Didn't you bring home the oyster shells and the—"

"Yes, I got all that, Bennet, but"—Annie might as well tell. Now was the time. "You see, Bennet, when I baked a spice cake yesterday, I baked one just like it for Mrs. Warehouse in town."

"Mrs. Warehouse?" scowled Bennet. "And who is she?"

"Just a lady I learned to know in town."

"Well?"

"Then I sold Mrs. Jones two pounds of butter."

"Two pounds of butter?" Bennet exploded. "How could you do that? What's left for us, and who gave you the authority to sell butter in town?" He was on his feet now, one shoe on and one shoe off.

"I've been doing it for months, Bennet."

"Months?" he bellowed loudly. "How can this be and I didn't know it? What else have you been buying behind my back. Bring it out and show it all. Who's running this place, you or I?"

"Please—please, Bennet!" said Annie gently. "Sit down, and while you put your other shoe on I'll tell you all about it."

"That's a pretty way to do; tell me after it's done."

"Well, Bennet, it's like this." Annie leaned hard against the dresser. Her heart was pounding violently and tiny beads of sweat stood out on her forehead. Her arms trembled. "Joseph needed stockings and so did I."

"Yes, go on; so did I."

"But we never got them."

"Huh?"

"I've needed underwear ever and ever so badly for a long time. Joseph needed mittens to wear to school and —so I thought of a way to get them."

Bennet looked at his shoe.

"I've been selling cottage cheese in town on Saturdays." Bennet looked up sharply and an icy chill passed over Annie. "And garden things we could spare, and little things I can bake when there's no garden, and—"

"Now, if this isn't something!" Annie could see that his temper was hot now. She felt weak and sick on her stomach.

"And who knows about all this?" He panted now. "I suppose everybody in town and the church knows this but me."

"I didn't know what else to do, Bennet," came Annie's tired, sad voice. "I had to do something."

"Why didn't you tell me you needed these things?" He was beside himself now. When he talked the saliva stood in the corners of his mouth. It looked almost like foam.

"I tried to, Bennet." Annie sank into a chair. She could not stand another minute. "And—" she choked, "if you loved me you could see what I need—without my begging for it. I'll never do that." Two tears fell on her new blue dress.

"Well," answered Bennet, scrambling desperately now for words, "if you've made such a success at peddling, maybe you can get me—"

Joseph appeared at the bedroom door.

"Father," he announced, "we're going to be late to church. Didn't you—" he stopped short and held his breath. What was wrong with Mama? Her face was white and she looked sick.

"What?" shouted his father.

"The clock in the kitchen struck nine-thirty. Virginia and Lowell are in the buggy."

Never had J. Bennet Armstrong been seen coming into church late. He was vexed now.

"You three go on then," he said angrily. "Mama and I aren't going today. Go on! If anyone wants to know why we didn't come, just tell them your mother isn't feeling well."

Joseph said very little on the way to church. He was appalled at the strange look on his mother's face. And why was Father cross? He was certain he heard stern words from the bedroom when he entered the kitchen.

"What's wrong with Mama?" asked Virginia for the fourth time on the way.

"I just don't know," answered Joseph for the fourth time.

"She looked so pretty in her new dress when she tried it on yesterday. And now," said Virginia with a keen sense of regret, "she won't even get to wear it."

Virginia and Joseph were as thrilled over the prospect of seeing their mother wear a new dress to church as was their mother. Why shouldn't they be? Hadn't Virginia greased the cake pan for Mama, and run to the cellar after the eggs; and hadn't Joseph been praying and suggesting and helping for weeks to this end?

*   *   *

Brother Grissley Steward was reading reverently from the book of Ephesians when Joseph felt a light tap on his shoulder.

"You're to go home at once." It was Uncle Tom Bradly whispering in his ear. "A man came to the door and said your mother is awful sick."

Terror numbed Joseph. He sat stiff and speechless.

"Joseph," he heard Uncle Tom saying as in a dream. "If you want to see your mother alive you'll have to hurry."

Up got Joseph as if he'd been shot. Out of the church he went, half walking, half running, stumbling down over the steps. He ran to the shed, and forgetting that Virginia and Lowell were there, he jumped into the buggy and backed out. Down the road they dashed, the capless boy now standing, now sitting, now staring wide-eyed and pale.

"O God!" he prayed aloud, tears streaming to his neck. "O God! please—please let her live to speak to me —just once more."

He ran into the house; great tears blinded both eyes. Bennet was standing beside the bed, his hands clasped tightly across his breast. Joseph could hear him breathing before he entered the room.

"Mama," cried Joseph frantically.

No answer. She lay stiff and cold. Her lips and fingernails were blue—but—but Joseph could see at once she was still breathing.

"Can't she—can't she talk, Father?" cried Joseph.

"No. She's unconscious now."

"What—what happened, Father?" Joseph wrung his hands. He wanted to yell, but he couldn't.

"I just don't know," answered Bennet, shaking his head. "I was out to the barn a while, and when I came in I found her on the bed here, and—and I noticed she was breathing sorta strange. I shook her and put cold rags on her head but she wouldn't come out of it. All she would say was "Call Joseph," so I rode Mike down to Hunter's and told Michael to go up to the church and call you out."

"Oh!" Joseph groaned. He bent over his mother and touched her forehead—her hands, her lips.

"Mama," he called.

She moaned.

"Mama," he repeated.

She moaned.

"It's Joseph, Mama." He put his face close to hers and he could feel her breath on his lips. He took one hand in his and rubbed her arm.

She opened her eyes a little. They didn't look like his mother's eyes. She made one great gasp for breath and shook all over.

"Mama," pleaded Joseph pitifully, "don't die yet, please. If you'll only live I'll try to do more to help you. Mama." He rubbed her other arm. All the while Bennet stook back and kept his hands clasped across his breast.

"Did you send for the doctor?" Joseph looked over at his father.

"I told Michael to." Bennet walked back and forth at the foot of the bed, clearing his throat occasionally.

Joseph knelt beside the bed and buried his face in his mother's arm.

"Dear Lord," he cried.

Bennet left the room.

"Everything will be so dark if Mama leaves. I can't stand it. Oh, tell me how I can be better to her and help her more so she won't need to work so hard."

The woman stirred. She opened both eyes.

"Put my head—up on two—pillows, Joseph. Oh, I thought I'd go—before you got here."

By the time the doctor got there Annie was sitting up in the rocking chair by the window.

"You must take it easy for a while now, Mrs. Armstrong," he said. "I'll leave some pills and the next time you feel one of these spells coming on, put one of these under your tongue at once. It will help. And be careful about going up steps. And," Doctor Hudson Lindquist gave Bennet a quick glance out of the corner of his eye, "try not to worry over things, Mrs. Armstrong. That's hard advice for women to take, especially mothers, but worry and anxiety of any kind cannot help but be hard on you with a heart condition such as you have. Isn't that right, J. B.?"

"Sure," answered Bennet.

CHAPTER XVII

As the months became years, the devotion that Joseph had for his mother grew to esteem. The more he comprehended the difference between his parents, the higher mounted his honor for his mother. He found genuine pleasure in showing her every consideration and enjoyed talking things over with her. Joseph and his father never talked over any problem small or great. That boy never received anything from his father but orders, threats, and criticism. Joseph had washed dishes at the age of three, but as soon as Virginia was able to reach the dish pan from a wooden stool, she was made to take Joseph's job so he could spend more time doing outside work. There were fences to be painted, trees to be felled, and new trees to be planted. Only on an occasional Saturday evening was he allowed any leisure time. Those were the times Freddie came over to spend the night.

"Mom," said Freddie one Sunday night after church. "Uncle Bennet isn't jolly at home like he is when he comes over here."

"He isn't?" inquired his mother with surprise. "I wonder why?"

"I don't know, but he isn't. He talks cross to Joseph, and I'd rather have Joseph come over here."

"Well, maybe you boys misbehave over there."

"No we don't, Mom," answered Freddie. "He talks plenty cross to Virginia too, and I heard her tell Aunt Annie she wanted a doll and a set of little dishes for Christmas, and he told her she'd do well to get an orange and some candy, and toys were—were—I can't think what he said, but—I wish we could get her something for Christmas. Joseph said he wished he had a wagon like ours. Mom, is Uncle Bennet poor?"

"Poor? Why Freddie, he's got lots more than your father has, yes, a good deal more, unless he's lost it."

"Well, Mom, how's come Joseph and Aunt Annie sell things in town every Saturday so he can have his three cents to take to Sunday school and—"

"Why, Freddie!" gasped his mother in surprise. "Who said they did? Sell their eggs, you mean?"

"Why they do, Mom, and I don't mean just eggs. Joseph told me so. That's why they leave Virginia here when it's cold."

"Freddie!" and Sara Stokes put a hand on each hip, "how long—do you mean to tell me—Freddie Stokes, are you telling me the truth? Why, Aunt Annie has a bad heart and—why—it's uncalled for, and—why, Freddie, I can't believe it. Sell what?"

"Why, they peddle things from house to house every Saturday, and they've been doing it for a long time because Uncle Bennet won't let them spend his money."

"Freddie, this is impossible. I'm going to ask Joseph myself the next time he comes over here. Annie's never let on to me and we've been living here over a year now. She always seems so happy and so sweet, and I thought Bennet Armstrong was a Christian. You're not mistaken, Freddie?"

"Mom, I know Joseph don't lie, and yesterday they sold popcorn balls, five dozen, and a spice cake, and cottage cheese, and—"

"Freddie Stokes!" gasped his mother, holding up both hands.

*   *   *

By the time Joseph had completed the fifth grade he had gone through the sixth- and seventh-grade arithmetics. Amos Pennewell was astounded. He hardly knew where to place Joseph, for he was always through with his lessons before anyone else in his class. There were but a few books in the school library and those were old histories. Joseph read each of those through twice.

When Joseph was fourteen he was taller than his mother. His cheeks were well filled out and his voice was beginning to change. On his face one could read a healthy blending of pleasantry and depth. He was neither fickle nor dull. Some called him handsome, especially Mrs. Irons.

Bennet brought in the mail. With indignation on his face and in his step, he approached Joseph who was standing behind his chair at the table. The meal was ready and the family stood waiting.

"And who are you getting mail from, Joseph Armstrong?" snorted Bennet angrily.

"I don't know," answered Joseph honestly, looking his father full in the face.

"Don't know?" he sneered. "Then maybe I can open it and read it for you."

So saying he tore it open and unfolded a sheet of tablet paper.

"Dear Joseph,

"I always liked you very much. You know it, don't you? We are going to move to Wisconsin in a couple of weeks. Since my grandfather died my father is to take over the farm. Just think, we may never see each other again, but I'll never forget you. I'll write to you if you'll write to me. Your sweetheart,

"Rosie Magee."

Joseph got cold, then hot, and both hands gripped the chair in front of him.

Bennet held the letter in his hand and looked sharply at Joseph. "Well," he snapped, "and who is Rosie Magee, and how long has this been going on?" He glared at the boy, who was almost as tall as himself. "Well answer," he said hotly. "Who is Rosie Magee?"

"Just a—girl—in—school," answered Joseph blinking. He bit the corner of his cheek nervously.

"And how long has this been going on?" Bennet demanded an answer. There was no dodging it.

"It's not been going on, Father," answered Joseph meekly.

"Don't tell me that, young man. This sounds like it's not been going on. Indeed. 'Your sweetheart.' " Bennet flung the words at Joseph until they stung. "How many letters like this have you written to this Rosie Magee?"

"None," answered Joseph.

"Then why did she write this to you?"

Joseph's face burned and his knees shook.

"I can't answer that, Father."

"Yes, you can. What girl would be so silly and brazen as to write such a letter to a boy who didn't write one like it first? Answer that."

"I did not," answered Joseph, "ever write Rosie Magee one letter. I passed a couple notes to her across the aisle in school already, but I never wrote her a letter, and I never called her—a—"

Bennet laughed mockingly now. " 'Your sweetheart,' and you know it." Bennet curled his lip with contempt, and scorn was written on every line of his face. "And you claim to know so little about it. So if it's nothing to you then"— and here Bennet stepped to the cookstove and lifting a lid, dropped the letter into the flames— "right here is where it belongs." Down came the stove lid with a bang. "Now care if you like," and Bennet licked his lips as though he relished the cruel words he had spoken. "And," he shook his two first fingers at Joseph, "just you let me catch you writing a letter to

Rosie Magee or any other girl at this age. One thing I know, either she's crazy or it's you. Come, let's eat."

Joseph thought (he wasn't sure) he heard his mother groan. By the look in her eyes he knew she meant they'd have a long talk as soon as they could get together.

"Joseph," whispered Virginia after Father left the room. "I—I believe you."

"Believe what?" Joseph's voice was husky.

"If you—you said you didn't write to—to her—you know—why, I know you didn't."

"Thanks—sis—" It made Joseph feel better.

It so happened by the hand of Providence that Bennet was called to Michael Hunter's to assist with a sick horse.

"Joseph," said his mother softly. (Not so long ago, it seemed to her but yesterday, she held him on her lap and told him stories from the Bible, and now their eyes were on a level. How big and strong Joseph looked today. How capable of doing things.) "Tell me, do you care that Rosie Magee is moving away?"

"Care? Why, Mama, why should I care?" Joseph smiled slightly. There was no need to feel nervous or embarrassed when his mother talked to him.

"Then it's true you never wrote her a love letter?"

"Love letter?" said Joseph taking a heavy breath. "You mean?"

"I mean, did you ever tell her you loved her?"

"No, of course not."

"But you do like her?"

"Everybody in school likes Rosie Magee—everybody but Alpha Smith, and she's just jealous of Rosie's curly hair. It makes her peeved because she likes Jason and Jason likes Rosie best."

"Rosie must be a pretty girl, then."

"She is." When Joseph heard his own voice it sounded strangely solemn, almost reverent. It rather startled him.

"But of course, Joseph, you realize," continued his mother softly, "that you're too young to be thinking seriously of any girl."

"Sure," Joseph looked out the window.

"And I'm sorry Father was so harsh with you." She touched his arm lightly. How handsome he would be someday. Annie caught her breath. "I couldn't approve of his attitude, and I'm sorry for what took place in front of the children and Earnie. I thought it couldn't be—but—but Joseph," she hesitated, "if the time comes that you really do love—someone—you'll promise me—won't you, that you'll tell me about it?"

Joseph looked straight into his mother's eyes. "It's not necessary for me to promise you that, Mama. You know I will."

*   *   *

Joseph was cutting dry weeds along the road when he passed. It was Fonzo Bullet, driving Squire McCracken's six fine white horses.

"Whoa." Fonzo Bullet drew back on the reins and stood up in the wagon. He rolled his eyes over to Joseph and showed his white teeth.

"A-da," he nodded.

"Good day," answered Joseph politely.

"Makin' hay, heh?" Fonzo chuckled.

"We burn this kind," said Joseph.

"Looks lak you's gwine hab some. Say, Marsi, ken ye tell me, is dat ar bridge wash out ober yonder hill whar de ol' Hampton place sets?"

"I don't think so," answered Joseph. "Why?"

"Wall, didn't dat ar storm strike through dese parts las' night?"

"It rained some here, but not bad; hailed a little too."

"My sakes! I wish you'd been whar I was las' night. I neber drive in sich a hurry in my life. Sure war a storm 'cross de mountain. Neber heard tell a' worse one dis time o' year since in 1892. Thought fer a while dem what has wouldn't hab, an' dem what hasn't would get took from—sech blowin' an' lightnin' an' tearin' up o' trees, an' water pourin' down. I," Fonzo stroked his chin slowly and a serious look crossed his face, "sure done call on de Almighty, an' fer a' dat I al'ays try ter hev my 'counts settled up, fer I'm one of dem what believes in keepin' your slate clar."

Joseph stood almost spellbound. This was the old black Fonzo who would come and get him if he disobeyed. It made Joseph smile now. Why he didn't look nor talk like he'd kill a jack rabbit.

"So you say, Marsi, de storm didn't strike here?"

"No, Mr. Bullet, it didn't storm here last night. Not bad."

"How you know my name?" Fonzo smiled and the radiance that shone from that black face touched Joseph's heart.

"My father knows your name," answered Joseph respectfully, "and I've seen you pass several times."

"Wall, I'll be gwine on if you're sure dat bridge ain't wash out. Squire McCracken's specken me ter bring back a barrel apples afore dark. I'll hafter go on. 'Day, an much ablige, Marsi. What yer name?"

"Joseph."

"Sure nuf? Good a name as is. If ye eber chance ter come our way," and Fonzo pointed back toward the hills behind him, "why stop an' see me. I'll show ye roun' de mansion same's de res' of de folk."

"Thank you, Fonzo." Joseph waved good day and continued cutting weeds. Father said they must be burned before snow fell. Joseph hummed a little as he worked.

CHAPTER XVIII

It was announced in church on Sunday morning that a minister by the name of Palmer Trenem from a distant state would begin a series of meetings the following Sunday. Of course the Armstrongs would go. Only sickness or death would prevent that. Although Bennet felt in his heart he could scarcely quit his work early enough in the evening to get to church on time every night, yet he'd rather do that than have the brotherhood inquire about his absence. Just why Bennet Armstrong enjoyed going to church may be a subject for long discussion, so before the discussion is started let it suffice that he was always there.

Palmer Trenem was not only strikingly handsome, but also a powerful speaker. His manner was unlike any Joseph had ever witnessed. He announced first that he had come into their midst for a threefold purpose; namely, to conduct a revival; to awaken in the congregation a greater interest in Bible study; and to make them all more conscious of the sins of the age.

Joseph sat rapt. One minute he was lost in the delight of some beautiful Bible story, and the next smitten to the heart with fearful dread of what might come upon him should he not be ready to meet God face to face. The longer he sat under the sound of this preacher's voice, the more sin-conscious he became. Not because he had been a wayward boy; surely not because he had committed great sins; but because for the first time in his life he realized he was condemned to eternal death unless he confessed Jesus Christ as his personal Saviour and accepted His atoning blood. Brother Trenem made that plain. Joseph wondered if Freddie felt the same way. He wondered how it could be that his father could listen to those stirring soul-searching words and not be convinced he should be kinder to his mother. And yet at the close of each service Bennet Armstrong was shaking hands with all the brethren and nodding in assent— "surely was—you're right—that's as fine a sermon as ever came over that pulpit." He even pressed Brother Trenem's hand and said, "God bless you for that wonderful message."

"Joseph." It was Uncle Tom Bradly. He was drawing Joseph to him in the side aisle. "Don't you think, son," he said with earnestness, "that God may be calling you?"

Joseph looked up with both surprise and gratitude in his blue eyes. Why should Tom Bradly call him son—and why should he care? Joseph was touched in his finest senses. How often a person's life is like a picture, and just one stroke from an artist's brush is what it takes to bring out the details it seems to lack.

Joseph had on his first suit. His father had worn it a number of years, and Annie had skillfully altered it to fit her son. It was a little large, but Joseph was growing. He fumbled with a small comb in his coat pocket, and Uncle Tom could hear Joseph's thumbnail running over the teeth. He recalled that one day he had done the same thing when his grandfather Fortner had asked him if he didn't think he ought to give his heart to God. That was over twenty years ago and he had been about to be married. Conviction in those days did not seize young men as early in life as now. Undoubtedly it was due to the fact that few revival meetings were conducted when Uncle Tom was young and Sunday school was held only once a month. Yet if the facts would be brought to light, there were numbers of teen-age boys in those days who struggled under the awful burden of sin and failed to realize what it was. Conviction is a strange thing and causes people to do strange things. To be guilty by law upon indisputable evidence and deserving of punishment is one thing, but to declare oneself guilty of sin, sin no one else knows about without accusing witnesses, is another thing. The hardest battles ever fought have been those between a man and his own conscience.

Joseph cleared his throat and looked into Uncle Tom's brawny face. Those kind eyes seemed to be pleading earnestly for an honest answer.

"Maybe so," said Joseph.

"Then don't put it off, son." Uncle Tom pressed his hand and walked on.

Joseph couldn't sleep. All night long he heard that voice by the barn, then felt the warm pressure of Uncle Tom Bradly's hand on his. But his father had said emphatically that a higher education would give him a straight ticket to hell. What should he do? What could he do? What if that voice by the barn really was the voice of God, and if—and if he'd say yes—what if it would tell him to go to India someday, or China, or some far distant mountain district? If he'd go to India he'd have to leave his mother and—and maybe he'd never get to see her face again. Joseph tossed. Indecision and fear rendered him sleepless. This terrible feeling would kill him. Either decision looked hopeless. Unless he gave his whole heart to God and confessed Him publicly, he knew he was doomed; for Palmer Trenem had pictured the judgment in all its reality. There was no possible escape. Judgment was certain, and life was uncertain. He knew that. He had seen his mother lie unconscious. And tonight Joseph knew he was a sinner with the penalty of death hanging over him. But his father? And if that voice would call and he'd refuse to answer, then what? He'd be worse off than now. It would be like the man who put his hand to the plow and looked back. Brother Trenem said such were not fit for the Kingdom of Heaven. But his father? Yes, his father objected to his going on to school even for a good cause. There was no possible chance for him. If God called him to service, he'd have to know his Bible better. How did Brother Grissley learn so much? Did he ever go to school? And Brother Trenem? He preached as one with confidence and divine authority. Yet another obstacle mounted up before Joseph like an angry monster, ready to devour him: What if his father would make fun of the whole idea? Try as he would, he could not recall being praised for anything he had ever done. If he should try to tell his father he had heard God calling him, he was certain he'd be ridiculed and hooted at without mercy. Oh, if Father could only be just a little like Amos Pennewell or Uncle Tom Bradly. He had a notion to get up and tiptoe downstairs and waken his mother. She wouldn't mock him. She wouldn't doubt or treat lightly his feelings. He put one foot out of the bed, then two. It was cold. He sat on the edge of the bed and shivered. Someone below coughed. It was Father, so Joseph knew he must be awake. He pulled the covers closely around him. The moon shone in the east window, and Joseph could see the picture on the wall beside his bed. Though now he was twice as old as when his mother brought it home for him, he still prized it among his fondest possessions.

*   *   *

He was standing at the door of the church waiting for Freddie. They always sat together on Sunday mornings. Delores Bays stepped out of the carriage and came up the cement walk alone. Long, blonde braids hung below her waistline, and in her one hand she carried a blue lesson quarterly. Her plump pink cheeks were delicately sprinkled with a few freckles, and the dress that hung

out below her wool jacket was light, with red roses in it.
Joseph had seen Delores Bays many times before, but
today it was distinctly different to see her coming up the
walk alone. She walked so sedately, and her manner was
so refined. She smiled at him as she passed.

The meetings closed and Joseph Armstrong was not
among those who stood. The battle in his soul grew more
severe as time passed. He lived in constant hope that
his life would be spared until he could decide, and with it
the hope that God would not stop calling him. A duel is
usually fought with guns or swords between two persons,
or sometimes between animals in the presence of two
others called seconds; but this one was fought not with
swords or weapons of warfare, but between two living
spirits more powerful than regiments of soldiers.

In the spring of the next year the elders of the church
decided to have another series of revival meetings.
Brother Grissley Steward in particular thought they could
not afford to let this opportunity go by.

"Beloved," he said, standing behind the sacred desk,
"Brother Edson Myers, who has proved to be a success-
ful evangelist in the West, has written to let me know he
can be with us the first ten days of April. Shall we have
him come, or shall we not? We will ask the brotherhood
to vote. Those of you who want to see this church of
ours grow in truth and numbers, raise your hands."

Many hands were lifted. Yes, even Bennet Armstrong's was among those in the left wing.

Joseph missed but two nights, and that was because of
bad roads. He went to bed on those nights quite early
just to be alone to think. He prayed earnestly that God
would make it clear to him what to do. If he could see
just a little change in his father, he could decide, but
Bennet's attitude toward Joseph remained rough. Seldom
did he give his son anything but harsh words, and those

were spoken only to give orders. Joseph was shamefully reprimanded for not getting more done in a day, and he always went his limit. It seemed that Bennet expected Joseph to do the impossible many times. Only by the aid of the Spirit of God was he able to keep bitterness toward his father out of his heart. Joseph was more certain now than a year ago that if he told his father God had called him, he'd laugh in his face. Even small children like to be recognized as having some degree of judgment, but Bennet treated Joseph as one who lacked common sense. Joseph did not stand, although he wanted to.

He worked hard all summer. He was now able to keep up with Earnie Eloy shocking oats, wielding an ax, or handling a plow. Not once was Joseph praised for his work. Not once did he receive a penny for spending money. He was forbidden to accompany his mother to town on Saturday. Virginia was big enough now to go along, and Joseph was kept busy in the field from daylight until dark. By the middle of October he hoped to be back in school to finish his seventh grade English, but Father said, "no," so no it was. Joseph was not as brilliant in English as he was in arithmetic and history, and yet he had a longing to complete all the subjects taught. Kind, considerate Amos Pennewell had a warm liking for Joseph Armstrong. Although he never actually said so, he made several clever inferences that told Joseph he surmised his father's attitude. Amos Pennewell was shrewd.

Before Joseph had gone to school many days, (in the week of Thanksgiving, to be exact) another evangelist came to preach. The church was filled every night.

"Joseph." It was Uncle Tom Bradly again drawing him aside. "Don't you feel God calling you, my boy?"

Joseph's eyes filled with sudden tears. He turned away. Oh, if he could only tell Uncle Tom how he felt.

"I do, Uncle Tom," he faltered. It was hard to speak. His voice broke, "but—"

"Then why say, 'no,' Joseph? I'm praying for you. Remember, I was a boy once and I know." Uncle Tom squeezed Joseph's hand in his big strong one.

The night was long. All at once Joseph remembered the story his mother had told to him one Sunday evening when they hadn't gone to church. "And," he heard her sweet voice saying again, "your Grandfather Stokes said he likes to think that when Joseph was down in that deep, dark pit—maybe God sent a light down from Heaven to give him courage." Joseph sat up in bed and drew a long, deep breath.

CHAPTER XIX

Joseph cried during the entire service from the first song to the last. Lowell was beside his father three benches in front of Joseph. Virginia sat beside her mother in the middle section. Fully three hundred persons sat fascinated and with grave faces while the evangelist expounded the Scriptures. He set forth such details; he explained so clearly (for he had been a schoolteacher); he interpreted with such everyday homely illustrations the fuller meaning of the Scriptures, that it were as though he laid it all out open on the pulpit for the people to inspect. Joseph sat with his head bowed part of the time. Not for one minute were his eyes dry that evening. The struggle in his soul was furious. Freddie sat beside him motionless. Once he touched Joseph on the arm, not knowing what else to do to let him know he was trying to sympathize.

"I'll read my text just once more," said the minister, closing his Bible and laying his left hand over it. He stepped to the edge of the platform, and when Joseph raised his eyes, the man of God looked straight into them.

" 'He found him in a desert land, and in the waste howling wilderness; he led him about, he instructed him, he kept him as the apple of his eye. As an eagle stirreth up her nest, fluttereth over her young, spreadeth abroad her wings, taketh them, beareth them on her wings: So the Lord alone did lead him, and there was no strange god with him. '

"Dear people, I've tried my best to explain this portion of God's Word to you. I believe there is conviction in this audience tonight. I can feel it, and I can see it on some of your faces. Before we even begin to sing, is there someone who wants to get right with God tonight?"

Joseph's shoulders dropped for a moment, and taking hold of the pew in front of him, he pulled himself to his feet. A larger boy directly in front of him stood at the same time, and the evangelist failed to notice Joseph. His mother saw him stand, and tears of joy welled up in her eyes. No one shook hands with Joseph. Uncle Tom hadn't seen him stand. Bewildered and heartbroken, he walked out of the church.

"I'm so glad for you, Joseph," whispered his mother just before he went upstairs.

Joseph cried all night. Not because of the burden of sin, for now it was gone, but because no one cared that he stood. His father did not speak to him, Uncle Tom hadn't noticed, not even the preacher. Disappointment crushed him. As the long hours of the night wore on, he thought the terrible weight in his chest would crush his life out. Disappointment of this kind is one of Satan's clever devices to frustrate a well-meaning young seeker. If he can delude one into believing no one cared that he stood, the devil is highly pleased. If he can use this delusion then to balk that one's progress, he is still more pleased.

In the morning Joseph was nervous and self-conscious. The long sleepless night had left him weak, and dark under the eyes. If he had lain awake because of un-speakable joy in his heart (as some have), he would have come downstairs walking on air, but to lose sleep because of defeat and disappointment is disastrous to both mind and body.

Bennet was leaning against the kitchen wall, his hands in his pockets, both shoulders drooping. Bennet never stood like that unless he was greatly displeased about something. He sniffed when Joseph entered with the milk pails. Breakfast was eaten in silence. Nothing tasted right to Joseph.

His mother took him by the hand and pressed it gently. "Joseph," she said tenderly after Bennet had gone out, "I told your father last night." She hesitated and swallowed twice. There seemed to be a great lump in her throat that made speaking difficult. "He thinks you don't know what you're doing." Joseph's face was already warm. Now it got hot, and his mother could see the veins in his neck throbbing with each rapid heartbeat. "But I am confident, Joseph, that you do know what you're doing." She folded her arms and pinched them with her finger tips. "He says you'll never make it—but—by God's help you will, Joseph," she added looking deep into his eyes. "I'll be praying for you," she said with feeling. "He may not say a word to you, but don't let it bother you, please." She touched his arm. "Please don't be grieved; oh, Joseph—don't." He could not stand it any longer. So hurt was Joseph that he burst into tears he could not suppress.

"Well—why—" Joseph tried desperately to control himself. "Why doesn't Father have any confidence in me?"

"I can't understand it."

"I've gone through three revivals now, just on account of him."

"I know."

"I couldn't stand it any longer, Mama," he cried again. "I—was afraid he'd make fun of me."

"Oh, Joseph—don't. I'm sorry. I believe in you. You know I won't make fun— Oh, here comes Bennet! Joseph, go quick. Run upstairs until your face— Here, take a wet rag."

Two weeks passed, and not one word did Bennet Armstrong say to his son about his stand for Christ. Uncle Tom Bradly talked to him and told him how happy he was. Brother Grissley Steward shook Joseph's hand and gave him a warm and sincere, "God bless you, my boy." Lottie Woods and plump Mrs. Irons, who admired Joseph since he was a tiny boy, both gave him kind words of encouragement. Cousin Freddie said he was glad he and Joseph could be baptized together. The evangelist learned that he had made an unintentional oversight, and made a special effort to speak to Joseph the next evening, but—his father—his own father (who above all persons on earth should have clasped his hand and kissed him and knelt beside him after they got home and prayed for him), completely ignored him. Joseph was smitten. Sometimes when he thought he was about able to live above it, he would find himself almost buried in sudden grief. Annie could not help seeing what her son was going through. She went to her bedroom every afternoon, and, closing the door, poured out her heart to God in his behalf.

"Mama," said Joseph one evening, "you told me once that maybe sometime I'd be down in a deep, dark pit, didn't you?"

"Maybe I did, Joseph."

"Well, I almost feel like it sometimes when Father—"

"But Joseph," came her sweet voice that was always an inspiration to him, "you're not in it alone. I'm there with you."

"Mama!" He threw his arms around her neck.

"Remember that, Joseph. Don't you ever forget it. And God's light shines down on us all the time. Joseph," and Annie's voice almost broke, "I doubt if I'd be living today if it weren't for you. When I think of you it keeps me going. If I can just live now to see you happy and established in the faith, then I can be satisfied to go."

Do you suppose Joseph Armstrong could ever, ever forget the conversation with his mother that day? Do you suppose it buoyed his spirits?

*   *   *

Thirty young women, and fifteen boys, most of them in their late teens, sat on the front seats. The eldest bishop preached a fitting sermon, and after that, water was applied to each bowed head as they knelt face forward. Parents sat breathless and silent, and many eyes were wet with tears of joy. J. Bennet Armstrong sat erect and stiff, his eyes fastened on the wall in front of him. Virginia sat enfolded in thought. She was almost transported to the gates of Heaven when it came Joseph's turn to be baptized. It was Joseph, her beloved brother. She was ten, and only partly understood what it was all about, but she knew it was something good and right and glorious, and she was infinitely happy. It thrilled her until her toes tingled when the aged bishop took Joseph by the hand and said, "Arise. And, like as the Father ...," and kissed Joseph there before all the people. How tall and handsome he looked to her. How serious. Then, after all forty-five had had the water applied, and had received their blessings from the grand old bishop, he stood aside and one by one the ten ordained men filed down from the platform and shook hands with each of the converts. Uncle Tom Bradly spoke meaningful words in Joseph's ear after church, and so did several others, but his father remained speechless and stern. Months passed by, and never once did Joseph receive one word of encouragement from him. He was always watched with a critical and suspicious air.

*   *   *

"Annie," announced Bennet one morning at the breakfast table. It was Sunday, and Earnie Eloy had gone to spend the day with Alex Burns. "I sold the farm yesterday."

"This farm?" Her hand dropped.

"What other one could I mean? Yes, this farm. I've

decided," he cleared his throat without reason, "to invest the rest of my inheritance money and part of this in the Hendrick's Produce Company. And I'm going west this week to look for a new location." Bennet saw Annie's face becloud, and hurried on. "I've heard you say several times this house is too big to take care of without a hired girl, so I'll find a smaller one. We can get ahead once."

"Get ahead once? Why, Bennet," said Annie in astonishment, "I didn't know we were behind."

"We're not behind," he answered hollowly, "but why live on in moderate means if I have a chance to get rich?" He looked at Annie and the three children wisely and stroked his black hair rather indifferently. He brushed the dandruff off his shoulder in the same manner.

"Riches sometimes take wings and fly away, is a saying I—"

"Yes—yes," he broke in, "I've heard that too. But when that happens it's usually because of poor management. I think it's time for us to make a move. I—I—" Bennet's face colored up suddenly and he seemed to be groping for words, a thing he seldom had to do. "I heard a statement last Sunday that was plenty smart." His voice was strangely curt, and a sheepish look played around his eyes. He waited.

"What was it, Bennet?"

"Maybe you know all about it," he answered complainingly.

"I don't know what it is you have in mind, Bennet."

"It was your own brother talking to Tom Bradly. They didn't know I was around, but I heard part of it anyway." His breath came fast—fast—faster. His cheeks burned red. "I heard your very own brother Timothy say to Tom—" He was almost yelling now, and he unbuttoned his vest nervously. " 'Annie Armstrong would make an ideal deacon's wife, you're right, but Bennet would never make a deacon.' "

Now Annie's face got red. Spots came out on her neck. He looked at her gloatingly. New fear struck her in the breast.

"Do you know anything about this, Annie?"

"Indeed not," answered Annie.

"Well, someone's been running down my reputation. There's no two ways about that. I've been well thought of all these years, and why Timothy Stokes should make an impudent remark about me like that is what I'd like to know. You've been telling things, Joseph Armstrong. I can see it in your eyes. And you'll have to pay for this." Bennet picked up his fork and threw it down on the table. Joseph was struck dumb. The clock on the shelf ticked loudly. Lowell looked frightened and bent toward his mother for safety.

"The farm is sold," he announced again, "and the church can get along without us. Joseph, you're not going to Freddie's house today, and you needn't invite him to come here for dinner either. I told Earnie last night to look for another place. He will stay until I make sale. And Virginia, you needn't start crying about this. It's the thing to do any way you want to look at it. There's no chance for advancement here."

CHAPTER XX

Four sad faces watched Bennet Armstrong walk to the gate where Earnie Eloy was waiting to drive him to town. He had on a new doublebreasted, squirrel-gray overcoat and in his right hand he gripped the handle of a genuine leather traveling bag. There were no good-by kisses, no endearing words at departure, no solicitation for the family's prayers for the Lord's leading in this adventure. J. Bennet Armstrong felt very self-sufficient and satisfied with his own opinions. He needed no one's advice in business matters. The procedure he was taking was perfectly legitimate. It could not be otherwise.

"What all will we sell, Mama?" asked Joseph, wishing to break the awful stillness in the room. Everyone felt like crying, but each was trying to hide his feelings for the sake of the rest.

"Everything, I guess," came her sad answer.

"It'll be like starting all over again," Joseph said, stretching. How strange it would seem with Father gone for a week or more! How strange it would be not to be scolded and criticized with every turn! He put both arms up and crossed his hands behind his neck. He could even stretch and yawn if he wanted to without being called lazy.

"It'll be like starting all over again," echoed Annie.

"It will be hard to leave Freddie," added Joseph.

"It will be," echoed his mother.

"Well," she said, putting one foot before the other listlessly, "I suppose I might as well get to work."

"I'll wash the dishes, Mama," said Virginia bravely, "I'm almost as tall as you are now, see!" and she stood beside her mother and held her head high. She and Joseph had made out in secret the night before that while Father was gone they would put forth special effort to keep her spirits up. She had showed evidence of unusual fatigue the past several days, and Joseph in particular noticed a growing anxiety on her face. He likewise well remembered the words of Dr. Hudson Lindquist on the morning he was called home from church. Worry and anxiety could not help being hard on one with a heart condition such as she had.

"You wash them and I'll wipe them," said Joseph. "Mama, you sit down here and rest once. There's nothing that's got to be done right now, is there?"

"Oh, I could find something to do," she said.

"But rest this once, Mama," Joseph said, leading her to a chair by the bay window. "Sit down here and tell us about Grandfather Stokes."

"Yes, do, Mama," said Virginia.

"Yes, Mama," joined in Lowell.

*　　*　　*

"So you say yer goin' ter buy a ranch out west?" asked Earnie Eloy after they had driven a mile in silence. Earnie wasn't a man to ask many questions of any man, least of any, Bennet Armstrong, but since his days of laboring under him were going to be few now, he felt he could afford to run the risk of aggravating him. He spit tobacco juice and stroked his black mustache while he waited for the answer. At last it came, and Bennet's voice was neither hot nor cold. Earnie was expecting anything.

"I'm not saying what I'll buy. I'm going to see if there's anything worth buying. I know this, I'm not staying around here the rest of my life. Most of the folks that go to our church were born here—lived here all their lives, and their children married right in the church here. That won't do. This church needs some new blood in it. Everybody does just like their fathers did before them. There's entirely too many relatives in this church. Why, when they want to ordain a preacher or a deacon, you've got to vote for your own kin. That won't do. There's bound to be jealousy. I think it's time we're spreading out a little and get our children out of here before they're old enough to get marriage in their heads."

"Well, I reckon yer right, Bennet," drawled Earnie thoughtfully.

"I know I am," answered Bennet, with emphasis on the "know." "Now when I'm gone you see to it that Joseph helps get that corn husked, and keep the horses well fed so they'll be in good shape for the sale. If you can possibly get to it, polish up the spades and hoes, and paint all the wagon wheels. There's paint in the woodshed. See that Joseph gets up at the usual time. He's not to oversleep just because I'm gone. And I wish you and he would chop down that old pear tree at the edge of the garden and work it up. The wood ought to sell good this time of year. I told Annie to get all the pots and pans shined up good and use a little elbow grease on the heating stove; but if she forgets it you tell her I told you to remind her. You tell Virginia again (she's so childish sometimes) to take in those glass fruit jars out there on the fence behind the woodshed and get them washed up nice and clean. There's no need in giving a lot of that stuff away for nothing, or just leaving it set for the next fellow. I've been to sales already when the women folks just go for nice shiny pots and kettles. Annie's got one there she brought from home that's as good as new. And say, Earnie" (Bennet hadn't talked this much at one time to Earnie Eloy in all the years he'd been his employee; it surprised him and rather amused him too), "if Michael Hunter stops you on the way home, or comes over to borrow something while I'm gone, tell him you can't loan when Mr. Armstrong's gone. And if he asks you where I went and what for, tell him it's none of his business. I've never met a man in my life who reminds me so much of a woman as Michael. He even talks like a woman."

Earnie Eloy stroked his long, shaggy, black mustache. He sort of liked high-pitched Michael, even if his voice was falsetto.

*   *   *

"I thought sure," concluded Annie after talking to the children for twenty minutes, "that you, Joseph, would remember your Grandfather Stokes. I know I can recall a few things that happened when I was three."

"I think I do, Mama," said Joseph, wiping the last piece. The tea towel went round and round and round the bowl.

"Well, that's dry now," laughed Virginia. "Don't rub the flowers off."

"They're still on, sis." Joseph looked the bowl over and put it in the cupboard.

"Sometimes when I close my eyes, I think I can see an old man with a long, whitish beard."

"He was here only once," she said, "and he couldn't stay but a day. And," she went on demurely and with a muffled tone, "it was just as well he couldn't. I," she almost whispered now, and her voice sounded somewhat like a prayer, "didn't want him to know I wasn't happy." A faraway look crossed Annie's sweet, sad face. Her breast rose and fell, and her lips twinged as in sudden new pain.

"Say, Mama," said Joseph rising to meet the situation. He stood in front of her now and looked down into her face earnestly, "let's pop some corn after supper and sit around in a circle and sing, or do something nice."

"Let's do, Mama," chimed Virginia eagerly.

"Let's do," came in Lowell's voice with clapping of his hands.

During the ten-day absence of the head of the Armstrong household, the mother and the three children became remarkably attached to one another. They unconsciously bound themselves together with a cord of love and affection that could not easily be broken. They talked about living in a new home, and working, and pulling together.

"There'll be no more peddling in town," Annie said, softly brushing her hand over her apron, "because Father said I've done it for the last time. He doesn't seem to like it."

"He ought to be glad," suggested Joseph.

"He thinks I've done wrong to make so many friends behind his back. Maybe I should have asked him first."

*　　*　　*

The sale was made, and the Armstrong family went west to a country they'd never seen before except on the map. They rode several days on the train, and Bennet wired ahead to the land agent to meet them at the depot and take them to the hotel until the most necessary pieces of furniture could be purchased and set up in the house.

What wonderings, what anticipations, what words of foretaste were spoken when the four waited in the hotel room while Father went out to make purchases! They could hardly wait to see their new home.

"I hope it has a fireplace like Uncle Timothy's have in their living room," said Virginia beaming.

"I hope there's a pump in the kitchen, too," said Lowell, "so I don't have to carry water three times a day."

"Well, I hope I'll have a nice schoolteacher," ventured Joseph as soon as he could get a word in edgewise. "I hope he's as nice as Amos Pennewell."

"Maybe it'll be a lady," Virginia said.

"Maybe so."

"All I hope," said their mother, "is that the house is good and warm, and easy to keep clean."

As they started out to the place, four hearts were pounding with excitement. Those who have never made such a move can't realize that feeling. The air was fresh and cold, and they turned their collars up around their ears. The gray sky above them predicted snow before morning.

"Father," said Lowell, "there are no trees out here."

"Of course not. We're in the West now."

"The houses are so far apart," Virginia said.

"Of course, we're out West now. People don't run over to the neighbors to borrow this and that out here."

"The houses are all so little," said Joseph. "Just look at that one. It looks like a cow shed."

"People out West don't spend all they make for big houses and velvet rugs. Look at those cattle there."

Annie stared and said nothing.

"You children be quiet now, or Mr. Stalcup will think you've lost all the manners I've taught you."

Mr. Stalcup, the burly land agent, sat on the open wagon seat chewing constantly. If he heard what the children back of him said, he paid no attention. Whenever Bennet talked to him, he had to lean over and shout into his right ear. He turned his horses left, and Bennet jumped down and opened a place in the barbed wire fence. It wasn't a wooden gate on hinges like they had back home. Over an open space they went, and down a gentle slope.

"This is it," said Bennet.

Mr. Stalcup helped Virginia and Mrs. Armstrong to alight, and the boys sprang off. Bennet walked ahead and opened the heavy glassless door. The family followed him into a two-room, unpainted shack with a small lean-to kitchen on the north. The rough floor was uneven, and the walls were papered with plain brown paper that was cracked and hanging loose in many places. Through the cracks in the floor in the kitchen Annie could see the cold bare ground, so she knew before she asked that there was no cellar. She opened a door.

"And what is this?" she asked.

Mr. Stalcup was hard of hearing, and Bennet made no answer, so she repeated her question closer to his ear.

"That's the cattle shed," shouted Mr. Stalcup.

Annie would have fallen, but Joseph slipped an arm around her waist and whispered in her ear, "Don't cry, Mama, please!"

CHAPTER XXI

The few pieces of furniture which Bennet had purchased from a small secondhand store and which Mr. Stalcup had taken out to the house in his spring wagon while Bennet stayed in town to transact some other business were in one disorderly heap on the side of the room they first entered. The small heating stove was the only piece which had been placed properly, and Bennet had requested Mr. Stalcup to set it where it belonged and join the pipes so fire could be started upon arrival. Mr. Stalcup had graciously done that and a little bit more. He found a few sticks in the cattle shed, a greasy rag, a strip of soiled oilcloth, and part of an old harness, which he put in the stove and lit a match to it so he could say he tried to take the chill out of the house. The fire had gone out, however, before Mr. Stalcup had gone two rods. The house was cold. Annie shivered until her teeth chattered—part of which undoubtedly was due to nerves.

"Here's a chair, Mama. Sit down!" From the mass of things, Joseph pulled a chair out from under two mattresses.

As soon as Mr. Stalcup was out of hearing distance, which wasn't far, Bennet turned to Joseph and said rather roughly, "Well, get busy and do something. Here's a match. Rustle up something to burn. I asked Stalcup to bring out a wagonload of coal in the morning as early as possible, and a five-gallon can of kerosene, then after that Stalcup's through doing things for us. Look around out there," and Bennet pointed toward the cattle shed, "and maybe you can find a few cobs or something. Virginia, what's wrong with you?"

"I'm cold," she said. Both eyes were swimming in tears. Oh, this wasn't at all—at all the kind of a house she dreamed of. There was no fireplace in the living room, and to be honest, there was no living room; for the two largest rooms would have to be bedrooms.

"Well, open the suitcase and put on another pair of stockings if you're cold."

"I have to save those for Sunday." Virginia was crying now, and Lowell was leaning hard against his mother's knee, a dismal look on his chubby face. He would soon be crying too. He didn't feel one bit happy. Nothing looked right here, and it was dark already.

"Well, then," said Bennet, "I guess you'll just have to be cold. Hurry up, Joseph, and bring in something that will burn. Here," he scrambled through the jumbled heap and found the lantern he had purchased. It was wrapped in an old "Mourville Post." "Here's some paper. Try this." Bennet lit the lantern and hung it on a spike on the back of the one door.

"I got some bread and cold meat in town. It's supposed to be here somewhere. I know I put it on the wagon. Stalcup said I'd have to get someone in town to bring out the cookstove, so I'll ride back to town with him tomorrow when he comes with the coal. I guess we can— Come here, Lowell, and help me lift up this mattress. Here's a can of soup too. We can heat this on that stove."

"Did you think to buy a kettle, Bennet?" asked Annie feebly, still sitting where Joseph put her.

"Oh course," retorted Bennet; "do you think I'm a half-wit?"

"No, Bennet," answered Annie, resolving not to ask any more questions.

"I bought a pan. Here it is. I think I did pretty well to get all this together in one forenoon. I even thought of blankets, and here's a nice secondhand coffeepot. Joseph, let's get these beds set up first."

"Is there only one chair, Father?" asked Virginia.

"There was only the one that I'd consider buying. The others were all too expensive. We can sit on the beds until I have time to look around a little more. We can shift along for a couple of days, I guess."

Annie was too bewildered and sick at heart to get up and help; she just sat and watched Joseph and Bennet set up the two beds.

"We ought to have three beds."

"Well, Joseph," Bennet said irritably, "Virginia and Lowell can sleep with their mother until we locate a cot."

Then Joseph would sleep with his father. Never had he done that. How strange it would seem. Would Father kneel beside the bed and say his prayers?

"This bed is broken here, Father."

"Broken?"

"Right here at the back leg. Look, it came off. It was only pasted on, I guess. It came right off when I went to push it back."

"Well, why did you push so hard? We can prop it up some way until I get time to fix it."

"We had—" Annie caught herself. It would be best not to say it.

"Had what?" asked Bennet.

"Oh, nothing." She repented in her heart.

"Had what?" repeated Bennet, too curious to let it pass.

"I was just going to say," said Annie wearily, "that the bed we sold was a good strong one."

"Then what?"

"Well, I thought"—she coughed—"that we'd put that much money into another one. All our things sold so good."

"But surely you didn't think we'd put all that into furniture, did you?"

"No, not the outdoor things, but I meant just what the

furniture, and dishes, and bedding, and household goods brought."

Bennet laughed mockingly. "I bought half a section of land! Annie Armstrong, we're living in the West now. The people out here take pride in their land and cattle, not in their houses."

Bennet sulked. The rest of the furniture was placed with motions, but few words.

"Mama," whispered Lowell, "I'm hungry."

"We'll eat soon now. As soon as Father has time."

"I'm thirsty."

"Yes, dear, I am too."

"Joseph, the pump is down over the slope back of the house."

"Where's a pail?"

"A pail—a—well, a—that's one thing I didn't have time to get. Take that pan there. You children go easy on the water tonight. I'll go get the water and fill up at the pump." He said this after second thought. "Joseph, you help Virginia put the blankets on the beds till I get back. I'll have to take the lantern. I'm not used to the way yet, and it's pretty dark outside."

"Oh, Mama," cried Virginia after Father had closed the door, "how can we ever stand it here? Oh, Mama, aren't you disappointed?"

"I hate to say how I feel," came her sad answer. "I'm too heartbroken to talk." Her voice failed her, and through the darkness Joseph heard her suppressed sob.

"Well, I know one thing," said Joseph, trying desperately to make his voice sound brave, "we're going to stand together and make the best of it." He hesitated, then reaching over in the dark, he found Virginia's arm and squeezed it. "Aren't we, sis?"

"Why sure," she said catching her breath between sobs. "What else can we do?"

The bread and cold meat sandwiches were eaten around the stove, and immediately after that Bennet said it was time to retire.

"I've got lots to look after tomorrow, so let's get to bed."

Joseph waited until his father blew out the lantern, then he knelt beside the bed to say his prayers. With a poignant pain around his heart, which was more painful than a cut or bruise, he tried to find words which might bring some solace. He tried to measure his disappointment with that of his mother, and knew instinctively that hers was the greater. In the darkness he could hear her moan while his father slept soundly, often snoring. In the distance he heard the howl of a prairie wolf. Then again. Then again, each time closer. Joseph wondered if his mother heard it too, but he didn't want to call and ask her, lest after all she might be moaning in her sleep. Pillows were another thing Father hadn't had time to purchase, so Joseph had folded up a coat for his mother's pillow. She could breathe only with great difficulty without an elevation of her head.

Possibly around three o'clock Joseph fell into unconsciousness, when Virginia made a sudden pitiful outcry.

"What's going on over there?" asked Bennet huskily.

"Something's biting me, Father."

"You're just dreaming. Lay down and be quiet."

"She's not dreaming," said Annie through the thickness of the night. "They're biting me too. I haven't slept a wink yet. Bennet, there must be bedbugs in this mattress!"

"Nothing's been biting me."

"Oh, Bennet, please come and light the lantern. I can't stand it another minute. Both of my feet have swelled."

*   *   *

"Father," said Joseph in the morning, "where is the school from here?"

"So you've got school in your head already, eh? Well, it's a mile and a half north. I've already met the teacher. He happened to be in the store when I bought this furniture, and I talked to him." Bennet looked at Joseph sternly and wet his lips before he continued, "This is what I've made out with him. He lives in town, and, like most town folks, doesn't like to get up early. He said if you'd do the janitor work, go out by seven and build fire, he'd furnish you your books. And so you can go to school only under one condition, Joseph. If you'll help me load hay or whatever there's to be done from five to six-thirty, and help me after you get home, I'll let you go. Otherwise it's all off."

Joseph thought a minute and said, "I'll do that."

Of course he wouldn't leave his mother yet, so not until the family was better settled did Joseph mention school again. Bennet concluded the boy had changed his mind.

The wind whistled in through the cracks in the kitchen. Joseph worked for several days packing earth and sod around the foundation. His mother kept her overshoes on most of the day in order to keep her feet warm. He stuffed all the windows with rags as time permitted. Father was gone a good deal buying cattle and implements that he said were essential. Virginia was to milk twice a day, and Lowell was to carry water for his mother. Never were the children told twice to do a thing. Once was sufficient. They had learned that from their earliest childhood. Joseph had received many whippings in his life, and the other two children did not escape like treatment. Bennet, however, did not bear on quite so heavily when Virginia was the victim.

*   *   *

Mr. Karl Herrmann was as opposite from Amos Pennewell in appearance as it was possible for a man to be.

The difference struck Joseph when he opened the school door. It nearly made him stagger. And before a dozen words were exchanged, he knew he was opposite in disposition as well. The children sat in fear and trembling, afraid to turn their heads when Joseph entered a little late. He was ushered to a seat in the row of sixth graders. His heart sank when he looked over the English lesson on the given pages. The book was different, the teacher's methods were different, the entire school system was different. Joseph swallowed hard to hide his disappointment. Nothing would please his father more than to hear him say that he hated school and didn't want to go any more. But Joseph Armstrong was determined to stick to it and finish the eighth grade in spite of his disappointment.

On the third day that Joseph had performed his duties as janitor, he approached Mr. Herrmann with these words: "My father said I was to come home at noon today and help him work."

"Did you bring a written excuse from your father?" Mr. Karl Herrmann stood stock-still behind his desk, his weight resting heavily on his knuckles. His brown eyes, almost black, were piercing.

"No, I didn't."

"Then bring me one tomorrow," came the stern guttural voice.

Joseph stood up very straight and looked the teacher in the eyes. He drew a deep breath and said: "If you can't take my word for it, Mr. Herrmann, there's no use to promise to bring one tomorrow, for I could be lying and write the note myself."

Mr. Herrmann put his hands behind his back, and his stiff body relaxed a trifle. "Very well, son," he said, "you may go. Be back in the morning to make the fire."

CHAPTER XXII

Through biting sleet, against the stinging north wind, plowing blinding snow, or in the teeth of a prairie storm Virginia and Lowell walked to school an hour later than Joseph, or stayed at home. They could choose. Bennet purchased a sturdy secondhand buckboard in which to go to town, but he neither had the time nor the urge to take his children to school. He did want his children to learn to read and write, but Annie could easily teach them at home. To be able to handle figures was in Bennet's estimation the most essential achievement. He was secretly gratified over Joseph's ability with figures, but Joseph never knew it. History was a waste of time. What good could the past of men and nations be to any growing boy? It only made him dream, and hanker for adventure. English was another useless study for children. Children learn to talk from their parents, and isn't that enough? Why should they waste their time learning what a pronoun or a modifier or a prepositional phrase is? What child ever remembered, after he received his diploma, how to use compound predicates? Several times Bennet had glanced through Joseph's book and closed it with disgust. He was actually disappointed when December came and Joseph made no complaint about getting up at five and going off in time to make the schoolhouse warm for the earliest arrival. He was likewise surprised and disappointed that Lowell and Virginia didn't beg to stay at home. It was hard on rubber and leather to tramp that distance over rough, icy roads twice a day. And Annie was always mending mittens.

*   *   *

There was something unusually fresh about the western air that was strangely invigorating. There was a

ightness about the atmosphere that seemed to lift the
heaviness in one's breast. Despite the homely little two-
room shack with a gravel roof and crooked, lean-to
kitchen; despite the lack of soft rugs and fine furniture
inside; despite every imaginable baffling experience Annie
Armstrong had undergone since the day Bennet announced the farm had been sold, her health improved.
The vast open prairies, the gorgeous sunsets, the wild rab-
bits, the bucking bronco, the sweeping wind that turned
and twisted one's skirts, and even the weird howls of
the coyotes, all had a physical and mental effect on Annie.
Something she could not explain surrounded her constantly. Her cheeks got pinker. Joseph in particular
was aware of this noticeable change. It made him so
happy that often on his way to school he sang at the top
of his voice some new unwritten song that best expressed
his joy.

"But I can't get used to this crowded feeling," he told
his mother one day.

"I know."

"I have no place here to go to pray alone, but in the
cattle shed."

"I know."

"That's why I like the janitor job."

Annie's face shone. "I wondered if you had dropped
your secret prayers since we came here."

"I couldn't."

"I'm glad."

"It's nice in the schoolhouse for that."

"I'm so glad to know."

"Mama." He stood back a step and looked at her.
"You're getting better, aren't you?"

"Joseph—it seems almost like a happy dream that I
feel this good here. I wouldn't have believed it when we
first came. And I sleep so good at night."

"Since we got rid of the bugs." Joseph laughed and made a funny face.

"Yes. Wasn't that something? I hope none of our friends ever find that out."

"I must go. 'By."

"Your lunch!"

"Oh, yes."

One evening Joseph said, "Father, I wish you would give me a postage stamp."

"A postage stamp?" Bennet's expression suddenly sharpened, and he answered abruptly by adding, "Are you writing a letter to Posie?"

"Who?"

"That Posie, or Rosie, whatever that Magee girl's name is you wrote to."

"But I didn't, I said."

"Oh, you didn't?" His question was curt, and Joseph knew his statement was not accepted.

"I want to write to Freddie."

"What for?"

"For anyhow. I have lots to tell him. I haven't written yet and I want to hear from him."

"Well, you can just let Freddie Stokes rest for a while. I think you two boys were entirely too thick anyway. You might slip a note to Rosie through Freddie. And what's more," Bennet rammed both hands into his pockets and fumbled with some loose change, "since Tim made that smart-aleck remark to Tom Bradly, I can't feel so near and dear to that family. And I think you—or your mother—" here he gave Annie a quick sidewise glance, "told something, I don't know what, that prompted such a remark. No, I haven't any postage stamp for any of Tim Stokes's children."

That was the first time Joseph had ever heard his father call Uncle Timothy, Tim. And according to the

English lessons Joseph had been studying, his father used pretty good grammar even when he was cross. But "Tim," just now, sounded quite disrespectful.

Joseph could not squelch the hurt look on his face even though he did in his voice. He was positive his father called Rosie Magee Posie just to torment him. He didn't care a whole lot about that because he had seldom even thought about Rosie in the past year, and Father evidently forgot Rosie now lived in Wisconsin; but it did actually pain him to the inmost part of his heart that he objected to his writing to Freddie. That seemed unreasonable and unjust. There was no use for him to try to convince his father that he had never intentionally said anything to run down his character. If Freddie gleaned anything unfavorable from his overnight visits in the Armstrong home, Joseph wasn't responsible for that. Freddie was sixteen when the boys separated, and Freddie wasn't a stupid boy.

"Well," remarked Bennet, his face written full of opposing thoughts ready to be expressed. "Why don't you say something?"

"What is there to say?" asked Joseph, not meaning to be impudent. He stood as tall as his father, and although his shoulders were not quite so square and wide, they were not far from it.

"Well, you're not homesick to go back there, I hope?"

Joseph couldn't answer. He pulled at the skin under his chin and looked at the floor.

"Well, *I'm* not." Since Joseph couldn't answer, Bennet did. "And I doubt if the folks even miss us. Did the church have a big farewell for us? No! And did Uncle Tim's have us over for a turkey dinner? No!"

"But—" Joseph bit his tongue. He could say a whole paragraph, but he didn't. As often as he had seen his father angry, he could not get used to it enough to wish

to view it again. He could have reminded his father that
Uncle Timothy invited them over for a meal and had been
told emphatically that they were too busy to go to anybody's house to eat. He could have reminded his father
that Freddie told him Agnes and Maryanna cried all
night when their father came home and said Uncle Ben-
nets weren't coming, and even after they had planned the
menu; and Virginia cried too. Yes, and he could have
reminded his father how Grissley Steward drove over in
the hard rain to bid them all good-by, and how Lottie
Woods came dashing out on the platform at the depot
after they were on the train, and with tears streaming
down both cheeks, waved good-by frantically and threw
kisses as the train pulled out. And how could Father
stand there and infer that no one missed them when right
beside their bed hung the beautiful motto Mrs. Irons had
embroidered in variegated yarn, and the class of mothers
had presented to Mama as a parting token of their love
to her.

> We seek in prayerful words, dear friend,
>   Our heart's true wish to send you,
> That you may know that far or near
>   Our loving thoughts attend you.
>
> We cannot find a truer word,
>   Nor fonder to caress you,
> Nor song nor poem have we heard
>   That's sweeter than, "God bless you!"

Joseph looked at it once more, and his face got hot
with shame that his father would actually be so rude and
ungrateful. That motto had been a daily inspiration to
both Annie and Joseph. Even Virginia had often admired, with words of ecstasy, the beauty of it.

* * *

Karl Herrmann was a very stern man who ordered his
school with harsh and rigorous words and uncompassion-

te threats which he carried out to the letter. His look
r frown frightened the children, from the smallest to
he largest. Even big Roscoe Hintch, who stood a head
aller than the German schoolmaster, shrank like a baby
rom a hot stove when Mr. Herrmann touched him with
is finger. But as hard and severe as he was, there
proved to be something in Joseph Armstrong that made
im more tolerant with him. More than several times
e let Joseph go home at noon to help his father, and
aid he'd pick the papers off the floor, and hide the keys
n a secret place in the coal shed for him.

To Joseph's utter astonishment Mr. Herrmann addressed him thus one morning,

"Joseph, you've done your janitor work exceptionally
well. I would like to give you a little Christmas gift for
this. What would you most wish for?"

"I could tell you that, Mr. Herrmann," answered
Joseph without thinking long, "but you don't need to do
that."

"I know I don't need to, but I want to. My wife is
glad I don't need to leave home so early since you've
come. Tell me what it is."

"I'd like a few postage stamps," answered Joseph,
dusting Mr. Herrmann's desk.

"Well—well—I thought you'd say something worth
more than that."

"I can't name anything that would be worth more to
me. I have a very close friend I want to hear from, but
I must write first."

"What's her name, Joseph?" smiled Mr. Herrmann.
Joseph had seldom seen him smile. How different he
looked that way.

"It's my cousin Freddie Stokes," answered Joseph,
returning the smile courteously.

"Ah, and you shall have your stamps, my boy."

At recess the children talked about hanging up stockings, and about chicken and turkey and candy and all that goes with Christmas talk and anticipation. It usually is greater than the realization for most children, especially first and second graders.

The conversations at school trailed along home with the children, the Armstrong children not the exception.

"Tut, tut," Father Armstrong rapped on the door casing. "What's all this I hear about dolls and sleds and ponies and collie dogs to pull sleds? Who's getting all this for Christmas?"

Lowell's countenance fell, and he looked to Virginia to make the answer.

"We were just talking, Father," she said with a demoralized air.

"Well, it better be just talk, because this ado over Christmas presents is all plain foolishness. You children get a lot of that in school, I'll bet. Now hush up this minute, and don't let me hear another word out of you. I'm trying to figure here. I'd be ashamed of myself, Virginia, to talk about dolls. A great big girl like you, almost as tall as your mother!"

Virginia blushed red. She was wounded in her heart and soul. The damage done to her finer feelings by that statement impaired her motherly instinct for years to come. She didn't think about it that she would be twelve her next birthday. She didn't realize she was almost as tall as her dainty little mother. All she did realize was that her longing for a pretty doll had never been satisfied, and she was only speaking out of the abundance of her heart's desires.

* * *

The children approached the table with open eyes and awe. Reverently they bowed their heads while Father made his silent prayer. Lowell peeked twice. On each plate lay a package wrapped in brown paper and tied with red twine. There was one on Mama's plate too, but the one on Virginia's was twice as large as the others. Could it be that after all Father had repented and got her a doll? Breathlessly and with their faces all aglow each opened his own package. Their hands trembled with excitement. Father sat smiling from ear to ear, a new strange twinkle in his blue eyes.

"Oh!" cried Lowell.

"Oh, Father!" cried Virginia.

In each package were several good-sized cinders bound up in some straw with more red twine.

"Oh, Father!" cried Virginia as though her heart would break.

CHAPTER XXIII

In the course of time Bennet found a two-seated carriage in which to take the family to church. Although it had been used by a man of the prairie for many years, it was still substantial and he considered himself fortunate in finding one so sturdy for the price given. Bennet Armstrong had made special inquiry about the location of the church of his choice, and of course this influenced his decision to buy where he did. The place for worship was situated near a little jog in the road on a barren, unattractive stretch of land, and any one of the four dozen or so members who chanced to be gazing out of the windows instead of at the preacher could readily detect who it was who was coming late. One could see out over the treeless plains for ten miles. How unlike the pretty white church back home so picturesquely nestled in a wooded glen just a happy riding distance from home. Now they had six miles to church—six long miles against a driving wind.

It was almost as exciting to go to another church for the first time as it was going into the new home. Every face was strange and new. Even the pews felt different. The hymnbooks were of a more recent publication, and most of the songs were new. The preacher's voice sounded younger and less experienced, too (not at all like dear Brother Grissley Steward's), for he would change suddenly from one tone of voice to another in the same sentence, until it reminded one of an unexpected key change in music. But there was a gentle, polished way about him that Joseph liked. His manner was graceful, his speech was refined, and the longer Joseph listened, the more he believed he enjoyed his modulated way of speaking. He soon concluded too that this strange preacher was a man with an education, for some of his sentences were elegant and delivered with great power and deep conviction. And the politeness he bestowed on each of them after the benediction was enough to make any stranger feel welcome. The Armstrongs were invited to go along home with him to dinner. All during the meal he talked about everyday occurrences with a spiritual emphasis, and with spiritual applications; and from every remark that Bennet made, he seemed to get inspiration for another spiritual reference. Joseph listened with both ears. So did Annie. Could it be that Father was enjoying this as much as he seemed to be, or was he only being courteous? The preacher's wife (who told Annie to call her Evalena, as though they'd been friends for a long time) was friendly, and made Annie feel at once that she had found a friend who could be a real companion to her. Even the silky-haired Irish water spaniel showed affection by sitting beside Lowell on the sofa, allowing him to play with his long drooping ears.

"We were talking of driving over to call on you folks," said Evalena, stacking the dinner plates in the corner cupboard.

"The reason why we haven't been to church before," Annie said, "was because Bennet didn't find a carriage until last week, and it was most too cold to drive six miles in the open buckboard."

"Of course! Milton thought maybe that was the reason."

"We sat at home for three Sundays, and those were the longest three Sundays I've ever spent in my life," said Annie.

"I shouldn't wonder you got a bit homesick."

"Well, we did! Everything here is so new and different, even the textbooks in school."

"But we do hope you'll learn to like it here."

"I hope so too," answered Annie.

"I wouldn't want to live anywhere else now. Maybe you don't know, unless I tell you, that I was born only twenty miles from the place where you were born."

"Wickville?" inquired Annie in surprise.

"Yes, indeed," answered Evalena.

"You don't say?"

From that moment Annie Armstrong and Evalena Collins stood on common ground. There wasn't a thing in Evalena's house she wouldn't have loaned or shared with this new friend if she needed it.

When it came time to leave, Evalena pressed Annie's hand and said, "We're so glad you came into our community, and we do hope you'll soon feel at home here. We're just awful common folks, all of us; and do come again. Any time that you come to church and you don't want to drive back home for dinner and no one else invites you, just remember our doors are open."

"Thank you," smiled Annie.

"Thank you," added Bennet.

"Mama, did you have a nice time today?" Joseph asked on the way home.

"Yes, I did. Did you?"

"Yes."

"That sure is a cute little dog they have," said Lowell.

"And wasn't the chocolate pie delicious?" spoke Virginia.

"Everything tasted good," said Annie.

"What makes everybody so friendly?" asked Virginia.

"I guess that's the way folks are out here," answered her mother thoughtfully. "I used to hear that people were more friendly out where the West begins, but I always thought it was just talk maybe."

"Then I wasn't so foolish after all to buy out here?" said Bennet.

"Did I say you were?" asked Annie in surprise.

"Well, you all acted like it."

*   *   *

Little by little the family became accustomed to the newness of the West. The children often longed for the kind ways and voice of Amos Pennewell, and they missed greatly the association of the cousins, but little by little one can get used to quite a few things that are different. The unhandy and crowded condition under which the family of five had to live in that little three-room shack was a vast change from the spacious eight-room house which had been sold, but each day they learned a little better how to make the necessary adjustments for comfortable living.

The letter in reply to Joseph's came on a Saturday when Joseph was not in school. Bennet had gone away early in the day on his new bay saddle pony, Quicksilver, to try to buy more cattle from some of the ranchers. He already had seventy head but wanted that many more before spring, so he told Joseph when he left that he likely would not be back before dark. If necessary, he would scour the country to find what he wanted. Before he opened the letter, Joseph tingled with joy and excitement. Had he been a few years younger he would have jumped up and down.

"And Mama," he exclaimed, "here is one for you."

He handed her the folded pages marked on the outside: "For Annie."

"It's from Aunt Sara," she said.

"Read it out loud, Mama," cried Virginia.

"All of you sit down and be quiet and I will. Joseph, maybe we'd all like to hear yours too, or are there secrets in it?"

"I don't know yet."

"Dear Annie," she read. "Freddie is writing a letter to Joseph, so I'll put one in for you. It seemed like years almost until we heard from you. Freddie got Joseph's letter just this morning, and he's answering it right away. He misses Joseph so much; sometimes he acts like a lost dog, especially on Sundays. We all miss you for that matter. I just thought I couldn't go to church another Sunday without some word from you. Everybody asks, 'Have you heard from Annie yet?' and 'What's Annie's address now?' Now next Sunday when folks ask, I can tell them we heard. Thanks to Joseph for writing at last. I suppose you are so busy getting your new home all fixed up that you just didn't have time to write. I haven't been able yet to get over it that we couldn't have you over for a meal before you left. It all happened so quickly—the sale, and then you were gone before we hardly realized it. So many things have happened since you left, I hardly know where to begin. We've had quite a mild winter so far, not nearly so much snow as the last several years; but there seems to be more sickness for some reason. Mrs. Irons has been bedfast for two weeks with arthritis. It came on her quite suddenly, and she suffers a lot. Maybe Freddie told Joseph about the accident. Wasn't it awful? Such terrible things can happen so quickly, and no one seems to know how it all happened."

"What was it?" asked Virginia.

"Well, I don't know yet. Joseph, is there anything in your letter about an accident?"

"Not yet." Joseph was still reading.

"Go on, Mama," said Virginia, bending forward. "Oh, Mama, I do hope it wasn't Maryanna or Agnes."

"When we were in town on Wednesday," Annie read, "we went to the hospital to see Earnie."

"Earnie?" shouted Joseph. "Earnie Eloy? What happened to him?"

"He was a pitiful sight. It blew part of his jaw off. They still have to give him something for pain."

"Well, what happened?" asked Joseph.

"Be still," said Virginia. "Go on, Mama."

"They say Alex Burns feels so bad about it that he's nearly losing his mind. Those two men have been old cronies for years, but that's what often happens when men go hunting on the Lord's day."

"Must-a got shot," whispered Joseph. The letter in his hand shook. His mother read on.

"Earnie knew Timothy right away and could talk a little through his teeth. He can't hardly move his lips at all, and they feed him liquids through a glass tube, just a few drops at a time. It took him a long time to get it out, a word at a time, but we made it out that he only wished he had had a mother like Joseph Armstrong had who taught him how to pray." Goose pimples came out on both of Annie's arms, and her eyes got misty. Joseph held his breath.

"Poor man," Annie read on, "hasn't a relative to go to see him, so there he lies and thinks. Timothy isn't any hand at helping people who need spiritual help, but I'm sure the experience did him good, and I hope it helped Mr. Eloy too. Timothy quoted to him a few verses he knows by memory, and prayed for him. He certainly did seem to appreciate it and held on to Timothy's hand a long time. He said he never could forget how one time he saw Joseph out kneeling beside a woodpile pra—" Annie choked, and a big tear fell on the paper. Joseph stood as though paralyzed. The little mother wiped her eyes with the corner of her apron and swallowed hard.

At last she could speak again, but when she did her voice was drenched with feelings of pity for poor old

Earnie and immeasurable gratitude for her son, who at an early age chose a secret place to pray. In a moment of time, as she sat there trying to bring under control her emotions, she lived over again many heartbreaking experiences in the years past that had driven her and Joseph both to their knees and bound them in love to each other.

As Joseph stood leaning hard against the table looking down on her he too recalled with special vividness those long tortuous months when he and Earnie Eloy stayed at home with Aunt Hepsi while his parents went north, and he couldn't understand why. Many a time he found solace from his troubles beside that woodpile. He did not know anyone had ever found him there. His face burned now to learn that Earnie Eloy, that rough unbeliever who almost worshiped his guns and knives, had one day discovered him there. He was glad he did not know it at the time—"beside the woodpile praying," read Annie, clearing her throat. "I wish Joseph could write him a letter. It might do him a lot of good. You wouldn't know him with his mustache cut off.

"Well, Annie, the folks who live on your place had it painted a lead-gray the first thing. I happened to take down my receiver one day just in time to hear Mrs. Foster saying to someone that she liked everything about the place but the color, and she never could stand yellow for a house, and her husband promised her when they bought it he'd have it painted right away. It's trimmed in white, and all the buildings match. It looks very nice.

"We're going to have revival meetings again in April. I think maybe Maryanna will stand. She understands and seems to know. I only wish I could be as good a mother to my children as you are, Annie. I think you must be a perfect mother the way Freddie talked every time after he'd been over to your place for a night. I

know I often fall short of my ideal." Annie stopped
long enough to clear her throat.

"Some of the women are talking of starting a sewing
circle to sew for foreign missions. I told them they could
meet here if they want to. Everyone would bring a
covered dish, and we'd try to begin about nine in the
morning and go home about three. It's just talk so far.
First we'll have to take up a collection to buy the mate-
rials to work with. Some of them said, 'Oh, if only
Annie Armstrong was here to be our president.' Do
they have a sewing circle out there? I suppose not. I
guess in the West, if it's like Timothy says, you live so
far apart it's hard to get together. I wish I could drop
in tonight and see how you live. How do you like the
church there? Are the people friendly? How do you
feel there? Does the climate agree with you? And how
many chickens do you have? Will you have a big garden?
I can think of lots of questions. Did you have a nice
Christmas? We surely did." Annie's voice faltered.
"Timothy got me a new roaster, a big one like I've been
wanting for years. It will hold two big chickens easily,
and room for dressing too. I wish you could all come
back on a visit around Easter time. We'll be married
twenty-five years on the fifteenth of April. I told Timothy I wish we could celebrate together. Timothy said
if everything goes well he'll try to get us a new set of
silverware." Annie's voice faltered again. "Please think
about this. You and Bennet will be married twenty years
in April if I remember right." Tears rolled down both
cheeks. "I must close or this letter will get too long. Oh,
yes, Lottie Woods had a date with William Ashelford
last Sunday night. He took her home after church. Please
do write!

"My sincere love,
"Sara."

Annie slowly folded the letter and pressed it to her breast. "Well," she said at length, "Joseph, do you care to read yours out loud?"

"Dear Joseph," he read. "It's about time you wrote. We just about decided you didn't care much for the Stokes cousins any more. Believe it or not, I made 100 in English test last Friday. Mr. Pennewell gave every one in the school a candy cane for Christmas. He read to us 'The Redemption of David Carson' last month. Did you ever read it? It's a good story. I wanted to go hunting today, but Papa said, 'No.' You will probably get a letter from Uncle Tom before long. He asks me every Sunday if I know what your post office is. Is Admore a big town? I tried to find it on the map and couldn't. You must have a stern teacher, but that was sure nice of him to give you stamps for Christmas. Spend the rest of them on me. Joseph, I sure do miss you. If you were here maybe we could go coasting on Ellder's hill. How many boys are there in your Sunday-school class? Don't forget your promise to me. Write soon—sooner than the last time.

"In love,
                    "Freddie."

CHAPTER XXIV

It had been dark for an hour before Bennet got back, but Joseph and his mother both knew without asking by the way he stepped into the house and smacked his lips as he hung up his cap that the purpose of his expedition had been realized. They knew, too, that he considered his purchases a bargain. Nothing pleased J. Bennet Armstrong quite so much as the assurance that he had made a real buy, or the prospect of making a good sum from his investments.

He was never ready to pay the "pretty penny" unless he could see profits ahead. He was not satisfied with the dividends he received semiannually from the Hendrick's Produce Company, but like Dickens's Scrooge, the more he got the more he wanted, and his eyes saw money everywhere. To Bennet the leaves on the trees in summertime seemed as so many fluttering greenbacks, and the stones in the ground were as glittering coins. Even hymn number 297 in the sacred songbook read to him two hundred and ninety-seven dollars, or two hundred and ninety-seven head of beef cattle worth ten cents a pound on the Chicago market.

Little did the good brother next to him dream what covetous thoughts went through Bennet Armstrong's mind as he sang out lustily, "Teach me in every state to be content to be Thy child." Annie could not help but wonder how much he was going to put into the offering plate after they had sung "Give to the poor along the way, Give to some needy soul today," when she remembered Virginia's ill-shaped shoes that were shoddy when Bennet bought them. Not that she didn't hope Bennet put in liberally out of his abundance, but she simply couldn't help but compare and contrast his shoes of superior quality with Virginia's inferior ones.

159

Virginia was almost a young lady now, and without dispute she was the poorest-clad girl in the congregation. She was at the age when girls care very much how they look, and she did care. It made her shy and sensitive. If her father would have been struggling to make ends meet, Virginia could have willingly worn what she had without any great tendency to having her finer feelings touched, but she knew her father cared more for his money than he did for her personal comforts. Virginia pondered over this more than once until the consciousness of her shabby appearance made her wretched.

She had a lovely form and a pretty face, and those two God-given blessings magnified the beauty of everything she put on. Her mother was often secretly glad for that, and so was Joseph. He cared what his younger sister had to wear. Every time they went to church he longed for the day to come when he could work for wages and get his sister and his mother some new clothes. Thinking too well of oneself, or glorying in what one has is not only an abomination to God but also offensive to others, but self-respect is far from self-conceit. The pride Joseph had in his heart for his mother and Virginia was just and proper. J. Bennet Armstrong cared very much how he himself looked to others.

*   *   *

The meat Annie prepared for supper was a little tough, and during the conversation Virginia said sincerely, but quite artlessly, "I know poor Earnie Eloy couldn't chew this meat."

"Why Earnie Eloy?" asked Bennet. "He had as good a set of teeth as anybody I know."

"Yes—but—but Father, he can't chew now."

Joseph looked at his mother and she looked at him. Both wondered what should be said. Father hadn't heard yet.

"He was accidentally shot in the jaw, Bennet," ventured Annie, her voice trembling slightly. She shivered. "I didn't tell you yet that I had a let—"

Bennet dropped his fork.

"Yes—a letter from Sara—Saturday while you were gone, Bennet, and she said Alex Burns and Earnie were out hunting on a Sunday and somehow Alex shot Earnie in the jaw and he's in the hos—"

"Well, why didn't you tell me when I got home?"

Annie couldn't honestly say she never thought of it all evening.

"Huh?"

"Well, I can't say just why I didn't, Bennet. I just didn't get around to it yet. You've been so busy."

"So busy?" he shouted. "Well, we ate supper together Saturday night, and drove all the way to church together Sunday, and came home together, didn't we? Where's the letter? You didn't burn it, did you?" He cast her a stabbing look.

"No, indeed, Bennet." She hastened to get it. It was in her Bible on the dresser, and Joseph's with it. "Here they are."

"They?" he shouted. "How many?"

Her hand trembled when she held them out, for she was certain there was more than one thing in the letters that would rouse his feelings. Joseph ate with bated breath while his father read. He saw the color in his cheeks rise and deepen, and he could hear the exaling of his breath get louder and heavier as he turned the pages.

"I call this an insult," he shouted angrily, turning to Annie first. "And you, Joseph Armstrong," he hissed hotly, turning next to the boy beside him, "are a sneakin' rascal. I thought you were supposed to be a Christian. Christian indeed! I told you you couldn't write to Freddie Stokes, so you go sneakin' to Mr. Herrmann and beg stamps off of him behind my back. You're not too big to have a good strapping if you are as big as I am. I'll just show you" (and Bennet rolled up both shirt sleeves and displayed his muscle) "who's boss on this ranch. Get up off your chair young man, and get ready for your dues." Bennet was furious. He all but frothed now.

"But, Father," said Joseph getting to his feet. "You didn't say I couldn't write to Freddie. You said I should let him rest a while, and I did. You said you didn't have a stamp, and—and I didn't beg Mr.—"

"That's enough out of you," and Bennet would have struck Joseph, but Annie jumped up and caught him by the arm.

"Don't strike him, Bennet," she cried. "Sit down and let's talk this all over first. Let Joseph explain just how he got his stamps from Karl Herrmann before you punish him." Bennet stepped back. He was almost shocked into numbness.

Annie Armstrong had never in all her years of married life done a thing like this. Something she didn't realize she possessed rose up within her in defense of her boy who was now almost a man. In the past years Joseph had received too many punishings which had been laid upon him unjustly and sometimes even knavishly. If the child would have been given a hearing in court they would have been pronounced unwarrantable. Annie Armstrong possessed an evenhanded and reasonable amount of sound judgment, and right now in view of the sacredly precious, priceless, and solemn contents of the letter on the table beside Bennet's plate, his outburst of anger seemed to her almost villainous. How could he stand there and accuse his son of not being a Christian when he displayed such a violation of the laws of Christian con-

duct himself? How could a lawbreaker rightfully punish another? Annie couldn't stand it. She stood up very
straight and looked Bennet square in both eyes. She
rebelled this time.

"Bennet," she said quietly but earnestly, "I can't for
the life of me see that Joseph did wrong to write to
Freddie. Mr. Herrmann gave him stamps for a Christmas present, and I think it was mighty nice of him. What
was there in either of those letters that made you so
angry?"

"I'm not angry," he panted. "You're the one who is
angry."

"No, I'm not angry, Bennet," came her calm answer.
"I'm only trying to be fair. What was it that Sara or
Freddie wrote that you don't like?"

"The whole thing is wrong," he shouted. "I'm clear
out of the picture already. Why didn't Timothy write to
me and tell me all this?"

"He didn't know where to write until one of us wrote
first, Bennet. All they knew was that we moved out here
to the West. Didn't you get that in the letter? No one
knew our post office."

Bennet gulped twice. He didn't answer. His face got
redder and redder. "And where's any more letters you've
gotten behind my back?" He pointed to Joseph. He was
so angry he shook now, as he flung the words in Joseph's
face.

"I have none," answered Joseph.

"Don't you feel awful sorry for Earnie?" asked Annie,
touching Bennet on the arm.

"Sorry? That's what he gets for going hunting on
Sunday."

"But I pity him anyway."

"Course you would," he pouted, "after the bouquets
Sara says he gave you."

"Forget all that, Bennet," answered Annie. "I do feel sorry for him. And did you ever invite him to go along to church with us instead of going fishing or hunting on a Sunday?"

"It's not in my place to invite folks to church. That's the preacher's work. He knew where the church was."

"I know," Annie said sadly, "but maybe he was just waiting to be asked."

"Well," Bennet swallowed. "Well," he repeated, "I don't meddle into other people's affairs, but I still think Joseph deserves a good strapping for going ahead and writing to Freddie without my permission." He couldn't bear the idea that his wife should alter his intentions or frustrate his plans in any way. "First of all, Joseph, you may go get me the rest of your stamps and hand them over."

"You mean?" gasped Annie. "You mean you won't let him even write a letter to Earnie?" Annie swayed for a moment with sickness of soul, and her face turned a deathly white. She would have fallen with her face against the hot stove, but Joseph caught her in his arms. Virginia screamed, and Lowell cried out in terror.

"Father," cried Joseph. "Father," he repeated breathlessly. "Oh, she's going to get one of those terrible spells again! Quick, Virginia! Get a cold rag! Where's one of those pills? Father, get one quick and—put it under her tongue, one of those pills Dr. Lindquist—"

Bennet walked across the room, scrambled through the dresser drawer and finally found one. Together Joseph and Bennet laid the prostrate woman on the nearest bed, and while Joseph pried her teeth apart with his fingers, Bennet dropped the pill under her tongue.

"Open the door, Lowell," cried Joseph. "Mama— Mama—" he called, patting her face. He rubbed one arm frantically. "Rub her other arm, Father."

Bennet did what Joseph told him. He rubbed rather awkwardly.

"Help—me sit up," she whispered after several minutes. "Fan—me—dear." Bennet's Sunday hat was the first thing Joseph saw, and so he used that.

"Do you want a drink, Mama?" Virginia grabbed a glass off the table at Joseph's suggestion. She shook her head.

"Father," she looked up into Bennet's face, "you—you won't—will you?"

"Won't what?" he asked in a throaty voice.

It was hard for her to talk yet. She raised one hand. "You—know," she said weakly.

Bennet stopped rubbing her arm and sat for a long time tapping the floor with his heel while he held his tightly folded arms across his chest. He seemed to be pondering something to answer. She waited. She waited.

"Close the door now," said Annie softly. "You won't, will you, Bennet? I believe—it will—kill me—if—you —do."

"If I can forgive—you surely ought to," he said at last, getting abruptly to his feet. "Let's forget it," and so saying he walked to the door of the cattle shed, opened it, and stepped out into the dark. After that night whenever a letter came to the Armstrong ranch, unless it was addressed to Bennet, he showed no interest in it whatever. He listened to the news from home with an unconcerned, indifferent attitude and pretended that he was completely absorbed in his own thoughts.

*　　*　　*

Earnie Eloy asked the nurse to open the letter for him. "Who's it from?" he asked through his teeth.

"Someone at Admore—the state is so blurred I can't make it out."

She handed it to him, and as he turned it over and saw Joseph's name signed at the bottom, a strange light came into both eyes. He could not smile for the bandage on his face, but above the bandage the nurse could see that he was highly pleased. She closed the door leaving him alone to read.

"Dear Earnie:

"Aunt Sara wrote and said you are in the hospital, so I want to write and let you know I'm thinking of you and hope you'll be out again before too long. It seems like a year already since we left home. Where did you go after we left? Everything is so different here, even the books we use in school. Our teacher is not half as nice as Mr. Pennewell. I get awful lonesome for Freddie, and I'd like to see you again too. Mama is better since we live here. The air seems fresher or something. Father has 150 cattle out on our ranch. I have plenty to do, and I do the janitor work at school to pay for my books. I prayed for you last night, Earnie, and twice every day since I heard about your accident.

"Best wishes,
"Joseph."

The man in the bed read the last sentence again and again, and slowly folded the letter.

CHAPTER XXV

Joseph received two letters, one from Freddie, and one from Tom Bradly; and his mother had one from Lottie Woods disclosing with rapturous words her engagement to William Ashelford. Part of it read thus:

"We've been secretly but immensely interested in each other for over a year, but he promised his mother he'd never marry until after she had passed on. I don't know when the departure of a saint took me so close to the heavenly portals as did dear Mother Ashelford's. She was buried on Sunday. Of course we won't get married for several months yet. William wants to do some papering and remodeling. Wasn't it wonderful of William to show such devotion to his aged mother? Every time I see William, he makes me think of your Joseph. He always seemed to be so devoted to you from his early childhood. I suppose he is quite a big boy by now. He was as tall as you when you left; of course you're not a big woman. Please keep my secret, Annie. I know I can trust you; that's why I was free to tell you all this. Tell the children hello, and tell them that our missionary child support fund this past year amounted to eighty-two dollars and sixty cents."

Uncle Tom Bradly's letter wasn't a long one, but Joseph did appreciate it beyond any words to express it. Nor did he try. He read it over twice and handed it to his mother.

"Dear Joseph," she read silently.

"I'm a poor stic at riting letters but if you can't make it out copy it and then read it. How's my boy Joseph? Member your promise to stay close to God way out there in the west. Be a man, my boy. I can't think of nothin more to rite, so I'll send you this little piece I cut out of the *Herald of Truth* that came today.

Life is more than stocks and bonds,
Love is more than rate per cent,
He who gives in friendship's name
Shall surely reap as he has spent,

"Your friend,
"Uncle Tom."

"P.S. I'm sending you something."

Annie smiled and handed the letter back to Joseph. "I'd never part with that," she said softly.

Joseph put it in the inside pocket of his Sunday coat.

"I do wish I had a room of my own," he told his mother.

"I wish, too, you did, Joseph," she answered sympathetically. Little did Joseph realize when his mother answered how she pitied him living in such close quarters. Any boy eighteen or under likes to have a room of his own and a place to keep his own things. Every boy wants to be the owner and master of a few personal possessions. Every boy likes at least to turn around without others seeing how he did it or why. There were times when Joseph would have cherished a room to go to where he could close the door and be alone. Lowell had eyes, Virginia had eyes, and so did his mother, but none were as penetrating and critical as his father's.

The package from Tom Bradly contained a small Testament with Psalms. Joseph carried it in the hip pocket of his overalls. As he had opportunity he read from it when he was out alone with the cattle. It wasn't many days until Quicksilver manifested a special fondness for his master's son. He liked Joseph's tone of voice and his caresses. His pats were kinder than Bennet's, and even a dumb brute knew the difference and pawed the ground for joy whenever Joseph came near. As the months passed by, Joseph and Quicksilver became real pals.

"Let's just stand here and rest a while," said Joseph one day when they were out on the prairie alone. "I want to read a little more in this book Uncle Tom sent me."

Quicksilver gave a quick little neigh and stepped over. Joseph had started at the beginning and had read through to the twenty-eighth chapter of Acts. For days he had been searching for it—those words in the text the evangelist had used the night he stood. It was something about being in a desert place and being led about and kept and instructed, and something about an eagle's nest. Joseph hadn't found it yet. There was something about the stillness and vastness of the prairie that made Joseph think of it. Once he saw a large bird soaring high in the distance, and as he watched it, it carried him back to those Sunday evenings when Father went to church alone on horseback, and his mother told him stories while he stood at her side with his arm around her neck. He thought he could smell that certain freshness of her body and the starch in her white apron, and as the cool autumn wind blew across his face, he thought he felt her soft brown hair against his cheek again, and the pressure of her arm around his waist. Just that morning his father had talked harshly to him and accused him of mislaying a letter he had received from Hendrick's Produce Company, when Joseph declared he didn't touch it. Sometimes he was almost tempted to despise his father, but his mother's gentle voice and tender ways would loom up before him, and again and again he heard her say, "Maybe Father will be kinder someday."

"O God," prayed Joseph all alone out on the treeless stretch of land, holding both arms up above his head and lifting his face to the open sky above him. "Why, oh, why, does Father act like he hates me? Won't he ever be different? Why can't he be kinder to Mama and Virginia and us boys? What chance do I have of being anything worth while? O God, when I was a boy way back East I thought You called me by my own name one evening, and Mama said someday I'd understand about that fruitful bough. What does it mean, O God? I'll soon be twenty years old, and what chance have I got? What have I ever done for anyone yet? What have I ever done for You? Nothing, Lord; but once I read an essay in church which wasn't any good. Why does Father always misjudge and criticize me when I've tried so hard to please him? And how can he go to church and take communion when he treats Mama the way he does? O God, is there some sin in Father's life he's trying to keep covered? Sometimes I wonder. Help me to be more obedient. Help me be true for Mama's sake, and O God, somehow help Lowell and Virginia to grow up to be good. I can't see any chance for any of us unless You help us out. I hope Uncle Tom prays for me. I hope Brother Grissley hasn't forgotten me, and Amos Pennewell, and Earnie Eloy. Help him, Lord, to find You in spite of the life Father lived before him. Brother Collins seems like a true Christian. O God, he is a real true Christian, and maybe someday I can have a talk with him. Lead me, God, for the way is often hard and the pit is dark, but—but Mama is in it with me. Bless her, O God, and if Father will never make her happy, help me to be able to do it."

Across the valley beyond the distant mountains a streak of lightning flashed in the heavens. The bay saddle pony whinnied, and Joseph threw his arms around his neck and rubbed his cheek against Quicksilver's nose. "Don't be afraid," he whispered.

*　　　*　　　*

Spring came again to the little family in the West. It was nearly nine months after Bennet purchased the last bunch of cattle that suddenly he announced to the family one evening that early the next morning two ranchers were coming to help him drive forty head of beeves to the stockyard at Admore and that Annie was to pack his suitcase and fix some lunch, for he was going to accompany his carload of cattle to Chicago for market.

"I might be gone a week," he said. He was shaving. He looked at Annie in the mirror on the wall. "And Joseph," he said, wiping lather and whiskers on a piece of paper beside the basin, "I'll tell you what to do and not do while I'm gone. I want you to learn how to handle Quicksilver now like I do. I'm going to teach you how to take care of cattle out on range. There's money in cattle, and before you're of age—" For some reason the man decided not to finish that sentence. He studied Joseph's frame as a mechanic would a tool under consideration for a certain piece of work. Joseph could feel the blood rush through his veins as his father stared at him.

*   *   *

In the throng of men at the stock market Bennet pressed up against one with a familiar face. "Aren't you Squire McCracken?" asked Bennet, tapping the gray-haired man on the upper arm.

"Hello—a—McCracken's my name, sir, but I can't speak yours this moment."

"Armstrong."

"Sure enough. You live not so far from me over by the—"

"No, not any more. I sold that place and moved west on a ranch. We left over three years ago."

"Like it?"

"Sure do. There's money in beef cattle. You got some here?"

"I brought in a carload last night, and one two weeks ago. How many did you bring in?"

"Forty head now. I'll have more ready before long. I didn't know you raised cattle."

"Oh, I try a little of everything. But I'm going to have to cut out some things now pretty soon. I'm not young any more and it's hard to find enough help these days. Every married man wants to go into something for himself, and single men aren't any good."

"So? Well, I had a single man for ten years or more, and he was a real worker."

"That Eloy?"

"Yes."

"I've heard he was a worker, but he was what you'd call a bachelor. That's different; but these young fellows who want to be out sparkin' a girl twice a week or more aren't any account. Now you take a growing boy who wants to lay up money to buy himself a horse and a buggy, but isn't ready to run around yet, they sometimes make pretty good workers. I've heard tell you taught your boys how to work."

"Isn't that the way to do?"

"Sure," answered Squire McCracken, scratching his head above his right ear. He jingled change in his pocket with his other hand and he looked at Bennet Armstrong in deep study. "Say," he said at length, twisting his gold watch chain as he always did when a wise plan which he was about to explain ran through his head, "haven't you got a boy who's about ready to start working out?"

"I've got a boy that's as big as I am already, maybe not as heavy."

"I've got an idea," spoke the Squire, still twisting his watch chain. "I've got ten acres of the finest kind of grapes grown this side of the Mississippi that I'd like to lease out for crop rent to someone who wants to make some money."

Bennet's ears went up.

"Last year," continued the Squire noticing his hearer's attention, "I just couldn't get the help I needed and a lot of grapes went to waste. But the year before I cleared a hundred dollars an acre on—"

"You say you have ten acres you'd lease out for crop rent?"

"I'd like to. I have more than ten acres of grapes, but I'd like to have help on at least ten acres. There's a lot of work with grapes, but it's not such hard work. I enjoyed it when I was younger, but my wife's after me all the time to get rid of some of my property since Fonzo had a stroke."

"Who?"

Bennet heard what the Squire said.

"My best colored man had a stroke five months ago. I'll never find another like old Fonzo Bullet. If ever a darky gets to Heaven, old Fonzo will."

"So?"

"He has a heart of gold, old Fonzo has. I fixed up a nice room for him in our basement and hired a trained nurse to come and take care of him while he was in bed, and if I'm living when he dies I'll see to it that he gets a decent burial. Funny how a white man can become attached to a black man now, isn't it?"

"I s'pose so. I never had one work for me," came Bennet's reply. "What crop rent will you ask for your ten acres?"

"Are you interested, Mr. Armstrong?" asked Squire McCracken.

"Well, I'm going to find something for my son to do pretty soon now. He's out of school, and before he gets it into his head to run off to some academy, and on to college, I'd like to get him tied down to something worth while. The house we're living in is too small for five of us; and another thing, when a boy is past twenty it's time he gets out from under his mother's heels. You know a mother can spoil her boy in more ways than one, and a separation might do them both some good. He humors her and she humors him."

"Well, well," said Squire McCracken. "Has he been a disobedient boy?"

"Oh—no—not exactly that," answered Bennet, fearing the Squire might not consider such a boy. "No," he added quickly, "I can't honestly think of one time when he was willfully disobedient, and he can really work too. Joseph is a pretty good boy, but as I was saying he's at that age now where—a—where he's a little hard to—a—where I mean, he might be better satisfied working away from home since we're so crowded there."

"Yes, I see, I see," said Squire McCracken twisting harder on his gold watch chain. "We've got to be moving on, Armstrong. I'll see you again after dinner. Meet me in the lobby here."

"All right," answered Bennet, with an impressive note in his voice. "What crop rent did you say you'd rent for?"

"Oh, maybe one third. We'll talk things over later, talk business."

As Bennet Armstrong pressed on with the crowd, Squire McCracken saw him moving his lips as though he were juggling figures.

CHAPTER XXVI

Joseph was washing for supper when the door opened, letting in a soft breath of fragrant April air as Bennet entered.

"I've got a lease here," he said drawing a paper out of his pocket and flourishing it so the family could all see it, "for a ten-acre vineyard on the Squire McCracken estate."

"A what?" asked Annie in surprise. She almost dropped the pan of gravy she was holding in her hand ready to pour out into a bowl.

"A three-year lease," answered Bennet with stiff formality. "And Joseph is going back there to take care of it."

"Joseph is?" gasped Annie with still greater surprise. "You mean alone?"

"Yes. It's all settled," went on Bennet wetting his lips and blowing his large Roman nose. "It's all settled," he repeated with greater importance in his manner. "I saw Squire McCracken in Chicago on this trip and I had a big notion to go along home with him and see it, but I'll wait and go sometime later. I thought I'd better come on home and take care of my cattle. It pays to take care of them. Have you been doing it right, Joseph?"

"You mean you got a good price for the ones you took to market?" asked Annie evading the question he asked Joseph. Of course Joseph had done his best.

"Not bad at all," he answered almost pleasantly, pulling a chair over to the table. He rapped his fingers on the oilcloth and continued, ready to meet his opponents in the struggle that was bound to start soon. "Joseph," he said first, "you're going back to look after that vineyard. I'll take you to town on Saturday and get you the clothes you'll need and buy your ticket. I," Bennet saw Annie's countenance change and saw her breast rise and fall with fast breathing. He hurried on. "I want you to leave the last of next week and get busy. The Squire will show you how to prune the vines; that's the most important thing right now. He said a few posts would need to be replaced and some of the wire mended before the leaves come out too far. During the summer you'll have to cultivate and pull weeds and—"

"But, Bennet," gasped Annie, pale-faced and trembling, "do you mean Joseph will go away—way back there and not get home for three years?"

"I didn't say that, Annie. I didn't say that," he repeated coldly. "I'll see once how much it pays when the first crop is sold. Of course if Joseph can't handle it I'll find someone else, or do it myself, or—or maybe, well, Lowell here he's too young yet and he's still in school. Joseph is old enough to get out and work."

All the while Joseph was standing beside the cookstove listening. If he was right, Squire McCracken's estate would be within walking distance of the church if he got up early enough. And he'd manage somehow to be with Freddie once in a while. Joseph's heart pounded within him like a drum.

"The Squire said he was certain Joseph could room and board at the Bantum place on the hill right back of the vineyard. I'm going to write to them tonight and find out. We'll hear before—"

"But, Bennet," put in Annie feebly. "Are you sure we can spare Joseph?"

"We?" Bennet laughed. "I can. Can't you?"

"I don't know," she answered with feeling, "but if Joseph really wants to go, I won't say no."

"Of course you won't say no," he retorted, meaning to be witty. "And he can't say no now. Here are the papers. It's going to be a paying proposition."

"And what will Joseph get out of it?" asked the mother meekly.

"What will he get out of it?" asked Bennet. "Why, he'll get some good experience out of it, and a free train ride, and his room and board and clothes. Isn't that enough? Joseph isn't of age yet. If I pay his room and board and furnish his clothes, what more does he need?

Annie did not answer. As yet Joseph hadn't opened his mouth to say a word. Bennet was dazed. He thought sure Joseph would bring up at least one objection. "He's not old enough yet to want a horse and buggy. What would a boy his age do with money?"

"Well," said Annie, "he'll need stamps to write home."

Bennet laughed again. Annie never appreciated those laughs.

"Whenever you write, you can send him a stamp to answer," said Bennet.

This did not satisfy Annie altogether, for maybe Bennet would not furnish her with stamps as often as she'd want them. Would he let her have two stamps a week? Would he?

"Do you want to go, Joseph?" asked his mother, searching his face seriously.

"Shall I?" he asked, searching hers.

"Of course you're going," voiced Bennet, rapping the table with the fingers of both hands. "You're not old enough yet to say what you'll do or not do. Annie, why do you put such ideas in his head?"

"I—I—never meant to, Bennet. I only wanted him to express himself. This is a complete surprise to all of us. It—it somehow makes me feel like we're growing old already, Bennet, to have a son leaving home." She swept her cheeks with her eyelashes, and when she spoke again her voice was quite unsteady. "It's going to be hard, in a way, to see him go."

"Now Annie," said Bennet rebukingly, "it's time he's showing what he's made of. I'm anxious to know if he's going to be an Armstrong."

"What else can he ever be?" asked Annie with a twinge of distress in her tone.

"Of course," mumbled Bennet, "but you know what I mean. The Stokes are a good sort of people, I suppose, but they never seemed to know how to get ahead."

Annie was hurt. The family pride in her bosom welled up within her, and tears quivered in both brown eyes. "You never heard of a Stokes in my family receiving charity," she ventured delicately, "and my father owned his own farm."

"Maybe so, but not more than a farm, and that wasn't a big one, and all the buildings on it were run down when he died."

"That's all true, Bennet," answered Annie, and those two quivering tears started rolling, "but he wasn't run down in his spiritual condition, and if Joseph grows up to be as good a man as Grandfather Stokes I'll be satisfied. There's something higher in life worth striving for besides—"

There was a loud knock at the door, and the pawing of horses' hoofs was heard.

"Armstrong," came a man's husky voice from without, "come on out. There's a stampede on." Before Bennet could get into his coat and cap there came another louder knock. The entire door shook. "Armstrong," shouted a man gruffly, "can't you hear it?"

"Coming," answered Bennet breathlessly. He opened the door and called back as he ran. "Joseph, get on Quicksilver and come. I'll try Do."

Joseph leaped.

"Do your best, old pal," he said jumping on the saddle pony. Away they dashed out over the prairie toward the panic-stricken herd in the distance. He could see a moving cloud of dust ahead.

"Come on," said Joseph, slapping Quicksilver as they went; "help me show Father I'm an Armstrong with enough Stokes in me to make me decent."

Do wasn't as nimble and surefooted as Quicksilver, and Bennet had a hard time catching up with the pony ahead of him. Do, who had never helped in a stampede before, stumbled twice, almost throwing his rider headlong. Bennet hadn't had him two weeks yet.

"What's frightened the cattle," said Joseph to his pony. "Do you see anything, Quick? There's no storm."

Two hundred head of frenzied cattle were rushing headlong in the dusk in one mad flight toward the cliffs where the swift Denifer River ran dizzily over large rocks thirty-five feet below. Joseph caught his breath and held it.

Possessed with sudden knowledge which he had never learned from previous experiences, the pony ahead dashed straight for the cliffs, outrunning the leader of the frenzied herd, cutting slowly but surely to the left just eight feet from the edge of the cliff. Five head of cattle were following at such speed, and in such a delirium, that before Bennet reached the cliff on Do they were pushed over the edge and hurled madly into the foaming cold water below.

"Stop—stop," shouted Bennet at the top of his voice, and the sixth steer came very near pushing him and Do over the brink. Only a divine hand could have been responsible for the escape. Joseph looked back for a moment just in time to realize his father was in danger of his life. He closed his eyes.

"My God!" he cried shivering.

Just then Bennet sighted a wolf.

"For a gun! Oh, for a gun!" cried Bennet hysterically. In his haste he had forgotten to stick it in his belt. What could he do? He was almost beside himself. "Charlie," he yelled to the neighbor rancher, who had knocked on his door. "Where are you, Charlie?" Bennet whistled his loudest whistle and in the dust Charlie answered the call.

"Shoot, Charlie, quick, shoot this wolf!"

It seemed to Bennet an hour before Charlie fired. Shot after shot pierced the night air, echoing in the valley below and re-echoing over the prairie.

Annie stood in the open door, her hands clasped across her breast as if in prayer.

"What is a stampede, Mama?" asked Virginia, her face drawn with sudden terror at the sound of the distant discharge. "Who's shooting, Mama? Look, there hangs Father's pistol."

"Listen," whispered the little mother. "The wolves are howling dreadfully. They must be savage tonight. Listen, children, let's pray that no one gets hurt. Joseph is not used to such as this."

While Lowell clung to his mother on one side and Virginia on the other, Annie Stokes Armstrong asked God to spare her husband and son from harm. And as she was praying the moon high above a far-off cluster of hills came out from between two floating clouds and shone down on them in the doorway.

"Look, Mama," whispered Virginia, pointing to the shining body, "Everything looks so bright now."

"It's just another light from Heaven," the mother said softly, "and somehow for me it means—"

"Means what, Mama?" Both children asked it at the same time.

"How shall I say it?" she said, taking a deep breath of the fresh night air. "We were talking of such sad things before the knock on the door—so—so quickly our thoughts can be cut off—so quickly our plans can be changed—so often I've been in the dark, but—like I used to tell Joseph when he was a little boy, God sees us in the dark, but we often forget it. We were standing here in the dark, wondering and fearing; then suddenly the clouds parted and there was the moon. It was there all the while, but we didn't realize it. Look, children, the whole prairie is lighted now and perhaps it means someday things will be brighter for all of us."

"How do you mean, Mama?" asked Lowell earnestly. "Listen, the howling is dying down and you can hear Father shouting. I hope no one got hurt."

Breathlessly the three stood listening. A cloud of gray dust loomed against the distant horizon.

"How did you mean?" repeated Lowell, "that someday things will be brighter for all of us?"

"Oh, it must be," answered Annie, putting her whole self into her words. "You both know we could have a happier home, but I want you to know that I dearly love you, and you've both been wonderfully good to me. And Joseph's been a good boy too. When I think of that it's always like a light from Heaven shining down on my life. I have much to be glad for when I stop to think of it— if only—Father could be more like—"

"Like what, Mama?" whispered Virginia.

"Oh, like I thought he was going to be," came her sad answer. "But," she added, quickly unclasping the hands that were crossed on her breast, "maybe if we all pray every day things will be brighter sometime."

"And Father won't ever do that again on Christmas day?" asked Lowell, his voice full of disappointment even this long afterward.

"Oh, wasn't that awful," cried Virginia.

"It truly was," sighed Annie, "but let's never tell a single soul. Let's all love Father anyway, and let's try to figure out how we can do something real nice for him sometime. That makes me much happier, for then I know God never takes his eyes off of us, even in the dark, when I keep such thoughts in my heart."

CHAPTER XXVII

"But Mama," sobbed Virginia, "it won't seem at all like home any more if Joseph is gone."

"But his spirit will be with us, Virginia, dear. We'll talk about him and pray for him each day, and he'll write to us."

"Oh, I have an idea, Mama," said Lowell standing up very straight. "Maybe I can do the janitor work at school next year and get stamps from Mr. Herrmann."

"Lowell," came the mother's answer, "don't suggest it to Father. He can afford to buy your books, and he can afford to keep us in stamps too. Anyway, you're too young to have any more put on you than you already have. I pray every day of my life that none of you children will have your health ruined for life. When I think of how hard Joseph had to work when he was a little boy, I know it's only by the mercy of the Lord that he has strong arms and a stout back, and a good heart today. God has certainly spared his life for a purpose." And there in the Heaven-lighted doorway once more Annie Stokes Armstrong repeated to herself those words she found in her own Bible one evening more than ten years before. "Joseph is a fruitful bough by a well; whose branches run over the wall: The archers have sorely grieved him, and shot at him," Annie shivered, "and hated him." Annie shivered again.

"Are you cold, Mama?" asked Virginia throwing an arm across her mother's shoulder.

"No," she answered dreamily. "But his bow abode in strength," she quoted to herself reverently, her sweet face uplifted, "and the arms of his hands were made strong by the hands of the mighty God of Jacob." A smile played around her half-parted lips.

"There they come," shouted Lowell, pointing to two

dark figures approaching. "We'll finish our supper now, won't we?" he asked.

"That's right, we haven't eaten yet. Everything is cold now."

As Annie entered the lean-to kitchen, the odor of fried meat and cold lima beans, mingled with the smell of the pickled crab apples, gave her a sickening feeling. The conversation of the previous hour had robbed her of her appetite, leaving her weak and nervous. She had endured a good many similar experiences in past months, yes, years, but nothing had affected her quite like this. Annie was always conscious of the fact that she was the one who wanted the children, not Bennet. Could it be he would have wished for them if he could have been sure they would all be all Armstrong? That smote Annie as much as anything Bennet had ever said. She thought he would be glad if the children had some of the character-istics of the Stokes. She had heard her father say one time that in his lineage as far back as he could go there had not been one idiot, or criminal, or adulterer, and not one pauper. All had been respectable people, some were schoolteachers, forty were preachers of the Gospel, a number were doctors, and several were poets or hymn writers. Secretly Annie had been proud of her ancestry, and though her father did not give her a farm when she was married, he did give her pure blood and a very im-portant factor in character building, an inner life of high ideals and an honest name. More than once she had heard her father say what Milton wrote, "A good man is the ripe fruit our earth holds up to Heaven," and again quoting from Horace Greeley, "Fame is a vapor, popularity is an accident, riches take wings, those who cheer you today may curse you tomorrow, but character alone endures." Yes, it was true; her dear old father owned but one farm, but at his funeral hundreds filed by his casket to pay their last tribute of respect to one whose character had influenced their lives for good. That meant more to Annie than several farms would have.

She didn't get to go home to his funeral, but Timothy had written all about how impressive the service had been, and told her some of the remarks that the officiating ministers had made. "Sister," he had written at the end of his letter, "we've buried a grand old father." And now, could her children ever say that? her very own flesh and blood children she brought into being in tears and prayers? Joseph, her first-born child, whom she had longed and prayed and waited for? would he ever be able to say "my grand old father"? Could he ever be able to say "I've inherited from my father an inner desire to do God's divine will"? Annie felt cold and sick. Just as surely as parents transmit the color of eyes and hair, and types of faces, so they transmit strength or weakness of body, tempers, prejudices, social bents, and religious inclinations. She had never studied psychology in school, but she knew nevertheless, that the home, the school, the church, and the community her children lived in were molding their characters day by day. This truth drove her to her knees many a time when she was alone in the little shack out on the western prairie. She wanted her children to love and not hate. She wanted her children to take an interest in the beautiful and cultivate an appreciation for the fine arts. She wanted to teach her three children home and church loyalty and reverence for God. Annie tried. Sometimes she even prayed that if God could look ahead and see that any of the three were going to live to bring Him shame, He would in mercy take them out of this life before that day came. Sometimes when she was alone in the little house and she sat with her open Bible on her lap, she seemed to see the hands of all her ancestors reaching down from Heaven pulling her upward, while a fragrant mist of her parents' prayers surrounded her like heavenly incense. Without these experiences her husband's harsh words and criticism would have dragged her to the depths of despair. He deprived her of many comforts of life, even necessary clothes, but he could never deprive her of these personal soul experiences. Little delicate Annie Stokes Armstrong knew a secret that many kings have not discovered. Bennet was a very stern man and he could refuse this or that or dictate to his family; yes, he could tell Joseph he must leave soon to take care of a vineyard, but he could never give him orders to lose confidence in his mother, or tell her to stop praying for him. The burden of training the three children in the right way now rested on Annie's shoulders heavier than ever before. She felt sick and weak.

Bennet was crying!

"Oh, dear, are you hurt?" Annie ran to him with outstretched hands. "Lowell, help Father to the bed. O, Joseph, tell us what happened!"

"Where are you hurt, Father?" asked Joseph, stepping close to him.

"I'm—not hurt," he sobbed. "It's those poor—cattle that are hurt. Five or six or—maybe ten head went—over the cliff. I can't stand it!" Great tears rolled down both cheeks and he shook now with sobs.

A terrible feeling went through Annie and her three children as they stood by watching; a feeling that was almost weird.

"Joseph," he choked, "get me the lantern and light it. I'm going back out there."

"And—do what?" asked Annie, with a strange fear gripping her.

"Why, I'm going to go back out there and stay till daylight and see just how many went over. This is a—" he heaved as if in great pain, "a terrible loss."

Loss! Loss! This was what made Bennet weep. Once before Annie had seen him moved to tears when Pete died. The memory of that scene on the back door steps brought nausea to her. There are serious losses of health. Bennet hadn't shed any tears when his wife had passed through two heart attacks and death hovered near. Numbers of times he had wrongfully accused Joseph and had broken his heart and hers as well, but he showed no regret over that loss of confidence. He had wilfully deprived his family of the comforts they deserved and robbed his children of the company of their favorite cousins, but these personal injuries to the ones he should love most were not considered loss worthy of mention. They were like the loss of a half-used pencil in comparison to this now. This was a personal loss. Those beef cattle were his. They were valuable. They were almost ready for market. They were worth eighty dollars apiece, maybe more. Bennet cried as though his heart would break.

Joseph handed his father the lighted lantern and watched him get to his feet. He staggered like an old man.

"You're not going to eat any supper, Bennet?" Annie followed him to the door.

"How could anything taste good to me now?" he cried. "I may not be back before morning."

Forlorn were the four who sat up to the table that night. Each felt miserable and neglected and depressed. There are times when words can't be found to express one's feelings. There are times when a shake of the head comes nearest expressing one's thoughts. The table seemed to groan for them. The lamp flickered sighs. The brown paper on the walls cracked and drained bitter tears, and the entire house was filled with a heavy atmosphere of unquieted pain. It was an awful feeling.

"Folks," said Joseph, at last breaking the dreadful silence, "let's not let this get us down. Father shouldn't feel so bad because a few cattle went over. He came very near going over himself."

"Joseph!" cried Annie.

"It's true, Mama. I just closed my eyes and shuddered. It's only a miracle—but—let's talk about something else." He saw his mother getting white around the nose and a strange stare come into her eyes. "Pass the beans, sis, and Lowell, take some meat and pass it on. It must be nine o'clock or after. I'm pretty hungry."

"Well, Joseph," began Virginia, "tell us—Oh, well, I'll wait until some other time." She saw Joseph shake his head.

After Lowell and Virginia were fast asleep, Annie and Joseph talked in the corner of the kitchen. Joseph stirred up the fire and put in some coal.

"Tell me honestly how you feel about me going back there, Mama."

"Tell me first how you feel about it," answered Annie.

"Well, Mama," began Joseph drawing a deep breath and leaning on the chair he was standing behind. "I've been praying every day for years now that God would lead me in the way I should go. I've been hunting for weeks," and here Joseph pulled out the small Testament from his hip pocket and ran his fingers across its pages, "for the text that the preacher used that night I stood, and I can't find it anywhere."

"But, Joseph, that was in the Old Testament, I think in—just a minute, if I get my Bible I can find it, I'm sure."

"Sit still, Mama, let me get it for you."

"Here it is, Joseph; I marked it. It's in Deuteronomy 32. What were you going to say?"

"Well, I remembered there was something in there about being led about and—"

"I'll read it to you. 'He found him in a desert land, and in the waste howling wilderness; he led him about, he instructed him, he kept him as the apple of his eye. As an eagle stirreth up her nest, fluttereth over her young, spreadeth abroad her wings, taketh them, beareth them on her wings: So the Lord alone did lead him, and there was no strange god with him.' "

"That's it, Mama. I want to copy that off and learn it. Perhaps—perhaps God is using this way to—to—"
She waited.

"I—I—can't say it, Mama," and Joseph burst into tears.

CHAPTER XXVIII

There are hallowed spots on earth that are sacred only to one individual or a restricted few. It may be a spot where a promise was made and sealed with a kiss. It may be a certain step on the stair where an important decision was made. It may be a board in the floor of the old home place where some father or mother knelt to pray. It may be by a tree under which someone stood and won the victory over sin. It may be a place in the barn, or along the road, or on a certain street corner where something unforgettable was heard that changed the destiny of a soul. The little crooked lean-to kitchen was from that moment on a hallowed and sacred spot to Joseph Armstrong and his sainted mother.

To be understood is enough to lift one's spirits. Joseph could feel by the way his mother breathed that she knew what he couldn't say for choking. She was skilled in understanding her son: why shouldn't she be? Together they had experienced trials and disappointments. She had lived on for him and he had worked on for her. She knew the meaning of his every look. She comprehended his desires and ambitions. She had watched him grow in stature and intellect from week to week. She thought and thought while she was lengthening his trousers. She dreamed while she ironed his shirts. She hoped when she stood at the window and watched him going out over the prairie on Quicksilver and noted his broadening shoulders. She prayed as she mended his socks. Every stitch was fastened with love and devotion. Of course she understood him now. His strong youthful body shook with sobs, but how utterly opposite from those sobs that shook his father's frame such a short while before. Yes, she understood why he couldn't talk.

"Perhaps you are right, Joseph," came her gentle voice. It sounded almost like the voice of an angel to him. "You know it will be hard for us to see you leave but—" a tear fell silently on her sleeve and she quickly brushed it away—"but if this is the plan for your life, I wouldn't say no for the world."

"Thanks, Mama." Joseph wiped his eyes and sat down. He didn't realize until now how tired he was. To know that his mother could willingly let him go took all the stiffness out of his muscles, and he relaxed. He had been on tension all evening. It had also relaxed his nerves to cry a little. He had shed many tears in his younger days, but not so many of late. Joseph was almost a man. But the ability to prevent tears is no sign of manhood. In fact, some of the greatest men who have ever lived have been men who wept, not at personal injuries, but over a touching story, the affliction of another, or at the thought of the nearness of the holy God or of motherhood. The strongest men are the most tender.

"Thanks, Mama," he repeated tenderly. "It will be easier now for me to go. You know how I've been wanting a room of my own."

"Yes, I know."

"And Father has never once praised me, no matter how hard I've tried to please him."

"Yes, I know."

"Maybe if I go away to work he'll be different."

"Maybe so, Joseph." She picked at the edge of her blue apron.

"Tell me, Mama," Joseph bent forward until he almost touched his mother, "what do you think is wrong with Father?"

"I've tried to figure it out, Joseph, but—as yet—I'm puzzled."

"How long did you know him before you were married?"

"Well, most of two years," came her subdued answer. "I hope Virginia and Lowell are both asleep, for Joseph, I've confided in you things I've never confided in another living soul. Your father came into our community and found work not far from my home at Wickville. He was quite handsome and wore nice clothes. He soon won the confidence of all the people in the church there, and a number of girls were just wild about him. I wasn't, but when he asked me for a date I was pleased. My folks thought he seemed like a nice young man, and he was free to tell us how much his father was worth. I remember that in particular now. He was not lavish with his love, and if he had been I probably would have resented it. I had never read any books on love or courtship and I didn't know exactly how to read a man's character. He said he was a Christian and always went to church—and —I trusted him." She twisted the corner of her handkerchief. "Before we were married a week I was shocked at the temper he had. It shocked me more and more as time went on. He got aggravated at almost nothing, and never praised anyone unless it was a preacher. He suspects almost everyone or misjudges his motives, but I've often wondered why he likes to praise the preachers when their sermons hit him so hard."

"Do you think—"

"Yes, I think it's because he wants to hide his real self from men of God."

"But Mama," whispered Joseph bending forward still farther, "don't you remember what Brother Collins said in one of his sermons just recently about people like that?"

"Yes, I do, Joseph, and it grieves me very much. All we can do is pray for him."

"But I should think he could soon see what a difference there is between himself and you."

"Is there, Joseph?"

"Is there?" Joseph got abruptly to his feet and walked back and forth across the kitchen. "Oh, Mama," he cried, and the next thing Annie knew she was folded in his arms and he was kissing her on the cheek.

"Mama," he whispered, taking the chair in front of her once more. "If all I had to inspire me to be a Christian was my father, I'd have given up in despair years ago. In fact I'd never have tried it in the first place. You remember?"

"Yes, Joseph, I remember."

"You've been a real mother, Mama."

She didn't answer. Her lip quivered and she couldn't speak, for her heart burned with emotion.

"If anything happens before—before I get back—well—I'll say it now—to your face. Mama—if I ever—amount to anything—it'll be—" he shook with sobs again, "it'll be because of—you."

There are hallowed spots on earth that are sacred only to one or two. The dumpy little lean-to kitchen—that one special corner of it—would always be a never-to-be-forgotten spot for Joseph and Annie Armstrong. It seemed that all the hands of all the Stokes who had gone on to glory were reaching down through that graveled roof pulling those two, mother and son, upward to them. Just as there are hallowed spots on earth, so there are uplifting memories that are attached to them. Uplifting, upward experiences that can never be cast aside. Men have made such statements as this after their mothers had returned to dust, but Joseph told her now. The day of his going would come all too soon, and maybe they would never have a chance to be together like this again. Her face, though seasoned with sadness and age, was no less beautiful to him. Not a hair on her head was gray, and her brown eyes were kind and trustful. Joseph wished he might be an artist to paint her face as she looked at him that night, trusting him, loving him, willing to die for him and the right if need be.

"And perhaps, Joseph," answered his mother at length, "if Lowell and Virginia ever amount to anything it will be because of the life you've lived before them." She meant it. She spoke out of a sincere heart, but Joseph waved it aside.

"No, no, Mama. It will be because of you. Are all of Father's people as stern and critical as he and Aunt Hepsi?"

"I couldn't say. All that I know have a peculiar opinion of themselves being— Oh, Joseph, I'd rather not say it. Shall we have prayer together once more like we used to back home—just you and I?"

"It would mean much to me," and so saying, each slipped an arm around the other and mother and son knelt beside one chair.

Tears fell on that chair. Some were hot and sad, some were glad tears.

"And now, dear Lord," prayed Annie, "in closing let me ask just one more thing of You, dear Lord, that if this my son has been found in a desert land and has found favor in Your blessed sight, that You will lead him and instruct him and keep him as the apple of Your eye wherever he goes, and keep him from any strange god, and make of him a fruitful bough, even a fruitful bough by a well. Keep these convictions ever before him and let no evil person harm him in any way or lead him astray, and make him strong by Your mighty hands, O God. And if it please You, O gracious Father, extend unto me your mercy that my days may be numbered to see that day come when these prayers be answered, blessed Lord. In Jesus' name. Amen."

*   *   *

Bennet did not come in all night. About an hour after daybreak he stumbled in. His face was drawn and his eyes were bloodshot. His hair was disheveled and his trousers were soaked to the knees and torn.

"I'm afraid you will become sick," said Annie, offering him a cup of hot coffee.

"I'm already sick," he said sinking into a chair and dropping his head in his arms on the table. "That was the most pitiful sight I ever saw."

Annie did not ask him how many were lost. Somehow it did not matter to her. To care seemed to her worse than for a half-grown child to cry over a broken toy.

"Let me fix you an egg, Bennet," she said softly.

"I've got to eat," he said.

"Yes, Bennet, you've got to eat."

"Is this Tuesday or Wednesday?"

"This is Thursday, Bennet," she said, breaking an egg into the skillet. She filled the sugar bowl and set out some bread.

"Thursday?" he asked dazedly. "Thursday?" he repeated. "Why don't the children get up? Where's Joseph?"

"He's gone after water."

"I thought that was Lowell's job."

"It is. But he seemed so tired last night, I let him sleep for once."

"For once—sleep for once. I must lay down just a minute. I'm dead on my feet."

Bennet sipped a little coffee, ate the egg, and one slice of bread, and sprawled out face downward across the empty bed. He was snoring when Joseph entered a few minutes later.

"Sh! Let him rest," whispered Annie. "Come outside a minute; I want to tell you something."

Joseph followed and closed the door behind him softly.

"Father said last night he was going to write for a place for you to room and board."

"Yes."

"He didn't get it done, you know."

"Yes."

"Do you suppose he's forgotten it, or this stampede last night has unstrung him so that—he—"

"Perhaps he'll be all right after he's had some rest. Mama, don't worry about it. You mustn't worry." He placed a hand on her shoulder. How tall and strong he looked. He stood looking down at her straight in her eyes.

"No, I mustn't," she answered, thoughtfully looking away. She bit her lip.

"Who's that coming? Look, Mama, someone in a buggy."

A half-grown boy with sandy hair jumped out and faced the two standing just outside the back door. He was quite out of breath, and he stuttered when he tried to speak.

"Ma w-w-w-wants to n-n-n-know if you can c-c-come over right away. M-m-my little s-s-s-sister has s-s-s-spasms—awful bad." The boy's face was red to begin with and was redder yet till he got that much out. "T-t-that was my d-d-dad who h-h-helped you out last night, an' he s-s-s-s-said you'd h-h-help us out now."

"It's Charlie Ledfetter's boy, Mama. They live in the first place on the west road."

"Oh, of course. I'll—you mean, you want me to go along back with you now?" asked Annie sympathetically.

The boy nodded and motioned to the buggy.

"Just a minute. I'll get my coat and scarf."

The boy rubbed his dirty hand over his face and climbed into the seat in the buggy.

"Maybe you'd better hang around, Joseph," she said in undertones as she passed. "Have Lowell and Virginia get up at once. Tell Father where I went. I'll be back as soon as possible."

CHAPTER XXIX

The man across the end of the bed slept soundly for over an hour. The episode of the night just past had completely exhausted him. He must have had a wild dream, for he gave a strange outcry and woke with a start. He got to his feet and shook himself.

"What's going on here?" He staggered into the kitchen, running both hands through his black hair. Virginia was washing dishes and Lowell was wiping them. They were talking in undertones when their father appeared in the doorway, a strange look in his deep blue eyes. He stared at them.

"Where's your mother?" he said huskily.

"Joseph," called Virginia, opening the door of the cattle shed, "where'd you say Mama went?"

"She went over to Ledfetters."

"To where?" asked Bennet.

Joseph was milking, but stopped right there and came into the kitchen. He was not afraid of his father exactly, but he liked to be near the rest of the family whenever he thought he might go on a tantrum. He would likely be wondering why he was milking this morning.

"Sammie Ledfetter came over in a buggy while you were sleeping, Father, and asked Mama to come over. His little sister has spasms."

"Spasms?" shouted Bennet. "Well, is that anything so serious they have to call in all the neighbors?"

"I don't think they called them all in, Father," spoke Joseph; "the boy just asked for Mama. He said his father sent him over."

"Huh! Spasms. Anyone ought to know what to do for them without running four miles after the neighbors. When will she be back?"

"She said she'd be back as soon as possible."

"Soon as possible? Well! And how will she get back?"

"I suppose Sammie will bring her back. He came after her in their buggy."

"Buggy?" repeated Bennet. "Well, they took a lot for granted, didn't they?"

"I guess they knew she wouldn't refuse, Father," said Joseph. How deep his voice sounded this morning. Virginia looked up in wonder, surprise, and admiration. Why—Joseph's voice was as deep as Father's this morning, and much, much richer. "You see, Charlie helped you out last night, Father." Joseph hesitated. He didn't like the look on his father's face. He stepped closer to Virginia at the dishpan. "If he hadn't noticed the commotion out there, maybe all the cattle might have been—"

"Yes, might have been," mocked Bennet stroking his black hair. "If I only would have grabbed my own pistol I might have saved them all. Charlie was so slow and stupid. It will take me a long time to get over this."

"But it could have been much worse, Father," suggested Joseph with fervor.

Bennet cleared his throat and adjusted his shirt collar.

"Is this Thursday?" he asked.

"Yes, this is Thursday," answered Joseph. "You just came back from Chicago last evening."

"That's right. I didn't—did I? No, I haven't written that letter yet to Sol Bantum. I must get that in the box before the mail carrier comes along. Virginia, wipe your hands and clear off a place for me to write. I must get me another roll-top desk. After Joseph leaves maybe we'll have a little more room around here. Now you all be quiet while I try to write." When he opened his leather suitcase Virginia saw a square white box. Out of this her father took an envelope and a sheet of paper and a stamp. He closed the suitcase, locked it, and pushed it under his bed.

*		*		*

Annie was away most of the day. In fact it was after three when the same boy who had come and got her, brought her back.

"You're very welcome, Sammie," Virginia heard her say as she opened the door, "and you tell your mother anytime she ever needs me again not to hesitate to send for me. Good-by, Sammie, and I'm glad we had a chance to get acquainted."

*		*		*

Bennet took Joseph to town on Saturday as he had planned. He knew it would be the middle of the next week at least before he could have an answer from Sol Bantum, but he had written on the bottom of the letter, "Answer at once," and had underlined it twice. So surely by Thursday or not later than Friday, he should have the answer. So confident was he that the answer would be favorable that he was ready to take every step to get Joseph ready. First he took him to the shoe store and had him fitted with a pair of heavy work shoes that laced half-way to his knees. He grumbled a little at the price, but when he was convinced there were none in town as sturdy for the price, he bought them. He got him four pairs of overalls and told Joseph very emphatically those should last him at least a year and he was to take care of his clothes. He got him a straw hat that one merchant had left over from the summer before (since this was a little early for the straw hat season to begin, and since the hat was a trifle dusty and out of shape he made a nice little reduction which suited Bennet right and did not impinge upon his pride), six pairs of heavy work socks, four heavy blue cotton shirts, three bandanna handkerchiefs, three pairs of canvas gloves, a denim jacket, and a short, pocketed apron to match, in which to carry tools. From there they went to the hardware store and Bennet selected a hammer, a pair of long-nosed pliers, a large box of staples, and a ball of binder twine.

"I'll need a Sunday shirt," ventured Joseph, dreading the reaction. He had seen his father hand the clothier a twenty-dollar bill and get less than three back in change.

"A Sunday shirt?" gulped Bennet. He blinked. He sniffed. He scowled. "Well," he panted at length, holding his purse halfway in and halfway out of his pocket, "I thought I was sending you back there to work. Where do you think you'll be going that you'll be needing a Sunday shirt?"

"I—I hope I'll get to church sometimes—Father," he answered. He was sure the man at the other counter could have heard, for Father talked quite loudly. Joseph blushed. Just then the man turned and it was none other than Brother Milton Collins, their honorable and much-esteemed pastor. He tipped his hat graciously and made a slight bow.

"Why, good day," he said, extending his friendly warm hand.

Bennet grabbed it and shook it vigorously.

"Why, good day, Brother Collins," he said pleasantly. "Nice day, nice day, isn't it?"

"Yes. And how is everyone at your place?"

"Just fine," answered Bennet, smiling and making obeisance.

"You'll all be out to church tomorrow, I suppose?"

"Of course. If nothing prevents you can count on us being there."

"I—I—thought I heard—heard your son saying something to the effect—"

So he had heard! Brother Collins of all persons! Joseph's face burned with a feeling of disgrace for another's improper conduct.

"I'm getting him fitted out with clothes to go East next week," came Bennet's quick cautious reply. "I've leased a ten-acre vineyard not so far from our old home place and he's going back to take care of it."

"I see, I see," answered Brother Collins. "So Joseph is going to be a husbandman! Well, there's a story in the Bible about the husbandman who—"

"Yes, I know, Brother Collins. Yes, I'm getting Joseph all ready for his trip. It will be quite a new experience for him."

"He'll get to attend church back there, I suppose?"

"Oh, of course—a—that is, I hope so. It's quite a distance to walk and, a—well, if the good Lord wants him there He'll make a way, I guess," and J. Bennet Armstrong chuckled as though he had quoted a very wise proverb. "Yes," he said genially, "we were just talking about buying him another Sunday shirt."

Another Sunday shirt! Joseph's face burned down to his neck and up into his hair.

"Well, Joseph," and Brother Collins stepped up close to him and took hold of his arm firmly, "we'll miss you here in our little church. We don't have many young men like you here. I think we need you, but God bless you when you leave us. I've been wanting to tell you I enjoyed that essay you read. I'm sorry I've waited until now to tell you. I suppose all your old chums will be ready to welcome you back."

"I hope so," smiled Joseph warmly.

"Well, we must be moving, Joseph," said Bennet, "or we'll not get home by chore time. Sorry, Brother Collins,

but we must be moving on," and Bennet tipped his hat
again.

*·   *   *

The day came for Joseph to leave home. Negotiations
with the Bantums had been completed and in twelve days
after Bennet came home with the lease, Joseph was all
packed and ready to go.

"There is just one more thing I think he needs," said
the mother, as she tied a string around his lunch, "and
that's a Bible."

"A Bible?" quizzed Bennet banteringly. "Haven't I
spent enough on him yet?"

"But he has no Bible."

"He has a Testament."

"But many of the Sunday-school lessons are taken
from the Old Testament, Bennet," said Annie.

"But the readings are printed right there in the quarterly."

"Yes, I know," she sighed wearily, "but I would feel
so much happier about his going if he had a Bible."

"Would he take care of it if he had one?"

"Bennet! He's not a child any more."

"But think of the loss I've just had, and his ticket
cost a small fortune."

"This is how I feel about it," said Annie seriously.
"The boy wants a Bible, and he needs a Bible, and it
may pay you in more ways than one to get him one."

"How do you mean?" Bennet looked up sharply and
his lips parted.

"I mean," she said thoughtfully, "that if you don't
get him a Bible you may lose a lot more yet."

"You think?" A new fearful look crossed the man's
face and he rubbed and rubbed his large Roman nose.

Bennet hadn't counted on taking the family along
to town to see Joseph off. He would take him and his

baggage in the buckboard. He would avoid as much chance for a display of emotion as possible. Anyway, he told Annie, he wanted to bring back some coal.

Joseph said good-by to Quicksilver first, then Lowell, then Virginia, kissing them both fondly on the lips.

"Be good," he said, "and good-by."

"Mama!" He clasped her to his breast and held her there. Her soft hair brushed his cheeks. He whispered something in her ear. Bennet hurried with the baggage. He stopped long enough to tighten one strap. He stumbled. Joseph kissed her twice as her tear-stained face was uplifted to meet his. Neither could speak. The fondness each felt for the other was unutterable. Both understood. He pressed her to him once more, then tore himself loose. Blinded with tears, he walked toward the buckboard, climbed on, and waved his hand.

Annie and her two children watched the wagon until it was out of sight, waving occasionally. Joseph answered each time he chanced to see them. His father sat beside him stiff and with set jaws. He spoke only a few sentences all the way to town. In front of a general dry goods store in Admore he went in and soon returned with something wrapped in pink paper. He handed it to Joseph.

"Here's a Bible for you yet. Your mother said you needed one."

CHAPTER XXX

"Now here's your ticket, Joseph. Take care of it. I told you how to do when you change depots in Chicago. If you forget, ask a red cap. That's what they're for. Yes, your trunk is checked. You've got the key. Don't fall asleep when it's time to get off, and don't talk too freely with strangers and tell them everything you know and don't know. I put that alarm clock in your trunk. Be sure and use it."

All the while Bennet was addressing Joseph he was looking down the tracks. He pulled out his watch. "The train is due in about six minutes, so I'll be going on back. I think I've told you about everything. Ask Squire Mc-Cracken how to prune those vines." Bennet had told Joseph that at least six times in the days just before. There was no firm handclasping, no kissing, no fond farewell, no tears, no waving good-by, no display of emotion. The next thing Joseph knew he was standing alone on the north side of the little red brick depot at Admore, looking east at the long stretch of tracks that ran out across the level prairie. He straightened his shoulders and lifted his head and the warm afternoon April sun bathed his ruddy face. A sudden consciousness that he was no longer a boy but a full-grown adult facing life alone took hold of him, soul and body. He had wept when he bade his mother good-by. He could not keep from it, but he didn't feel like weeping now. He felt a new strength and courage envelop him. A noble dignity swept across his healthy face.

The train came in on time, snorting, steaming, rumbling, grinding as it came, until the earth under his feet trembled. Joseph took one long look at the tracks out ahead and boarded the train. As there was plenty of space, he chose a seat on the left to avoid facing the sun.

It's quite impossible to sit without thinking, although some faces look empty and wanting for something worthy of thought. Joseph's meditations were an equal blending of sorrow and happiness. He anticipated with joy seeing Freddie and all those he had learned to love and respect in his boyhood days.

But more grievous than the anxious concern for his mother was the stinging thought that his father cared nothing more for him than that he could be used to make more money. If Bennet Armstrong ever was glad he had a son, it was now, and Joseph knew it. One minute he wanted to revolt, and the next he wanted to show the world he was an Armstrong with enough Stokes in him to help him make a worth-while contribution to society.

Joseph sat and thought and thought and thought. When two elderly ladies across the aisle and forward two seats opened a shoe box and started nibbling on some sandwiches, he opened his box and ate his sandwiches too. His mother had packed enough lunch for six meals, and she had wrapped each meal separately. Then a likable-looking gentleman came in from another coach and sat down beside him. Joseph looked up in surprise.

"You on your way to New York, too?" he asked, smiling broadly enough to show two gold teeth.

Joseph remembered what his father had said about making up with strangers and answered at length, "Is that where you live?"

"I live there part of the time. A traveling salesman has several homes. See? Anyhow I have. I'm going home to see my wife this time. You got a wife?"

"No, sir. I'm only twenty."

"Only twenty? No kiddin'? You look over twenty. Took you for a married man. Must be used to hard work. Just look at my hands besides yours. Goin' 'long with me to the diner?"

"No, sir, I just ate my supper."

"Sure 'nough? Well, I'll be seein' you later. Only twenty? Wish I was twenty again. Think of it, I got married when I was twenty and I know I didn't have the sense you look like you have. You aren't much of a talker, are you?" Joseph smiled. "Well, that's one of my failings," went on the man, "but I'm just wound up that way, I guess." He shrugged his shoulders and straightened his red silk necktie. "They say a salesman has to be able to open a conversation with anyone, and I guess that's me. I never feel like a stranger anywhere. I was put out when only a little shaver of seven. Had to sell papers on the streets of New York City and make my own livin'. I know all about the hard knocks of life, don't think I don't. Never knew a mother's love or a father's care. I've read a lot about such stuff and wondered how it really would be to know all that.

"I get over the country a lot an' the world's awful wicked, kid, awful wicked. You know it? You look like you come straight off the farm an' never took a swig. Well, if you never have, don't begin it when you get to New York. Wish I'd a never started it, but it's pretty hard to live straight an' be a salesman.

"What do you think of President Taft? Pretty good speech he made. Could you tell, is he against liquor? I know I had just a little too much this afternoon, but a fellow has to get relief of mind somehow once in a while. Makes you feel like a million sometimes, but I must go. He said 'last call' didn't he?" The man moved on, reeling a little as the train swung him this way and that.

The lights in the coach were dimmed, but the man never came back. Two hours passed, but he never returned. Joseph curled up on his seat as best he could and fell asleep.

He made the transfer in Chicago without any difficulty and spent another long day on the train.

"Are you Joseph Armstrong?" A tall smooth-faced man tapped Joseph on the arm.

"Yes, sir."

"Well, I'm Sol Bantum. I got the telegram."

"Telegram?"

"Yes, your father sent word for me to meet this train. You got any baggage?"

"I had my trunk checked."

"All right, we'll get that next. I came in my spring wagon. It's right over there. Did you have a nice trip?"

"Well—yes, I guess. I got pretty tired sitting for two days. I'm not used to that."

"S'pose not. I never cared a lot about traveling."

Mrs. Bantum was a plump, rosy-faced woman with big brown eyes and a dimple in each cheek. Her appearance, like the house, was immaculate. The odor of frying ham greeted Joseph just inside the yard gate. A red- and white-checked cloth was spread on the kitchen table, and a blooming narcissus stood in the center on a ruffled doily.

"Take the young man on up to his room, Sol," said Mrs. Bantum after the introduction had been made. "Supper is ready as soon as you two are. Girtie is done milking and will be down in a minute."

"All right, Katy. If this young man's as hungry as I am, he won't need to be coaxed to come down. We'll take this trunk right up, Joseph—I guess we'll just start right in calling you by your first name. We leave that Mister off around here. Just call me Sol. Everybody else does. Now this is the room we fixed up for you."

He passed two doors and turned a corner.

"I hope you can make yourself at home in it. Katy and Girtie cleaned it all up for you and aired it out good. No one's used this room since our boy died three years ago this June. They changed the furniture all around, I see. The bed used to set right along here. Katy always said she'd never let anyone else occupy this room, but after we talked it over when we got your father's letter —well, she sorta changed her mind. If she takes a liking to you, it'll be all right. She was awful fond of Jerry. Katy's that way. She has strong likes and dislikes." The man slapped Joseph on the shoulder. "I hope she'll like you. She never met your mother, but she's heard a heap about her through some friends of ours in town who used to buy your mother's cakes and cheese and things. They said they sure did miss your mother when you moved away. If it hadn't been for that, I doubt if Katy would have considered keeping you."

Joseph's heart thumped and a cozy, comfortable feeling filled his breast.

"I have a wonderful mother," he said, hanging his cap on a hook beside the door, "and I hope your wife—" Joseph didn't know exactly how to say what he wanted to. He was sorry he had entertained those fleeting thoughts of rebellion toward his father. He was heartily ashamed that he was even tempted to despise him now when he heard this remark about his mother. It recompensed or made amends. He had something to live for. He had something very precious to strive for, and maybe after all there might be a chance for him to make good if his mother had made lasting friends just by peddling her wares in town on Saturdays.

"I hope she will—" again he tried to say it and didn't know just how. Above the years of hard work and repeated whippings; above the cruel misunderstandings, and harsh words; above the stream of bitter tears he had seen his mother shed; above every false accusation, every privation, every injustice, his mother's noble face stood out a silent phantom aglow with a heavenly radiance. In fancy he saw her smiling at him through her tears.

The finest gift one can bestow upon another is beautiful thought, for it enriches the one who receives it. Little did Sol Bantum realize what eternal good that one beautiful thought of his mother did for Joseph just then on his initiation into his new home. It accompanied the setting of the little old-fashioned trunk on the floor. He'd remember it every time he opened the trunk. His mother had something to do with his being admitted into this lovely corner room. His mother, completely unconscious of the fact, had years before prepared a way for him to have a room of his own, the thing he so long had been craving. Frilled white curtains adorned the windows, one to the east and one to the south, overlooking the vineyard.

"If you're ready, I'll show you where to wash for supper."

Joseph followed.

"Well, now this is Girtie Maples, our hired girl," Sol said when the two all but collided at the kitchen door. "Girtie, this is Joseph Armstrong."

Girtie blushed and smiled and said, "How do you do," and Joseph said the same without blushing, for his handsome young face was already flushed with excitement.

"This will be your place right here," announced Mrs. Bantum, tapping the back of the chair in front of the cupboard.

The supper was delicious. If this was a fair sample of Katy Bantum's cooking, Joseph knew he would be satisfied with his board.

"Take some more potatoes," beamed Mrs. Bantum. "You must eat. Take some more ham. Don't be afraid to ask for what you want. I know you're used to good cooking and maybe mine don't taste like your mother's, but I hope you won't get homesick first thing."

"Your supper tastes very good, Mrs. Bantum," spoke Joseph, "and if I get homesick it won't be because you can't cook as good as my mother. This tastes very much like hers."

Of course that pleased Katy Bantum. Why shouldn't it?

"I see you folks have a phone," said Joseph after supper.

"We haven't had it long," Sol said.

"I wonder if Timothy Stokes have one? Do you know?"

"Yes, I know they do. Let's see, their ring is 4 on 29. Isn't that right, Katy?"

"I think so."

"Do you care if I use it?"

"The phone? Of course not. I suppose you know the Stokes?"

"Timothy's my uncle."

"Your uncle! Well. Sure, go ahead and talk to them. I don't know how well you can hear, but you can at least try it."

"Is Freddie there? Please call him to the phone. Hello, Freddie. Don't you know me? Don't you know me, Freddie? It's Joseph.—Yes, Joseph Armstrong. I'm over here at Sol Bantum's—Sol Bantum's.—Yes, just this evening.—I'm going to room and board here and work in the vineyard.—Yes.—Father leased a ten-acre vineyard from Squire McCracken. Just recently.—Yes, he sent me back here to look after it.—All summer I guess, I don't know exactly.—I suppose it's seven or eight miles over here.—I don't know; I hope so.—Well, I'm anxious to see you too. Yes—Yes.—Pretty good.—Yes.—All right.—Can you tell me anything about Earnie Eloy?—He is?—Well.—I hope someday I will get to see him.—Yes.—Yes.—It was a long tiresome trip, two nights and two days.—Yes.—I hope so.—I couldn't go to bed without calling, after I saw this phone here.—You do that, Freddie."

What a hubbub and asking of questions! What ejaculations! What exclamations filled the room when Freddie hung up the receiver!

"Think of it!" shouted Freddie. "Joseph is just about eight miles from here right now!"

CHAPTER XXXI

Joseph's hand hesitated. He was about to knock at the door when he heard from the half-raised window the sound of a man's voice singing. It was the sweetest voice he had ever heard. He lifted his head and listened, amazed at the beauty of that voice.

All o' God's chillun got a robe.
When I get to Heab'n gonna put on my robe,
Gonna shout all ober God's Heab'n,
Heab'n, Heab'n! Eberybody talkin' 'bout Heaben
      ain't a-goin' der,
Heab'n, Heab'n! Gonna shout all ober God's
      Heab'n.

The quivering voice within sang with innate passion and tender childlike faith, and as Joseph stood rapt, he wondered if it could possibly be old Fonzo Bullet, the colored driver he had met on the road several years before. The McCracken mansion was surrounded with so many cement walks and so many porches and doors, he was at a loss to know on which door to knock. He had chosen one of the side doors on the east. The warm morning sun was playing on some potted plants on the wide window sills on either side, and snowy dotted Swiss curtains were tied back with gold cords.

I've got a harp, you've got a harp,
All o' God's chillun got a harp,
When I get to Heab'n gonna play on my harp,
Gonna play all over—

"Singin' again this morning already?" Joseph heard someone say within, and footsteps came close to the window on the right. "If you're through with your tray I'll raise this window while I make up your bed. One of these days it'll be warm enough for you to sit out on the lawn."

"Minnie," said a voice, and instantly Joseph recognized it as that of old Fonzo, "I had de pretties' dream las' night 'bout angels standin' round my bed a-singin' to me."

"Oh, Fonzo," chimed the other, "I never had a dream about angels. I guess I'm not good enough for that." Then she laughed.

Joseph knocked. A young girl in a blue gingham dress with a white collar opened the door.

"Good morning," Joseph tipped his hat. "If it's not too much trouble, could you tell me where I might find the Squire this morning?"

"The Squire? He's probably in the drawing room just now listening to his wife playing the piano. She plays for him every morning right after breakfast, while he reads. After that he takes a ride on his horse. I can give him your name if you like, or do you have an appointment with him?"

"No, not exactly," answered Joseph. "My name is Joseph Armstrong, and my father has leased—"

"Who is it, Minnie? Did he say Armstrong?"

Joseph stepped into the open door and lifted his hand. "Hello there, Fonzo," he said. "Do you remember me? I'm Bennet Armstrong's boy. You met me along the road one day when I was cutting weeds and you were on your way after some apples for Mr. McCracken."

"Sure, sure 'nuf. But how you've done growed up since dat day! I spect you'se growed a foot."

Joseph laughed.

"You dunno I was struck by a stroke 'bout a year back?"

"No, I didn't know that," answered Joseph.

"Sit dar," motioned Fonzo to a chair beside the window. "I'm sorta he'pless since I was driv' to my bed dat day. Thought sure 'nuf I was gwine to go. Mars McCracken war mighty kine ter me. Dey done tole me southern folk dey ain't white ter darkies, but Mars McCracken sure 'nuf is. Mees Minnie thar takes ker me like a chile since Mees Snow lef. Are you de boy what's come ter take ker dat ar vineyard?"

"Yes, I am, Fonzo," answered Joseph taking the chair. "I got here last night. I'm staying at Bantum's up on the hill, and my father told me to be sure and have the Squire show me how to prune the vines."

"Dat's right," Fonzo said, stroking his black face with his wrinkled hand. "He knows all 'bout dat. He knows 'bout most things. Mees Minnie, reckon ye better tell Mars McCracken he's here afore he goes trottin' off," and the girl picked up a pewter tray full of blue-willow dishes, and with dexterous movements swung out of the room, holding the tray high on the palm of her right hand.

"So your father puts lots o' trus' in you ter sen' you way back here ter look arter sech."

Joseph fumbled with the bill on his cap. For lack of appropriate words he refrained from answering. He sincerely hoped his father trusted him a little, yet he doubted it.

"You orter make good, nothin' hinderin'. I've he'ped take wagonloads o' fines' grapes ter town fer shipment."

"I'm going to try my best. My father is very particular, and if it doesn't pay he'll be very much disappointed. Fonzo," added Joseph bending forward, "I heard you singing when I came to the door a while ago. It sounded fine."

Fonzo's old black face beamed. A glory rested on it that made him radiant.

"Wall," he drawled meekly, "I'se no 'count fer work no more a'ness God a'mighty teches me. Dees legs don' work right fer me somehow, but bress God I kin sing yet. I kin member de day when I war a boy an' we lived in a log cabin hut an' 'twar cole an' we had near ter rags fer close, jes' cas'-off stuff, toes stickin' out our shoes, an' my ole mudder'd sing ter us chilluns, 'I's got-a shoes.' " Fonzo started singing again. Splendor and devotion possessed his soul. "All o' God's chillun got-a shoes, When I get to heab'n gonna put on my shoes, Gonna walk all ober God's—"

In walked the Squire, buttoning his double-breasted coat as he entered.

"Good morning—good morning," he said extending a warm hand to Joseph, who rose to his feet to clasp it.

"Good morning, Mr. McCracken," he said.

"To my knowledge," spoke the Squire, "we've never met before."

"No, sir. This is the first time I've seen you, although I've heard about you as far back as I can remember."

"Yes?" The Squire unbuttoned his coat and hunted for his gold watch chain. It was there all right and he twisted it fondly. "And so you've come to look after the vineyard?"

"Yes, sir."

"And you want to begin today?"

"Yes, sir, I'm ready to begin if you can take the time to tell me how. My father—"

"Certainly, certainly, Joseph. Your father told me that was your name."

"Yes, sir."

The Squire pulled out his watch and glanced at it and said musingly but very pleasantly, "You might walk on over and I'll come directly on my horse. Come out here with me and I'll show you where I'll meet you."

"Good-by, Fonzo," called Joseph over his shoulder. "I might be back to see you someday."

"Do dat, Joseph," said Fonzo happily. "Dis pore ole broke-down crittur might not las' long nohow. If you be a prayin' lad, send up a pretty one fer me ter night, will you?"

"I will," answered Joseph.

The Squire took real pains in giving Joseph a demonstrative lecture on pruning grapevines, and by the time he was finished, Joseph was convinced he knew his business well, and the Squire was convinced Joseph was an intelligent young man capable of being taught and willing to be taught. Joseph not only seemed willing, but he was also eager to learn. This pleased the Squire. He showed him how to repair the wires and tie the vines, and how to watch for destructive insects.

"Well, my boy," he said, "if you want to know anything more, don't be afraid to call on me. I wish you success, and unless we have a big hail storm, or something happens beyond our control, I believe the grape crop will be good. We're having an ideal spring so far."

"And thank you for your trouble and help," Joseph said, as the Squire mounted his fine, black horse.

"You're welcome, my boy."

For two days Joseph worked from sunup till dark, and the third day was Sunday. The Bantums served breakfast an hour later on Sunday mornings than during the week and it was a quarter of eight when Joseph started out on his six-mile tramp to church. Classes had already assembled by the time he got there. Not exactly with a faint heart, but rather timidly he entered the side door and paused, hesitant and quivering. Almost breathlessly Freddie had been watching that door for at least forty minutes. At sight of Joseph he rose halfway out of his seat and motioned to him. The young men's class now convened on the two back seats of the long chapel and before them stood none other than Uncle Tom Bradly. As Freddie Stokes half rose out of his seat and motioned in the direction of the side door, Uucle Tom cut his sentence abruptly in two and turned completely around and came up the side aisle to meet Joseph. He closed his big brawny hand over Joseph's and all but clasped him in his strong arms.

"It's good to have you back, Joseph," he said earnestly. "Freddie told me first thing this morning. Sit right in there beside your cousin. Can it be, Joseph? You've grown so since we last saw you." The boys pinched each other for want of a better way to express their joy over meeting.

"We were just discussing the twenty-second verse. The lesson is found in the fourteenth chapter of Acts, Joseph. The last part of that verse reads, 'We must through much tribulation enter into the kingdom of God.' Paul had just healed a crippled man at Lystra who had never walked, and he was then stoned. Think of it. Now most of us seem to think a life without any troubles or hardships is the ideal life. We all feel like running away from trouble, but when Paul was stoned it somehow brought the best out of him. It showed up what he really was made of. That's the way it works.

"I remember one time during the Civil War the rebels knocked on my father's door one night and threatened to burn our house down and burn our church if my father wouldn't give him all his horses. My father told him to go take the horses. Then the rebels tried to make my father promise to spy out on the Union men, and when he refused, they got out their matches and held them up in front of my father's face. 'I cannot be a spy,' my father said. 'All right then, you can choose,' they said, and we were driven out of our home that night and watched our house and church both burn to the ground.

"My father stood there and said to my mother and us children, 'Don't cry; they can burn our houses but not our peace. We'll build again when we can.' Many times tribulation can be met in such a way as to make our lives richer and nobler than ever before."

Joseph thought of his own little mother way out west. No doubt she and the rest of his family were at this same time sitting in church listening to Brother Collins preach. Down in the front of the church directly below the chancel sat the group of mothers among whom she used to sit, and to the right, back several pews sat the class in which his father had taken an active part for years. There stood Eli Mattson as eager-faced as ever, talking enthusiastically in the direction of Scudder Madox. A peculiar feeling of reverence surged through Joseph as he recalled past times of sorrow when he and his mother had found comfort in this very room; and where he had struggled under the weight of indecision. It was like coming into a holy sanctuary, and silently Joseph thanked God for those hard trials his mother had endured that had polished her true character and endeared her to him.

Brother Grissley Steward preached.

"Of course you're going home with us for dinner," said Freddie, taking hold of Joseph's arm after the benediction. "Then I'll drive you home in the afternoon. If it wasn't so far, I'd do it after the evening meeting."

CHAPTER XXXII

"But Freddie," answered Joseph, "I'd love to come, but your carriage is full already without me getting in it yet. I'll walk out."

"No, you won't. Papa got me a horse and buggy for my birthday."

Joseph stood back and stared in mute wonder.

"Wasn't that great? Come on. You're to go with me in the buggy. Of course—" Freddie stepped aside while plump Mrs. Irons shook hands with Joseph and made extravagant exclamations about his size and good looks. Then Lottie (Woods) Ashelford wanted an interview with the returned boy, and she like many others wanted to inquire about his family, his mother in particular, and it was twelve-thirty before the two boys drove out of the churchyard.

"How does it feel to come back home?" asked Freddie.

A healthy color had crept over Joseph's face while meeting all these old friends, but his cheeks burned warmly when Delores Bays walked shyly down the aisle. She didn't exactly speak, but her lips parted and she smiled faintly when she passed him. He couldn't remember now whether he had returned her smile or not, but he felt like it. He wanted to. In his mind he did, but there were so many people standing around and Riley Doane was asking him a question just then and he had to answer.

"Oh, it feels good," answered Joseph taking a deep breath. "Don't ask me how I feel. I can't explain it. But tell me, Freddie—you say your father got you this outfit for your birthday?"

"It's like this, Joseph. Now don't you laugh at me. You've grown up as much as I have since we last saw each other. I had a long talk with Papa one night

220

before my birthday, and he said if I find me a nice girl in the church he won't object if I have dates.

Joseph unbuttoned his shirt collar and folded and unfolded his hands.

"Well, then what?"

"He said I've stayed at home longer than a lot of boys have, and he'd get me a horse and buggy if I'd promise to stay by him another year. After that I can work out or he'll pay me wages. I promised I'd stay and help him another year, so he got it for me. Isn't it a dandy?"

"It surely is, Freddie. Your father was awful good to you."

"Yes, Papa's always treated me right. I don't mind staying at home another year."

"And, and, you've got a girl?"

"No, not yet. I've just been thinking about it. I haven't made up my mind yet who I want to ask first."

"Well—a—who have you been thinking of?"

Joseph cleared his throat. He could think of no one but Delores Bays. For some reason she seemed to be the only girl in the entire church right now, but there were a dozen of them. He held his breath awkwardly and looked at the fence along the road.

"Well, there's Martha Denlinger. I think she's a mighty nice— What's wrong, Joseph?"

"Nothing, why?"

"What made you take such a long, deep breath? Don't you like her?"

"I scarcely know who she is," answered Joseph. "Sure, she's a nice girl. I'd ask her if I were you. Who else appeals to you?"

"Well," answered Freddie, readjusting his hat, "I think Lillian Bond is nice too. A little prettier than Martha, in a way. Have you had a date yet?"

"No, not yet."

"You're old enough."

"Am I?"

"Why, sure. You're not much younger than I am. Some day let's start out together."

"How do you mean?"

"I mean I wish you'd look around and spot a nice girl in the church and then we'll, we'll, oh, well, maybe we'll write them letters and ask if we can't come to see them and oh, I don't know."

"But I've got no way of getting around. I've got no horse and buggy, so I'm out."

"Well, we could figure that out somehow. I've got a buggy. Do you like it over there at Bantums?"

"Yes, very much."

"Do you have a nice room?"

"A lovely room."

"Good eats?"

"Swell."

"Have you started working in the vineyard yet?"

"Yes, I worked at it the last two days. I like it. I love my room all to myself. That's something I didn't have at home. I have time to read evenings after Mrs. Bantum gets done talking. She sure can talk and talk and ask a fellow more questions. I like her, though. She's so jolly and good-natured and kind. I tell you, Freddie, I certainly don't want to ever go with a girl just for fun —I mean if I'm not sure it's—it's God's will."

"How do you mean?"

"I mean life is too serious to fool with a girl and make her believe I love her if I don't. I've see too much in my life already."

"What do you mean, Joseph? You talk like an old man."

"I mean I'd rather stay single all my life than to fool a girl or be fooled. If I ever get married I want to really be a father and not just a boss. Let's talk about something else, Freddie."

Perspiration stood out on Joseph's forehead and he wiped it off with his handkerchief.

"No, let's not," returned Freddie. "I've been thinking about this myself for months. I've just been longing to talk to you about these very things. I feel the same way you do. If I ever get married I sure want it to be a happy marriage, and I want to be a good husband, too. I want to be a real father to my children like Papa is to us. I'll say that he really is a good father."

Joseph's cheeks burned and great drops of perspiration stood out on his forehead.

"Mother fusses at him sometimes more than she'd need to, I think, but he's always so patient and takes it all. But I don't want a wife that will nag or fuss at me. Oh, I couldn't stand that. I want a girl that's not too big nor too little. She don't have to be beautiful, just so she can cook and knows how to treat children and help me decide things in life."

"And how about loving you?"

"Of course—of course I want to be sure she loves me. Now, you make a speech. Joseph, I'm in earnest. I'm not foolin', I mean every word I said."

"I mean every word I said, too," answered Joseph. "I've been wanting to talk to you, too. Now, I've—I've never said this before, and it hurts me," he hesitated and his eyes glistened with tears. "It nearly kills me to say it, but if I can't be a better husband and father than Bennet Armstrong has been so far, I—I don't—want to marry. And you know Mama's a Stokes. She's a real mother. She's your father's sister. If I can find a girl as good as she, I'll be doing well."

"Well, let's look around from Sunday to Sunday and decide on somebody. We've got to make a start sometime. We're getting old." Freddie laughed.

"Let's pray about it too, Freddie. That will help, won't it?"

"I guess it will. I know Papa's really concerned I don't make a big mistake like some have. And he don't want me to go with every girl in the church, either. He said if I do that he'll wish he'd never given me this horse and buggy."

"That wouldn't be fun, do you think?"

"Some seem to think so. Bill Thenshon brags about it that he's gone with twenty different girls in one year."

"That isn't even smart. He'll probably end by marrying the most unlikely one of them all, or he'll keep on until no girl will want him. I have no desire to do that. Of all the girls I've ever seen yet, only one appeals to me."

"Who is it?"

"Let me think it over before I say. I've just come back."

"Come on, Joseph. Tell me. I told you who I had in mind."

They drove past two more trees. Joseph folded and unfolded his hands. He drew another deep breath.

"It's Delores Bays," he said at length very softly.

"She's not a bad-looking girl," Freddie said. "All I've ever heard about her is good. Agnes told me one time like this. She said, 'If Joseph lived back here yet he and Delores Bays would make an ideal couple.'"

"Agnes said?" Joseph sat up very straight.

"Yes, Agnes said that."

"What made her say that?"

"I don't know. Oh, yes, I do, maybe. She overheard Mother talking on the phone one day to Mrs. Irons, and something was said about you folks and—oh, well, I can't repeat it all, but Mrs. Irons said to Mother that she supposed you were quite a young man by now and would probably find yourself a wife in the West, and she just hoped you'd find someone as nice as Delores Bays."

"Mrs. Irons said that to Aunt Sara?" Joseph felt like standing now. The seat could hardly hold him.

"Yes."

"Freddie, you're just making this all up, and you know it."

"I'm not making this up. That actually happened."

"When?"

"Just a couple weeks ago."

"Freddie!"

"What?"

"What does this mean?"

"I guess it means Mrs. Irons thinks a lot of you, and she must think a lot of Delores Bays, too."

"Mrs. Irons ought to know."

"She ought to."

"But why—why?" Joseph cleared his throat and brushed some lint off his suit. "Well, why didn't you mention her name?"

Joseph looked straight into Freddie's face and searched it.

"Well, I don't know exactly. I don't dislike her, but I just like those big eyes of Martha Denlinger and the way she walks, and Lillian Bond has such pretty dimples, and haven't you ever noticed how she can sing?"

"No, I never noticed." Joseph's voice sounded far away and dreamy. He was seeing only the face of Delores Bays as she smiled faintly when she passed him in the church aisle less than an hour ago. She had appeared so womanly and walked with such graceful ease.

All the cousins wanted to talk to Joseph at once. How big he was! How tall! How handsome! And how big was Virginia? How big was Lowell? What kind of house did they have? The questions they could ask!

Slowly and honestly Joseph tried to picture their western home, breaking gently the factual news that their home was small and not elaborate in any way. They sat at the table and talked for an hour after dinner was over.

"But why," asked Agnes, "didn't you graduate until you were eighteen, Joseph?"

"When we got out there all the books were so different. The teacher showed me the eighth-grade books first and I couldn't be honest and say I was ready to enter that grade, so he put me in the sixth grade."

"The sixth?" shouted Agnes.

"Yes. I took the sixth grade all over again. I missed so often to help father that I was always behind. The teacher finally helped me with homework and graduated me or I'd still be in school!"

"But Joseph," gasped Agnes, "that wasn't fair for Uncle Bennet to keep you out so much. Didn't you get awfully discouraged?"

"I was often discouraged, Agnes, but I was determined to finish the eighth grade if I had to go till I was twenty-five."

"Twenty-five?" Dennis whistled. "Eighteen is bad enough. Freddie was through when he was fifteen, and I'll be through when I'm fourteen."

"I'm glad for you," answered Joseph.

"I'm sorry, Joseph, but we'll have to go or I can't be back in time to go to church."

"That's right, Freddie. We'd better go."

"It's a shame you can't be at the evening service," said Aunt Sara.

"I'd love to, but it's almost too far to walk home afterwards."

"Yes, you did well enough to walk in this morning."

"Thanks for the good, good dinner, Aunt Sara."

"Don't mention it, Joseph, come often, anytime you can."

"Thanks."

"Oh, Mother!" cried Maryanna after the two boys left the house, "isn't Joseph nice!"

CHAPTER XXXIII

"Freddie." The two drove out of the lane.

"Yes."

"Oh, nothing." Joseph's blue eyes looked away.

"What is it, Joseph?"

"Oh, I was just going to ask if we'd have time to drive past our place—I mean the place that used to be ours, but I guess—"

"Sure, we can go that way. It won't be much farther. The Squire made a new road from his estate over to the turnpike just beyond the tollgate."

"When?"

"Oh, last year already. Joseph, a lot of things have happened since you left. You won't know the place when you see it since it's painted. It's a drab or gray, trimmed in white, and you should see the border of peonies they planted on both sides of the walks. They may be in bloom today. Getup, Queen. They were in bud already last week when I went by. Foster put up a new windmill and cut down that big oak tree by the corner, and they either built a new chicken house or remodeled the old one. You think your father did well to sell out and buy out West?"

"I don't know," answered Joseph soberly.

"Don't know?" asked Freddie.

"That's a question I couldn't answer, Freddie," answered Joseph. "Maybe you know such things, but I don't. Father never tells us anything. We think he's doing well, but we don't know."

"Not even your mother?"

"Not even Mama." Joseph's voice was calm and steady but strangely sober. They drove past the schoolhouse.

"Isn't it sorta funny?" said Freddie after an awkward silence. "We say Papa and you say Father. It's been

Papa and Mom at our house since I can remember, but now since we're growing up we're trying to learn to say Mother. I think it sounds more respectful. Why do you children always say Father?"

"Well, I guess because he told us to," came Joseph's answer.

"I never learned to know Uncle Bennet very well."

Joseph coughed a dry little unnecessary cough and said almost under his breath, "Neither have I, Freddie." They passed the Hunter place next. A sad look crossed his face as they neared the field where he had plowed corn day after day when but a child, and had suffered for want of a drink. Strange how years afterwards one can feel again the agony of certain painful experiences, but stranger still is the fact that pain is more easily forgotten than joy, for, as soon as the big front window of the living room came into view, that pain left.

In fancy he could see his mother several feet behind the curtains sitting on her armless rocking chair, her white starched apron hanging down over her blue dress and a little boy in woolen knee pants and a polka-dotted shirt standing beside her, his left arm around her neck and her right arm around his waist. Yes, he even thought he could see Tabby, the yellow cat, sitting on the window sill between the blooming begonias. Somehow begonias and yellow cats and white aprons always would be associated with the things his mother had told him one Sunday morning while Father was at church.

"Isn't that a beautiful sight?"

"Who, what? Oh, yes," answered Joseph coming out of his reverie, "the peonies are beautiful."

"We get that from the Stokes, don't we?" chuckled Freddie.

"What?" asked Joseph.

"Appreciation for the beautiful. That's what Mother says. Papa notices pretty things a lot more than most men do. That's one thing Mother likes about Papa. He takes as much interest in fixing up the home as she does. He likes to bring home a pretty dish or a picture, or a piece of goods for an apron for Mother. She tells us children she hopes we'll all be like that. Does the place look natural to you?"

"No," answered Joseph thoughtfully. "It seems like a dream, in a way, that I ever lived there."

"Do you wish you still lived there?"

"No, it's best the way it is. It does make me think of Earnie."

"That's right, Joseph. Let's take time to drive past Alex's shack and see if he's there."

"Could we?" asked Joseph eagerly.

"It's not much out of the way. If I don't get back on time, I'll just be late." They drove past the lane, past the barn. The woodpile wasn't there any more. Joseph looked in particular, but it was gone.

Visitors at Alex Burns's hut or shanty were so few and far between that both men stuck their heads out of the door in curiosity before Freddie said "Whoa."

"Who is it?" shouted Alex gruffly.

"It's Joseph Armstrong," came a low friendly reply.

"Who?" shouted Earnie Eloy, stepping outside and holding his hand above his eyes.

Joseph walked swiftly toward him. Earnie hesitated a moment, then making a grunt of recognition he clasped Joseph's outstretched hand in both of his. "Joseph," he gasped joyously and his lips quivered. "Can it be possible? You went away a boy, an' come back a man."

"It's good to see you," said Joseph, "even though you've changed—since your accident."

"Yes," answered Earnie a little unsteadily. "I've done gone through somethin' since I last seen you, my boy. But I pulled through. I'm surprised you know me a-tall."

"Maybe I wouldn't have if we'd met on the street, but Freddie knew you were staying here and I knew that wasn't you." Joseph pointed to the man standing in the open door.

"That's Alex Burns."

"How do you do, Alex. This is Freddie Stokes, my cousin."

"Howdy. I've heard heaps 'bout you an' your raisin's."

"My raisin's?" Joseph smiled good-naturedly.

"Sure. Earnie here done told me how you've had ter work fist an' skull from little up, an'—"

"Keep still, Alex," warned Earnie. "Joseph, you're lookin' like a prince."

"Hardly that, Earnie."

"You sure do. You've got your dad beat fer size an' looks both. You're lookin' swell."

"Now, Earnie."

"Don't hush me up like that, Joseph. I guess I know. I ain't fergot nothin'. If a rocky raisin' had anything ter do with your growin' up an' bein' somethin', you've sure got the startin' of bein' a man. How's that little mother o' yourn?"

"She's quite a bit better, Earnie. Yes, the West seemed to do her good."

"Coughin' yet?"

"Not nearly as much as she did back here."

"An' do you still say your prayers, my boy?" Earnie's scarred face twitched nervously.

"Yes." Joseph looked into Earnie's dark, deep-set eyes, and the snap they used to have wasn't there. That long, straggly black mustache was gone, and the man's whole face had a mellowness on it Joseph had never seen there

"Yes, Earnie, I still pray."

"That's one of them things that sticks ter me. That an' the whippin' you got onct, an' it was my fault. I told on you an' I've often wished since your father would o' used that belt on me fer tattlin'."

"Now, Earnie."

"Gets me ter this day I done such a trick. After that night I wouldn't a-cared if you would a-rummaged through all my things. 'Member how I tucked you inter my bed one night?"

"Yes, I do, Earnie. I remember well."

"An' you used ter tell me stories your mother done told ter you, an' I said I couldn't believe that stuff?"

"Yes."

"But you 'member I told you ter believe everything yer mother told you?"

"Yes."

"You been a doin' that, hain't you?"

"I've been doing that, Earnie. I always did think my mother was a wonderful woman and knew what was right, but the older I get the more I realize it is true. She has meant a lot to me." Joseph looked at the ground and rubbed the toe of his shoe over a small stone.

"An' ter me," added Earnie.

"How, Earnie?"

"I weren't blind when I lived at your house them years. I weren't deaf either. Yes, sir, Annie Armstrong is a real woman ter my notion. You ain't found you a lady yet, eh?"

"Not yet, Earnie." Joseph tried to make his answer sound both unconcerned and indifferent, but he put such emphasis on the "yet" that Earnie couldn't help but smile a little.

"That's all right, Joseph," he said, bending over and nipping off a blade of grass. "You believe in goin' slow an' kerful like, don't you? If you can't find what you want, stay single like me an' Alex here."

"We must be going," Joseph said, putting on his cap. "How about coming to church some Sunday?"

"Who? Me?" squinted Earnie.

"Yes, I mean you, Earnie, both of you men."

Earnie looked at Alex and Alex looked at Earnie, and Alex spit tobacco juice cleverly through his teeth. Neither said a word, but a look of strong disapproval crept across the face of the older of the two.

"We ain't never been to no sech place," said Earnie, snapping his suspenders.

"It's not too late to start," Joseph said kindly.

"I reckon we'd feel orful wicked settin' in sech a crowd," Alex laughed scoffingly.

"Just the same," said Earnie after the two young men had driven away, "church is all right fer them that lives it, an' that thar Joseph won't go fur wrong if he sticks ter the raisin's his mother give him."

*   *   *

Late the next afternoon when Joseph was working in the vineyard, he discovered, to his surprise, an old-fashioned open well. Several young branches were reaching anxiously toward the side of it; and as he looked more closely, he noticed one vine had already fastened itself to the rough surface of the stone wall. Over the center of the well hung a bucket on a chain, and as soon as Joseph turned the wheel he knew it had not been used for some time. He lowered the bucket and brought up some water that did not look very appetizing. He poured it on the nearest vine, and as he did so a peculiar feeling possessed him. Hadn't his mother told him once—once one evening (the evening he heard someone calling him by name in the barn) something about a—a well and a bough by a well—and he was too young then to understand it? And didn't she tell him that night so sweet and earnest, "Someday I believe it will be revealed to you?"

Joseph stood and looked at that well and he tingled from head to foot. If he couldn't have stepped up and touched the well, he would have thought he had seen a vision. But there it was! He shook himself. Wasn't it less than a month ago his mother had prayed for him in the little old lean-to kitchen and asked God to make him like a fruitful bough by a well? "Keep these convictions ever before him," he heard her praying. As clear as a bell he could hear his mother's prayer ring in his ears, and a conviction, the strength of which he had never felt before, took hold of him.

CHAPTER XXXIV

"Sol," began Katy Bantum one Sunday morning as she was tying her apron in front of the dresser, "why don't you offer Joseph, Daps to go to church on. He's been walking every Sunday, and we could eat breakfast a little later if he wouldn't have to leave so early."

Sol looked down at Katy, smiled warmly, and said, "I thought of it, but I've been waiting for you to make the suggestion."

"Me? Why me?"

"I was waiting to see if you thought that much of him."

"That much? How much do you think of him?"

"I think he's a pretty nice chap myself, and it's all right with me to let him use Daps."

"He's always doing something for me," Katy said, fixing the combs in her pretty hair. "Yesterday he mowed the back yard after dinner before he went back to his work—finished where you left off."

"I supposed Girtie did that."

"Girtie nothin'. It was Joseph. Then before supper he fixed the hinge on the cellar door and brought in two pails of water. Friday he swept the walk and brought in an armful of wood. He's picked up the clothesline props and put them away more than once, and pulled weeds in my flower beds, and shakes the rugs in his room twice a week ever since he's been here. Why, Sol, I couldn't mention all the little things he's done already all of his own accord. I think he's a pretty nice chap, too, and you can tell he's had some real home training. He must love his church to start out walking. Did you notice that picture he hung up in his room, Sol, of Christ with the light? He told me how he got that when he was a small boy. He must have had a hard life in some ways."

"How?"

"Oh, I don't know. He never just said exactly, but he's hinted a few times. Sol, I do hope you won't care."

"Care? What about?"

"Oh, you'll see," and Katy hurried to the kitchen.

After breakfast Sol offered Daps to Joseph.

"It's very kind of you, Sol," said Joseph, hesitating at the door. "Please don't think I expect it."

"If you expected it," answered Sol, "I wouldn't be so quick to offer."

"I'll take good care of him."

"I know that. And if your cousin will feed him, you may stay for the evening service if you like."

"Really?"

"That's what I said," answered Sol.

"I can't tell you how I appreciate this."

"Go on," Sol said, withdrawing from the room, smiling pleasantly as he went. Although he seldom went to church himself, he claimed to be a Christian believer and admired anyone who held to a good creed. He was watching Joseph Armstrong with silent wonder. Not once had he heard him use profane language or even the current slang expressions most folks used. He noticed in particular that Joseph never went out at night, but went to his room after a pleasant chat, saying he wanted to read and study. Sol Bantum noticed, too, that Joseph carried a small black Testament in his hip pocket every day.

Sol stood at the open door and watched Joseph walk toward the barn.

"Looks mighty nice in that gray suit, don't you think, Katy?" He turned. "Oh, you're here too. I thought you were in the kitchen. Makes me think of Jerry, somehow."

"Didn't you recognize it?"

"Recognize what?"

"The suit."

"What suit?"

"That suit he's got on."

"It looks kinda like the one Jerry had."

"Kinda like it? Why, Sol, it is Jerry's suit. I gave it to him yesterday."

"Gave—" gasped Sol, "gave Joseph Jerry's suit! Why, Katy!"

"Why, what?"

"You said you put it away and you were going to keep it for always."

"I know I said that," came her soft answer. "I know I said that," she repeated, "but—but Sol, he's so nice and—" she picked at the rickrack on her apron pocket —"the suit was just like new almost—and—I thought it's a shame to let it maybe get moth-eaten when it just fits him."

"Well, how did you know it would fit him?"

"Why, I got it out and pressed it and told him to try it on. Didn't you see how shabby his clothes looked last Sunday?"

"I didn't think much about it."

"You didn't? You didn't notice, Sol? Why, Sol, I did. Just see how it fits him over the shoulders."

"Katy," and Sol Bantum put an arm across her shoulder, "I wondered if you'd take a fancy to him. I hoped you'd like him enough not to be sorry we let him come here, but I never dreamed you'd like him or anyone else enough to give him Jerry's suit. You said—"

"I know I said, Sol, but a person can make rash statements and afterwards change their minds, can't they? You don't care, do you?"

"Care what? That you like him?"

"Care that I gave him Jerry's suit. You couldn't wear it."

"No, I know I couldn't wear it. No, I don't care since he'll be gone all day while he's got it on. Makes me think of Jerry."

"I know. It does me, too, but we can't help that. Every time he laughs I think of Jerry, too."

"Well, if he can wear his suit I suppose he could wear his shirts, too."

"Of course. I already gave him three. A white one and two nice striped ones."

"Katy!"

"What?"

"I'm surprised."

"Why?"

"I didn't think you'd ever like anyone that much."

"Neither did I."

*   *   *

After a long talk by the fence along the clover field, Joseph and Freddie agreed to go to the house and each write a letter. Freddie said he'd furnish the stationery and stamps for both. Freddie wrote to Martha Denlinger.

"Dear Martha:

"For some time I have been wishing for a date with you. May I come to your house next Sunday evening? Please answer by mail.

"Sincerely yours,
"Fredrick Stokes."

Joseph sat with the pen in his hand and had but two words written when Freddie folded his letter.

"What's the matter, Joseph? I thought we both agreed to write. You're not going to back out now after I've offered to furnish you the buggy."

"No, I'm not going to back out."

"Then why don't you write?"

"I'm going to, but I'm afraid she'll turn me down."

"Well, you'll never know unless you try."

"That's right."

"That's right," added Freddie. "Mine is done. See there! It's sealed and stamped and ready to mail."

"I see."

"Can't you write it with me here beside you?"

Joseph chuckled. "Maybe that's it."

"Well, I'll sit over on the other side of the room if you want me to."

Freddie crossed the room and picked up a book that lay on the library table and started leafing through it with no intention of reading.

"Dear Delores," Joseph had written. Only yesterday it seemed he had seen her coming up the walk toward the church with braids hanging below her waistline. Today he had seen her again, vivid and eager-faced with the fresh bloom of womanhood, so rosy, so bright and hopeful-eyed as she passed him on the cement steps after the service. It seemed she had changed from a carefree girl to a serious woman. It gave Joseph a serious feeling too. Love has a purifying influence on one and Joseph wanted to be sure he was doing the right thing.

"It would make me very happy," he wrote thoughtfully and slowly, and a new strange joy overwhelmed him, "if you would permit me to call on you next Sunday evening, June the 20th; please let me hear from you, in care of Sol Bantum.

"Sincerely yours,
"Joseph Armstrong."

He read it over carefully, folded it, and put it in the envelope.

"Done?" asked Freddie.

"Done," answered Joseph.

"Feel better now?"

"I'll feel better after I hear, Freddie," said Joseph at length. "If she turns me down I'll always wish I'd never written."

"If Martha turns me down I'll try Lillian."

"Well, I've got no second choice," answered Joseph after a moment's hesitancy.

* * *

Annie read Joseph's letters at the supper table. Twice she had sent him a stamp, and this was the third letter. Joseph would have written oftener if he could have been sure his mother only would read them. Always and always he had to keep in mind that if he would write personally to his mother, Father might get angry.

"Dear ones at home," Annie read. "I'm enjoying the work in the vineyard more every day, and summertime is really here. It was very warm today. Sunday Sol Bantum loaned me one of his horses to ride to church. Brother Grissley preached the best sermon I ever heard him preach. I was at Uncle Timothy's for dinner and also attended the evening meeting. Mrs. Bantum gave me a nice suit that belonged to her son that died. Many people ask about you, Mama. Lowell, how is school going? Virginia, Maryanna wants me to tell you to write to her. I think she is about your size. I saw old Fonzo Bullet again this week and he sang for me one of his Negro spirituals. Father, the grapevines are looking fine. I'm sure you would be pleased if you saw them. I like it here at Bantums and I surely do enjoy my room. Mother, I promised you years ago that if I ever found a girl I thought a lot of, I'd tell you."

Bennet Armstrong sat up straight. He held his breath. "Do you remember Delores Bays?"

Bennet dropped his fork with a clatter. Annie looked up and both arms sagged until the letter lay on her lap.

"Well, go on," said Bennet. "Don't stop there."

"There isn't much more to read," answered Annie almost in a whisper.

"Read it," he demanded.

"I'm going to have my first—" Annie cleared her throat and hesitated a little—"date with her next Sunday evening.

"With love,
"Joseph."

"Delores Bays!" shouted Bennet sarcastically. "A date with Delores Bays!"

"You object, Bennet?" asked Annie softly.

"Object?" roared Bennet. "Yes, I do object. Of all the girls in the universe, why would he choose Delores Bays?"

"What's wrong with Delores?" asked Annie. "The last time I saw her she was a very attractive girl."

"Attractive?" shouted Bennet, panting. "How could a girl of Jeddie Bays be attractive?"

"Why, Bennet," said Annie, taking a sip of water before she spoke again. "What's wrong with Jeddie Bays? I always thought he was one of the outstanding men in the church."

"Outstanding in what way?"

"Why, for his fine Christian character, Bennet."

"Character, indeed," mumbled Bennet resentfully. "I would call him one of the offscourings of the church. Of all the stupid, outlandish, ridiculous stunts for a boy of mine to do. I'm going to put a stop to this before it goes much farther." And Bennet Armstrong pounded the table with his fist until the dishes rattled.

CHAPTER XXXV

Her answer came on Thursday. From the moment he sealed the letter to Delores he prayed that, if it were God's will that he should care for her at all, her answer would be favorable.

"Dear Joseph," she had written in a beautiful hand. "Your presence will be pleasantly accepted.

"Sincerely,
"Delores Bays."

That was all—just one little sentence of six words—but it sent happy, fresh life flowing through Joseph's veins. It welled up within his breast, rich and strong. For the first time he felt like a man. Could it be true that this beautiful young lady, rosy with the ardor of young womanhood and health, actually meant she would be pleased to have him come! "Pleasantly accepted," the words rang in his ears all afternoon. The oftener he heard them, the harder and faster he worked. By evening he had decided to tell his mother. He could not keep the happy news to himself overnight. She must know it. She would be pleased, he was quite sure. Delores Bays was the very kind of young woman his mother would want him to be interested in. He was confident of this.

The well in the center of the vineyard reminded him again of his mother's prayers and that voice he had heard from Heaven; would Delores Bays be the kind of girl who would be sympathetic toward his convictions? Would she? Joseph could not imagine anything less than sympathy and understanding from one so ladylike, gentle, and refined, though he had never yet exchanged half a dozen words with her. Her face was open, free, and honest, and her walk and manner sincere and proper.

Joseph's hands actually trembled with joy and anticipation as he pulled weeds that afternoon. Several times he caught himself gasping with the glad wonder of her answer. He had read those six words over and over. Katy Bantum could tell that something made Joseph's face glow over the noon hour. She had handed him the letter when he came home for dinner, and he had hurried to his room to open it.

"Must have been from a lady friend," remarked Katy to Girtie Maples after dinner.

"Why?" asked Girtie, watching Joseph cross the yard.

"Didn't you see how pleased he was when he came down, Girtie?"

"Um-huh." Girtie fixed her hair.

"If you didn't have Arnold maybe you'd be—"

"Now Katy," cut in Girtie, blushing red, "you know good and well I'm too common for Joseph Armstrong, and anyway, he'd never look at a girl who wasn't a member of his church. Now, would he?"

"I was only teasing, Girtie," laughed Katy, walking swiftly away.

It occurred to Joseph when he wrote the letter that his father would likely be at home and learn the news too. It occurred to Joseph that his father might have some kind of remark to make about it because he had never yet known anything but criticism from him, but it did not occur to him that he could object seriously. Where could there be a girl finer or more beautiful than Delores Bays? And surely Father could not say he was too young to have dates if Uncle Timothy said he wasn't. Joseph had a notion to write a personal note to his mother, but then that could prove very disastrous to him and his mother both. Aunt Sara would likely make some reference to it when she wrote or Mrs. Irons might, or Maryanna might write it to Virginia, and so, after much deliberating, Joseph decided to write what he did with all good meaning and in faith. He knew when he mailed it that his folks would not get the letter until after he had had his first date.

Joseph shaved with extra pains Sunday morning. He had polished his shoes the evening before and picked out his best white handkerchief and put it on the corner of the dresser. Katy Bantum had laundered the white broadcloth shirt that used to be Jerry's, and had cut his hair on Friday night after he had stood by and watched her cut Sol's hair first.

"You didn't believe Katy could do it, did you?" laughed Sol, sweeping together the hair on the porch floor.

"I'm not saying what I thought, but I'm ready to say now it looks as good as the barber in town could do."

"Want me to cut yours?"

Katy brushed her apron and smiled pleasantly; both dimples showed.

"Would you do it for me?" asked Joseph eagerly.

"Sit down here on this stool and I'll show you."

"I'll pay you for it."

"Pay me?" and Katy's rosy cheeks spread with a ringing laughter. "No, indeed you won't. When you get married and thrash your cats you come over and settle with me then."

"What?" Joseph sat down on the stool and Katy pinned the towel around his neck. "I never heard that one."

"That's one of them sayings her grandmother handed down," said Sol, sitting on the banister. "My mother used to always say 'Charge it to the dust and let the rain settle it.'"

"Well, I want to do something for you for this," Joseph said to Katy.

"You've already done it," answered the woman, snipping hair. "You mended the garden gate for me last evening, and I've been waiting for three weeks for Sol to do it."

"Now, Katy," drawled Sol. He yawned.

"It's the truth," she said, snipping faster.

* * *

Joseph went to church on Daps, and at five o'clock the two young men started out in Freddie's buggy. Daps was put away in his Uncle Timothy's barn.

"We'll drive past Bays first," Freddie said, "and I'll let you out there. I'll go on to Denlingers, and I'll be back for you about nine."

"All right."

"Three hours will be about long enough for the first date, don't you think?"

"I think so," answered Joseph.

"I hope Martha will talk."

"I hope so, too," added Joseph.

"You mean you hope Delores will talk."

"Yes, and I hope Martha will too."

"Why? What's that to you?"

"Well, Freddie," Joseph said, "I want you to have a good time, too."

"Thanks. Do you feel you will?"

Joseph smiled faintly. Along the road, wild honeysuckles scented the air with their spicy perfume. He drew a deep breath. Life never seemed so worth the living as tonight."

"I'm expecting to have a happy time," answered Joseph softly.

"Agnes said she heard that Delores got six letters from boys last week asking for dates."

"No!"

"That's what Agnes heard, so if she turned down five for you, you're a lucky man."

Joseph knocked at the front door. Through the screen (for the door was open) he could see a lustrous green rug on the floor, and on the table in the center of the room, a glass bowl of red roses. He swallowed twice, for a strange feeling came up in his throat.

"Good evening." A short, black-eyed girl answered the knock.

Joseph removed his hat and stepped aside.

"Is this where Miss Delores Bays lives?"

"Yes, sir. Come in. She's expectin' you, but not this soon. She's out milkin' yet."

"She is? I didn't realize I was too early."

The girl held open the screen door. "Come on in and take a chair. I'll tell her you've come already."

"Thank you." Joseph sat on the first chair right inside the door. He could smell the roses from where he sat.

Before the black-eyed girl had a chance to inform her, Delores came into the house quite out of breath, for she had seen Joseph get out of the buggy and walk toward the house. She put the milk on the kitchen sink and softly told Bessie to take care of it for her. There was no other way to get to her room but by the stairway which opened into the living room. Blushing, she walked in. Her plain blue chambray milking dress with full-gathered skirt was somewhat soiled, and she had on her oldest shoes. Her blond hair, which was pinned around her head in two thick braids, was coming loose and in front it was clinging to her warm forehead.

"You kinda caught me—didn't you?" she said sweetly in a gentle voice. She smiled and brushed the hair from her forehead. She did not extend her hand or come close to him, but blushing a deep peach pink she hesitated with one hand on the knob of the stair door.

"That's perfectly all right," said Joseph rising and bowing slightly. "Perhaps I am a bit early."

"I'll be down in a few minutes," she said and disappeared.

He could hear her feet running up the carpeted steps. "Oh, wasn't she beautiful!" he said to himself. "Even in her milking clothes, she's beautiful." Joseph waited almost breathlessly. When the door opened he was stunned. Delores appeared in a long-waisted brown silk dress, made simply with a pleated shirt and a white narrow edging around the neck. She had exchanged her old shoes for black patent-leather slippers. Her hair was neatly put around her head, and in her left hand she carried a white handkerchief with a dainty lace edging. She crossed the room and held out her hand.

"Now I'll say good evening, Joseph." She looked up at him and smiled a little.

"Good evening, Delores," he said in his rich, deep voice. "Your answer made me very happy."

"Did it?"

"Very happy," he answered softly. "Have your parents gone to church already?"

"No, they went to Illinois to a funeral. My mother's sister passed away on Tuesday. Albert and George have gone to church. They left early so that they could stop and see some friends before church."

"And who was the girl that met me at the door?"

"That was Bessie Wiggers. My folks hired her to come and help me till they get back." She looked into his blue eyes sincerely.

"Do you have lots to do?" he asked.

"Enough. But not too much."

"You understand why I couldn't take you to church tonight?" He looked down at her thoughtfully.

"Yes, I understand," she answered.

"Maybe someday I can have a horse and a buggy of my own."

"I hope so. Shall we walk through the garden and the orchard, or shall we stay here and look at some pictures, or what would you like to do?"

Joseph hesitated a moment, then said, "I'd like to see your pictures if you'd care to show them to me."

CHAPTER XXXVI

From the drawer in the library table, Delores took out a large brown album and, crossing the room, she invited Joseph to sit beside her on the green velours sofa at the end of the living room. Over their shoulders the evening sun played through the leaves of a catalpa tree at the edge of the strawberry garden.

"Will we get too warm here?" she asked, opening the album, and looking at him cheerily.

The sun flickered gold across her face and neck. Joseph took hold of the lid with both his hands, and his eyes fell on the picture of a young, eager-faced couple standing just inside an open gate.

"I won't if you don't," he answered smiling. "Is that your mother and father?"

"I was just going to ask you if you could guess."

"If it is—" answered Joseph, wanting to look at Delores again and hardly daring to. He wished he wasn't so timid and shy. It wasn't that he was scared or ashamed. It wasn't that he was a coward or nervous, for never before had he felt so unafraid and unshrinking as now; but to be sitting for the first time beside the one he had long inwardly admired filled his heart with such profound appreciation and adoration he could not look at her just then. "If it is," he repeated softly, "you look very much like your mother used to, only you are—" Joseph cleared his throat, "you are prettier." He almost whispered the last words. His heart pounded fast, faster. He had not anticipated saying any such thing tonight. For only a moment a strange hush lasted. If Delores heard it, she made no sign of recognition. Could it be she had heard and disapproved? Joseph was smitten, but not for long, for her next sentence was spoken in so pleasant a manner and with such a brightness on her face that it destroyed all his fears. It can hardly be imagined what a delightful hour the two had, looking through that brown album. Every picture furnished a perfect introduction for another interesting topic for discussion. This old picture reminded Delores of something her grandmother had said or done, and that one reminded her of something amusing that happened when she was a child. There was Uncle Dewey with his wooden leg, and Aunt Emma with her two sets of twins, Cousin Homer who died in India, Cousin Eleanor, a schoolteacher; more aunts and uncles, and cousins, friends, and close friends. Joseph saw her as a baby, a bashful schoolgirl, a zealous-faced graduate, a girl ever and constantly growing in charm and beauty. Invariably he sought her out from the others in a group and his gaze lingered on her face only.

"And when was this taken?" he asked bending forward a bit.

"That was taken the day I was baptized," she answered.

"The day you were baptized?" Joseph lifted the album so he could look at the picture more closely. "We must have been gone then."

"Yes, you were. You were gone about three months when I was baptized."

"You remember?"

"Yes, I remember, Joseph. I remember when you folks moved away. And I remember when you were baptized too."

"You do?"

"Of course I do, Joseph," she said with pleasant seriousness, "and I remember some of the things Brother Grissley Steward said that morning." Her eyes shone and she tucked back a loose strand of blond hair as she continued eagerly. "He's a grand old man, don't you think?"

"I certainly do."

"A good many things he says seem to stay with me longer than what some other preachers say. Do you know what he said that day you were baptized, the thing that I remember above all else?"

"No. Tell me, Delores. What was it?"

"He said, 'There are some fine young men and women in this group before us today. God only knows, but in this group there may be some future Sunday-school teachers, deacons, ministers, bishops, or foreign missionaries. With every soul born into this world, his work is born with him.' Why, Joseph, don't you remember?"

"Yes, go on."

"Go on?"

"Yes, I like to hear you talk."

Delores smiled.

"Well, he said like this then. Maybe I can't repeat it just exactly, for that was six years ago, but he said, 'With every work born with a soul, God provides the tools with which to do that work, but the sad part is that some people are too lazy, or too blind, or stubborn to use those tools, and many die with their work undone!'"

"Do you remember all that, Delores?"

"Oh, yes, Joseph, and something more too. He said, 'I would feel highly honored to be the father of such a group as sits before me today.' I can see him yet, how his face glowed as he said that, and his long beard; you know, Joseph, how he strokes it at times."

"Yes."

"'But I'm not,' he said, 'but I have a love and fatherly concern in my heart for every one of you, and I appreciate deeply this consecration you have made. I cannot be a father to you all as I am to my own sons and daughters, but I can appreciate you all, and that is far better than to have you all for my own sons and daughters and not be able to appreciate you.' I never forgot that." Delores picked up her lace-edged handkerchief and tucked it in her sleeve. "I wonder why he said that that day?"

"I wouldn't know," answered Joseph thoughtfully, "but I've always appreciated him very much, and Uncle Tom Bradly. Another person that I admired when I went to school was Amos Pennewell."

"What is it about people that you most admire, Joseph?" she asked. She closed the album and laid it on the sofa beside her.

"I think," answered Joseph, "the thing I admire most about a person is kindness."

"Did you know my aunt?" Delores asked, "the one that died? She sent me a card for my birthday last year, and it had a pretty little verse on it that said, 'Kindness is the only language that the blind can see and the deaf can hear.' Isn't that a lovely thought?"

"It is," answered Joseph. "That's a beautiful thought, and I believe it's true too."

"Tell me about your mother, Joseph. And I'd like to hear about Virginia and Lowell too. I wonder if I would know them if I'd see them."

They talked until the long band of gold slanted across the western sky, and the longer they talked the more each discovered they believed alike. Without trying, each revealed to the other his ideals and convictions. She lit the lamp. As Joseph sat and listened to this pleasant-voiced friend, the more determined he became to hold to those ideals he had read in the lives of those he admired. There was something about Delores Bays's very being that made him want to be good and true. She had made him feel that way long before he had ever asked her for a date, and now that he was sitting beside her in her own home, listening to her voice (and every word she spoke was to him) it seemed that the very atmosphere around her was sacred or hallowed. Never before had he felt such an inner urge to be a man, the best man possible. Every good thing his mother had ever taught him now seemed to be emanating from this charming young woman.

"Can it be," she said at length, "that it is nine o'clock already?"

"Nine o'clock? Surely not already! Freddie said he would be by for me about this time."

"So soon?" she asked in the gentlest voice, sweetly. "Before you go we should sing a hymn or two together, don't you think, since this is the Lord's day and we missed going to church?" And before Joseph could answer, Delores took the Aladdin lamp and placed it on a small stand beside the organ.

"Come," she said, winding the stool around twice. "What is your favorite hymn?"

"I don't know that I have a favorite," answered Joseph looking down at her. "Let us sing your favorite."

"You may be surprised when I tell you what it is," she said opening a songbook and turning to it at once. From the organ soft solemn music came. "You know it, I'm sure." She looked up for a moment.

"Surely."

Together they sang all four verses of that simple, stately old hymn, perhaps the greatest ever written in the English language because of its deep religious fervor and solemn passion for the suffering Christ, "When I survey the wondrous cross, on which the Prince of Glory died."

"Why is this your favorite hymn?" asked Joseph.

"I don't know if I can tell you why, Joseph," she answered, "unless it is because it was the first song my mother played after we got the organ. You know Father got it at a sale about a year ago for only seven dollars, and the day he brought it home he made me promise I'd never play anything on it on Sundays but sacred songs. My mother never finds time to play much except on Sundays, and we usually sing a while before lunch."

"It's nice you can play."

"Mother taught me how. Do you think Freddie will come soon?"

"I'm afraid he will, Delores. I can't tell you how I've enjoyed the evening with you."

"You haven't enjoyed it any more than I have," came her soft answer, "but before you leave, we're going to have a little something to eat."

She hurried to the kitchen and soon returned with two dishes of crushed fresh strawberries on a tray with sugar, cream, and thick slices of delicious pound cake.

Nothing Joseph had ever eaten tasted so delicious. They ate and talked, and soon fifteen minutes flew by and still Freddie did not come.

"Who did he go to see?" asked Delores.

"Martha Denlinger."

"Oh! She must be showing him an interesting time."

"Do you know what Freddie's sister told him?" asked Joseph.

"No. What sister?"

"Agnes, I believe."

"What was it?"

"Maybe I shouldn't mention this."

"You make me inquisitive."

"She said," he hesitated, "you had received several other letters last week besides the one from me."

"Yes," she answered, blushing a little, "I did, but— yours was the only one I—" She did not finish her sentence, but she looked at him trustingly for an instant and an excited little gasp escaped her parted lips.

Joseph stood speechless with happy wonder, and a strange glory seemed to rest upon his shoulders and burned warm in his breast.

"This is the happiest evening I've ever had in my life," he managed to say at length.

"I'm glad you have enjoyed it," she answered sweetly, "and when you write to your mother, be sure and give her my best regards. I think she's one of the sweetest little women I've ever seen."

"Thanks," Joseph said sincerely; "that makes me very happy. But I did not know you knew my mother well."

"Well, I really don't know her well, Joseph, but I've heard so many nice remarks about her through others. Oh, that must be Freddie now! The evening has gone so quickly, hasn't it?"

"It has—but it's nearer ten than nine."

She handed Joseph his hat.

"Thank you," he said, "and it would please me very much to come again next Sunday evening."

"Would it?"

"Indeed it would, Delores."

"Then,"—she looked at her clasped hands a moment —(Freddie was at the door) "then—you may," she whispered.

CHAPTER XXXVII

A happier young man never descended the steps of the Bays home than did that night.

"You must have had a real good time, Freddie," said Joseph after they were both in the buggy and on their way.

"Oh, I don't know," stammered Joseph's cousin, scrambling for words. "Did you?"

"I had a wonderful time," answered the other.

"Wonderful?" asked Freddie. "How wonderful? What do you mean?"

"I just enjoyed every minute of it, and I'm going back again next Sunday evening."

"Whew!" Freddie whistled softly through his front teeth. "I wish I could say that. I didn't have nearly as nice a time as I expected."

"What was wrong?" asked Joseph.

"Oh, I don't know." Freddie's voice was almost forlorn. "I was disappointed, just between you and me. Don't tell anyone, though. Maybe I'll try her once more, and maybe I won't. I haven't decided yet."

"Then you didn't tell her you had a nice time?" inquired Joseph. His own heart still burned within him, warm and comforting.

"No, I didn't. I won't ever say that unless I mean it."

"Neither will I," added Joseph.

"Well, what did you two do all evening? We couldn't think of anything to talk about."

"You went to church, didn't you?"

"Sure, but we didn't sit together. She said she'd rather not. I guess she thought we might get teased. And you actually had a good time, you say?"

"Freddie," answered Joseph. "I wouldn't have asked to go back if I wouldn't have had a good time."

The boys drove on in silence.

* * *

On Thursday Joseph walked over to the McCracken place to ask the Squire how to treat a certain insect that was working destruction on the grape leaves in the lower end of the vineyard. On approaching the mansion from the east he noticed a girl standing outside holding a handkerchief over both eyes.

She looked up abruptly when she heard his footsteps on the sidewalk. She ran toward him.

"Oh, don't knock," she said brokenly. "Poor old Fonzo is a-dyin'," and tears quivered in both eyes.

"You're the girl I met one morning."

"Yes, I'm Minnie, and, oh, I just can't stay in there with him another minute," she sobbed.

"Is he alone?" asked Joseph.

"No, Miss Snow, the nurse, was called this morning. She's in there. He took another stroke last night, and a while ago he started seein' angels or somethin' an' I just had to get out. I remember you." Minnie wiped her eyes.

"Does the Squire know he's dying?" asked Joseph.

"Oh, sure," answered Minnie twisting her wet handkerchief nervously. "He comes in every now and then to see him, but he went up to his room a bit ago to drink a cup of coffee. His wife is takin' it awful hard. We all think as much of Fonzo as if he was a white man, an' maybe more. You can't know why we all like him so."

"I like him too, Minnie," answered Joseph warmly and with genuine fervor in his deep voice. "I don't know him as well as you do, I know, but there's something about him that I like."

"He's so kind to everyone," cried Minnie, tears trickling down her cheeks. "Oh, I do hope he won't be disappointed."

"Disappointed?"

"Yes. Oh, I do hope he really will get to Heaven. He's countin' on it so. If only God will give him a little corner somewhere. There's some what says darkies won't get there, an' they die like horses an' birds an' things, but I can't see how God could turn Fonzo down when he's been so good and kind to us all."

"He won't," said Joseph earnestly. "God won't turn him down if he believes."

"Are you sure, Mister? Oh, I do hope you're right."

"In God's sight Fonzo is as acceptable as anyone. He died for all, black as well as white; 'whosoever believeth on him shall be saved' includes Fonzo."

"Are you sure, Mister?" The girl looked up into Joseph's face almost beseechingly.

"I'm absolutely sure, Minnie."

"Oh, maybe I can stand it then to watch him die. Miss Snow is all alone with him now."

Minnie walked toward the door on tiptoe. "Want to go along in with me?"

The nurse had Fonzo's head propped up on three pillows. His eyes were half closed, and Joseph saw at once that his black face was drawn a little to one side. His tired black hands that had worked so faithfully for years lay limp and still across his breast. Miss Snow was dampening his parted lips with a piece of wet cotton; then she fanned him gently.

Suddenly Fonzo opened his eyes and, gazing toward the ceiling, smiled and said in an audible but low voice, half chanting, "Swing lower—sweet—lower—sweet." Then he gasped once and his breath came no more. Life departed and a terrible hush filled the room. Squire Mc-

Cracken walked in, closing the door softly and carefully behind him. He stood speechless.

"Well, Joseph," whispered Mr. McCracken, placing a trembling hand on the young man's shoulder, "this is a day I'll never forget. Fonzo Bullet was a good old soul, and we'll all miss him." He shook his gray head slowly, almost reverently. "There's one man I've never known to say or do a mean thing all these years he's lived here. I've never asked him to do anything he refused to do, and I'm going to be as good as my word—I'm going to give him a decent burial."

"I'll be back some other time, Mr. McCracken," whispered Joseph.

"What was it you wanted, son?"

"There's some insects—"

"Come out to my shop with me. I'll give you something. Minnie, tell Mrs. McCracken to call the undertaker and tell Miss Snow I'll have someone drive her to town in a few minutes. Come, son, I'll have a few minutes with you. You can't let those insects get headway this time of year."

Katy Bantum always stuck Joseph's mail in a crack beside the telephone. When Joseph got home there was a letter there for him. After supper he retired immediately to his room, and taking a chair in front of the open window he tore open the letter and read:

"Dear son Joseph,

"Before I do anything I want to write you a letter this morning. We took dinner yesterday with the John Williams family and enjoyed getting better acquainted with them. Brother Collins preaches better all the time. Gradually Lowell and Virginia are getting acquainted with the young people here. Father gave his first talk in the Young People's Meeting last night. He talked on the 'True Marks of Discipleship,' and he mentioned love, patience, and understanding. Joseph, it was all good what he said, if only—pray for him, Joseph. I know you do. Virginia is doing very well in her school work, but she can hardly wait until she is old enough to work out. I wish I knew of some way to earn a little to get her a couple new dresses and a coat.

"I am so glad you got to see Earnie, and that you like your work in the vineyard. I wonder if you enjoyed your first date, Sunday. I thought about you all evening, and prayed that you would have a nice and profitable evening, as I remember Delores was a nice girl when we left. I know this, that if she will be as fine a woman some day as her own mother, she will be an example to everyone. May God bless you in your friendship to His own glory. This is my daily prayer. Father did not seem so pleased," (Joseph held his breath) "but I cannot tell you just why. Virginia seemed almost thrilled over it. Joseph, she and Lowell think what you do is about right. Don't ever forget this.

"I had the nicest letters last week from Aunt Sara and one from Mrs. Irons. Today I had one from Lottie, and maybe you know that Mrs. Bantum wrote to me. I'm so glad she likes you, Joseph. I wish Father would soon begin to fix up the place a little. He expects to take another carload of cattle to Chicago the end of this week. He always went the first part of the week before. Lowell wants to learn to handle Quicksilver, but Father thinks he's too young. He really does miss you. I mean Lowell. Tell Mrs. Bantum I'll answer her nice letter one of these days. Father thinks I ask for too many stamps, but my friends mean a lot to me, and I like to get letters, especially from you. Evalena Collins fills a real place in my life, but as yet I've never been *real* confidential with her about some things. You are the only person on earth I've told some things to. I get real lonesome to have a good long talk with you, Joseph. You must be careful what you write home. You understand, dear. I only hope some day it will be different, but don't write much about Delores Bays just now. I'd love to hear all about her, but it's best now if you don't. I must get busy and wash the breakfast dishes. It is going to be a pretty warm day, I fear.

"I was just reading last evening in Psalm 92 about bringing forth fruit in old age, and I just thought I'd pass this on to you, that it is what young people do, and believe, and strive toward today when they are growing young men and women that will help them bring forth good fruit in old age. What is more inspiring and beautiful than a happy, radiant, old person? God bless you, my beloved son Joseph. Pray for us all.

"Lovingly,
"Your Mother."

Joseph folded the letter and bowed his head in silent prayer. It used to be his mother's face that stood out in fancy as he prayed, that sweet, sad, honest face that always seemed to breathe confidence and courage into his soul; but tonight and for several nights two faces hovered near. The one was his mother's, and the other was Delores Bays's. For an hour Joseph sat thinking.

*   *   *

It was Sunday morning. Someone pulled on Joseph's coat sleeve. Herbert Lanyard, the youngest minister in the church, stood beside him. "Step aside, Joseph," he said. "I'd like to speak to you just a few minutes."

"Certainly," answered Joseph, stepping out from the group. They walked a few rods out across the church-yard.

"Over the next week end," Herbert Lanyard said, "I'm to preach in a little mining town forty miles from here across the mountains at Asterlow, and I want to take someone with me. Brother Grissley suggested you to me. Would you like to go along?"

18

Joseph thought a full thirty seconds, then answered. "That would be something interesting all right. When would you need to start?"

"We'd start early Friday morning about daylight."

"When would we come back?"

"We'd start back early Monday morning."

Joseph thought fast. Delores—the vineyard—how could he do it? And yet, what a chance. Never had anyone invited him to go along on such a mission. Why had Brother Grissley mentioned his name? There were plenty of other young men in the church.

"I'm interested," said Joseph at length. "And thank you, Brother Lanyard. Could I call you up tomorrow sometime and let you know?"

"That will be all right, Joseph," answered the young minister. "But please don't wait later than tomorrow to let me know. If you don't go along, I want to ask someone else." He started to walk away. "I hope you decide to go," he called back over his shoulder.

CHAPTER XXXVIII

This time Delores and not Bessie Wiggers met Joseph at the door. A small white apron was tied around her waist, and she wore a soft blue dress the shade of a robin's egg. Her delicate pink cheeks, her kind eyes, her blond hair, her sincere smile, and graceful manner again filled Joseph's heart with overwhelming joy as he stepped into the house. Tonight she seemed to be crowned with a womanly charm he had never seen on any other girl.

"Good evening, Joseph," she said.

"Good evening, Delores," he answered, smiling.

"I see you have a buggy tonight." She looked toward the gate as she spoke.

"Yes," he answered. She took his hat. "Mr. Bantum loaned me his for tonight."

"Then we'll go to church?" She looked up at him.

"Would you like to?"

"Yes," she answered. "We should always be in church whenever possible."

"That's right, Delores. It would make me very happy to take you to church."

"Would it?" She looked happy.

God has manifested Himself not only in the beauties and wonders of nature, but also in human life. There is in the heart of every normal man a divine craving and hunger for companionship. Joseph craved something spiritual, something refined and comforting, something real that Delores Bays expressed without trying. It was not something she put on for the occasion, but an atmosphere, an invisible influence that surrounded her, that reflected her pure beauty of soul that made Joseph's respond. The happiness he had enjoyed in this room just seven days before had never left him. A distinctly uplifting feeling had possessed him then, and now he felt a

263

fresh outburst of fervor in his soul that marked an upward movement in his Christian experience. He could not have explained it had he tried ever so hard.

"It would make me very happy, Delores," he said softly in a deep rich voice, "to take you anywhere, but especially to church."

"Then everybody will know," she said, sweeping her cheeks with her lashes.

"I won't care, if you won't."

"I won't care," she whispered, looking up.

"Good evening, Joseph." Jeddie Bays walked briskly into the room, extended a friendly hand.

"Good evening, Mr. Bays," Joseph said, clasping the hand.

"It's a fine evening," said Mr. Bays.

"A very fine evening," answered Joseph.

"Take a chair."

"Thank you."

"We'd better go soon, don't you think, Joseph?" Delores asked.

"Before too long," Joseph answered.

"Would you like to eat a little lunch now or would you rather wait until we get back?"

"I'd rather wait, wouldn't you?"

"I'd rather." She smiled and left the room.

"Well," began Jeddie Bays tilting back in his chair, "so you're taking care of a vineyard."

"Yes, sir."

"Rather monotonous, isn't it?"

"No, I wouldn't say that, Mr. Bays. I rather like it."

"I suppose your father will come out and help you when harvest time comes."

"I don't know," answered Joseph.

"He surely will," said Jeddie, fumbling with a toothpick in his vest pocket. "That will be a busy time and more work than one man can handle, and if I know anything about it they've got to be picked at the right time and no delaying."

"I guess you're right, Mr. Bays," said Joseph.

Delores returned with her mother, who gave Joseph a cordial handshake and a few pleasant words. She made him feel welcome. Not with gushing words, not with great ado or lavish expressions; but in one simple sincere sentence she gave him a kind reception into their home, and this was another source of inspiration to Joseph. He was moved with deep emotion. Hadn't his mother said in her recent letter that Mrs. Bays was an excellent woman, an example to others? The esteem he felt for his own mother helped him appreciate this woman all the more. She was Delores' mother.

The sky was still glowing with the summer sunset, the air was balmy but not hot, and the ride to church was perfect. There was something interesting and worth while to talk about all the way. When love is in evidence there is always something rich and beautiful to talk about. One of the finest arts of life is to have pleasant thoughts to pass on to another. To express one's joy to another only makes that joy grow, and to express one's grief diminishes it. Joseph discovered in Delores Bays that something that brought sunshine into his life. He had long lived under the shadows. And she was not hesitant to express herself about spiritual things. He soon learned that she had a very real and vital experience with God and a sincere desire to do His will in her life. It unconsciously encouraged Joseph to renew his own honest heart searching to learn the Father's will for him. Those boyhood prayers beside the woodpile meant something now. The effort he put forth to do the janitor work that he might be permitted to finish his schoolwork was well worth it now. Those prayers in the cold empty schoolroom had not ascended in vain—not if a girl like Delores Bays would turn down six requests in preference to his, and write "pleasantly accepted." All the harsh words he had ever received from his father, all the unjust whippings, all the unlove faded into insignificance now when Delores spoke.

"You are so different from all the other boys I've ever known," she said, looking up at him in the deepening dusk.

"How do you mean?" asked Joseph, catching his breath.

"Well," she answered clasping and unclasping her hands twice, "you seem more—more sincere, I guess. Of course," she added quickly, looking away, "I haven't known you long. Once—" she hesitated.

"Once what?"

"Well," she cleared her throat and sat up very straight. "Once I thought—someone was—was sincere too, but he really wasn't after all."

"You went with him?" Joseph drew a deep breath.

"A few times."

"He didn't mistreat you, did he?"

"Oh, never! Not that. He was very much like a gentleman when we were together, but in a crowd—oh, just many times I noticed he was very shallow. I never could quite feel he truly believed all the good statements he made."

"Would you mind telling me who that was?"

"You might know him," she answered shyly.

"You'd rather not tell me?"

"You'll never tell anyone?"

"Never."

"I might tell you sometime."

"Delores," said Joseph in a calm, quiet voice, "if you ever feel that I am not sincere, I want you to tell me."

"Oh, Joseph!" She looked up startled.

"Please do. If I know my own heart I am, but—"

"You mean you believe in yourself?" she asked.

"If that is the way you care to put it," he answered thoughtfully, "I do."

"Oh, Joseph," cried Delores smiling, "I'm so glad you didn't say no. You should believe in yourself, for you know yourself better than anyone else does. At least you should. I suppose your mother believes in you, doesn't she?"

"Yes." He said it very softly.

"And she knows you real well."

"Yes."

"And your father believes in you too, doesn't he?"

Joseph's heart almost stopped. He felt a chill creep over him. He did not answer. His hands which gripped the lines trembled.

"Doesn't he, Joseph?" she repeated softly.

"Delores," he choked, "I hope so—I—a—we'll sit together, won't we?"

"I—I thought we would," she answered sweetly.

A strange new fear gnawed at Joseph's heart during the entire service. How could he answer her question? How could he without reviewing the unpleasant things of his life? He was trying to forget them. Why had she asked such a question? Did she know something of his unhappiness. If he did tell her, what would she think? How could he convince her that his father seemed to hate him without a cause? And yet if he refused to answer her question, she would have reason to suspect his sincerity.

How delighted he was to be sitting beside Delores Bays! Love beat high in his breast, and he tried desperately to shake off that weight of fear, but it clung there tightly until they were over halfway home.

"Joseph," she said, "what was Herbert Lanyard saying to you this morning after church? I noticed him taking you aside."

"That's just what I was going to tell you next," he answered confidently and warmly. "He is to preach in a mining town forty miles across the mountains next Friday night, Saturday, and Sunday, and he asked me to go with him."

"Oh, Joseph!"

"You mean you're glad?"

"Glad? Joseph, that is quite an honor, I think. You mean he chose you to accompany him on such a trip?"

"He said Brother Grissley suggested my name."

"Oh, Joseph! It makes me very happy."

"Why, Delores?"

"To think Brother Steward would suggest you. Now I know"—she hesitated, and she was glad Joseph couldn't see her cheeks turn crimson.

"Know what?" he asked softly.

"Know you *are* sincere—if—if a man like Brother Grissley would suggest your name above all others. You're going, aren't you?"

"I want to," he answered fervently, "but I won't be back to see you on Sunday night. We won't be back before Monday evening."

"Well," she said musingly, "I'll be praying for you. I want you to go."

"Why, Delores?" He smiled lovingly at her.

"Oh—for several reasons, Joseph. If I were a young man I'd surely accept an invitation like that."

"What would your parents say then if I'd come to see you on Wednesday night?"

"I know what," she beamed; "come in time for supper, then we can all play a game of croquet before dark."

"All who?"

"Father and mother and the boys—all of us, I mean. You can't imagine what good times we have once a week or so."

* * *

Sol Bantum answered the knock. In the doorway stood a middle-aged man in a dark suit. He tipped his hat. "Mr. Bantum?" he asked. He seemed a little out of breath.

"Yes, sir," said Sol.

"Is Joseph Armstrong here?" he asked rather sternly.

"No, sir, not yet," answered Sol.

"Could you tell me where he is?"

"Well," said Sol a little carefully, "I reckon he's out with his girl tonight. He borrowed my horse and buggy fer that purpose. He's due in here most any time now." Sol looked at the clock. It was just getting ready to strike ten thirty.

The man on the other side of the screen door cleared his throat and pulled at his large Roman nose. He scowled and said resentfully, "Well, I sent him out here to look after my vineyard and not to run around with the girls. I—"

"You're Mr. Armstrong. Well, well, come in," and Sol opened the door. "Come in," he repeated. "I'm sure Joseph will be here any minute. He never stays out late. Fine boy you've got, Mr. Armstrong; fine young man. Take a chair, sir. How did you come?"

"I came on out from Chicago," answered Bennet Armstrong still scowling. "I took a carload of beef to market and decided to run on out and see how things are coming."

"I see. Well, that must be Joseph coming now."

CHAPTER XXXIX

"The gods we worship write their names on our faces."

A stifled exclamation escaped Joseph's lips at sight of the man within.

"Why, Father," he said in surprise. He hung up his hat and crossed the dining room. "When did you come?"

"Just a bit ago," answered Bennet. He did not get up and shake hands, but frowning, he said coldly, "Since I just took a carload of cattle to market, I thought I'd better come on out and see how things are going here."

"I'm quite sure you'll be pleased when you see the vineyard, Father," said Joseph trying to look pleasant. "Whose horse is that out there?"

"It's the one I rented from the livery stable. You don't suppose I walked out here in the dark?"

"No, of course not," answered Joseph. "I just hadn't thought that far yet. This is quite a surprise."

"Sorta caught you, didn't I?" And Bennet eyed Joseph sharply.

The loud knock at the door had wakened Katy Bantum, who had been in bed for over an hour. She could hear distinctly from the half-open bedroom door each voice in the adjoining room. She listened breathlessly. She sat up in bed. Was the man joking? She listened; no one laughed, not even Sol.

"You're going to stay overnight, I suppose?" Joseph spoke in a voice that sounded a little hurt.

"I couldn't see much vineyard in the dark, could I? Can't you give me half your bed this once?" Bennet did not smile. His stern face was set.

"Why, yes," came Joseph's ready answer. "Of course I will. I'll put your horse away for you; then we'll go to bed. I suppose maybe you're tired."

"I thought you'd be in bed surely," Bennet said icily.

"Have you had your supper, Mr. Armstrong?" asked Sol, somewhat embarrassed. This unexpected visitor and his sour, disagreeable manner made Sol a little ill at ease. Joseph looked very happy when he first stepped into the house, but when he went out Sol noticed a sadness on the young man's face which he had never seen there before.

"I ate in town," Bennet answered. "How long's this been going on, Mr. Bantum?"

"What do you mean, Mr. Armstrong?" asked Sol.

"Him running out like this at night?"

"Joseph? Oh, let me see, I think this was his second Sunday evening out. Mighty fine girl he's got, Mr. Armstrong. Yes, sir, Jeddie Bays's daughter is a right nice girl or you can know Joseph wouldn't be interested in her. Never knew a finer young man than this son of yours."

J. Bennet Armstrong cleared his throat and ran his left hand back over his black hair several times.

"And what does he pay you for the use of your horse and buggy for these frolics?"

"Pay?" Sol laughed good-naturedly. "I don't expect him to pay anything. I told him he could take it. He didn't ask either; I offered it to him. It's been a pleasure to have your son in our home, and my wife, she'd do most anything fer Joseph."

Sol wasn't exactly sure, but he thought he heard the man make a grunt of disapproval.

"Could I get you a fresh drink before I go to bed?"

"Maybe a drink," Bennet said. "You say you think Joseph has been paying attention to his work?"

"Been workin' like a trooper. There's not a lazy bone in that boy, Mr. Armstrong, and if your crop don't bring the top price, it won't be his fault."

Bennet smiled faintly. The severe lines softened a bit and he wet his stern lips.

"Thanks," he said. "That is pretty good drinking water you have here."

"We have good water," Sol said. "That's the first thing my wife requires. She can make herself at home anywhere if she has good drinking water. What kind of water do you have out there where you live?"

"Good. Makes nice fat cattle, at least, and I guess what's good for cattle's good for men."

"Well, since Joseph is in now and I can't do any more for you, I'll say good night. I'll see you in the morning for breakfast."

"Good night," answered Bennet blinking, and Joseph led the way upstairs to his room. He lit the lamp on the dresser and closed the door.

"Don't you think I have a nice room?" Joseph pushed a chair over to his father.

Bennet did not answer. He stood up very straight and folded his arms tightly in front of him.

"Now look here, young man," he began, "I came out here to inform you that I heartily disapprove of what's going on here."

"What do you mean, Father?"

Joseph was going to sit down, but since his father remained standing, he did too.

"You know what I mean," he panted. "I sent you out here to look after the vineyard and not to run around with girls. How do you suppose you can do your work and stay out this late at night?"

"It is very little later than if I had come straight home after church."

"Huh! And who is the girl you were out with tonight?"

"I was with Delores Bays, Father."

"Delores Bays," he mocked contemptuously, "and who is she?"

Joseph's cheeks got hot, and his head ached above his eyebrows.

"She's Jeddie Bays's daughter."

"And is that the best you could do?" hooted his father.

"I don't know how I could do any better," answered Joseph.

"Any better!" shouted Bennet. "You must have closed your eyes and thrown in a hook, and that's what you got."

"Father!" cried Joseph. "How can you say that? You haven't seen Delores Bays for years. You should see her. She's a beautiful girl. She's refined and ladylike, and she's a—"

"Beautiful?" shouted Bennet scornfully. "How could one of Jeddie Bays's children be beautiful? She certainly can't get any good looks from him." He unfolded his arms and rubbed his hands.

"I've seen lots worse-looking men," answered Joseph, trying to stay calm. "Her mother is a fine-looking woman, and even if Delores wasn't pretty, her character would be enough to attract me."

Bennet sniffed. He ran his hands deep into his pockets, and he fumbled with some loose change.

"I wanted you to get a girl out west. That's one reason why I moved out there."

"But, Father," said Joseph, taking hold of the end of the bed, "I didn't see anyone out there that appealed to me in the least."

"Appealed," scoffed Bennet. "What do you know about appeal in a girl? I suppose if a girl has a nice head of blond hair, or a dimple or two, you call her appealing. Indeed!"

"Delores Bays has everything," (Joseph's voice broke a little; he could hardly swallow the lump that was choking him) "everything that I long for in a friend."

"Long?" snapped Bennet. "Is it actually that bad? And you've gone out twice with her. I hope you don't mean you're engaged already?"

"Certainly not," answered Joseph. "I've never made love to any girl yet."

"And you'd better not let me hear of it either. A boy your age has no business out with the girls this hour of the night. This is scandalous."

"Father," said Joseph, stepping a little closer to him, "if Mother was right, and I'm positive she was, she said you were married at my age."

Bennet Armstrong's face grew red. The cords in his neck throbbed and throbbed, and Joseph could see that he was angry now.

"Don't get smart now, young man," shouted Bennet furiously. "When I was your age I had some sense." He swallowed twice. "And what's more, I had in sight a— a—Joseph, why on earth don't you find yourself a girl out west who comes from a worth-while family?"

"What do you mean, Father?"

"Don't act so stupid, Joseph," mumbled Bennet. "What's Jeddie Bays got to show for? Nothing. He's a middle-aged man already, and what's he got ahead? I'd call it a disgrace to have a son of mine marry into that family."

"A disgrace?" Joseph's knees shook and he felt sick all over. Hot tears welled up in his eyes, and he felt as if the floor under him was moving.

"I would call it a disgrace and nothing less."

"If I ever marry," Joseph said slowly, "I hope it will be for love only. I hope I'll never be guilty of marrying any girl for money."

"Money and love are more reasonable and sensible than love and beauty without money," Bennet said curtly.

"I don't see it that way," answered Joseph. "I believe in letting God direct me in this. I mean this with all seriousness, Father." Joseph's lips quivered and he could hardly control himself now. "I've been praying about this for months. Before we ever moved away from here, Delores Bays appealed to me. I liked her looks, and I liked her ways. Everyone in the church and community thinks highly of the Bays. I've had numbers of persons tell me Delores was a fine girl. The happiest two evenings I've ever had in my life have been with her. She's as pure as a lily, and I know this; I'm a better Christian already after spending just two Sunday evenings with her."

"And if this keeps on," cut in Bennet sarcastically, "you'll soon be a religious fanatic. You'd better do as I tell you and quit her before you go any farther. She's just got you under some hypnotic influence. I want you to promise me you'll not go with her another time."

"Father!" cried Joseph, and he shook now with sobs uncontrolled. "Father!" he choked; "you don't realize what this means to me. You can't—or you wouldn't ask —this—of me. I have felt God's leading in this matter. It's a sacred thing to me. I can't cast it aside—that— easily. Did your father tell you who to love?"

Bennet Armstrong was furious now. He felt like slapping Joseph. He would have, but his son was now larger than he.

"And you mean you refuse to promise me this?"

A prolonged silence filled the room. Each could hear the other breathing heavily. The clock below struck twelve. It seemed every strike of that clock was dealing a death blow to his heart. That strange, new fear that had gnawed at him in church, now gnashed at him. Such a blow he had not felt for years, not since the morning his mother had told him her days were numbered. Oh! were disappointment and misunderstanding going to be his portion forever? Would his father like to smother all the joy in his life? Why was he always so harsh and so cruelly misunderstanding?

"Must I promise that, Father?" cried Joseph. He felt weak and dizzy now.

"You claim to be an obedient boy, don't you?" said Bennet. "I told Squire McCracken you were always an obedient boy, so I'll give you a chance now to prove to me whether or not you're still obedient. Let's go to bed."

CHAPTER XL

"And where and how did you get that new suit you have on?" blinked Bennet, taking a step toward Joseph as though he were going to snatch it away from him. He didn't however. He didn't even touch it with his finger tips.

"Katy gave it to me," answered Joseph sadly. He buttoned the coat with trembling fingers. He hadn't shed tears since the afternoon he had kissed his mother good-by. With rankling, cutting, crushing pain, he again lived some of those boyhood experiences when punishment was laid upon him without mercy. He had often wondered if other boys, any other boy, had cried as often and hard as he had. He was growing out of that stage now. Since the hour he stepped into Sol Bantum's home, life had been so utterly different. There had been no occasion for tears here. His newly-found joy in Delores had helped him forget to a great measure those trying days when he lived under constant criticism and sententious rule. He surely didn't expect to cry tonight before he went to bed after such a pleasant evening. Was he always going to be a target to be shot at time after time, always before the former wound was quite healed over? His eyes burned and smarted. He sincerely wished he hadn't cried over what his father had said, but he simply couldn't help it. The man before him who should have been his understanding comrade had struck the most delicate spot in his heart.

"And who's Katy?" yelled Bennet frantically.

"Sh, Father," whispered Joseph. "She'll hear you. Katy is Mrs. Bantum, Sol's wife. This suit used to belong to their son who died."

"Of all things," gulped Bennet. He blew his nose. "I'd be ashamed if I were you. What I got wasn't good enough for Jeddie Bays's daughter, so you had to beg a dead boy's clothes."

"I did not beg." Joseph stood up very straight, and walked across the room. He removed his coat and put it carefully on a hanger. He hung it in the closet. "You're tired, Father," he said wearily, "let's go to bed. What time must you leave tomorrow?"

"That depends on how things look to me," answered Bennet starting to unlace his shoe. "I'm provoked at you, Joseph, and I want you to know it. I can't get over it that you'd even look at that Bays girl. You wrote it home and Lowell and Virginia both heard it. After this I'll read your letters first, and if you have anything in them that's not fit for the children to hear, I'll burn them. I gave them implicit orders not to tell anyone. There's more than one girl in the West a heap nicer than the Bays girl. Now don't act like you're not listening, Joseph. I'm in earnest about this, and this is the main reason why I came out here. I meant it. Are you listening? If this continues I can move the family back here and we'll take care of the vineyard, and I can send you out west to take care of the ranch. Are you going to—" Bennet looked up at Joseph with a penetrating, acid look. "Are you going to promise me before we go to bed that you'll never have another thing to do with that girl?"

A terrible hush fell over the room. The prolongation of it became tense.

"Speak!" came Bennet's tense voice, breaking the silence.

Once before Joseph had been the victim in a similar situation, and his mother had come to his rescue and pled his cause. But his mother was not here this time. That same something that rose up within her that night, rose up within her son. He stood straight and tall beside the light on the dresser.

"No," he said in a deep, firm voice, "I will not promise you that." Joseph did not stagger or falter. His voice came sure and steady. "And," he added, "if you are not satisfied with my work in the vineyard after you've inspected it—remember, Father, I'll soon be twenty-one, and I can get a job and support myself and buy my own clothes, and also get a few for Mama and Virginia sometimes." Joseph drew a deep, deep breath. He had never before spoken to his father like this. He had never dared to. He had always stood in his presence in terror and dread. Tonight he stood up above him strong and strangely brave. For some reason he almost pitied the smaller man before him who had such a lean conception or appreciation for the finest things in life. Did his father ever have a tender thought? Did he ever consider another's feelings? Did he ever know love and affection?

The father's indignation now rose to wrath, and in his sore displeasure he shouted in exasperation, "Joseph —you're crazy!" Crazy! Once before Joseph had heard his father use that adjective, and he remembered distinctly when he used it. It was the day he got a letter from Rosie Magee. He could still hear the stove lid slam when his father's anger rose.

Both father and son prepared for bed. Neither spoke another word. Long after Bennet was snoring, Joseph was on his knees beside the bed, his face buried in both hands. He felt no guilt of conscience, but the longer he prayed, the more calm and unperturbed became his spirits. It was an unparalleled quietness of heart that even his father's snoring did not disturb.

*   *   *

Bennet Armstrong came to the breakfast table carefully shaved. His shoes had been dusted, every speck of lint had been picked off his handsome blue serge suit, and the part in his thick black hair was without a hair's mistake. He smiled and shook hands with Katy Bantum and Girtie Maples, and made a few pleasant remarks about the fairness of the morning. He ate heartily of Katy's pancakes and sausage, and even laughed several times when the conversation afforded such a reaction. In fact, had it not been that Katy had heard with her own ears the entire conversation in the living room the night before, and louder, crosser talk in the room overhead, she would have concluded this was not the same man that had knocked at their door.

"Oh, Sol!" Katy had cried, "what on earth is going on up there? He's angry with Joseph—just listen."

"He's got no reason to be angry so far as I can see," whispered Sol.

"I have half a notion to go to the stair door and listen."

"You'd better not," Sol said. "Joseph may tell you all you want to know."

"And he may not," answered Katy. "Poor boy. I told you once," she whispered softly, "that I figured he's had a hard row because of a few little remarks he's made. I wonder what's wrong. Just listen, Sol!"

And neither Katy Bantum nor Sol fell asleep that night until all was quiet upstairs.

An orange crate can be overlaid with gold or ivory and make quite a magnificent piece of furniture but it is still an orange crate. Joseph could not but think at the breakfast table (glad as he was that his father could appear so pleasant in front of the Bantums and Girtie) what Delores had said about sincerity on the way to church the evening before. The veneer of courtesy and geniality which Bennet put on seemed to Joseph so thin and ornamental that the glaze was almost nauseous. He ate very little, and his face remained serious and thoughtful.

"You must eat, Joseph," Katy said, anxiously eyeing him with a motherly concern.

"Thanks, I'm eating," came Joseph's grateful answer.

"A little more water, please, Pet," said Bennet softly, lifting his tumbler and winking at Girtie, who was sitting around the corner at his left.

Girtie almost jumped, and hurried to get the water pitcher. She spilled a little on the man's coat sleeve.

"That's all right, that's all right," he chuckled, wiping it off with his napkin.

"I'm sorry," Girtie said, blushing a deep red.

"If you never do anything worse than that, you'll be all right, Pe—" He caught himself. Joseph was looking him straight in the eyes across the table. Bennet put his napkin over his mouth and coughed almost convulsively. He took a drink and wiped his forehead. When Bennet raised his eyelids, Joseph was still looking at him across the table.

"Would you care for another cup of coffee, Mr. Armstrong?" asked Katy. "That might help your cough."

"Maybe it will," smiled Bennet.

They walked to the vineyard, father and son. They walked swiftly and without conversation. The warm sun brought the perspiration out on their faces, but only the father wiped his frequently, and oftener than necessary. They walked between the first two rows and back through the center. Joseph led the way, lingering now and then to answer a question the older man would ask. He could see that his father was well pleased, although no such remarks escaped his stern lips. Occasionally Joseph could hear him give a certain guttural sound which meant gratification over something. Joseph remembered that sound from his earliest childhood, for his father had always made it when he saw money ahead—always.

"Hi, there, Armstrong."

A man on a handsome black horse made a sudden appearance on top of a near-by knoll.

"Hi," waved Bennet, answering the call. "Just the man I wanted to see. Come on ever."

The Squire came, fumbling at his historic gold watch chain.

"Bantum called me up and said you were out here, so I thought I'd trot over, as I go out for a little ride every morning anyway."

"Good," shouted Bennet, slapping the Squire on the shoulder. "How do you think the vineyard looks?"

"Looks like money to me," answered the Squire. "I can't remember such a crop since the second year I put Fonzo to it. He sure had a magic touch with fruits, it seemed. Never saw the like. I suppose he told you about his death?"

"Whose death?" asked Bennet.

"Fonzo's," answered Squire McCracken. "I buried the best man I ever had, and I'd like to meet the rascal that ever started that report that he'd go nab children whenever they were bad."

Bennet wiped his warm face, his neck, and his forehead. He cleared his throat and spit on the ground. "Huh," he said clearing his throat again and looking at the clusters of grapes nearest him. "Seems to me I heard that once, too—but— Look out there, Joseph!" he yelled. "There's a snake!"

CHAPTER XLI

Joseph stepped back. A full-grown rattlesnake had his grooved fangs ready to puncture Joseph's ankle and inject his poisonous fluid. He did not scream nor act overly excited, but picking up a large flat stone, he threw it squarely, crushing the serpent's head. He put his weight on the stone to make sure his efforts were accomplished.

"Pretty good shot," said the Squire. "Pretty smart boy you've got," he added, turning to Bennet. "I wouldn't be surprised if he has done as good in this vineyard as you could have done yourself."

Bennet smiled feebly, meekly, intricately, as through a maze or confusion of thoughts, then suddenly he pulled out his watch and looked at it.

"I'd better be going," he said, "if I'm to catch that noon train. I want to stop at the Produce Company. What time have you got there, Mr. McCracken?" Bennet wound his watch. He tried to hide the fact that he was a bit uneasy.

"I've got 9:45," answered the Squire.

"You'll show Joseph how to pick the fruit for market, and when?"

"Oh, sure," assured the Squire warmly. "All Joseph needs to do is to ask what he wants to know. We're pretty good friends."

"I'll have to be going," Bennet said next. "I want to stop at the house and settle with the Bantums for your room and board, Joseph. I'll write to you about shipments, or I may drop back in about thirty days. From now on every move counts." He talked as he walked backwards.

"He's all business, that Dad of yours, isn't he?" asked the Squire after Bennet was gone.

"He puts it before anything else," answered Joseph, and the Squire thought he detected a grieved tone in the young man's voice. He looked at him intently for a moment.

"Well," spoke the Squire, twisting his watch chain again, "if your father isn't satisfied, let him try his hand at it, or get someone else, and I'll hire you to work for me."

Joseph smiled, and the smile lit up his whole face. He stepped on the stone again.

"I wouldn't mind working for you," he answered, looking up.

"I'll go home and mark that down in my book."

After the Squire left, Joseph caught himself humming a little as he worked. One tune ran into another until he was singing snatches of "When I Survey the Wondrous Cross." The July sun was hot, and as it beat down upon him, it gave him new energy. For a while, the night before, he had felt heavy and weak and sick, but now his hands were steady again and he felt a new endurance that would give him the power and grace to suffer anything without breaking—if only Delores would understand and give him a chance to prove to her he was sincere. He hoped she would not find out his father had called on him. To be sure he would not tell her the unkind things he had said.

After calling Herbert Lanyard on the telephone, Joseph wrote a letter. He wrote as fast as he could.

"Dear Mother—

"There is nothing else for me to do but write this. This is meant *only* for you, but if Father reads it he'll just have to. He was here to see me last night—was waiting here when I got home from spending a pleasant evening with Delores. He was very angry with me and tried to make me promise I'd never have another date with her. He said he wants me to go with some western girl whose father has money. Money seems to be the main thing that counts with him. Mother, I think an awful lot of Delores. I think more of her each time I am with her. She's gold herself, even if her parents aren't what Father would call rich. I've prayed lots about this, and I feel sure God has led us together. If I'm wrong, I'm willing to be shown, but it will take more than Father's unkind remarks to change my mind.

"He tried to make me feel I'm disobedient when I refused to promise him. I couldn't do it and be honest with myself or God. If the Bays are so good-for-nothing, why is Father the only person who sees it? I'm invited to their house for supper Wednesday. They treat me nice. I wish I could tell you what a sweet girl I think Delores is. I am not hypnotized as Father accused me of being. I have not lost my head either. I'm as old as he was when you were married, am I not? Mama, if you write and tell me I'm not to have another date with Delores, and you can give me a good reason, I'll listen to you. Please answer at once.

"In case you are out of stamps, I'm enclosing one for an immediate reply. Katy Bantum gave me several. I'd give anything to talk to you a while. I know you've been praying for me, and I know I can depend on your answer. I couldn't bear to go against your wishes in this. Mama, if you could only see her and know her, you would surely love her.

"Maybe this is a risky thing to do to write like this, but I've just got to. Father left this noon. I can hardly quit writing, but I guess I'd better. I'm going to work for Sol until dark tonight because he's going to go over the vineyard for me Friday and Saturday, as I'm going on a trip across the mountains with Herbert Lanyard. He's got three preaching appointments in a mining town near Asterlow.

"Write soon, Mama—Mother, which shall I call you since I'm older? I think 'Mama,' but I write 'Mother' sometimes. When I get home on Monday I hope there's a letter here from you. I'll be back Monday evening, I hope.

"In love,
"Joseph."

There was something comfortable about the Bays home. It wasn't because they had an expensive dining-room suite, for the table and chairs did not match exactly, and the china closet didn't either. The rug on the floor in the dining room was a little worn in spots, especially in front of the sideboard, but it was still a beautiful rug and soft to walk on. Joseph couldn't tell just exactly why there swept over him such a friendly, cozy feeling whenever he stepped into this house, unless it was because Delores lived there. It was the same sort of feeling that possessed him whenever he went to Freddie's house, only it was more evident at Bays the Wednesday evening he went there for supper.

Houses have smells. Certain definite, peculiar, distinctive smells. It always smelled the same at Freddie's house. It always had, and it still smelled the same when he came back several years later. Joseph could have told it was Uncle Timothy's house had he been blindfolded. It was a pleasing, comforting, characteristic odor—not exactly fragrant—not like perfume or spices; not like vinegar or boiling meat; not like soap or new wallpaper; but a mixture of something no one could analyze—a clean smell that reminded him of that starchy scent on his mother's Sunday apron, and it made him feel comfortable and happy.

The Bays home had even a more delightful, friendly odor that gave him a cozy, easy sensation. It made him feel like sitting down and staying there a while. It made him confident that whatever was served would be good to eat. It gave him that "at home" feeling. The way the furniture was placed, the tailored curtains, the mantel clock, the hooked rugs, the pictures on the walls, the bowl of goldfish, the snowy linen tablecloth with the blue border, and the two armchairs, all lent a homelike atmosphere. And then Delores lived there. These were the rugs she walked on and swept. These curtained windows were the ones she looked through. Perhaps she had ironed that tablecloth, and wound the clock with her hands. Maybe those were her goldfish. There was something there that looked and felt and smelled just right. Joseph was conscious of it, but he couldn't have explained it had he tried. It made him happy.

The supper was delicious. It tasted like Katy Bantum's, only better. The old-time philosopher who started the saying that "love is blind," and the other one who added "also deaf and dumb," have had many to comment on their statements. Those who have been disappointed in love think the adage very wise, but those in love usually pass it over with a smile of disagreement. Wise or unwise, Joseph Armstrong did not imagine he felt comfortable and at home under Jeddie Bays's roof, nor was he under a false notion. Joseph was a man capable of acquiring a true conception of things. He observed, he listened, he felt, he sensed here a true Christian home that measured up to his ideal. Jeddie was kind and thoughtful to his children and to his wife. He spoke to them all with true affection. It touched Joseph deeply. Once Jeddie stooped over and straightened out a rug one of the boys had tripped on. Joseph had never seen his father do that. Mrs. Bays, whom Jeddie addressed as "Mother," had a look of perfect contentment on her bright face. She was neither plump nor thin, and just tall enough to come to Jeddie's shoulder. He called her Mary with great tenderness several times.

The heat of the day had been lifted by a pleasant evening breeze, and there wasn't one thing that marred the close of the day. Only once Delores caught Joseph dreaming. He stood with his croquet mallet over his shoulder.

"It's your turn, Joseph," she called across the lawn.

"Pardon," Joseph answered. Jeddie had made a remark that sent Joseph's brain whirling.

"You know," Jeddie had said, "isn't it funny how you see faces that remind you of someone you know. I saw a man in town this forenoon in front of Hendrick's Produce Company that looked enough like your father to be his twin brother."

"My father?" Joseph asked. Something like a shock went through his body. He twitched.

"I know it wasn't him," added Jeddie, taking his turn. "Now look at that, would you! Come on, Mother, see if you can beat me. Don't worry about those dishes; I'll wipe them for you this once."

"Once?" laughed Mary Bays. "Now Jeddie, that sounds like you've never done it before."

After the game of croquet they all sat on the porch a while and talked; then Delores showed Joseph the gardens. There was the flower garden beside the house, the strawberry patch, and the vegetable garden. An old lawn swing under the cherry tree needed a coat of paint badly, but it was still stout enough to hold two or more, and the two sat there watching the purple shadows deepen into black. They talked and laughed and talked.

"Mother," called Delores.

Her mother answered from the open kitchen window.

"Please let the dishes go. I'll do them in the morning."

"I've got good help," came her mother's pleasant answer. "We'll let you off this time."

"You won't mind sitting in the kitchen, will you?" Delores stood beside Joseph and the breeze blew the soft folds of her pink dress against the swing where his hand was resting.

"Mind?" Joseph's smile was warm and sincere. His face beamed. "No, indeed! I like to sit in kitchens."

"Then come, let's go in; I want to help. And then I hope we can sing a few songs before you go. Mother and Father both sing well. Don't let on that I've told you, Joseph; they both have beautiful voices, but they're timid about it. If anyone says a word, they act worse than children. Since you are here maybe Albert and George will come in and help too. They think you're quite—" She stopped abruptly.

"Quite terrible for coming so often?"

"Oh, no, Joseph, that isn't what I was going to say."

"What then?" They were at the kitchen door.

"I'll tell you next time," she answered softly.

CHAPTER XLII

From his earliest childhood, Joseph had wondered what it was like on the other side of those mountains. That long, jagged stretch of rocks and trees against the western horizon seemed to divide his world from another beyond. Often he had looked at them and imagined crossing over, but never did he dream his first trip across would be with a young minister, and in a two-seated surrey drawn by four horses. Before the sun was up, the two had been on their way for over an hour.

"It's going to be a real pull," Herbert said.

"I believe it's going to be as steep as it appears to be from below," answered Joseph looking back. "You can't imagine how I've wanted to cross these mountains."

"The first time I crossed over was in the month of April when I was a boy about fifteen. I went with my father to get a load of coal. It took us two days to come back. The horses got awful tired, and we ran out of food and water before we got home. The road has been improved considerably since then."

"Have you been to Asterlow before?"

"Twice. I was there the first Sunday in May and the first Sunday in June. It's an open field, and I like to go. Those folks seem hungry for the Gospel. Some are Hungarians, some Polish, and some Bohemians."

"Do they know you are coming?"

"Oh, yes, I wrote to one of the foremen I learned to know. I told him to announce that I'd speak tonight. He urged me to come back both times I was there. I wish I could go every week end, but I can't. It's too far. You know what I hope?"

"What?"

"I hope I live to see the day when automobiles will be common enough that I can have one. Then I could go and take my family. Just think," said Herbert Lanyard, "how soon we could get there at twenty-five miles an hour, or even twenty. It will take us all day with the team. It'll be upgrade till after twelve at least."

"Where there is no vision the people perish," and this young minister had visions of a greater work to be done. Small visions have no inducement to stir men's blood. High aims, noble plans, and big visions may not be realized by those who are inspired, but are often carried on, and grow, and become real after the one who instigated them has died.

All day long they drove, stopping several times to water the horses and let them rest.

"You're a man of God," said Joseph earnestly, toward the middle of the afternoon, "and since we've been talking about the church, I'd be interested in knowing how God called you to the ministry."

"Well," began Herbert Lanyard, "from my earliest recollections I heard the Bible read in the home. My father had family worship until the day he took sick. I was seventeen then and the oldest. Father asked Mother to gather the family in the bedroom and read, and she did, and she led in prayer. Father died that week; died of pneumonia fever, and mother was so broken up she asked me to take the lead. I couldn't have done it, but I pitied Mother so. She had a lot on her with seven younger than myself, and I knew she depended on me. I couldn't refuse her. Mother had made a wonderful impression on me when I was a small boy. She nearly died one night."

Joseph sat up straight and held his breath.

"She called me to her bedside, and put her hand on my head and said, 'Herbert—my boy, I'm afraid my end is near. You are young, but I must tell you before I leave, that you are a child—an answer to prayer. God has called

you to serve Him. I have known it since the day you
were born, so be true, Herbert. Never say, no, to God.
Do whatever He asks of you. Be obedient to your
Father.' "

Joseph felt prickly all over. Goose pimples covered
his body. "Did—did she die?" Joseph asked.

"No, she got well. She was sick several weeks, but
when she told me that, I knelt beside her bed and prayed.
I can remember yet what I said. I was only five, but I
know God heard my prayers. And that night when I was
on my knees, I believe I heard my first call from God."

"You mean—?"

"I mean I felt a consciousness that God touched me
with His own hand. I've never been able to get away
from that experience. I tried to, but I couldn't. It was
real to me."

"You never told anyone?"

"What do you mean, Joseph?"

"Did you ever tell anyone you felt God called you, or
—or touched you?"

"Never. Never. I kept it to myself. It followed me
when I went to school, and when I worked in the field.
It followed me everywhere. Mother got well, and every
now and then she'd say something that made me know
she felt I would some day be in special service, but I never
came right out and told her how I felt until after I was
ordained. I told her then. Father died when I was
seventeen, as I said; I wanted to go away to academy—
then I couldn't. Then Brother Grissley suggested I take
correspondence work until the way would open for me to
go to school."

"And you did?"

"Yes, I took two years of academy work by correspondence. It took lots of time, but I did it. I felt all
the time God was helping me."

"Then," Joseph cleared his throat and he looked Herbert Lanyard square in the face, "then you don't think an education gives a person a straight ticket to hell?"

"To hell?"

"Yes—that's what—what I heard someone say once."

"Who said that?"

"I—I wouldn't want to say who it was—but—"

"It all depends on what a person wants to get an education for, Joseph. In some cases maybe an education has led persons away from God. Certainly that has been true in some cases, but to desire knowledge to be able to serve God better certainly can't be wrong. Every young man who feels the call of God should get all the education he can, if he can do it honestly and use it to the glory of God. I'm sure Brother Grissley Steward himself would say that, though he's never had more than the eighth grade. He's a man who has read a great deal. You have never seen his library?"

"No, I haven't."

"He's loaned me some of his books often."

"You only had two years of academy work then?"

"That's all, Joseph. I wish I had more. I went to a winter Bible school twice. Different preachers have helped me choose the right kind of books to study at home. There is no end to learning. The more I study, the more I realize I have much yet to learn. I'm only beginning."

"And you have been preaching—?"

"Only a little over three years, Joseph. I've got lots to learn."

"Did you ever fight conviction? I mean, did you ever try to make yourself believe it was just notion and not of God?" asked Joseph.

"Did I, you say? Yes, more than once, Joseph, but I couldn't shake it off. It was always there. I tried once to—oh, I won't say what, but it followed me even there."

"And you never told anyone?" Joseph nipped off a weed as they drove along and broke it into bits.

"Never. That would have spoiled the sacredness of it if I had. Why should I have told it? God knew, and that was enough. Brother Grissley said once that when men must inform others that they are called of God, it makes him doubt whether it really was God who did the calling. No, Joseph, I never told a living soul. You folks moved away before the voice of the church was taken. There were three of us in the lot. My mother lived just long enough for me to tell her that experience."

A sudden lump came up in Joseph's throat. He looked out over the great valley below, and quickly he brushed away a tear that blinded him. Why was Herbert Lanyard telling him all this? His heart burned within him as they drove on down the mountainside. As they talked, Joseph added another name to his list of men of God who had impressed him for good. He felt that here was a friend he could regard as a confidant.

"Do you know Jeddie Bays?" Joseph asked after they had driven another hour.

"Of course I know Jeddie. Why?"

"I've had two—dates—with his daughter, Delores." Joseph breathed faster. His face got warm.

"So I heard."

"You did?" Joseph turned and looked him full in the face.

"Yes, news like that travels pretty fast." Herbert Lanyard chuckled a little.

"What do you think of it?"

Joseph had been wanting to ask Herbert Lanyard this question all afternoon. At last it was out. He held his breath and waited. His heart pounded within him.

"Well, you wouldn't know it, I don't suppose," answered Herbert slowly, "unless I told you that that's one of the reasons why Brother Grissley suggested you to go with me today."

"What?" asked Joseph. He sat on the edge of the seat. "What do you mean?"

"Well, I mean this, Joseph," came the man's kind answer. "Brother Grissley said to me, 'I hear Joseph Armstrong is going with Delores Bays. If that's the sort of girl he's interested in, it means something to me.'"

"What did he mean?" Joseph asked the second time. Herbert Lanyard smiled.

"He meant a young man is known by the kind of company he keeps. So evidently Brother Grissley is pleased. If he is, it must be quite all right."

Joseph drew a long, deep breath and sat back in the buggy seat, and that same quietness he had felt as he knelt beside his bed late Sunday night possessed him again, soul and body. It made him tingle with joy.

*   *   *

The school building was unlocked when they got there. They ate the last of the lunch that Herbert's wife had packed in a large shoe box, and they drank water from the old iron pump in the schoolyard. Though brown with rust, it satisfied their terrible thirst.

The people gathered in early; men, women, and children, simply clad; children barefooted, men in overalls, and women in colorful cottons. Eager-faced and wide-eyed they came, singly and in groups.

"You're going to lead the singing, Joseph," said Herbert Lanyard, looking at his watch. "It's almost time to begin."

"But I never led singing in my life."

"Then you can begin tonight."

"But I can't," whispered Joseph.

"Yes, you can," answered Herbert. "I brought you along to help me. I can't take no for an answer now. That's right, I forgot to bring in the songbooks. They're under the back seat of the surrey. Will you bring them in?"

CHAPTER XLIII

There was nothing for Joseph to do but to get those songbooks. He brought them in and distributed them among the people. He wondered how many of the people would be able to read if they did have books. Only one refused, and that was an elderly woman. She shook her head when Joseph came near. He held out a book.

"Ken no—ken no," she said. Joseph felt like running away and hiding. How could he possibly do the thing Brother Lanyard asked of him? He had come along for company, not to assist in the meeting. Not that!"

"Let's turn to number sixty-three," said Brother Lanyard. "It's time to begin our meeting, and I'm sure we're going to have a good time together here in the name of the Lord. I brought Joseph Armstrong along with me, and he will lead the singing for us."

What could Joseph do but get up? He faced the audience. He looked at the song. He held his breath. He felt his heart pounding violently. He breathed a silent prayer, then opened his mouth; to his surprise music came from his lips. He had the right key. Voices took up the strain, and by the time he had finished the first verse, though many were off the pitch and a step or two behind, he felt quite confident he could start the second. Joseph Armstrong was leading the singing! But little did he think that two women were praying for him at that very hour; one in a little house out on the western prairie, and the other in her bedroom in Jeddie Bays's house. The congregation of eager-faced foreigners sang, not out of personal experience, but with wonder, strange longing, and childlike astonishment, mingled with excitement. Joseph was leading the singing and enjoying it.

While Brother Lanyard preached, the people sat spellbound. Sometimes heads nodded in agreement, again deep sighs were heard. One man in particular sat with his mouth open, and each time a new truth dawned upon him, he'd make a funny little grunt. At the close of the service several men came forward and confessed their sins.

"Where will we spend the night?" asked Joseph.

"Right here in the schoolhouse," answered Herbert Lanyard.

"Mr. Zeitgi will drive our horses home and take care of them for us, and he has invited us to his house for breakfast. These people are very friendly, as you will soon learn. I hope you won't be sorry you came along, Joseph."

"I'm not sorry yet," came the answer. "I am very glad I came along."

"Even if you had to lead the singing," Brother Lanyard smiled.

All day Saturday Joseph accompanied the young minister as he called from house to house in the village, inviting people to the services, sometimes reading a short portion of Scripture, sometimes offering a prayer. It was all a new experience to him, but interesting and wonderfully enlightening. In three days with Herbert Lanyard, Joseph increased more in Bible knowledge than he had in several years going to Sunday school. That desire for more education had never left him, and now it took fresh hold of him.

During the meeting on Sunday night sudden lightning flashed. It flashed again and again, followed by sharp claps of thunder. Brother Lanyard walked to the door and looked out. With a seriousness on his face, he made a few remarks and closed the service.

He told the people to go home without delay.

Lightning zipped like fiery bullets.

"Let's strike for home tonight yet," he said to Joseph. "I don't like the looks of the sky. If this storm that's coming keeps up all night, it may rain all day tomorrow too. We'd better go, Joseph. If those mountain roads get soaked they'll get bad, or there could be a landslide at several places."

"You know best," answered Joseph. "I'm ready to go whenever you say."

"Then let's go at once."

They started toward the mountains with lightning flashing all around them.

"Maybe we can get out of it yet, or the worst of it," Brother Lanyard said. "Come on, Pete, come Doc, step up a little." He used the whip. Great drops of rain fell. Lightning flashed, thunder cracked and rolled.

By midnight they were nearing the top of the mountain and the worst of the storm was behind them. It was pitch dark. Only now and then the sky lit up with a sudden blinding flash. It seemed the whole mountain trembled. Then again they were in darkness. It was so dark they could not see the horses in front of them.

"Joseph," said Herbert. His voice was throaty.

"Yes."

"You're not asleep, are you?"

"No, indeed."

"Awful dark."

"Awful dark," answered Joseph.

"Joseph," he repeated.

"Yes."

"There's danger ahead. I feel it. Don't you, Joseph?"

"I feel it, yes."

"What shall we do?"

"We can't turn around and go back," Joseph whispered.

"No, of course not. It's almost straight down at this place if I know where we are. Narrow road."

Herbert Lanyard sat tense and straight. He gripped the lines tightly. He bent forward, but strain as he would, he could not see the horses. They drove on in silence for an hour. The darkness grew thicker—denser.

"Careful, Doc—Pete, watch your step! Don't you fall asleep, Joseph."

"I won't. Never saw such darkness. Don't worry, I won't sleep. I'm glad you're not alone."

"So am I, Joseph."

They reached the crest of the mountain at last. Each breathed a sigh of relief.

"I wonder what made us feel that way," asked Herbert.

"I wonder too," came Joseph's solemn reply.

"Will you drive a while, Joseph? I'm sorta tired and a little unstrung."

"Yes, I'll drive." Joseph took the lines.

"You'll have to hold them back a little now. It's down hill you know. Easy now, Doc. Easy, Pete. Not quite so fast."

In silence they drove on. Only now and then a word was spoken. They could hear the rain behind them, pelting, pouring as in a torrent from the heavens. Occasionally the entire mountain was lit up with sheet lightning; only for an instant, then it was pitch dark again. Herbert pulled out his watch and waited for another glare.

"It's two-thirty," he said. He put his watch back into his pocket. "Would you care if I'd snatch a little nap now?"

"Brother Lanyard," Joseph replied, "wait—just a little. That feeling hasn't left me yet. There's danger ahead," his voice was strained and breathy. "Don't you feel it?"

"Well—yes—or maybe I'm not quite over my former feeling. I won't sleep if you'd rather I wouldn't. You know these three days have been quite a drag on me. If anyone thinks it's an easy life to be a preacher, let him try it once. In a way it's harder work to talk to people about their souls than to plow corn. I really feel tired."

"O God," breathed Joseph. He caught his breath and held it. "God," he prayed silently. In the dark his lips moved slightly. "Prove Yourself—to me—tonight—Lord—if Delores is—the one—You'd have me—to love—" Every nerve in his body was tense.

Halfway down the mountain Joseph spoke again. "Something's wrong," he whispered. He touched the other on the shoulder.

"I know it. What is it?" Herbert Lanyard sat up straight. He leaned forward.

"I don't know. The wheels are all on good, aren't they?"

"Oh, yes. Maybe there's been a landslide ahead."

"I'm cold all over. There's danger ahead. I—I feel it."

"Let's pray, Joseph."

"I have been all evening. I never felt like this."

No sooner had he spoken the words than the two horses ahead shied suddenly to the left. Joseph got to his feet. His heart stopped. Out of the dense bushes to the right, something white appeared. A flash of lightning revealed the figure of a large, black-haired man. He had on a white shirt. He leaped upward and tried desperately to stop the leading horse. Joseph grabbed the whip, and, bending forward, he lashed that horse as hard as he could. He shouted at the top of his voice. The horses reared up on their hind legs, then ran furiously, snorting, down grade for half a mile before Joseph could check them.

"My," said Herbert Lanyard, "that was a close call."

"God surely was with us," Joseph said, drawing a deep breath.

"He wouldn't have gotten much off of me. I doubt if I have ten dollars in my pocket."

"I haven't a cent on me," answered Joseph. His breath came in bunches.

"He might have knocked us out and taken our horses. This is the first time I've tried to cross the mountains after night. Maybe we should have waited till morning."

"Surely God was with us," repeated Joseph, and as he said it another flash from the heavens lit up all the earth around them.

"He sees us even in the dark," he whispered to himself, and from that hour, on that memorable night, Joseph did not question or doubt God's leading him in his love for Delores Bays.

*   *   *

He knew the answer before he opened his mother's letter that evening.

"My dear son Joseph,

"Father was out on range when the mail came today. He said very little about his visit with you, but gave me to understand he was wrought up terribly over your interest in Delores Bays. He says he will stop it one way or another, and I believe he will try it. You know Father when he sets his mind. Joseph, if you have prayed about this, I would not for a minute think of asking you to quit Delores. I believe it that she is a fine Christian girl. 'Children, obey your parents in the Lord,' and I believe you are doing that. God bless you, and God bless Delores. I hope some day soon Father will see his mistake. I am greatly interested in your trip to Asterlow. I'll have Virginia mail this on her way to school. Don't worry, the letter reached me in safety and was soon put into the flames. Whatever comes, Joseph, be true to God, and remember God never takes His eyes off His children. And, as I have often told you, we may have some very dark experiences in life, but God will be with us even in the dark, and His light shines through the darkness, for He Himself is light.

"Lovingly,

"Mother.

"P.S. Call me *Mama* or *Mother,* I don't care which."

*　　*　　*

"Annie," said Bennet the next evening, "Mr. Carl Hendricks from the Produce Company may come one day this week to look over the ranch and talk business. We may make a trade or a deal of some sort. In case it goes through we'll go back—"

"Go back east again?" Annie's mouth dropped.

"Yes, that's what I mean."

CHAPTER XLIV

"You're going to tell me all about your trip," said Delores on the way to church Sunday evening. Her face glowed, and she spoke in the tenderest voice, sweetly. Her hands lay on the soft folds of her peach-colored dimity dress, and she looked up at him trustingly.

Joseph's heart beat rapidly. The happiness he felt was almost ecstasy. It surpassed any joy he had ever known, for now he knew she was the one he loved and was to love. She was his God-planned one. The secret in his soul was too wonderful to be true. Of course he would tell her all about his trip to Asterlow, but how could he, and leave out the conversation with Herbert Lanyard, his prayer, and the answer to it? Should he tell her that? Would she understand? The words in his throat were too great for his tongue to express. He yearned to tell her all—yes, even what Brother Grissley Steward had said about her —and yet it seemed so unbelievable, so impossible, so much like a beautiful dream! Could it be true? Would he dare tell her? How beautiful, how pure, and dainty she looked tonight! How wonderful it was to have her beside him in the buggy! Yes, it was Sol Bantum's buggy, but maybe someday he would have one of his own. That would be glorious. There are no hopes too high, no dreams too holy for those in whom God dwells, and Joseph felt that indwelling Presence.

"It was a wonderful trip to me from the time we left until we got home," he said.

"Tell me, Joseph. I can hardly wait." Again she looked up at him with those hopeful, trusting eyes.

Joseph talked, and Delores listened. Breathlessly she listened when he related the homeward journey over the mountains. Several times he almost told her the contents of his prayer, and yet he kept it to himself—the best part.

"Oh, Joseph," she cried, and both hands went to her throat. "Oh, maybe the man was Jesse James! Do you suppose?" Her face spoke horror.

"Maybe so, but I doubt," he answered thoughtfully. "At least I won't forget that experience as long as I live."

"Of course you won't," came her soft answer, and she wanted to tell him she had prayed for him several times each day while he was gone, and yet she didn't. She kept it to herself.

No, Joseph would never forget, and as long as he lived he'd know with deep assurance that God used a storm, a mountain robber, and a flash of lightning in the darkness of night to reveal His will to him about this girl at his side. He wanted to tell her, and yet at his happiest moments with Delores there would flash across his mind those words in his mother's last letter, "He will try to stop it one way or another." Should he tell her about his father's attitude? He would have to tell her someday. Every time he entered his room now, he saw again his father's stern face and heard his harsh voice. It reminded him of that distant threatening thunder in the mountains. Just two weeks ago tonight his father was waiting for him when he got home. Would that happen again? He had said he might be back in thirty days. But why worry about that now? Delores looked so happy and dear. She was smiling and talking to him all the way, and she would soon be sitting beside him again in church. Mrs. Irons had said they were an ideal couple, and Brother Grissley, the senior bishop, approved of the romance, so why let Father's attitude spoil the evening?

There sat Freddie with Lillian Bond. He had told Joseph that morning he had a date with Lillian. More than once when they were alone Joseph had a notion to tell Freddie about his father's visit. But each time he was about to—he decided not to—hoping—hoping that before his father came again he would change his mind.

"Delores," said Joseph after they had finished eating the pumpkin pie with whipped cream she served after church, "I can't tell you how delicious this was. It was nice of you, and I can't tell you what a pleasure it has been to me to take you to church again tonight. It seems each time we're together I enjoy your company more."

"Well," she answered taking the plate, "I—I—believe I feel the same way about you, Joseph."

Her eyes shone in the light of the Aladdin lamp like two evening stars, and her cheeks glowed a deep rosy pink with the fresh bloom of womanhood. He had seen that same bloom before, but tonight she was more strikingly beautiful than ever. Oh, if his father could only see her once. Surely he would never again mention the fact that her father was a man of only ordinary means. What amount of land or gold could compare to that open, pure, joyous look on her fair, sweet face? Delores Bays had something that money could not buy, and Joseph knew that he loved her and that something that belonged to her. Over and over in his mind he confessed it. He wanted to tell her. It was like a warm fire now that nothing could put out or smother.

"And then," he said in a deep, rich voice, "you'll let me come back again next Sunday evening?"

"You may." She smiled sincerely.

"I wish the Sundays weren't so far apart," he said, still looking into those deep, shining eyes.

"So do I," she said softly.

"Good night, Delores—dear."

*　　　*　　　*

When J. Bennet Armstrong decided he would exchange his ranch for more stock in the Hendrick's Produce Company and see to it that he'd break up this silly love afair, he meant what he said. He meant both. He would not lose any money in the trade, and he would be where he could control that disobedient boy of his. Maybe Joseph didn't think he meant what he said this time, but he'd show him. Maybe Joseph was almost of age, but he'd fix that. There was more than one way to stop this thing. He clothed his fatherly concern for his son with a religious garb he called duty.

Annie held her peace. Any number of words she might have spoken would have been in vain—that she well knew. She was secretly glad about the trade—but the other! Annie held her peace and pondered much in her heart. Lowell and Virginia were ready and glad to go back where their cousins lived. Why wouldn't they be? It was like an answer to prayer. Little did they suspect what their father had in mind. With eagerness they helped with whatever they could to get ready for the trip. It was almost like getting ready to go to the "promised land" to think of seeing Agnes, and Maryanna, and Dennis, and Freddie again. Happy visions danced in their heads. Yes, even in Virginia's, though she was now sixteen. It did not seem like many days after Bennet's visit until another letter came from Annie.

Dear Joseph,

"Things have been happening fast here. Get ready for a surprise, for Father has traded the ranch for more stock in the Hendrick's Produce Co. He will be taking cattle to market the last of the week. Maybe two carloads. He'll be coming on through then, and you'll soon be seeing him. He's going to look for a small farm that he and Lowell can handle alone, and I'm not sure whether he expects you to take care of the vineyard another year or not. I can't tell you what he has in mind. He may be back to get us after he finds something, or he may stay,

and send for us. We don't know what his plans are. We
will just have to wait and see. It seems quite a while since
your last letter, but I understand. Take courage, my
boy, and be true to God whatever comes. Remember,
I'm with you in every right undertaking.

"Lovingly,
"Mother."

*   *   *

The grapes were maturing fast. They would soon be
ready to pick. Thousands and thousands of luscious full
clusters dazzled and glistened, some purple and some
like transparent gold in the morning dew.

"From now on every move counts," Bennet had said
the morning he left. Joseph had the letters in his shirt
pocket, the one from his mother, and one from his father.
They had arrived together, and he had put them with the
letter his mother had written about Delores. He had
carried this letter with him ever since its precious confidence had brought joy to his heart. He held the reins
in one hand, and with the other unfolded his father's
letter once more. There was no salutation of any kind,
not even his name without a "dear." It was more like a
telegram or night letter, short and to the point.

"Get a team and go to town for express in my name.
100 baskets and 200 boxes. Will be there Saturday."

"Father."

Joseph wasn't sure whether his father meant he should
go to town on Saturday, or that he himself would be coming then. In view of what his mother had written, Father
might be coming any time, and this was the end of the
week. This was Saturday morning and he was on his
way to town in Sol Bantum's spring wagon to get what
his father had ordered.

The sky predicted rain. The leaves on the poplar trees along the road rustled and curled wrong side cut, and the horse's mane shifted this way and that. Spirals of dust swept across the road in front of him, and in the distance, thunder rumbled. Joseph read the note once more, and, tearing it into tiny bits, he opened his hand, and let the wind whip them out of his sight. A peculiar quietness crept into the valley, and darkness, like a gray blanket, hung over the treetops. Joseph used the whip, but the rain beat him to town, and all he could do was wedge through it. He got soaked. The letters in his pocket stuck to his wet shirt, and when he drew them out, his name pulled out of place on the one on top and bits of it remained in his pocket—tiny inky spots that didn't matter on a work shirt. He patted the one letter with his handkerchief, the one he would never part with, folded it, and put it into his hip pocket in the dry. The last letter from his mother he read once more, then reluctantly tore it in pieces too and dropped them on the ground beside the wagon.

Before Joseph reached the depot, he could see that the express was there. Three stacks of baskets, and the wooden boxes were on the end of the platform, and in front of them stood a man with a lived-in opinion on his face, as set as the concrete foundation around the building behind him. An unpleasant sensation swept over Joseph.

"Nasty morning," he said before Joseph had time to alight.

"Pretty hard rain," answered Joseph.

"Might spoil the grapes," he added complainingly, viewing the sky.

"I hope not," Joseph answered.

"Well," blinked Bennet fretfully, "let's get busy and load these things. Every move counts from now on.

Why didn't you start out earlier? I've been waiting here over an hour."

"I couldn't have the wagon till Sol and I emptied it first. He had a load of—"

"Well," bellowed Bennet resonantly, not caring what Sol had in his wagon, "I told you every move counts from now on, rain or no rain."

"Every move counts," Joseph said to himself as he helped load boxes. "Yes, every move counts."

CHAPTER XLV

Occasionally fresh rain splashed, and silver beads dropped constantly off the edge of the roofs and trees. In his haste Joseph had the misfortune of ripping his his little finger on a nail on one of the wooden boxes. It wasn't bad, but he pulled his handkerchief out of his hip pocket to wipe the blood. As he did so, something white fell to the ground. Quick as a wink Bennet put out his foot and stepped on it, and while Joseph had his back turned he picked it up and stuck it in his own pocket—it was the letter in which Annie had reassured Joseph of her confidence in his choice of Delores.

"Too bad this isn't Sunday," Bennet said on the way home.

"Why Sunday?" asked Joseph.

"Sunday's the best time for it to rain," answered Bennet with perverseness in his voice. His eyes scanned the sky rebukingly.

It drizzled lazily all the way back to Bantum's. Dinner was ready, but Katy insisted Joseph should put on dry clothes before they sit down to eat.

"You might take your death of pneumonia," she said, "and we'll wait. And you look drenched too, Mr. Armstrong. Even if it is summer, you might take a cold."

Therefore both the Armstrongs put on dry clothes.

"Sol," said Katy while the two were upstairs. "If that man came here to abuse Joseph, I may let him know what I think of him." She bit her lip.

"Tut-tut, Katy," Sol said tapping her gently on the shoulder. "You stay clean out of it. Joseph is mighty near a man now, and I think he can handle himself without your help."

"Well, he never said his father was coming. If he knew it he should have told us. I'm not fixed."

"Put a little water in the soup. He won't know the difference."

"I'm not having soup, Sol, and I already cut the pie in four pieces."

"Well, give him my piece this time."

"Oh, Sol, you never get excited over anything. I have to do all the fretting and stewing. That man makes me nervous, and I can't help it."

"Calm down now, Katy," Sol said, stroking her on the arm affectionately. "He may only be here a day or so, and if it's longer, he'll make it right with us. By the time that vineyard is cleared, he'll have his pockets full."

*   *   *

"I suppose you came to help Joseph pick the grapes?" ventured Sol after the potato dish went around.

"I don't know yet," answered Bennet without looking at Sol. "I thought maybe I could hunt up Earnie Eloy, if he's in the neighborhood, and have him help. I have some other business to look after right away." He spread another piece of bread. He had spread one already. He sat for a moment like a glass of fizzing ginger ale, and a hissing noise escaped his stern, parted lips.

A brief silence followed. Bennet expected Joseph to ask something, but no question was asked. He lifted his thick eyebrows and took a drink.

"Do you happen to know where there's a small farm for sale around here?" he asked at length, looking at Joseph's plate but not at him. "Not too far from town?"

"A small farm?" Sol asked. "One for Joseph to live on?"

Sol Bantum asked the wrong question. He knew it before his words were dry. The effervescing within Bennet boiled over.

"For Joseph?" shouted Bennet Armstrong, and his voice puckered at the edges with sarcastic bitterness. "What makes you think I'd be hunting a farm for Joseph? He's not getting married."

The food in Joseph's throat stuck there. It would go neither up nor down. The hand that was about to lift his glass, dropped, and when he met his father's glance across the table, those blue eyes seemed to thrust a dagger into his heart. For a while a grim shadow seemed to hang over him. Delores had looked very sweet and beautiful Sunday night! He had called her "dear" very, very softly when he had said good night. Maybe she didn't hear it, but it had made him very happy to say it. For the first time in his life he had called a girl, "dear." Tomorrow night he had dreamed of saying it again a little louder. And now Father had come and cast another gray shadow over his dream. Oh, why did this have to be when he'd tried so hard all his life to do right? Over and over he had tried to find his way out of these depressing experiences, only to find himself again in the thick of another hideous cloud. It was not just a make-believe. It was not just an ugly dream out of which he could waken each morning, to bathe his face and meet the world untouched. No, those clouds were real. One day his heart was filled with dazzling sunshine, the next crushed and bleeding. Was it fate that dealt him so many heartaches? From the day he could remember, his mother had been mending those wounds, and now as he sat there at the table he couldn't think of any wound that had been inflicted by anyone but his father. He had been the cause of all his tears. He had been the object of all his dreads and panics.

"I want a small farm for myself," blared Bennet, and then he added in a softer voice after taking a long, deep breath, "We've lived on the ranch long enough, Mr.

Bantum. It's time to come back. I had too good an offer to let slip. I may enlarge the vineyard by another year. It all depends."

"Well, now, let's see," said Sol. "I heard Al Johnson has his place up for sale."

"Al Johnson?"

"Yes, and it might be just about what you'd want, too. It's north of four corners—"

"I know where it is," Bennet said. "I didn't suppose he'd ever sell that place."

"Well, I don't know the particulars," Sol said, "but I was told Al had a rich uncle that died, or maybe it was an aunt—anyhow some rich relative left him a nice sum, so he's going to retire and live in a modern house in town. That's what you heard, wasn't it, Katy?"

"Yes, that's what I heard. Take some of that pickle relish, Mr. Armstrong. Joseph, pass the bread again. They're having sale this afternoon."

"This afternoon?" Both Sol and Bennet spoke at once.

"It's to begin at one o'clock. Sol, you knew it; you just forgot."

"I'd like to go, wouldn't you, Katy?"

"No, I believe not. There's nothing I need unless it would be a good butcher knife, and I don't care to go and stand around all afternoon just for a knife, and then have to buy a bunch of stuff I don't want just to get it."

"It's clearing off," Bennet said, looking out the window.

"Want to go?" Sol asked.

"Sure I do! Joseph, you unload those baskets and boxes on the east side of the vineyard." He looked at his watch. "It's almost one already."

Bennet was quite elated when he came back from the sale. Joseph could tell before he spoke that he was exultant over something. He could tell it by the way he walked.

"Well, Katy—Al didn't have a hard time getting rid of his things," Sol said at the supper table. He said this for Joseph's benefit because he knew Joseph wondered, and he knew Bennet hadn't told him anything yet.

"Tell us about it," answered Katy. Curiosity curled on every corner of her plump face.

"Mr. Armstrong bought the place and most of what was left when we got there."

"Well!" Katy blinked and looked at Joseph. Most sons would have asked questions galore, but Joseph just sat there wide-eyed, staring at nothing. "Household goods too?"

"Yes," Sol said. "I guess you could pretty near start living there tomorrow, couldn't you, Mr. Armstrong?"

"I guess we could if the Johnsons were out. I told Al how it was, and he said things were fixed so he could vacate within a week. If I can get Earnie to help Joseph this next week, that is, if the grapes will be ready, I guess I'll go over there and take care of things. Al said I could have one room. The Mrs. and the children can come out without me, I guess. I haven't decided about that yet. I would like to be here when the fruit goes to market."

"But, Father," ventured Joseph. He could contain himself no longer, "how—how can Mama pack all by herself, and—?"

"Well, Joseph, you don't understand," Bennet said rather coldly. "The family has decided to fit themselves into my plans. Don't worry about that."

*   *   *

Joseph was hunting for it. He was sure he had folded it and put it in his right hip pocket before he got to town.

He looked on the floor in the closet where he stood when he changed his clothes. Again he looked in his pocket. Bennet eyed him with a mocking grin on his face.

"Hunting for something?" he said, sitting on the edge of the bed.

Joseph didn't answer. His eyes widened with apprehension, and it was as though the knuckles of a fresh disappointment were about to punch him another blow.

"Maybe this is what you want," and Bennet pulled the crumpled letter out of his pocket and dangled it tantalizingly before Joseph's eyes.

CHAPTER XLVI

Joseph's face got hot. Perspiration like tiny beads came out on his forehead. He took a step toward his father and held out his hand. He waited.

"Oh, no, you don't get it back," snapped Bennet angrily. "You and your mother. Huh! You didn't know you dropped it on the ground at the depot, did you?" He put it back into his pocket. Joseph's face got red now.

" 'Be sure your sins will find you out,' my boy. So your mother had Virginia mail this to her dear son. Well! I'd give a penny to read the one she burned. So you think your prayers are the sort God can hear? Huh! I've got a good notion to go straight to Brother Grissley with this. Your mother has always petted you, and it's time someone puts a stop to it."

Without saying a word Joseph turned and went downstairs. He bathed his face in cold water and took a drink. He walked out behind the barn and, falling on his knees beside an old tree stump, he buried his face in both hands. He did not cry, but now and then a stifled groan came from his lips. He stayed there until several stars appeared. When he went back to his room, his father was in bed, his face to the wall.

Long before breakfast Bennet was seen coming in from the direction of the vineyard.

"Now just what do you call that, Mr. Armstrong?" began Sol when Bennet stepped inside the door. "Luck, or Providence, or management, or—or what—that you came in here and picked up a farm right off the bat? Not many have done that."

A smile played around Bennet's firm lips, and stepping close to Sol, he said in an undertone, "Let me tell you something, Mr. Bantum. Where's Joseph?"

"He's outside somewhere, I think."

"Listen," and Bennet tapped Sol gently on the arm. "I wouldn't want Joseph to hear this, but—you can call it luck if you want to, but someone told my father once like this—'I've never seen it to fail yet that an Armstrong didn't get what he wanted!' Ha. You can call it luck if you want to."

Sol Bantum stepped back as though he had been struck. Somehow he didn't appreciate the remark nor the haughty smile on the man's face. Both seemed so utterly incongruous, so inconsistent, so out of place coming from the lips of one who professed to be a Christian. Sol Bantum had been as certain the man was going to attribute the finding of this farm to divine Providence, as he was that the day was Sunday. He was expecting to launch a conversation of a religious nature. Sol was stunned.

"Well," said Sol, scratching his head, "that's more than anyone ever said about the Bantums. We've all had to plan, and scratch, and figure, and work hard against reverses, and then seldom got what we wanted. I thought a Christian didn't believe in luck."

The screen door opened and Joseph stepped in. Bennet cleared his throat nervously. He rubbed his large Roman nose.

"Don't misunderstand me, Mr. Bantum," Bennet said apologetically. He put his hands in his pockets and walked back and forth in front of the fireplace. "I didn't say I called it luck. It's all in knowing how to make every move count."

Every move! Why was Father talking about that this morning? What was that he was telling Sol? Joseph had heard his father say that before recently. It gave him a sad, weary feeling. It almost bored him.

"You'll be going to church with me, won't you, Father?" he asked.

"Did you ever hear of me not going to church on Sunday?"

"No, Father, never." Joseph washed his hands. "I'm invited to Uncle Timothy's for dinner. You'll go too?"

"To Timothy Stokes?" Bennet stared at Joseph. *"I'm* not invited."

"They don't know you're here, Father. Surely they would ask you if they knew."

Bennet coughed.

"We'll talk about that on the way."

*   *   *

"Sol."

"Yes, Katy."

"It's ages since we've been to church."

"Ages?"

"Hasn't it been?"

"It's been quite a while, I guess. Why?"

"Oh, I was just thinking."

"Thinking what?"

"It doesn't seem right to stay at home and see Joseph go every Sunday."

"Why not? I don't care that he goes every Sunday."

"I don't care, either, Sol—but it makes me feel almost —like we're not living right. Maybe we ought to get started again once."

"Well, if every church member was as sincere as Joseph, I'd feel like going again too, but there's too many that aren't. I guess we live as near right as a lot of them that goes. Don't we, Katy?"

"Maybe so, Sol. I didn't mean we'd have to go back to that—church if you don't like it there."

"Where then?"

"Well, we could try Joseph's church once, couldn't we? Sometime?"

Sol Bantum stood at the kitchen door looking out over the back yard. It had been a long time since he and Katy had been in a church service. In fact, they had seldom gone since Jerry died. The minister unconsciously had said something in one of his sermons that Sol thought was meant for him. He wouldn't go back the next Sunday or the next. Katy got tired begging, and all her pleadings did not convince him that the offense was unintentional, nor could she persuade him that to stay at home on the Sabbath was the greater offense. This was the first and only time Sol Bantum had ever displayed an obstinate disposition. He had said, "I'm not going back there, Katy." He stuck to the statement even though he realized more than once afterward that it was said at a rash moment. Sol stood and twisted the hook on the screen door.

"Not if they're all like Joseph's father," he answered at length.

"And what if they're all like Joseph?" asked Katy.

"Then," said Sol, "I'd be interested. Who wouldn't be? But they're not."

*   *   *

Bennet didn't talk about it on the way to church. He didn't talk about anything. He asked Joseph for his quarterly and he studied the lesson. He certainly wouldn't go to Sunday school without being prepared to answer questions. Not J. Bennet Armstrong! He studied the lesson until they drove into the churchyard.

Everyone took for granted Bennet Armstrong would go to his nearest relatives' home for dinner, so no one else invited him, though many gave him a warm handshake.

He found himself sitting at the very table he vowed once he'd never sit at again. He was sitting next to

Timothy Stokes, his wife's brother, and Aunt Sara was addressing him thus:

"Uncle Bennet," she said in a gracious voice just like a pleasant memory. "I know you must be pleased over the romance."

"Romance?" choked Bennet. "What romance?"

"Why, Joseph's romance," Aunt Sara answered.

"Pleased, you say?" panted Bennet as though he had been running and had to stop to catch his breath.

"Everyone around here seems to think it's about the loveliest thing that's happened in a long time, and Joseph came back just about the right time too or he might not have fared so well."

"Fared so well? What do you mean?" Bennet dropped his fork.

"I mean there were other boys who were trying to get Delores Bays, and—"

"Well," came Bennet's icy reply, "I wish to goodness one of them would have."

The pause that followed was depressing. Aunt Sara saw the look that crossed Joseph's handsome face. It was almost pathetic. Uncle Timothy fumbled and scrambled for another topic on which to talk and finally started on cattle raising, and the meal was finished with a few dry remarks.

Immediately after dinner Bennet said he was going to take the horse and buggy and drive over to see Earnie Eloy.

"I'll be back here in time for us to go to church." This he said with his eyes fixed on Joseph.

Joseph followed his father to the gate.

"I won't be here when you get back, Father," he said softly.

"And where then will you be?" asked Bennet turning sharply.

"I have a date with Delores tonight."

Bennet Armstrong glared at his son. He bit his cheek. He bit his lip. He opened his mouth and all that came out was a gust of breath. He was too angry to speak.

"Tell me, Father," said Joseph, "tell me, please—why do you dislike Delores Bays?"

"I never said I disliked her," retorted Bennet.

"Then why do you object to my going with her, Father? I'd like to know why."

"I told you I wanted you to go with some girl from the West."

"Why the West?"

"Because I said so. I've got good reasons and that's enough. I see you are determined to disobey me, so you'll have to take the consequences. If you were a little smaller I'd take you out behind the barn and strap you good."

"If that would make you feel better," said Joseph, "you can do it right now. I'll loan you my belt."

Bennet was furious now. Both eyes bulged. He opened his shirt collar.

"I'm going now," he said. He walked a few steps and turned back. "You are too stupid to know when a father is giving his son good advice. Some day you'll be sorry when it's too late. If you really wanted to make good, if you had half an eye for business, you'd listen."

"Wait just a minute, Father," called Joseph. He hurried toward him. He took hold of his arm. "Don't be angry with me, please. I wish you could understand. I love Delores and I can't help it. I do, Father, and I'm not ashamed of it. All the girls the West can offer don't attract me. I'll never be guilty of marrying any girl for her money. I'll never marry for anything but love."

"So!" shouted Bennet indignantly. "Quite a speech you made there. Must have practiced up on it. Very well,.

then. If you can't fit yourself into my plans, you're out, that's all."

"What do you mean by that?"

"You'll see what I mean," and Bennet walked away.

Joseph watched his father drive out of the lane in Sol Bantum's buggy—the buggy he was going to use to take Delores to church.

CHAPTER XLVII

The truth was out now. The entire Stokes family had been watching from the windows and knew Uncle Bennet was giving Joseph a piece of his mind. Strung between love and shame, Joseph walked to the orchard. He had to be alone for a while before he could face anyone—even Freddie.

"My God, my God," cried Joseph. "If I'm ever a father, help me love my boy. It can't be true. Oh, it can't be true that Father has so little heart. He hates me. I know it now, but why? I can't understand it," and in spite of himself, tears streamed down his hot cheeks.

He was perched on the rail fence, his back against an apple tree, when he felt a hand on his elbow.

"What's the matter, Joseph?"

Freddie climbed over and sat beside him.

"It's nothing pleasant to tell," Joseph said in a low, low voice.

"You'd rather not?"

"Well, you can guess from what Father said at the table, can't you?" Joseph looked in the opposite direction. He wiped his eyes.

"It sounded like your father doesn't like Delores for some reason."

"I can't understand it, Freddie. All I can get out of him is that Jeddie Bays hasn't money."

Freddie's eyes widened. "Money?"

"Yes, he wants me to go with some girl whose father is rich." Joseph turned and faced his cousin.

"Why?"

"Your guess is as good as mine. Money, money, money! That's all I can figure out. He's got it on his mind. For some reason he seems to have it in for Jeddie Bays, even called him an—oh, I'm not going to repeat

324

it. Jeddie's a real man—a Christian too. I can't help what Father says. Freddie, I've prayed about this—" Joseph jumped down from the rail fence and paced back and forth. "No one will ever know, but I know, I know before God she's a good girl—and I, my conscience doesn't condemn me. God proved Himself to me—and I *know*."

"I wouldn't worry then," Freddie said at length.

"I'm not. It's not that exactly. But how would you feel if you were in my shoes?"

"I don't know how I'd feel."

"I know you don't. No one knows what I've gone through. I've never told. If it wasn't for—for Mother, I'd have been glad many a time if I'd have died when I was a baby."

"Joseph!"

"It's so, Freddie. You don't know. I'm up against it now."

"How do you mean?"

"I've got no way to take Delores to church tonight."

"I'd loan you my buggy, but—"

"No, I wouldn't do that. Aren't you taking—?"

"Yes, I have a date with Lillian, but I'm not as thrilled over my girl as you seem to be."

"What's the matter?"

"Oh, I don't know." Freddie kicked at a clod of dirt. "One day I think I like her, and the next I don't know. Let's all four go together tonight. Maybe you and Delores can teach us how to have a good time."

Joseph broke a twig off the apple tree and tossed it across the fence.

"That doesn't appeal to me, to be honest, Freddie. Thanks anyway."

"Then I'll let you off at Bays and you can figure out the rest."

"The rest? Yes, and the rest is quite a bit to figure out, too. How will I get home? Walk? Think how late it would be, and then—"

Neither spoke. For a while it seemed to Joseph the whole world was suspended in space. He was hanging, and would soon drop.

"You'll soon be of age, Joseph," said Freddie.

Joseph smiled blankly.

"I know it."

"Then what?"

"Why, I'm going to work out."

"I wish we could go to academy together."

Joseph shifted his glance, and when he spoke his voice was almost inaudible. His lips twitched with an ironical smile.

"And go to hell together?"

"What'd you say, Joseph?"

"Father said if I'd go to academy that would give me a straight ticket to hell."

"Why to hell?"

"I don't know," answered Joseph in a voice that was shockingly loud for Joseph Armstrong. An odd, far-away look came into his eyes.

"God knows," he went on. "I'll go if I ever have a chance. And I'll do some more things, too, if I ever have a chance."

"Some more things like what?"

"Like a fellow like you could do with a father like Uncle Timothy. I tell you, Freddie, you ought to be thankful you have a father that understands you. Mine doesn't even try. Please, Freddie don't ever tell this to anyone."

"I won't."

"Please don't."

"I said I wouldn't, Joseph; but doesn't Delores know?"

"No, not yet. That's what hurts." Joseph put both hands in his pockets and walked back and forth again.

"I'll have to tell her. I'll *have* to now. I think—I can't."

"You really think a lot of her?"

"Do I?" Joseph looked from the ground to the fence, and from the fence to the sky. It was as blue as the dress Delores had on one night. "I think the world of her."

Freddie stood amazed.

"Maybe I'll find the one for me when I go to academy."

"You're joking, Freddie."

"No, I'm not. The folks said I could if I'd find work to pay my board. I wrote for a bulletin. Anyway, Joseph, how can a fellow know who he wants until he's tried a variety?"

"A variety?"

"Sure. I'm more unsettled now than I was before I ever had a date. Why don't you try Lillian next Sunday night and let me try Delores?"

"Freddie!" The color left Joseph's cheeks. A dazed, unbelieving look crossed his face. His lips trembled.

"Do you mean that?" he said, looking Freddie straight in the eyes.

"Sure I mean it. I'm not ready to get serious with any girl yet, and you shouldn't either. Try it once and see what your father has to say to that."

Sweat trickled down Joseph's face. What ailed Freddie? Was he jealous? Joseph stood speechless and stunned. Gasps of astonishment and despair escaped his slightly parted lips. Could it be that Freddie, his best loved cousin, Freddie, would try to take Delores from him? Freddie Stokes, the one he had implicit confidence in?

"I'm not jealous," Freddie said, twisting a blade of grass. "I'm only trying to figure a way to help you out."

To help him out? A mass of incoherent thoughts jumbled through Joseph's brain. His father was trying to help him out too. He too had made comments, and threats, and speculations, and criticisms. A cloud now seemed to hang over all his unlived days. It was not only over him, but also out beyond him for miles—for years. Would happinesss and security ever be his?

Joseph jumped the fence.

"I think I'll start out and walk," he said.

Freddie followed.

"You mean over to Bays?"

"I'm going to see Delores tonight, if I have to wade fire."

*   *   *

Delores looked up in surprise. She was sitting on a rug under the maple tree, reading.

"Why, Joseph," she said going toward him. "What time is it?" She looked down over herself and blushed a little.

"I walked from Stokes. I don't know what time it is. I have no watch."

"You walked?"

"Yes, Delores. My father is here and he went to see Earnie Eloy and I—I didn't think he'd be back in time with the buggy."

"I saw him in church this morning. Did he come just to see you?"

"He came—" Joseph unbuttoned his coat, "he came to help—well, he came to buy a farm really. I guess the family will be moving back soon."

"Back here? Oh, Joseph! How lovely!"

Delores smiled, and the beauty of the gleam in her eyes almost stabbed him.

"Delores," he said in a low, deep voice. "Shall we sit in the swing a while?"

"Why, yes."

Side by side they crossed the yard.

"I have no way to take you to church tonight," he began. "Father took the buggy. I'm sorry."

"Well," answered Delores smiling, "that's all right. I guess he had no other way to go. I suppose he hasn't seen Mr. Eloy since he was hurt, has he?"

"No, he hasn't."

"Well, I don't blame him for wanting to go. We can go with Mother and Father tonight in the surrey. That is, if you won't mind riding with them."

"Surely not—but how about George and Albert?"

"Well, they aren't going tonight anyway, Joseph. Albert has had a terrible sick headache all afternoon. I believe he needs glasses, and George is going to stay at home with him, so you see it's quite all right."

"You're not awfully disappointed then?"

"Not enough to let it spoil the evening, Joseph. No, my parents won't mind, I'm sure, for they—my father especially—seems to enjoy talking with you."

"Delores, I appreciate that," said Joseph. "I only— wish—my father took the same attitude."

"Attitude about what?" she looked up at him.

"About—" (oh, how could he say it?) "about—my coming to see you," he said.

"You mean?" Delores sat up very straight and looked Joseph full in the face. "You mean—" and an excited gasp of wonder came from her lips, "you mean he objects?"

"Delores!" Joseph wanted to catch both her hands in his and hold them still. She was clasping and unclasping them nervously. "My father has some very peculiar ideas about some things," he said, looking at her slippers instead of her hands. He gripped the swing. "My father wants me to go with a girl in the West."

"Who is she? You mean you had a girl in the West your father—?"

"No. No!" It's no one. Delores, believe me, I had no girl before I came here. It's just an idea my father has about girls in the West. I don't know why, but it's his notion."

"Then—" Delores was on her feet now facing him— "then he thinks you're too good for me?" Her cheeks were getting red. The look on her face wasn't exactly a resentful, or indignant, nor bitter one, but a sudden smitten look.

"It hurts me to tell you this, Delores." Joseph got to his feet also. "I'd rather take a beating, but I know I've got to tell you. My father has always criticized everything I've done. I cannot please him, no matter how hard I try. But my mother isn't that way. She doesn't object. My mother is pleased, and she will be anxious to meet you again. I've tried to tell her what a nice girl I think you are."

"And—and to what extent does your father object, Joseph?"

"To what extent?" Joseph's voice was husky and a little unsteady. "Do you really want to know?"

"Of course I do," she answered. "You should tell me! You must tell me!"

"You mean then that it will make a difference with you what my father says?"

"Of course it will. What all has your father said? You make me inquisitive."

"I'm going to be honest with you then, Delores." He hesitated. He tried to swallow the lump that came in his throat. "He said," he looked away. He could not say it and look into her sweet face. "He said," tears came into his eyes now, "he'd break it up one way or another."

"He—he—if he said that, Joseph, he must have a reason."

CHAPTER XLVIII

"The only reason I know of isn't worth mentioning," Joseph answered quickly. "It's not that he dislikes you, Delores, because he doesn't know you. If he did, he couldn't help but like you."

"What then is the reason?"

"It's too trifling to mention."

"Tell me."

"He wants me to go with some wealthy girl."

"Wealthy?"

"That's all I can get out of him."

"Why that?"

Joseph shrugged his shoulders. "There are things about my father that I cannot understand."

For several minutes they stood, both gazing at nothing in particular.

"If this makes a difference to you now," Joseph said at length, "of course I couldn't blame you."

"It makes a difference," she answered pinching one hand with the other, "of course it makes a difference. Wouldn't it with you?"

"It wouldn't make me think any less of *you*," he said softly. "Nothing would change that."

"Nothing?" she cried, looking up in surprise.

"Nothing except yourself."

She brushed her cheeks with her lashes.

"I—I did think you were sincere," and when she spoke her soft eyes got misty. Tiny tears rolled out to the edge of her lashes and hung trembling.

"Before God I think I am, Delores. I can't help what my father does or says, and I can't help what he believes. Nor can he choose the one I'm to love. I admired you years before we ever moved away," he said in a low, warm voice. "I thought you were—the nicest girl I ever saw."

"And you—never had—another girl, ever?" she took a step back and looked at him intently.

"No other girl, Delores. No other girl ever appealed to me."

What was Joseph saying? His own words surprised him, and yet they sent warm circles around his sad heart.

"Father may try to break up our friendship, but he can never break my love for you. But," he added in a hurt, serious tone, "if it makes a difference to you, and you—"

"Delores," called Mrs. Bays, "You'd better get ready or you'll be late for church."

"Joseph," she said, "I—I—do you want to wait here or come into the parlor?"

"I'll wait here," he answered.

"Mother," said Delores as she hurried toward the stair door, "Joseph and I are going to ride with you two in the surrey tonight."

"Why with us?"

"His father has the buggy."

"His father?"

"Yes, I'll explain when I come down."

Jeddie Bays was in unusually good spirits for some reason. They all talked about this and that on the way to church; but more than once Joseph noted a touch of sadness on the face of the girl beside him on the back seat; and her laugh had a strange little cripple in it. She sang in church, but the ring in her voice sounded somewhat like one that comes from a cracked bell.

She and Joseph both saw it at the same moment—Bennet's stinging glance across the church immediately after the benediction.

"Joseph," said Delores after they were on the outside, "unless you go on home with your father, how will you get home tonight?"

"I'll have to walk."

"But think how far it is, Joseph. And it's dark tonight. You wouldn't get home before morning, would you?"

"Hardly."

"Then you'd better go with him—and—anyway since he doesn't approve of your going with me, maybe we'd better—drop it for a while."

"Drop our friendship?" A weakness swept over Joseph as they walked toward the surrey—a weakness that made his knees shake, and he broke out with a cold sweat.

"We'll always be friends, Joseph," she said, "always, I'm sure—but I'd like to talk this over with Mother and Father and see what they have to say. I didn't suppose your father objected like this."

"I'll soon be twenty-one," he said, in a low, hurt voice, "and then—"

"And then," she said, "if things are different, you may come to see me again."

"But not next Sunday?"

"Oh, Joseph!" cried Delores. "This hurts me so. I had no idea. I must have time to think this through. There must be a reason why your father takes this attitude. If he changes, then you may come—but—but not next Sunday, yet."

"Good night, Delores," he said with difficulty. "Thank you for all you've done for me."

"Good night, Joseph." He could see tears standing in her eyes.

"Good night, dear," he said softly, "and if you change your mind, write me a letter, will you?"

"Yes."

Almost blindly Joseph walked across the driveway to where his father stood watching. He staggered toward the buggy.

They were halfway home before Joseph could speak a word.

"Father, did you get to see Earnie?"

"Yes, and he'll be around in the morning."

In the morning. Joseph almost dreaded to see the light of another dawn, because it would remind him of the sweet, fresh look on Delores Bays's face. He was young, and strong, and vigorous; the work in the vineyard had been anything but a drudgery since each morning meant it was one less night until Sunday, but now—he was glad it was dark so he could not see the face of the one who caused all his heartaches. In the morning—oh, would it ever be morning for him again—morning in the heavens so blue, blue like the dress Delores wore one night, and in those dear and dreaming eyes the kind Father had revealed and unfolded His tender love for him? Would his father ever be different, and would Delores ever, ever let him come back? Before they were home, it already seemed weeks since he had been alone with her and seen her bright smile.

"To help me?" asked Joseph. His voice sounded strangely hollow.

"Yes, to help," answered his father.

"Are you going back to get the family then?"

"That all depends, Joseph."

"Depends on what?"

"Are you going back to see that Bays girl again next Sunday night?"

"No," came Joseph's weary answer.

"Then I'm going."

If Joseph would have been alone that night he might have walked the floor or tossed, but since he had to share the room with his father, he had to hide his emotions. That was torture. The night was long and dreary, and in the black stillness his soul was steeped in thoughts no words could describe—sinking memories of past days and forlorn. Although he could not see it, he looked sadfacedly and longingly toward the picture on the wall beside the dresser; not as a child, but as a man with thinking eyes, and with an honest prayer for victory to his struggling soul. He realized now, in a measure, his mother's patience.

Bennet snored, and it seemed to Joseph that with each new sound that came from his father's throat, he could hear him trying to say in his sleep, "Every move counts from now on." It was nearing daylight when Joseph finally dropped off into unconsciousness.

* * *

They had worked side by side before—Earnie Eloy and Joseph. It seemed almost like old times for both to be taking orders from Bennet Armstrong.

"He's not changed a bit, has he?" asked Earnie.

"Not a bit," answered Joseph.

The week passed more swiftly than Joseph had imagined. Earnie came on horseback at seven in the morning and went home to Alex's shack at seven in the evening. Bennet had bargained with Katy Bantum for Earnie's dinner. She told Sol she'd rather have Earnie Eloy there than Bennet Armstrong any day. Those were long full days for the two, but these were the days Bennet had been waiting for and dreaming about, and every move counted now. Wagon after wagonload of beautiful grapes were taken to town and shipped to New York City wholesale dealers. Bennet stayed long enough to know everything was being done right, then left.

"You've never been to church yet," Joseph said to Earnie one afternoon when they were working side by side.

Earnie squinted and rubbed his hand across his face.

"Been thinkin' on't," Earnie said.

"Supposing we go together Sunday night?"

"Huh?"

"I'll go in with you and sit with you if you'll go."

"That's tomorrow night?"

"Tomorrow night."

"I'll study 'bout it."

*   *   *

Everyone was surprised when Joseph Armstrong came
into church Sunday evening with a tall, lanky man with
a scarred face, and Delores Bays came with David
Hanley. Earnie Eloy was altogether unconscious of the
fact that he was making an excellent substitute that
evening. Without practicing, and without knowing why,
he played his role perfectly. Joseph simply couldn't keep
his mind on the sermon, even though he did not see
Delores until after church was over. And he was glad
he didn't, for when he saw her going out the side door
with David Hanley, he was so overtaken with surprise
and so bewildered that for a little while he forgot where
he was and who was with him. Despair seized him like
a man in a sinking boat with no hope of being recovered;
and with that despair came a terrible, an awful feeling
toward his father. He had prayed and prayed for God
to keep that sin of hatred out of his heart. He thought
he had reasons to hate, but he knew it was wrong. Under
the divine law there was no excuse. He would not be
justified. But to keep from hating just because the Bible
says that he that hateth is a murderer, and no murderer
hath eternal life was not enough. Of himself he was helpless. He knew it was a transgression against God to hate
anyone, yes, even his father. He also knew from years of
observation that his own mother possessed that heart
experience that enabled her to live out day after day
what she knew was right before God. Never once did
she act as if she hated Father. And yet, how she had
suffered! How did she do it? Joseph talked very little
on the way home. His mind was in a turmoil. What

would Earnie think of him? He ought to talk but he couldn't. The struggle in his soul surpassed anything he had ever experienced.

As he sat pondering in his own room, it seemed every mean thing his father had ever said or done loomed up before him like a hideous monster with horns and claws. It would kill him and send him to eternal doom. Then suddenly he heard once more his mother's gentle voice telling him the story she had so often told him in his childhood. "And the pit was deep and dark, and it was lonely down there too; but God loved Joseph all the time, and Grandfather Stokes used to tell us that he liked to think that when everyone else had gone away, God sent a light from Heaven to shine down on him."

Joseph sat with his face in his hands and thought and thought. The clock below struck one. Finally he opened his Bible and read Psalm 77, then Psalm 40. Still he wasn't satisfied. Turning to Deuteronomy 32 he read part of that. The clock struck one-thirty. He fell on his knees beside his bed, but he could not pray. Then he read Genesis 49, and before he closed his Bible that terrible feeling toward his father was growing less. He could not pray with it there. He had tried to, but the words only clung to the ceiling. "Dear Lord," he cried in anguish, "whatever it is that I need, please give it to me. Of myself I can't overcome this feeling toward Father; but give me that same spirit Mother has. I give myself up to You. It's all I know to do. Oh, it hurt me to see Delores with David tonight, but, dear Lord, keep hatred and bitterness out of my heart. I'm not able, but You are. Things look so dark to me, but let a little light shine down on me yet. Delores—oh, God bless her, bless her, and for all the heartaches and disappointments Mother has endured, help me bring a little happiness into her life somehow. I want to be true; Oh, God, I do want to be true to Thee!"

CHAPTER XLIX

His hands trembled when he reached for the letter behind the telephone. He ran upstairs two steps at a time and closed the door behind him. He read:

"Dear Joseph:

"Perhaps you saw me with David Hanley Sunday night. I saw you with Earnie Eloy. When I told my parents how your father feels about your coming to see me, it made them both feel awful at first. That's why I told David he could come. He called me up on Friday. But I did not enjoy myself one bit." Joseph caught his breath. He leaned hard against the door. "Before he came I wished I hadn't told him I'd go." Joseph's breath came in bunches, and his heart pounded. "I talked to my parents a long time on Monday, and Father said he knew your father had some peculiar ideas, but your mother made up for it. We heard today that he went home. If you think it would be best to wait until you are twenty-one to come again, it will be all right; but as far as I am concerned I won't let your father's attitude make me unhappy any longer if your mother doesn't care. Your Aunt Sara Stokes talked to my mother quite a while Sunday evening. I had no idea things were like that." Joseph got numb. What did Aunt Sara tell Delores's mother? "We are having a birthday dinner for Albert on Friday evening and you are invited. If you cannot come, call me by phone.

"Sincerely yours,
"Delores Bays."

The healing oil of gladness started trickling down over Joseph's broken heart that for ten days had been giving him pain with nearly every breath. Why is it that pain is more easily forgotten than joy? It is one of those mysteries of life.

Joseph folded the letter and buttoned it securely in his shirt pocket, and, dropping on his knees beside his bed, he shook with sobs. "Oh, God!" he cried, "I wouldn't want anyone ever to know I care this much. I'm so happy I can't—keep the tears back. Forgive me for ever feeling so hard toward Father. I'm ashamed now. O, God, help me be—"

"Joseph," called Katy Bantum.

"Yes."

"Dinner is ready."

"I'll be right down."

It was impossible for Joseph to hide the fact that something had greatly affected him, and Katy Bantum knew he had gone upstairs to read a letter. Although she asked no questions, she had noticed Joseph's appetite lag for days. Girtie had noticed it too.

"There was something in that letter that made him happy," said Katy to Sol after dinner.

"Well, I'm certainly glad," Sol said. "It gets me all woolly when that boy isn't himself."

"You're as bad as I am then," she whispered. "I'm sure he was crying before he came downstairs."

"Crying?"

"Didn't you notice his eyes, Sol?"

"I thought—but I wasn't sure. Anyway he looked happier than he has since the day his father came."

*   *   *

Delores was filling the water glasses when he stepped onto the porch. She put the pitcher on the table and hurried toward him.

"I've been looking for you," she said, opening the screen door.

She smiled, and as Joseph passed her he could smell the red rose she had pinned in the soft folds of her dress front.

"Am I the last one here?" he asked, as he handed her his hat.

"I guess you are, Joseph."

The living room was lined with young people. Most of them were from Albert's Sunday-school class, but there sat Agnes and Maryanna Stokes, and there sat Lillian Bond beside Freddie, and before Joseph had time to say good evening to everyone, that same "at home" feeling swept over him that he felt when he entered this house before.

The dinner was delicious. Two enjoyable hours were spent in playing games and singing, and, after some strong coaxing, Jeddie Bays gave a humorous reading he had learned when a boy in school.

"And now," said Delores, "I'm sure you'd all enjoy hearing about Joseph's trip to Asterlow with Brother Lanyard."

Joseph looked up quickly, half startled. He blushed. "But Delores," he said, "I wasn't expecting anything like this."

"I know, but you can do it. Please do, Joseph."

"Yes, do," said Freddie. "You didn't tell it to me yet."

"Yes, tell it, Joseph," Agnes said.

Slowly Joseph got to his feet. He stood behind his chair and hesitated a moment, then in a deep, rich voice he described his first trip across the mountains. He pictured the beauty and grandeur of the rocks and evergreens, and the graceful mountain laurel with their glossy leaves and pinkish white blossoms. He portrayed clearly the long warm journey, their thirst, the arrival at their destination, and the crowd as it gathered in the schoolhouse. He told also his embarrassment in being asked to lead the singing for the first time in his life. With surprising poise he described their visits from house to house in the mining village, Brother Lanyard's concern and passion for the lost in Asterlow, and his conviction to do a greater work in that district. The group sat wide-eyed and breathless as he related their homeward journey in the dark—in the brewing storm,

and their escape from the hands of the bandit. Delores
sat rapt. She had never heard Joseph talk like this. No
one had. He seemed to have a natural gift to speak
extemporaneously, and he revealed an inborn love for
the beautiful, and a deep reverence for God. When
Joseph sat down, one could have heard a pin drop. Everyone was dumbfounded.

"That was wonderful," Agnes said, breaking the
silence.

"Wasn't it?" whispered someone from the corner.

"Why, Joseph," Freddie said, "you'd better look out
or you'll make a preacher yet."

"Thank you for telling it, Joseph," Delores said, and
when she spoke something passed suddenly through his
mind—the personalities of all those that clustered around
his ideal; his mother, Brother Grissley, Uncle Tom,
Lottie Woods, Amos Pennewell, Herbert Lanyard, and
the beautiful daughter of Jeddie Bays. This was a
stimulating, a challenging experience for him. He surprised himself. He must make good. He must be true,
for there were those who trusted him. He must be strong
and brave and pure, for there were some who cared. He
must never hate Father. Never! And now if Delores
cared enough to invite him to Albert's birthday dinner,
and was interested enough to ask him to make a speech,
why shouldn't he be encouraged? If he could only prove
to her he was sincere, no matter what Father said.

"It was mighty nice of you to ask me to come tonight,"
he said after nearly everyone else had gone.

"Joseph!" She blushed, and looked up at him. "You
surprised me so."

"How?"

"I knew you could talk, Joseph," she said, "but not
like that. Oh, it was wonderful the way you told it.
Must you go now?"

"Must I go? Well, not just right away, I guess. Why?"

"Oh, I wonder so about some of the things your Aunt
Sara told my mother Sunday night."

"What did she tell her?"

23

"Oh, Joseph, really and truly I had no idea what a sad life— I mean how hard your father makes it for you. I just can't forget it. Since I know this I—I think I must do something to make you happy."

"Delores," said Joseph, stepping a little closer to her, "all I want—all I need to make me happy is you, dear. I must tell you tonight; I can't keep it any longer, now. I love you, Delores."

"Joseph," she whispered. She looked up into his handsome face.

"Surely you've guessed it a little, haven't you, dear?" he continued.

"Well," she said, "I thought maybe—the night I told you to go home with your father."

"You'll never know how hard it was for me to go on home that night. You'll never know how it made me feel to see you with David Hanley."

"Did it hurt you?"

Joseph drew a deep breath.

"David is a fine fellow as far as I know, and I told you if my father's attitude made a difference to you I couldn't blame you, but it did—hurt."

"It was so hard to decide what to do, but will you forgive me?"

"Gladly, dear." He looked down into her penitent face.

"I'll not do it again," she whispered.

"I love you, Delores. You're the sweetest little lady I've ever seen, and I'd love you if your father lived in a mud hut. I know I haven't a thing, but as soon as I'm twenty-one I'm going to work out."

"How soon will that be, Joseph?"

"In about three weeks."

"You won't have a hard time finding a job."

"I hope not."

"And your folks are really moving back?"

"Yes."

"Soon?"

"I suppose they will be coming any day now. You heard about the farm my father bought?"

"Yes. Oh, I'm going to try to be nice to your mother and Virginia and make them happy if I can, since I know."

"I'll surely appreciate that, Delores. My mother is a wonderful woman, if I do say it myself."

"I know she must be, Joseph, because—" she looked down and picked at the corner of her handkerchief, "there must be a reason why you're so—so different."

"Different?"

"You're so unlike any of the other boys around here."

"You're unlike all the other girls too. Let me tell you something, Delores. You must be different because of what Brother Lanyard told me while on our trip."

"What was that?"

"Well, I wanted to know what he thought of my going with you—since Father objected."

"Oh, Joseph!"

"Don't be frightened, dear. He thinks you're a fine Christian girl, and so does Brother Grissley."

"Brother Grissley?"

"Yes, that's what Brother Lanyard said he told him. So if he approves of our friendship, and a woman like Mrs. Irons does, surely Father must be mistaken, don't you think?"

"I hope he is, Joseph."

"Then you do love me a little?"

She touched him on the arm and looked up into his face beseechingly. "I wonder now what the people in church thought of me last Sunday night, Joseph. I'm quite ashamed. I had no idea anyone took such an interest in us."

"You haven't told me yet." He put his hand on hers.

"I'm trying to tell you, Joseph," she said in a sweet gentle voice. "You mean what your aunt told Mother?"

"No, not that just now. I can imagine that, and sometime when we can be together longer you can tell me. You know what I want to know."

"Maybe"—she looked down a moment—"maybe it's more than just a little."

"That's all I need to make me happy." He pressed her hand.

"I want to make you happy," she said sincerely.

"There's something else yet I've been waiting to tell you." They walked toward the door. "You know on our way home from Asterlow?"

"Yes."

"When I felt so sure there was danger of some sort ahead, I prayed."

"Yes, you said that tonight."

"But I didn't say what all I prayed."

"What was it?"

"I said to—to the Lord like this, 'If Delores is the one You'd have me to love, prove Yourself to me tonight.' "

"Joseph!"

"And He did, dear, so that's why I know before God it's right—no matter what Father says."

"Oh, I'm so glad you told me this, Joseph. That means an awful lot to me. If I would have known that before—" Tears stood in both her bright eyes.

"Please don't feel bad about that now. I wanted to tell you, but somehow I couldn't. I was afraid maybe you'd think I was too—" he hesitated.

"Too what, Joseph?"

"You know what I mean, don't you, Delores? I wanted to be sure you'd be ready to believe me before I told it."

"Believe you, Joseph?" she cried. "Didn't I tell you I knew you were sincere?"

"But you didn't know then about my father's attitude, and when you said it made a difference I was glad I hadn't told it yet. It was a very, very sacred experience to me."

"I'll never doubt your sincerity again, Joseph, no matter what your father says. When you come on Sunday evening I'll tell you then what your Aunt Sara told mother, but it won't make any difference now."

"Delores, you're a dear!"

CHAPTER L

In the deepest recess of the soul of many a young life there lies a sincere longing to be pure and true. Some experience a constant challenge of these virtues. Young people need friends; they need a church, a creed, a work, and a God to which they can dedicate the freshness and vigor of their lives. Joseph Armstrong experienced on the morning of his baptism that commitment of his life of Jesus Christ. Over and over in the empty schoolhouse on the western prairie he had surrendered his will to God's after tears and strugglings of soul. Little could anyone but his own mother guess how often he had to ask God for courage to be brave for that particular day, and for courage to face the dark future that seemed to offer no chance whatever. Other boys could go to school if they wanted to. All they needed to do was to say they were interested in getting more education, and somehow their parents made a way for them. And now it looked very much as if Freddie Stokes was going to get to go to academy before many months. All his life Joseph had his hopes thwarted, and yet in his inmost self he had a constant desire to be true and strong and brave in spite of every obstacle.

Since a child he had felt that ever-present, never-satisfied longing for a father's love. As a little boy he had dreamed of sitting on his father's knee as other boys did, but that dream never came true. As an eager-faced adolescent he had watched with longing eyes other boys playing ball with their fathers, and wondered how it would seem to have a father who would play with him. He never had a wagon or a box of toys like other boys had. He always felt a want for something. Instinctively his soul was forever responding to any kind voice, or to the delicate beauties of nature—more so in recent years than ever before; and without doubt there was a reason. Maturity made him more sensitive or conscious of the fact that his childhood had been a stinted one. He himself was in the blossom time of life now, and love for anything beautiful made a strong appeal to him. In his soul-hunger for love he found in Delores Bays that purity and delicate beauty. He had seen it all his life in his mother; so he could not be satisfied with anything less than the highest and best in womanhood. Every blooming flower reminded him of Delores Bays since she had admitted her love for him. The skies never looked so blue as now. There was something about those lofty mountains in the distance that called for the highest and best in him. For the first time in his life Joseph found an opportunity to express his deep heart yearnings to someone. He had often told his mother in part, but it was different telling it now to the one he loved. And Delores understood. That was such a consolation, such a relief, such a support. Every day he became happier.

* * *

The work in the vineyard was finished before fall rains began. Joseph heard his father tell Sol Bantum he was pleased with the yield and prices, otherwise Joseph might never have known definitely. Bennet didn't tell Joseph in so many words.

"And so you're going to leave us?" Katy asked, when Joseph came downstairs one afternoon.

"Yes," answered Joseph putting his suitcase down. "Mother wants me to come home, and of course I want to too."

"Of course you do, but we'll certainly miss you."

"You've been very kind to me," Joseph said, "and I've enjoyed my room, and the meals, and everything you've done for me."

"Well, I said more than once I'd never let anyone have Jerry's room, but I've not been sorry we let you have it. I see your father has come after you."

"Yes. He'll help me bring the trunk down."

"Good afternoon, Mr. Armstrong."

"Good afternoon," answered Bennet, removing his hat. He smiled and bowed to Katy Bantum and to Girtie, who was ironing in the kitchen.

"Well, are you getting straightened up over there?" Katy asked.

"We need a young fellow like Joseph to help. That's why I came after him. Have you got your things together?"

"Everything is packed, Father, but I guess you'll have to help me carry the trunk down."

"All right. Let's get it. That's why I called over, so you'd be ready."

Joseph thought surely his father was going to add "Every move counts," but he didn't unless that was what he was muttering under his breath as he followed his son upstairs.

"I settled with your husband," Bennet said to Katy when he went out the door.

"Girtie," said Katy, looking out the window when the two drove away.

"Yes?"

"We'll miss that boy, won't we?"

"Spect so."

"Girtie."

"Yes?"

"Did he call you 'Pet' when he went by?"

"Who?"

"You know who I mean."

"No," answered Girtie indignantly, "and he'd better not. I never even looked up."

"Didn't you say good-by to Joseph?"

"Sure, I did to him."

"I dread to go up to that room," Katy said, resuming her mending.

"Why, Katy?"

"Oh—it'll remind me of how it was after Jerry was gone. I never imagined I'd ever think so much of anyone as I do of Joseph. If he ever gets married I'm surely going to send him a nice gift."

* * *

"It's great to be eating your cooking again, Mother." Joseph's face beamed when he sat down to the supper table that evening.

"But Virginia got the supper tonight," reminded his mother proudly.

"So you got the supper? Well, Virginia, I can hardly believe how you've grown. And Lowell, I'm sure you're bigger than I was at twelve. Mother, this is a treat to be sitting around the same table once more."

"It s nice to have you here with us, I know," answered his mother fondly.

It was not so strange that her voice should be affectionate. Wasn't this her beloved son, her first born, the one she had longed and prayed and waited for, the one on whom she had lavished her love from babyhood, who had come back home? Wasn't this her little one that God had touched twice with His healing finger after she had carried him for days, fever-stricken, and only half conscious on a pillow? Wasn't this her little Joseph who had come to her countless times and sobbed on her breast because of his father's harsh words? Wasn't this her little one who plodded home from school through the snow and cold when other children got rides? Wasn't this her boy who had a secret place of prayer all his own out behind the barn where he went to beg God to spare her life? Wasn't this her son who had folded her in his arms and whispered something when he left home? Wasn't this her son who now stood head and shoulders above her? whose clean-cut face was stamped with an honest, open expression of sincerity and devotion? who had come home to help lighten her burdens? Why shouldn't her voice sound affectionate? Her heart pounded and her soft, brown eyes got misty. Bennet eyed Annie sharply across the table. Was she going to begin spoiling Joseph the first evening he was in the house?

"There's a lot of work to be done around the place," said Bennet. "I want to get the hedge fence all trimmed before Lowell talks about going to school, and I want to replant part of the orchard, and mend fence, and fill in that ditch in the corn field. I hope being over to Bantums hasn't made you lazy, Joseph." Bennet looked suspiciously at Joseph, then took a bite of bread.

"I hope not," answered Joseph.

"Well, I want you to come down by five. Not a minute later, and you too, Lowell. Every move—"

"Yes, yes," Joseph said. "We'll help make the moves count, won't we, Lowell?" and Joseph reached over and gave his brother a significant slap on the shoulder.

How good it felt to be sitting beside Joseph again. Although there was nine years difference in their ages, they were brothers, and Joseph was Lowell's ideal. Big and strong and handsome, young and radiant, Joseph appeared to Lowell; and although Joseph was not conscious of the fact, he won the lifetime admiration of his younger brother. Almost shyly, Virginia eyed Joseph, while in her heart she silently adored him. She would never forget how thoughtful and how kind he had been to her in her tender years of childhood, and how they had worked and planned together to be able to sell things in town so Mama could get a new dress. This was Joseph, her big brother, who was told to leave home and take care of Father's vineyard. How he had grown and changed in the months they had been separated. How happy and bright-eyed he looked. How deep and sure his voice sounded. And he was back again!

Then Sunday came. Joseph had been wondering for days how he would manage it. There was nothing to do but walk to Bays. He knew it was useless to ask Father for a horse, and of course he wouldn't consider taking one without asking.

*   *   *

"I've got it figured out, Joseph," said Delores after they had talked a little while. "The boys will ride Prince to church and we will go with the folks."

"But—"

"They don't mind, Joseph. Albert suggested it himself. Really he did. We can't affort to miss church just because you haven't a buggy."

"Some day before so long I hope it will be different."

"Has your father said much since he's back?"

"He hasn't said a word."

"Doesn't he know you came tonight?"

"I don't know. I milked early and left. Mother knows."

"And she thinks it's all right?"

"Of course she does, dear. Mother wouldn't know of a girl anywhere she'd rather I'd go with."

"And she doesn't care that my father isn't rich?"

"Of course not, Delores. Why, I think you have a lovely home here. It's nice enough for anyone. Your father isn't a poor man."

"No, not poor. We've always had all we needed. Why is he so set on riches, your father?"

"I don't know, dear. Let's not talk about that now. I want to tell you how lovely you look tonight, and how happy I am that you love me. You still mean what you said, don't you?"

"Do you think I might have changed, Joseph?" she answered, smiling up at him sweetly.

A strange foreboding had surrounded Joseph all day.

"Delores," said Joseph after she repeated what Aunt Sara Stokes had told her mother. "That is all true, but that isn't half. Aunt Sara knows only a little of what we've had to endure."

"Not half?" she gasped. "How is it that we never knew?"

"Mother kept all her sorrows to herself. She confided in me only when she thought she was going to die."

"When was that?"

"I was eight. We've tried all our lives to shield Father. We've tried to keep this, but now and then things leaked out. Aunt Sara, after all, knows very little. It's a sad, sad life my mother's had."

"Oh, Joseph," cried Delores. "This makes me love you all the more."

*   *   *

Bennet's jaws were set and he looked dark around the eyes. Joseph worked hard from daylight till dark helping trim hedge, and he was dressed and downstairs by five in the morning. Bennet waited until the family was at the supper table to say what was on his mind.

"Joseph," he began after the bread plate had gone around. "I have told you for the last time I don't expect you to go with that Bays girl, and you were with her again last night."

Bennet glared at Joseph, but Joseph made no answer.

"I thought you told me you weren't going back there. You lied to me."

"I didn't go back the next Sunday night," Joseph said, "so I didn't lie to you."

"You let me under the impression you were quitting her."

"You asked me if—"

"I know what I asked you," shouted Bennet angrily, "and I know what I'm going to tell you too. I've given you fair warning. I told you if you couldn't take a father's advice you could suffer the consequences."

Joseph's face did not get red, nor did he flinch. He sat calm and erect.

"Do you see that door there?"

"Yes, sir."

"Very well. You may get your things and leave."

Annie's face turned white, and she clutched at her throat.

CHAPTER LI

Joseph got to his feet and looked his father straight in the eyes.

"Very well, Father," he said in a deep, low voice. "I'll do that. I'll be twenty-one in a week, and I intended to get a job then anyway."

"Maybe you did intend to," snapped Bennet, "but I'll take the privilege of putting you out before you're twenty-one. You could have avoided this if you'd cared to."

"But I'll never marry a girl for her money or her father's money," answered Joseph.

"And you'll soon be back here begging for a crust of bread!"

Joseph pushed his chair up to the table and walked around to where his mother was sitting. He put one hand on her shoulder and patted her gently.

"Don't feel bad, Mother," he said tenderly. "It's best that I leave."

"Oh, Bennet!" Annie cried while hot tears streamed down her cheeks, "Does he have to go tonight without any supper? Can't he at least wait until morning?" Her entire body now shook with sobs. Virginia and Lowell were both crying too.

"Very well, then," said Bennet blinking. "Go sit down and eat your supper. I don't want your mother to have another one of them—"

Joseph whispered something in his mother's ear and took his place at the table. The meal was eaten in painful silence. Why did Father always explode at meal time? No one had an appetite now. Every one felt sad and sick. Even Bennet ate but a few bites.

Annie followed Joseph upstairs.

"Mother," he said softly, "it's best that I leave without any words or tears. Father and I seemingly can't live under the same roof any more. I love Delores and she loves me, and someday I hope I can marry her when I get ahead a little."

"But where will you go?" His mother's eyes were stretched with dread and sorrow.

"Please don't worry, Mother," he said. "I'll find a place. Mr. McCracken told me he'd give me a job."

"Squire McCracken?" whispered Annie.

"Yes. He told me that quite a while ago."

"Does Father know that?"

"No, I never told him."

"Wouldn't that just about make him furious?"

"I don't know. Why would it?"

"I think he wants to be in kinda big with the Squire."

"Well, I wouldn't tell the Squire any more than I'd have to. I don't care to tell anyone."

"You mean you won't tell anyone he put you out?"

"Of course not. I'm just going to go hunt for a job. I'll be of age next week."

"Yes, that's right. Oh, I'm so glad if you won't tell. I hate this so," and Annie broke out with fresh sobs.

"Don't, Mama, please don't feel so bad—Mother dear, don't!"

"Doesn't it hurt you?" she cried looking up through her tears.

"Not like it would have a year or so ago. It makes it easier now since I know Delores loves me."

"But, Joseph," cried his mother, "if she finds this out maybe it will make a difference with her."

"She already knows some things."

"Joseph!"

"I had to tell her, Mother! I just had to tell her some!"

"Doesn't she think it's awful?"

"I guess she did at first, but since Aunt Sara talked to her mother, she said she wouldn't let it bother her."

"Aunt Sara?"

"Yes."

"Oh, Joseph!" cried his mother. "What all does Aunt Sara know?"

"She doesn't really know much."

"How can I ever face people again?"

"Just like I do, Mother." He put his strong arm across her shoulder. How small and frail she felt. "Many a time I thought I couldn't go on, but don't you remember the story of Joseph you used to tell me when I was a little boy?"

For a minute she sat in deep thought. His strong hand was on her shoulder and he could feel her body shaking.

"Joseph," she said at length, "do you mean to tell me that has helped you all these years?"

"More than you have any idea, Mother," he answered. "If it weren't for the stories you told me about God when I was just a boy, I can't imagine where I'd be today or what I'd believe. I know this, Mother, if it weren't for the things you've taught me, I'd hate Father."

"Joseph!"

"I would. I know it. How could I help it?"

"And you don't?"

"I've been tempted to, I'll admit. I've had a terrible struggle keeping bitterness out of my heart, but every time I'd think of you and all you've taught me. Don't you remember what you told me about the deep, dark pit and God's light? If you can put up with all you've had to and keep sweet and see God's light shining through, surely I have no reason to get angry. The thing that worries me is Father's spiritual condition."

Silent tears trickled down Annie Armstrong's pale face. "I've thought of that often," she said sadly. "And I know this, that it will take me the rest of my life to leave the right impressions on Lowell and Virginia. I'm so glad you didn't show a temper at the table. I'm sure they will never forget as long as they live how you took it."

"There wasn't any use getting mad. And to be honest, Mother, I really don't care a lot, in a way. Of course I hate to leave you like this, but since Father never did show any love for me, I've really been looking forward to being of age."

"I know."

"And you won't lie awake and think about this all night, will you, Mother dear?"

"Not if you won't. I mean I'll try not too." She rubbed and rubbed her slender hands. How frail she looked.

"And you won't get a heart spell when I leave?" he asked, anxiously watching her neck flutter. It startled him.

"I'll try not to, Joseph."

"I'll put my things together tonight then, and leave right after breakfast."

"Good night, Joseph."

"Good night, Mama," and he planted a kiss on her lips. He followed her to the top of the stairs.

"Be brave, little Mother," he said. "And remember what you told me—God sees us in the dark," he held her back by the arm. "You believe it, don't you, Mother?"

"I've got to," she said, smiling faintly through tears. He watched her until she reached the bottom step.

Joseph did not drop off to sleep as readily as he thought he could. Happy thoughts, sad thoughts, mad thoughts, rolled and raced and tumbled through his mind, and finally after a good hard cry he fell asleep. He wasn't going to cry. He wasn't going to. Joseph was almost twenty-one, and strong. But long after the light was out and he thought of all the heartaches his mother had endured, tears would come uncontrolled. They were not tears of self-pity, but pity for the one who had suffered twice as long as he had, and from which there was no escape. He could leave and Mother couldn't. He had Delores to love and live and work for. But Mother! Virginia and Lowell could both look forward to the time when they could work out. But Mother! Just last night Delores had made him supremely happy. They talked alone for fifteen blessed minutes before he started on his long tramp home. It wasn't long, but long enough to assure him she really cared for him in a personal way. But Mother! But Mama! It was her he cried for, not himself this time. Father would never again say anything that would make him cry.

As soon as breakfast was over, Joseph put on his cap and picked up his bundle. After he had found his location he'd come back for the rest of his things.

"Good-by, Mother," he said. "Good-by, Mama—Mother."

"Just a minute, Joseph," interrupted his father. "I want you to do just one thing yet before you leave."

"What is that?"

"I want you to take the team and go over to Simpson's and ask to borrow his spring wagon."

"To Simpson's?" Joseph put his bundle on a chair.

"Yes. You're not twenty-one yet."

Joseph looked at his father and then at his mother. "All right," he said, "I'll go."

Joseph harnessed two horses. Straddling one, he drove them to Simpson's place just a mile beyond Timothy Stokes. He started home with the wagon. The horses were going an easy trot.

"Every move counts," he said to himself. The breast strap on the one horse evidently broke, for suddenly Joseph noticed the quarter strap dangling. Both horses became frightened and started running full speed down the road. Joseph pulled on the lines with all his might but the horses were entirely beyond his control. Both horses were strange to him and his voice only frightened them all the more. There was a downward sensation, a sudden crash and the sound of scraping iron—dust—and all was dark.

* * *

"Mother!" cried Agnes. "There's a runaway. Look!" She ran to the front door. "Look, Mother, come quickly! I'll bet someone got hurt! Look out there by the culvert!"

Agnes and her mother both ran. The culvert wasn't far from the house.

"Oh, Mother!" she cried. "It's Joseph! It's Joseph! Call Freddie and Dennis quick!"

"You go, Agnes; you can run faster than I can."

Sara Stokes knelt by the culvert beside the motionless body of her nephew and tried to brush the dirt off his face with her apron.

"Joseph!" she called.

No answer.

"Joseph!" she repeated.

Not a sound.

"Oh, my God," she cried. "Are you dead? Joseph!" she screamed.

No answer. He lay limp and motionless. She hunted his pulse. It was beating.

All five came running—all the Stokes family, even Timothy.

"Let's carry him into the house," Freddie said.

They put him on the couch in the living room and Aunt Sara bathed his face in cold water. She rubbed camphor under his nose and fanned him, but he remained motionless, and only once in a while a faint moan was heard.

Timothy called Bennet and Dr. Hudson Lindquist, who said he would come as soon as possible.

They waited. Sad-faced and silent they were all standing beside the couch when Bennet came on horseback.

"What happened?" he panted.

"He must have had a runaway," Freddie said.

"I figured something happened when the horses came running home. Where are you hurt, Joseph?" he asked, shaking him on the shoulder.

"He's not made a move since we found him," Timothy said.

"You think he's unconscious?" asked Bennet wide-eyed.

"We've called and called him," cried Aunt Sara. "He won't answer, not even with a grunt."

Bennet groaned. He wiped and wiped perspiration from his face. He blew his nose.

"Did you call a doctor?" he asked.

"I called Dr. Lindquist."

"What did he say?"

"He said he'd be here as soon as possible. Maybe that's him now. It is."

Everyone stepped aside when the physician entered. Bending over Joseph, he examined him thoroughly.

"This boy's got a bad skull fracture," he said presently.

Bennet stepped up close to the doctor and tapped him on the arm. "You think we'd better take him to—"

"He dare not be moved," answered the doctor gravely. "His condition is too serious for that. Is his mother here?"

"No, sir," answered Bennet.

"Well," said the doctor, rubbing his chin slowly, "you say it's the Armstrong boy?"

"He's my son," answered Bennet.

"Your son? Well, if I remember right, isn't it your wife that had a bad heart?"

Bennet cleared his throat nervously. He shifted from one foot to the other. "It's not too good, I guess," he answered meekly.

"She's still living then? I haven't seen her for a number of years."

"We've been out West."

"Well, J. B., you'd better go get her," he said meditatively. "Sometimes it takes a mother to bring to consciousness a boy in his condition."

CHAPTER LII

"Mrs. Stokes." The doctor motioned with his hand. "Will you please come here a minute?"

He talked to her in undertones just outside the door. "I'll be back in the morning," he said at length. "If you notice any fever let me know and I'll come out to-night, J. B."

"Yes, sir." Bennet stepped on the porch. He put both hands in his pockets and his eyes danced nervously.

"This is to be put to your account, I presume?"

"A—a—well," stammered Bennet awkwardly. He shifted from one foot to the other and cleared his throat.

"He's not married, is he?" asked the doctor.

"No, sir; no, sir," answered Bennet.

"He's working for you then?"

"He was when this happened—a—yes, sir," answered Bennet. His face got red and he rubbed his nose.

"Well, I just wondered. I hardly thought your boy was of age yet."

Bennet felt like smiting his breast. He felt like tearing his hair. He did neither—but sudden tears welled up in both eyes, and, leaning against the porch post, he cried in his handkerchief.

Another loss! If Joseph didn't snap out of this there would be a big doctor bill, and Simpson's wagon was ruined maybe beyond repair. Joseph was careless, that's what he was! He probably had his mind on that Bays girl. Now this! When he had so much to do. What a loss! Bennet cried until he shook. He cried until Doctor Lindquist was out of sight.

"Look at Uncle Bennet," whispered Maryanna. "The doctor must have told him—Joseph might die, don't you suppose? Mama, do you suppose?"

"Maybe so," whispered her mother.

"And what all did the doctor tell you out there?" Maryanna asked next.

"He was telling me how to take care of him, dear,' she answered softly. "You girls go and finish up your work now and be as quiet as possible. Joseph is a very sick boy. Poor Annie! This will be hard for her to take.'

"Don't you think we ought to call Delores and tell her?"

"Maybe so. But wait until Aunt Annie comes and see what she says."

It was after twelve when Bennet came back with Annie. Palefaced and trembling she tiptoed across the room.

"Oh, Joseph," she cried, taking his one limp hand in hers. "Can't you speak to me? Joseph—Joseph!" She stroked his face and hair. "Where are you hurt, Joseph?"

"He hasn't moved since we brought him in," Timothy said tenderly. "One of us has been here with him every minute."

"Oh, my poor boy!" and Annie buried her face in her hands, and, sinking into the chair to which Timothy led her she burst into sobs.

Bennet stood at the foot of the bed and stared.

Evening came and Joseph still lay motionless. His mother sat close by watching him. Now and then fresh tears rolled. Bennet walked back and forth across the yard nervously. Now and then he came inside and looked at Joseph, then went outside again.

"Do you think I ought to call Delores and tell her?"

"Yes, Agnes," answered Annie sadly, "call her. Maybe we should have called sooner. It will be dark now before long."

Fortunately Bennet did not hear. He was pacing back and forth between the two rose bushes, muttering to himself when Agnes called. And before Delores came Bennet had gone home.

"I'll be back in the morning," he told Annie before he left. "I don't suppose you want to go along, do you?"

"I want to stay," she answered heartbrokenly. Of course she wanted to stay. It would have torn her heart out to leave her boy.

Jeddie Bays came with Delores. Overwhelmed with grief Delores stood looking at the unconscious form of her lover. Her voice broke when she tried to speak to Joseph's mother. A lump came into her throat and she turned her face away and wept.

Anne caught her hand and said softly, "I didn't suppose we'd meet on such an occasion."

Delores shook her head and sobbed. How still Joseph lay! How deathly he looked! She shuddered and cried with a grief the like of which she had never experienced. Hers had been a happy life. She had never experiencd any deep sorrow or suffered any great pain. How could she endure it if he should die? Agnes had told her at the door that his condition was serious. She could see that. How limp—how helpless he looked!

"Neither did—I," choked Delores. "Are they doing everything—everything that can be done for him?"

"Yes, dear," answered Annie wearily, "there's nothing more to do but pray and wait."

Delores put her arm across Annie's shoulder and together they wept and watched.

Jeddie and Timothy talked in low tones in the furthest corner of the room, and Freddie and Maryanna sat staring at Delores and Aunt Annie. Oh, if they could only think of something to do or say to comfort them in their distress!

"Maybe we'd better go now," Jeddie said, touching Delores on the shoulder.

"You call him once," Annie said. "Maybe he'll answer for you. I've tried it over and over."

"Joseph!" called Delores. "Joseph!" she repeated, "it's Delores." She bent over him and touched his cheek tenderly.

No answer.

"Oh, dear," she groaned; "won't he ever wake up?"

"We'd better go, Delores," Jeddie said softly.

"I'll call in the morning," she said to Agnes. "Surely he'll come to by that time."

But he didn't. Day after day Joseph lay unconscious
By the end of the week Annie was so nervous and
exhausted she could hardly walk without staggering. She
had slept and eaten very little. She sent a note home with
Bennet for Virginia to send her the clothes she needed
Once Virginia came with her father and went back with
him. There was work to be done at home and Virginia
did what she could. What she couldn't do could wait
Lowell worked from morning till night. Not until Sunday
did he get to come along to see Joseph. What good would
it do? Joseph was unconscious and wouldn't know it
anyway. Only by begging with tears did Virginia per
suade her father to take her along that once. There
were too many going in and out as it was. Sol and Katy
Bantum had called twice. Lottie and William Ashelford
called and brought a beautiful bouquet. Grissley Steward
and Herbert Lanyard both came and offered touching
sincere prayers. Uncle Tom Bradly looked down at
Joseph and brushed away tears, and felt his hot fore
head. By Sunday Joseph had a high fever. Neighbors
and friends from far and near drove in Timothy Stokes's
lane and tiptoed through the room and whispered words
of sympathy to Annie, who sat nearest her son. Her
pale face was drawn and tired, and her sad eyes looked
sick. Lois and Riley Doane called, Amos Pennewell and
his good wife, young men, young couples, ministers, and
even the dignified Squire McCracken called and brought
a bouquet. No one seemed to be so touched as Earnie
Eloy. Slowly he walked across the room and stood beside
the stricken boy. Silent tears trickled down his dark
cheeks and he shook his head sadly.

" 'Taint fair—'taint fair," Annie heard him say. "You
never deserved this—nohow." His shoulders sagged, and
Annie wasn't sure but she thought she heard him curse
under his breath.

"Is Bennet here?" he asked as he passed Annie.

"He's here somewhere," she answered wearily. "Did
you want to see him?"

"No. I only wondered. Wisht I could do somethin' fer you, Annie, an' him."

"There's nothing to do but pray, Earnie."

"That's what gets me. He—he prayed fer me when I were in the horspital. Don't seem fair 'tall that a good boy like Joseph has ter suffer this a-way."

"He's not suffering so much when he's unconscious," Annie said.

"But you never know," Earnie said thoughtfully; "he maybe ain't sufferin' so much, but he surely must be in awful darkness."

"But even there," suggested Annie, clasping her slender hands and looking up at Earnie Eloy with a strange, sad, yet triumphant expression on her face, "I hadn't just thought of it till now, Earnie, but even if he is in the dark, God is with him. Oh, I know He is, Earnie, and if he never wakes up to tell me so, I know he'll go through the darkness safely, for God is with him."

"Wisht ter God," Earnie said, "wisht ter God he'd pull through. He's an orful sick boy. Ain't much show fer him now 'less some ken pray better'n I know how."

"Many are praying for him," whispered Annie.

Doctor Hudson Lindquist came every day for ten days. Joseph's fever increased until it was alarmingly high. Bennet looked troubled and dark around his eyes. He sat longer beside the bed now, frequently feeling Joseph's pulse. He said as little as possible. Occasionally he held his hand over his own forehead as though in pain or deep thought.

Poor Delores! Twice a day she called Agnes, only to hear that Joseph was still unconscious. She prayed and cried and waited anxiously, hopefully. Never once did she lose faith that he would recover. She couldn't! He must live!

"I'm not going to believe he can't live," she told her mother, "and as long as there's life I'm going to have faith."

"You must say 'Thy will be done,' " answered he
mother kindly.

Late in the afternoon on the eleventh day after th
accident, Joseph moved a little for the first time. Instantl
Annie was at his side stroking his hand and calling to him

"Joseph! Joseph! I'm right here. It's Mama, it'
your mother. Wake up, dear, and speak to me."

Joseph moaned several times. Then Bennet came. H
stood with his mouth open. Joseph moved again an
moaned.

"Can't you wake up, son?" Bennet called, bendin
over him.

"Moo—"muttered Joseph.

"What is it, son?" asked Bennet.

"Moo—"

"Say it again, Joseph."

"Moove."

"Move? You want to be moved?"

Annie rubbed his arms gently. "I know you must b
tired, Joseph," she said tenderly.

Agnes and Aunt Sara both came and stood close by
Oh, could it be Joseph was going to wake up at last
Breathlessly they watched.

"Move," he moaned.

"You want to be moved, Joseph?' asked Bennet.

"But you've been hurt, you know," said his mother
gently. "We'll move you as soon as we can, Joseph."

"Every—move," he spoke with great difficulty. His
tongue seemed to be partly paralyzed.

"What?" asked Annie, bending over him.

"Every—move—counts," Joseph moaned again.

Bennet clutched at his throat. He stepped back as
though struck.

"Every move," cried Joseph. He groaned again as if
in pain.

"Never mind those moves now," Bennet said huskily.

Joseph tossed his head to one side and lifted both
hands. They fell heavily at his sides. His fever-parched

lips were almost black. Bennet pulled a feather out of the pillow, and, dipping it in a glass of water, ran it across Joseph's blistered lips.

"Keep up the fight, son," he said, "keep up the fight, but forget about that work just now."

"But—but—" he moaned. He opened his eyes slightly and closed them again. "Every move—counts—counts—counts. Every move—counts—from now—from now on."

Annie stood wide-eyed and frightened.

"Why is he saying that?" she cried.

"He must think he's working," Bennet said. He dipped the feather in the water again and brushed it across Joseph's lips.

"Hurry, hurry," moaned Joseph, "get that—wagon. Every—move—counts."

"Forget those moves now, Joseph," said his father. "Forget about that wagon, will you? Here, let me wet your lips again. Don't flop around like that. You'll be all right if you lay still and rest."

"Then—every—move." Joseph opened his eyes and stared wildly at the faces beside him. Only for an instant did he see those faces in the light of the oil lamp, then all was dark again.

CHAPTER LIII

Bennet left very reluctantly. For over an hour he waited for Joseph to open his eyes again, or speak, but he finally went home disappointed. Annie sat beside the couch all night. No one could persuade her to lie down and rest. Joseph had opened his eyes once and he surely would do it again. She felt his forehead, and it wasn't nearly so hot as it had been that afternoon. She held his limp right hand in her left one and stroked it gently with the other. Though worn and weary and thin from long days of suspense and anxious uncertainty, she now felt a sudden new strength come over her since the moment her son showed the first signs of reviving. She watched him expectantly and with new hope.

"Yes, Delores," Annie heard Agnes saying. "I'm so glad you called. I have something good to tell you this time. Yes. No, not exactly, but he opened his eyes once and spoke a few words. Yes. Oh, something about moves counting. Yes. No, it didn't mean anything. I guess he thought he was working; at least Uncle Bennet seemed to think that. What? Yes, his mother and father were both here. No, he's gone home, but Aunt Annie is here. No. No. His fever seems to be going down. Yes. I knew you'd be anxious to know. Yes, he seems to be resting now. I'll tell her. Yes, I will, Delores. Good-by. I'll do that."

"Delores called, Aunt Annie," whispered Agnes. "If Joseph wakes up she wants you to tell him she'll be over in the morning as early as possible."

"Thank you, Agnes. My, my—you've all been so kind to us; we'll never be able to repay you for all the bother we're making!"

"Don't call it bother, Aunt Annie," and Agnes put an arm across Aunt Annie's shoulder. "We don't expect to

be repaid for this. We're willing and glad to do anything
to help Joseph get well. I forgot to tell you that was
Brother Steward who called just before supper."

"What did he say?"

"He said he was sorry he didn't get over today, but
he'd try to come tomorrow. And he also said I should be
sure and tell you a number of folks met at his home last
night and had special prayer for Joseph."

"That's wonderful," whispered Annie Armstrong, and
again she stroked the limp hand she was holding. How
white it was getting—both hands! For eleven days they
had done nothing. Yesterday she trimmed his finger
nails as she used to do when he was little.

"Do you know what, Agnes?" Annie looked up quickly.
She held her breath for a moment.

"What is it, Aunt Annie?"

"What is today?"

"Today is Friday."

"Friday the what?"

"This is the seventeenth. Why?"

"Then Monday was Joseph's birthday."

"His birthday?" whispered Agnes.

"I wonder if Bennet thought of it? I didn't! All I
could think of was to ask God to help him wake up."

"That's about all any of us have been thinking of.
Can I do something for you before I go to bed?"

"No, dear, go and get your rest. You must be tired."

"And what about you?"

"My rest will come some day when God sees I need it."

*   *   *

When Joseph opened his eyes again he looked straight
into the eyes of Delores. She was bending over him,
calling in the gentlest tones.

"Joseph, Joseph," she repeated. "It's Delores. I've come to see you wake up. Joseph! It's such a beautiful morning. Won't you open your eyes?"

Joseph stirred. It seemed to him he heard someone calling in the distance. He hesitated. He listened. He turned his head to the right. Wasn't that a familiar voice? He took another step forward.

"Joseph," she repeated tenderly. It sounded like the voice of someone he knew. It sounded like the voice of someone he loved. It sounded very much like the voice of Delores Bays. That was her name, wasn't it? Delores Bays? He stopped and listened.

"Joseph," she called pleasantly.

He tried to answer, but for some reason he could not. His throat and tongue seemed paralyzed. Where was she? There was a strange mist or fog in the direction where her voice came from, but in front of him all was clear and light. The walk led up to a beautiful white gate that shone with a heavenly brightness. He took another step toward it. It was swinging open.

"Joseph," he heard again. This time that voice sounded closer. It seemed to be beside him at his elbow. He turned and opened his eyes. The mist was gone and he saw the face of Delores Bays looking down at him intently. He had seen that face before, but never with such an eagerness on it. When had he seen her face last? Wasn't it the day before yesterday?

"Was that you calling me?" he asked.

"Yes, Joseph, I've been calling you for days. Do you know me this morning?"

"I know you—yes, I know you. Aren't you—Delores?"

"That's right, Joseph. I'm so glad you know me this time." She tingled with joy.

"You've been calling me—for—days?" he asked.

"Yes, Joseph, for days."

"But why did you call me back, Delores? I—I—was almost to that beautiful gate."

"What gate?" whispered Delores.

"Oh, I don't know unless it was the gate to Heaven. Where—am I?"

He looked to the right. He tried to lift his head.

"Why am I here, Delores? And—why are you here? I don't—understand this."

"You'll understand before long now, Joseph. Here comes your mother. I begged her to go eat a little breakfast."

Annie bent over her boy and clasped his one hand in both of hers.

"Mama," he gasped wonderingly.

"Joseph! You do know me—don't you, dear?"

"Why, Mama?" He tried to raise his head. "Of course—I know you, but why am I here? And Aunt Sara—and Agnes? Freddie—who brought me here?" He looked at them all. "Why am I here like this?"

"I helped bring you in, Joseph," Freddie said huskily. "You were hurt out here by the culvert. The horses ran away. Remember?"

"Sh!" whispered Freddie's mother. "Don't tell him everything yet."

"The horses?" Joseph stared wonderingly at those standing around him. "Where are they now? Father will think I'm never coming with that wagon. One of you had better tell him—what happened. I couldn't help it. I'll be—all right now. Just let me—"

"Don't try to get up, Joseph," said his mother. "You got a bad bump on your head. Father knows all about it, so don't worry about that; and the horses are back home where they belong. Wouldn't you like to have a drink?"

"Yes."

Agnes hurried to get fresh water.

"I'll give it to you with a spoon. Don't try to sit up until the doctor says you can."

"The doctor?"

"I'm going to call and tell him," said Aunt Sara, and she hurried to the phone.

"Mama."

"Yes, Joseph."

"Tell me."

"You mean what happened?"

"Yes. Father will be angry—but I tried to—"

"Never mind about Father's being angry, Joseph. It couldn't be helped, and all we care is that you get well now."

"That's all we care now, Joseph," Delores said, and glad tears trickled down her pink cheeks.

"Why do—you cry?" he asked.

"You've been so sick," she answered brokenly, "so—so long, Joseph."

"Not long," he answered drawing a deep breath. How weak he felt. How strangely weak and exhausted. "Just after breakfast I started out. What—what time is it now?"

"Joseph," answered his mother stroking his forehead. "It's longer—than you think. This is the—" she cleared her throat and hesitated. Maybe the shock would be too much for him. "You've been unconscious a number of days, Joseph. See, your arms are thin. Were you sleeping all this time?"

"I don't know. For—days?"

"Joseph," answered Annie feelingly. "You've had a birthday since that morning you were hurt."

"Birthday?" Joseph stared wide-eyed and confused.

"You are twenty-one now, Joseph, and have been for nearly a week."

"Mama, no!"

"Yes, dear, Delores knows I'm right. After a while you will realize it. Tell me, Joseph, was it very—very dark?"

"For a while, but—the road got brighter and that gate made a light in the distance. Oh, I was almost to it when I heard you call, Delores."

Before noon many of Joseph's friends had heard the glad news, and by Sunday evening Timothy Stokes' living room was literally flanked on all sides with the choicest summer flowers the valley could produce: roses, gladioli, Shasta daisies, snapdragons, phlox, sweet Williams, Canterbury bells, gaillardias, Veronica, and sweet-scented pinks and other flowers for which Joseph knew no name. Not the most beautiful bouquet, but perhaps the one he most appreciated was a bunch of blue and purple delphiniums, somewhat wilted, that Earnie Eloy had found along the way and had handed to Agnes rather hesitantly with apologies after he saw the other flowers friends had brought.

"Them was the best I could find fer you, Joseph," he said, approaching his bed slowly. An expression of surprise and gratitude lit up his brown, scarred face.

"They're nice, Earnie, and I like them a lot. Thanks."

"You've been a orful sick boy, I hear," Earnie said, "an' we're all tickled ter see you pull through like this. Spec yer mother is gladder'n anyone."

Joseph smiled as best he could. He had talked quite a little that day and was getting tired. He raised one thin hand and put it back of his head under the pillow.

"We're all glad, Earnie," came Annie's soft voice. There she was, sitting on yonder side of the flower-laden table, and Earnie hadn't noticed her. Beside her sat a sweet-faced girl and another girl whose face was familiar. Could that be Virginia? How womanly, how mature she looked. Earnie caught his breath and held it awkwardly.

"Are you—?"

"I'm Virginia," she said.

"You're growed up already."

She smiled and blushed.

"This is Delores Bays, Earnie," Annie said. "I think she's as glad as I am that Joseph is on the road to recovery. She was the first one to hear him speak when he really came to yesterday."

Bennet Armstrong shifted from one foot to the other, and a look of sore displeasure flitted across his stern face. He took a handkerchief out of his hip pocket and blew his large Roman nose. Not until then did Earnie notice him beyond the bookcase at the opposite end of the room. There seemed to be people and flowers everywhere. He did not speak to Earnie nor nod in recognition, but he cast an austere, unforgiving, almost cruel look at Annie and then at Delores Bays, and stalked out of the room.

CHAPTER LIV

In came Brother Grissley Steward with three books in one arm. As he stood beside the bed looking down at Joseph, the Sabbath's afternoon sunshine flickered through the rose bushes outside the west window and played on his snowy beard like a golden-winged butterfly. His face beamed with a celestial glory.

"God bless you, Joseph," he said; "our prayers for you have been answered, praise the Lord!"

Joseph smiled and that same glory on the elder's face was unconsciously reflected in his own. The hand that pressed his seemed to transmit some spiritual and physical strength.

"God has been good, hasn't He, Joseph?"

"Very good," answered Joseph.

"And faithful?"

"Yes."

"And kind?"

"Yes."

He held Joseph's hand in his and it seemed to be magnetized with the Holy Spirit.

"This experience has been good for all of us."

Joseph didn't answer. That seemed such a strange statement to make. How could this accident do anyone good?

"Brother Lanyard told me this morning he thought maybe you'd like to read some books I have in my library. I mean after you are stronger and have permission to read. I brought three along. I'll leave them here, and if you care to read them you may find some real help or comfort or enjoyment in them."

"I shall be very glad to read them," Joseph said.

"Then I have other books I shall be happy to loan to you later if you care to read."

25

"Care?" Joseph's face lit up. "I can't tell you how glad I would be to read some of your books, since I've not been able to go on to school."

"You may borrow any book you like," Brother Grissley said. "It has been a real joy and satisfaction to me to help others in this way. I have here, 'Ben Hur,' 'The Christian's Secret of a Happy Life,' and 'Absolute Surrender.' These are books that have not only helped me understand God better, but myself, and others as well. They've helped me understand how to realize those joys of a deeper consecration to God."

A deeper consecration, thought Joseph. Was there a time when this priestly man of God did not fully know those joys? Was there a time when Brother Grissley had not completely consecrated his own life? As long as Joseph could remember he had portrayed to him in human sacred pageantry the godliest of godly men: not by any ostentatious display; not by any vain or gaudy or proud words or conduct in the pulpit; but by his sincere, unobtrusive, humble, submissive, God-fearing life and preaching. As a small boy Joseph trembled at his very presence. When Brother Grissley arose behind that sacred desk in the chancel of the church, it seemed to him the entire sanctuary shuddered and quavered as he opened the Book and spoke the words of God. Joseph often wondered if others felt it too. Some slept. Joseph never did. His young soul was hungry for those life-giving words. His heart responded to that kind voice and those gentle eyes. They were so different from the voice and eyes of his father. And now that same man of God was standing by his bedside and was telling him this accident—this unfortunate experience—was good for all of them. All of whom? The church? Wasn't that what he meant? The entire congregation? How could it be? Something like a sudden bolt shot through Joseph's body and he twitched all over. Only yesterday he had seen Heaven's shining gate swinging ajar when Delores called him and he turned to locate that voice and come to earth. At first it had seemed so worthless, so disappointing to come back and start this long uphill road to recovery. Yes, even with a sweet face like that one he first looked into to spur him on; but here he was, and nothing could change it. Life was real and not a dream. The doctor had called yesterday and told him he would make it unless complications set in. Death! If that was death, it was nothing to dread! And this was earth and life! Life to live, and climb, and work! Life! From now on it *must* mean more than ever before! There sat his little mother, sweet-faced but pale; there sat Virginia and Delores. How he loved them all. And Lowell was somewhere close by. His heart yearned to live to do something for all of them, and there stood Brother Grissley Steward, his ideal of a Christian man, offering him books out of his library. Life seemed worth living, certainly it did! He wanted to live, he must live now—and yet how sweet that glimpse of the entrance to Heaven! Even the foretaste —just that fleeting moment of anticipation in advance of reality of entering through that gate was beyond any words to describe. The pleasantness of it lingered around Joseph for days as he sat propped up in bed reading the books Bro. Grissley had left for him. Those books seemed different and strangely precious because Bro. Grissley had touched them. No, Joseph Armstrong did not worship the man, but the influence of his Spirit-filled life was far-reaching. Is that strange?

* * *

"Joseph!" Uncle Timothy said one morning several days later, "one of these days you'll be up and walking."

"I hope so," Joseph answered.

"Now that you are of age I understand you are planning on working out?"

"That's what I plan to do, Uncle Timothy."

"Sara and Freddie and I have been talking of something that I hope will appeal to you too."

Uncle Timothy Stokes tilted back in his chair and ran his hands deep into his pockets. He looked Joseph full in the face.

"Freddie wants to go to academy. Maybe he has told you that."

"Yes."

"How would you like to work for me for a year, or until he gets back? I'll give you the same wages other farmers are giving. You haven't promised anyone, have you?"

"No, I haven't."

"Think it over, Joseph. Will you? Let me know in a few days."

"I won't need a few days to think that over, Uncle Timothy," answered Joseph. "I would like that well enough. I'll work a month for you without wages to pay what I owe you for all—"

"Be still about that, Joseph. You owe me nothing. Aren't you my sister's boy? The day you're able to begin work is the day I'll begin to reckon from. And take it easy, Joseph. You've been a sick boy. It will be almost a month yet before Freddie will need to leave. By that time you'll be feeling more like yourself."

"I hope so," answered Joseph.

"And you surely will if your appetite increases as it has the last day or so."

Joseph chuckled. It seemed good to hear him do that again.

A miracle of healing was wrought in Joseph's body in the days that followed. He read, he ate, he slept, he walked, he talked and laughed until he was glowing with the fires of exuberant youth once more. His eyes sparkled again, and before Freddie left home Joseph was stronger physically than he had ever been; in fact, there was a buoyancy about his step and voice no one had ever seen or heard before.

Without a doubt Delores Bays had something to do with this enrichment of his life. They exchanged letters during the week, and occasionally talked to each other on the phone. After Freddie was gone, Joseph had permission to use his horse and buggy until he could buy one of his own. Each hour spent with Delores became happier and more worth while. Joseph's heart was thrilled through and through with a strange deep sense of God's nearness, and His leading, as the beautiful character of this young woman was unveiled to him. As the weeks made months, he was sometimes struck dumb with excitement and wonder at the ready response and keen understanding she manifested toward his convictions. There was something about Delores that made him want to be the best, and truest, and noblest man that ever lived. It gripped his heart. Was his mother like Delores when she was young? Didn't father see it then? Didn't he feel it and appreciate it? How could he be so cruel and blind and misunderstanding! What torture, what anguish, what rankling pain his mother must have endured all these years. To speak a harsh word to Delores was the last thing Joseph could think of doing. He blushed with shame at the thought of it. He liked to watch her face light up with a smile. He thought of every possible way to please her. The more of Brother Grissley's books he read, the more he was inspired and spiritually impelled to live a more abundant life because of, and for, and with Delores Bays, and to know the joys of a fully consecrated life.

The surprise came one Sunday morning when the Sunday school superintendent asked Joseph to teach a class of nine-year-old boys.

Joseph shook his head. "I've never done anything like that," he said.

"But we feel you can, or we wouldn't have asked you."

Uncle Tom Bradly stepped up and placed a brawny hand on Joseph's shoulder. One day he bent over to touch Joseph's shoulder, and now he had to reach up. How tall and strong he looked!

"Don't say, no, Joseph," he said kindly. "Think what the Lord has done for you."

And as Joseph looked into the eyes of Uncle Tom, he was conscious of the fact that God had spared his life to serve. He knew it. It would be sin to shrink from it now. A half-shadowed arm seemed to be outstreched ready to bless his efforts if he would give himself humbly, wholeheartedly, prayerfully to this task.

"Those little shavers in that class need a teacher who can be a big brother to them," Uncle Tom said.

"How many will there be?"

"Oh, a dozen or so," said the superintendent. "Here's the lesson help for you, and the class will meet—"

J. Bennet Armstrong passed, and when he heard those words, a contemptible, mocking grin curled around his stern lips. It struck Joseph like a sudden blow in the chest. It sent a dart through his heart. Why should Father care? Why did he always look at him suspiciously? Didn't he hear his father saying to him, "Keep up the fight, son, keep up the fight"? or was that a dream? Joseph was walking along in the dark trying to find the right road when he heard his father's voice. Those were the kindest words he had ever heard him speak. Was it only a dream? He had asked his mother and she had assured him Father actually did say that the night before he woke up. Did Father really want him to live? Since the day he woke up, he had said precious little to him. Sunday after Sunday he had passed him in the churchyard or in the aisle, and never stopped to talk to him. He barely nodded, even when Joseph spoke first. Mother always made special effort to talk to him. She always wanted to know how he felt and what he had been doing. And now Father openly rebuked him with his mocking smile because he was asked to teach a class. His scornful glance had been personal. His unspoken words had been felt. Joseph's voice trembled.

"Can't you find someone else?" he asked entreatingly.

"You can do it," said Uncle Tom Bradly.

"We have no second choice," said the superintendent. "It's time to begin now." He looked at the clock on the wall.

"The boys meet in that classroom," and he pointed to the room at the left.

Joseph knew that room well. He remembered distinctly the impressions Uncle Tom Bradly had made on him when he was a small boy sitting in there. He remembered, too, how his father had answered him when he asked if missionaries went to school first. Even now he could hear that fist come down on the corner of the kitchen table and feel the blow it sent to his young heart.

"The boys will show you," and the superintendent walked away.

As Joseph took his seat, the kind, understanding eyes of his mother sought him out across the pews of people, and in them Joseph read courage, and dauntless fortitude.

CHAPTER LV

Three weeks later Annie Armstrong met her son on the walk at the side entrance of the church. She had waited fully five minutes for him. Bennet was walking toward the surrey and would be impatient, maybe angry if he had to wait for her. She drew Joseph aside gently.

"Father is waiting for me," she whispered. "But I can't go without talking to you a little. Are you getting along all right with your class?"

"I guess so."

"You're enjoying it?"

"Well—yes. It really makes me study. Those boys are live wires. They can surely ask the questions."

"Well, do your best, Joseph," said his mother.

"I'm trying to. And how are you, Mama?"

"Oh, so, so." She fumbled at the corner of her Bible and looked toward the surrey.

Joseph touched her arm. "Is your heart bothering you again?"

"Again?" she asked. "It never has quit bothering me, Joseph. But it seems to be worse again since—"

"Since when, Mama?"

"Since you never come home any more." Her lips quivered and her eyes got misty.

"Has Father ever mentioned anything?"

"Almost every Sunday morning I suggest inviting you to come along home for dinner, but he always shakes his head—always!"

"Well, then, of course, I wouldn't enjoy coming. Would I?"

"I guess not."

"He told me to leave."

"I know."

"Whenever he invites me to come back, I'll come. You know that, Mother." He stepped closer to her.

"Yes, but I get so lonesome for you, Joseph." Tears welled up in both eyes now and she looked away.

Joseph put a strong hand on his mother's shoulder and said in a deep, rich voice, "And I want you to know, Mother, I get just as lonesome for you. Mama," and his voice was almost a whisper, "seems I still like to call you Mama best sometimes. Is—is Father no better, Mama —no kinder?"

"Oh, no," she sighed wearily. "I thought your accident would soften him a little, at least."

"It hasn't?"

"Not that I can see. For about a week there when you lay unconscious he seemed troubled and very quiet; and that one evening when you first tried to talk, I thought surely a change was coming over him, but then when he found out Delores was there when you woke up he was no different at all."

"Is he angry with me?"

"He refuses to talk about you. He never mentions your name unless it's absolutely necessary."

"Shall I try to have a talk with him?"

"I wouldn't. It would only make him worse, I'm afraid; especially now since you have a class."

"He thinks I'm not fit to teach a class, doesn't he?" Joseph's voice sounded a little hurt.

"Either that or he's jealous, Joseph. But go on and do your best. But pray for me every day, Joseph, please. I need it."

"I do, Mama. I pray for you more than once a day."

"And remember Virginia. She's very much dissatisfied at home, and it will be another year before she would dare to think of working out. I must go, Joseph. Father is watching us." She took a few steps.

"How are you and Delores getting along?" she whispered looking up at him.

"Just fine."

"I'm glad. She seems to be a very sweet girl."

"Sweeter the better I know her. And Father still opposes it?"

"Very much, Joseph."

"I'm sorry he feels that way."

"I hope we can keep it a secret as much as possible for more than one reason. The day will come when it will make it hard for Virginia if everyone knows Father wants his children to marry into money." Annie gave a big sigh.

"Sometimes," Joseph said as he walked beside his mother, "sometimes," he whispered, "I wonder whether that's the real reason why father objects to Delores."

"I just must go," Annie said sadly. "I wanted to talk to you about other things but Father will be furious if I keep him waiting any longer."

When Annie reached the surrey, Bennet was looking sternly at his watch. The severe lines around his mouth were set as in graven stone.

"A minute longer and we would have gone on without you." The "we" included Lowell and Virginia who were sitting in the back seat, silent and in a strained manner. They never, never would get used to Father's severe countenance and words. With feeling and pity they watched their mother climb unassisted into the front seat. Seldom had she taken that place. That was where Lowell belonged beside his father, and Annie belonged in the back seat beside Virginia. Today evidently he wanted her beside him to scold her the better.

Bennet cracked the whip, and so unexpected was the lash that the horse jumped up on his hind feet and gave the four-wheeled carriage a sudden jerk.

"Mercy," whispered Virginia, and she clapped her hand over her mouth.

"That's what I say, too," shouted Bennet angrily. "God have mercy on all of us. The next time you and Joseph Armstrong have so much to talk about," and he cast Annie a piercing sidewise glance, "I'll just leave you at the church to talk, and I'll drive to town for my dinner."

"All right," answered Annie, calmly looking straight ahead.

"And what about us?" asked Lowell (a question any twelve-year-old boy would have asked with an empty stomach reminding him it was past twelve).

"You?" roared Bennet—but before he roared he made sure every parishioner had left the churchyard—"you will go where I tell you to go."

Of course Annie Armstrong wouldn't want such a thing to happen if she could possibly avoid it, and it never did. Several times when she had something special to tell her son, she wrote it on paper and slipped it to him when she shook hands with him after church. And more than once Joseph had a note for his mother too. She found herself longing for his notes. They were the nearest to love letters she had ever received.

Her heart condition afforded her few moments of actual comfort, but she kept most of her aches and pains to herself; at least as much as possible. Virginia always knew when she felt bad. She could tell by her mother's respiration; and at such times she was not slack in doing her utmost to help with the work.

The second surprise came a year later when Brother Herbert Lanyard announced to the church the results of the votes cast at the annual business meeting the previous week.

"Sunday school superintendent, Joseph Armstrong; assistant Sunday school superintendent, Riley Doane."

A cold sweat stood on Joseph's forehead, and he felt weak all over. What was that he heard? Sunday school

superintendent? At the age of twenty-two! How could
that be? Wasn't there a mistake? He, Sunday school
superintendent, and Riley Doane, assistant? Riley Doane
was as old as his own father. What could this mean?
Brother Lanyard surely got their names and offices
mixed; but the next minute he knew without a doubt,
for Brother Lanyard was saying in a voice that all could
hear, "Will Joseph Armstrong and Riley Doane please
come forward and receive their charge."

Trembling from head to foot, Joseph walked down
the center aisle, and three pews ahead Riley Doane met
him and walked beside him toward the rostrum.

"This important work has been put into your charge
by the voice of the church," Brother Lanyard said, looking down at the two below him. Joseph stood with his
hands clasped in front of him and his head slightly bowed.
"Will the congregation please stand while we offer a
prayer of consecration for these brethren. Those of you
who are ready to support these brethren by your co-opera-
tion and prayers, please show it by the raised hand.
Thank you. As far as I could see, the vote was unanimous."

Fortunately Joseph had his back to the audience, for
there was one who did not raise his hand, neither the
right one nor the left, and that one was J. Bennet Armstrong. He did not close his eyes during Brother Lanyard's prayer, but, drawing one deep breath after
another, he swept the pew in front of him with his cold,
blue eyes.

The next Sunday morning Joseph opened the Sunday
school by reading from the fifteenth chapter of John,
beginning at the twelfth verse. After much studying and
searching he had chosen this passage in connection with
the morning lesson, "Living the Christian Life Between

Sundays." Reading from the eighteenth verse he raised his eyes to look at the audience. "If the world hate you," he read, and, looking up, caught sight of his father's face, rigid and severe, and his gaze fixed on the west wall. Joseph's voice faltered. A lump came into his throat that he could not swallow. He finished the verse and called on Brother Grissley Steward to lead in prayer.

"You go ahead and lead in prayer, Joseph," said Brother Grissley in a kind, fatherly way; so Joseph prayed with great difficulty, not because he didn't know how; not because he was not familiar with those terms that make prayer a real, vital experience of fellowship with God; not because he was embarrassed and had to fumble for words; but because his father's countenance sent sudden woe into his young heart, and it was not easy to recover himself at the moment. Would it always be so that his own father would send new terror and grief and perplexity through his breast? Would it never be different? That afternoon Joseph's feelings got the best of him. With tears streaming down his cheeks he approached Uncle Timothy by the gate. He could contain himself no longer. He must tell someone.

"Just keep on, Joseph," said Uncle Timothy. "Can't you feel the whole church behind you?"

"Yes," choked Joseph, "but Father! I think sometimes I can't endure it. If I only could go back to him like a prodigal son, I'd go. I'd run back, but he's the one that told me to leave."

"Just keep on and go the second mile."

"I'd go the third and fourth to win his love," cried Joseph.

*   *   *

Art Olterham and Joseph had been friends for months. When Freddie came home from school, Joseph went to work for Squire McCracken, and Art Olterham (who worked for the squire by the day) was often assigned work with Joseph. Art was a clean, sociable, likable sort of fellow, and he and Joseph had more than one thing in common—but Art was not a Christian. He and Joseph not only worked together, but occasionally also went fishing together after working hours, and Freddie Stokes went along. There was something about Art that both boys liked. Without much coaxing they persuaded him to come to church. Art was not of the roguish or fraudulent type, neither did he use bad language; but he was not a Christian. He smoked only in private and never drank; but Art was not a Christian. He was ready to be a good Samaritan to anyone; but he never had accepted Christ as his personal Saviour.

"Art," said Joseph one morning after church, "why don't you give your heart to God?"

Art looked up in surprise and took a step backward. He put both hands deep in his pockets and looked Joseph straight in the eyes.

"You don't care," he said musingly.

"Don't care?" asked Joseph in surprise. "Why do you say that?"

"Do you honestly think my soul is lost and I'm doomed for hell?"

"If the Bible is true," answered Joseph, "and I know it is, unless you confess Christ you cannot be saved."

"Then why," asked Art, "If you actually believe that, why haven't you or Freddie spoken to me before? Not once in twenty months have either of you asked me if I'd—"

"Art!" cried Joseph. He was struck. It was as if a chastening rod had dealt him an unexpected blow. "But we've been praying for you."

"You have?" A faint smile played around Art Olterham's lips, and he walked away slowly.

*   *   *

"Delores," Joseph said that evening, "I've got something awful to tell you."

"Oh, Joseph!" cried Delores, "What is it? Has your father—"

"No, dear, it's not about my father. It's about Art Olterham."

"What? Tell me, Joseph!"

"I'm not fit to be a Sunday school superintendent."

"Don't tell me that, Joseph. I can't believe it. Oh, it can't be that he has dragged you into something bad. Why, Joseph!" and she stood trembling beside his chair.

"Not that," he said clasping her hands in his, "but I've completely failed as a witness for Christ; but from now on I'm going to try to do better."

CHAPTER LVI

The noon-day sun was shining intensely on the distant hills; at the same time a soft warm rain was falling so lightly that it could not be heard. That Sunday morning an old, old hymn was being sung as Brother Lanyard extended an invitation, and Art Olterham arose from his seat. Joseph's heart pounded within him, and a new-born glory sprang up in his smitten soul, giving him fresh courage, new joy, and a new appreciation for the sacredness of a human life. Manhood's strife for noble living took on new meaning that Sabbath morning. He had helped one soul toward God. As long as he'd live, he'd never forget that look on Art's face when he said, "You don't care"; or would he ever forget the sun on the distant hills—those hills he and Herbert Lanyard had crossed together one dark night; or the shadow that fell across his open Bible when Art stood; or the earnestness on Brother Lanyard's face as he held out his right hand and invited sinners to accept Christ.

"God bless you, Art," whispered Joseph as soon as church was over; and it was quite impossible to keep the glad tears from his eyes. From that day on, Joseph and Art were *real* friends.

* * *

The strawberries were ripe again, and Delores brought in two dishes, heaping full, a dab of whipped cream on top, pound cake and fresh water, all on a pewter tray. While they were eating, the clock in the dining room struck ten.

"Strawberries never were more delicious," Joseph said smiling.

"They were good tonight, weren't they?" Delores answered.

"Shall we sing together a while before you leave?"

"Whatever makes you happy, makes me happy, Delores."

She smiled at him, and the beauty of her personality, the ardor of her womanhood and her glowing health overwhelmed him with joy.

"Delores," he cried, "you are beautiful tonight."

"You told me that before," she said blushing.

"But every time I come you are more beautiful," he declared. "Delores," he said softly. He caught her by the hand and led her across the room. "Sit here beside me. I want to talk to you."

She sat beside him on the green velours sofa, and crossed her dainty slippered feet gracefully. She waited. Before he spoke, he looked at her a full minute.

"Do you know, dear," he said, "that we've been keeping company now for three years?"

"Yes," she whispered. She smoothed out her pink silk dress, and took a long deep breath.

"I've been working hard, and I've been saving all I could."

"Yes," she whispered again, "and Father said you bought your horse and buggy at the right time, for the prices have gone up since."

"I know. I'm glad for my own horse and buggy, but that isn't all I want. I want a little home to call my own, and I want you to come and live in it with me, Delores. Would you—would you consider being my wife?"

She stood up and faced him; then suddenly she clasped him around the neck. He could smell some kind of spicy perfume, and feel the softness of her sleeves against his cheeks as she said, beaming, "Of course I will, Joseph. I could never be a wife to anyone but you. You'll have to ask my father, of course."

"That won't be hard to do, Delores," he answered. "You're worth that much. I'll go ask him right now if he's still up."

"I'll stay here."

Jeddie Bays was in the kitchen getting a drink when Joseph entered. There was no heavy apathy weighing on Joseph's heart, no smothering fear, no halting step; but through his veins fresh vigor flowed. It welled up within him rich and strong, and love beat high in his breast.

"Mr. Bays," Joseph said in a low, mellow voice that was firm and splendid. "Delores is the best girl on earth, and I know she deserves the best any man can offer, and I am not rich; but I do love her very, very much, and she loves me; and if you give your consent, we'd like to get married someday before too long."

Jeddie held the glass of sparkling water in his right hand a moment, then set it on the corner of the table and leaned against the kitchen sink. He folded his long arms slowly and answered pleasantly, "If that's what Delores wants to do, it's quite all right with me, Joseph. By this time you already seem like one of the family, almost."

"Thank you, Mr. Bays," and Jeddie caught Joseph's outstretched hand and clasped it warmly.

"He said 'yes,' Delores," cried Joseph.

"I knew he would, Joseph," and she found herself folded in his strong arms for the first time and his lips met hers.

"Do you suppose we can get ready by September, darling?"

"I think I can. Can you?"

"We'll let the Lord decide the time for us. He brought us together, and if He wants us to get married He'll give us a place to live."

"Of course He will, Joseph."

"You're a dear, Delores. You're sweet and beautiful,

and I love you more than—how shall I say it—it's more than I can ever tell you."

"It seems now that we've always loved each other."

"It does to me, too," Joseph answered, "and that makes me sure we are meant for each other. Let's kneel here and thank Him."

Together they knelt by the green sofa and prayed.

*   *   *

When Joseph came to see Delores on Wednesday night, he brought her a box wrapped in white tissue paper and tied with a satin ribbon.

Trembling with excitement, she opened it carefully. A silver box lined with rose velvet contained a three piece dresser set of gray ivorylike substance trimmed in silver.

"It's beautiful!" she gasped. "Joseph, it's perfectly lovely!"

"I'm glad you like it, dear. And I've got something good to tell you. I talked with John Hawkers today, and he said he'd give me a job by the first of September, and we could live in half of his house. We can have all the milk, cream, butter, and eggs we want, firewood, our own garden, a pig, and twenty dollars a month cash. Before I came here tonight I drove over and looked at the place, and I believe you'd be satisfied."

"I'm sure I will, Joseph. Oh, it will be so much fun to get things ready. Mother will help me get some comforters and other things made; and do you want to see what I've been working on today?"

"Of course. Pillow cases! You do lovely work. Must we wait three months?"

"We'll be so busy, the time won't seem long."

"That's right, Delores. We'll be so busy and so happy getting ready that the weeks will soon make months. Let's take a walk through the orchard and talk."

*   *   *

The day came when Joseph Armstrong walked beside
Delores Bays for the last time before they would be forever joined as husband and wife. A long strip of gold
slanted across the western sky, chasing the gray dusk
into purple darkness. Her slender hand was in his, trustingly, confidingly, and final plans were being made for
the wedding. The marriage license was in his inside coat
pocket, and her dress hung in the closet, pressed and
ready.

"I'll come tomorrow evening about four, sweetheart,"
he said, looking down at her lovingly. "I'll drive by and
pick up Virginia, and Freddie said he'd meet us here by
four-thirty."

"You made arrangements with Bro. Lanyard?"

"Yes, dear; as far as I know everything is ready. I
can count the hours now."

"Before you leave, Joseph," called Mr. Bays from the
open door, "I want to talk to you a little."

"Let's go see what your father wants."

"This is what I wanted to tell you," Jeddie said, stepping out to the edge of the porch. "I can't do for Delores
like Clark Elliott does for his children when they get
married. He gives each of them a thousand dollars in
cash and a team of horses; but I'll do for you what I can.
I'll give you all the furniture you'll need for three rooms,
a good milk cow, and a pig."

"Why, Mr. Bays!" gasped Joseph. "That's a big gift.
That will certainly help us out a lot. I was not expecting
anything from you but your daughter."

Jeddie laughed good-naturedly and went inside so
the two could be alone.

*   *   *

Joseph was there at four o'clock, tingling with joy, and
a happy, confident expression in his eyes, for at last he

had come to get his God-promised one. The stair door was open, and from the top Delores called to him.

"Come up, Joseph," she said.

He went up.

The sight was beautiful. Delores was standing at the top of the stairs in a long white satin dress, cheeks a peach pink, eyes glowing, her soft blond hair half covered by her white, crisp prayer veil.

"Do you like my dress, Joseph?"

"Like it! Delores! It's too good to be true!"

"That's all I wanted, Joseph," she said softly. "You may go down again. I just wanted to make sure you liked my dress. I like your suit very much."

"I'm glad you do. I hoped you would, Delores."

"What is it, Joseph?" He hesitated at the top step.

"You know," he said seriously, "we're starting out on a great voyage, and—and—there'll be lots of opposition. Don't you think before we go to the preacher's house we ought to kneel down and ask God to help us?"

"Why yes—Joseph—maybe we ought to."

Together they knelt beside the bed, and sincerely and with feeling Joseph prayed first.

"Dear Lord," he said, "I thank You for the day You brought this lovely person into my life. I thank You for the way You have led our lives in love and into Thy love; but You know the attitude my father takes. Neither of us knows what lies ahead, of joy or sorrow; but with whatever comes, help us be true to Thee. Help me be a real husband to Delores, and bless us both with health and strength, and whatever it will take to follow Thee completely, for Jesus' sake."

Then Delores prayed.

"Dear Father in Heaven, I too thank Thee for the day Joseph came into my life. He has made me so happy these past three years and more. Help me to be a real wife and companion to him, and share whatever joy or sorrow that may come to his life, and give us grace to forgive his father, and help us treat him right; and oh, God, somehow bring about a reconciliation between us, and Thou shalt have all the praise. In Jesus' name. Amen."

They went in Jeddie Bays' two-seated buggy (Joseph and Delores in front, and Virginia and Freddie in the back), and at six o'clock in Brother Herbert Lanyard's living room, a simple, but impressive wedding ceremony was performed. For just a moment a holy hush lasted after Brother Lanyard finished his prayer and took his hand off theirs; then Joseph kissed his bride, then Virginia kissed them both. Numbers before them had stood on that same hallowed spot in Brother Lanyard's living room and had been pronounced husband and wife, but this did not lessen the newness of the joy Joseph and Delores felt. It was theirs alone. No one else could be happy for them. No one could rob them of it.

Few words were spoken on the ride back home. The two in front were too happy to talk, and the two behind were afraid to break the quiet solemnity of the hour. To talk would have seemed almost irreverent.

The dinner was ready to be served. Jeddie and Mrs. Bays greeted both daughter and son-in-law with glad outstretched hands, and extended their sincere congratulations and best wishes. The evening was perfect.

The next morning the happy couple left for a trip to a big city in the middle west. They wanted to be alone for a few days to think, and plan, and talk things over; things of life that cannot be sketched on paper, life—love—faith in each other—purity of soul—honor for God—truths of life that alone must be experienced in two lives united by God, the union of such who have made history brighter and worth recalling to our generation.

CHAPTER LVII

Joseph Armstrong and his wife went to housekeeping in half of John Hawkers' eight-room house, and Joseph worked for John. Joseph bought a likely horse and fattened him, and in due time sold him with a sixty-dollar profit. Every day he prayed that God would bless them both with whatever material blessings He saw fit. A year passed by, but Bennet would not invite his son and his wife to come home. Annie wept more than once about the situation. Hers was a lonely life now since Virginia worked out. Were it not for the fact that she enjoyed her daily communion with God, the disappointments and griefs of life would have completely overwhelmed Annie. Her personal devotion to God, that moment-by-moment witness-bearing of Spirit with spirit which has sustained many a weary soul that otherwise would be daily terrified by the events of life, gave calmness to her.—Annie Stokes Armstrong lived through her trials calmly, believingly, and in her soul God whispered daily His low sweet amen of peace, and her sweet sad face grew sweeter until every consecrated Christian marveled at the strange glory they saw there.

"Joseph," she said one Sunday. Always she wended her way through the crowd to her boy after the benediction. "Won't you and Delores come home today for dinner?"

"Did Father say so?"

"No. He said I wasn't to invite you, but come anyway. If he can't stand it he can eat after we get done."

"Mama!" and Joseph put a strong arm across her shoulders. "I want him to invite us. You all go along home with us today."

"It's no use, Joseph. He's said over and over he'll not come. Delores called up yesterday and invited us, but he said he absolutely would not go."

God moves in a mysterious way His wonders to perform, and faithful saints can take fresh courage when His mercy breaks through the hanging clouds. One evening Bennet Armstrong answered the telephone and a familiar voice came over the wire.

"You say it's Milton Collins? And you and your wife are at the depot? Most certainly. I'll be right in to get you. No, it won't be too much bother."

With a rather unsteady hand Bennet hung up the receiver.

"I'm to go to town to get Brother and Sister Collins," he announced to Annie who was stacking the dishes. "They will eat their supper in town so you won't need to bother about that."

"And—and I wonder what brought them here?"

"They are on their way to the coast to see some relatives, and want to spend a day or two here. Don't look so shocked, Annie," Bennet said rather sharply. "I call it quite an honor to be considered their friends. I guess I must have made the right impression on him at least," and so saying Bennet scurried to the bedroom to put on his Sunday suit.

Not five minutes had passed after their arrival until Brother Collins asked about Joseph. His eagerness and interest in Joseph provoked Bennet, but he tried desperately to hide the fact.

"Well, that's one place we surely want to go to before we leave," said Evalena. "Don't we, Milton?"

"Yes, indeed! There was something about that boy Joseph I've never been able to forget. Is he still as interested in spiritual things as he used to be?"

"I think so," Annie answered. "Wouldn't you say he was, Bennet?"

Bennet shifted from one foot to the other, and a confounded, almost defeated look crossed his face. What should he say? What could he say? He wanted to hoot, but he could not do that. If the phone would only ring! If someone would only knock on the door and interrupt the conversation! There sat Annie, looking straight at him, waiting for an answer, and there sat both Brother and Sister Collins waiting, too.

"Well," he answered at length, and his voice was a little throaty when he spoke, "the church seems to feel he is, the way they use him. I never before heard of a boy twenty-two being a Sunday school superintendent."

"Well, well," said Brother Collins. "That speaks well. That sounds interesting. I want to see Joseph. Maybe we could all go over there tomorrow for dinner. I don't mean to be inviting myself, but Annie, maybe you can arrange a get-together some way."

"Of course I will. They will be glad to have us come. Delores doesn't know you, but she'll be very happy to have us all come. Won't she, Bennet?"

"Why—of course," Bennet said, and he blew his large Roman nose.

What else could Bennet do but take his preacher friend and wife to his son's home? Little did they suppose he had never been there before. Bennet dare not let them know. All the way he talked about the weather, the crops, this farm, and that farm—anything but his son Joseph.

Delores met them at the door.

"This is such a pleasure to have you bring your friends," she said, kissing Annie fondly on the cheek. "Sister Collins, I'm happy to meet you, and you too, Brother Collins. Joseph has often spoken of you good people. Good evening, Father, let me take your hat. Come into the living room and find chairs. Joseph will soon be in."

"May I help you, Delores?"

"Thank you, Mother, but I have everything ready."

The delicious odor of food came from the kitchen. Joseph washed with special pains and hurried to the living room. There sat the four, talking in pleasant tones and smiling at each other fondly.

"Joseph!" Milton Collins crossed the room to meet him. "It's a real pleasure to see you—and in your own cozy home, and you have a nice little wife. God bless you, Joseph."

"Thank you, Brother Collins. It's wonderful to have you as our guests. Sister Collins, how do you do. So glad to have you here. Father, and how are you today?" He shook his hand warmly.

"Very well," Bennet answered.

"And Mother! I'm sure this was a happy surprise for you, wasn't it?"

"The happiest surprise I've had in a long time," she answered smiling, and in that smile Joseph caught a gleam he hadn't seen in those eyes for years.

No one could have found fault with the meal Delores served, and done it justly. No one could have gone home and said he did not have an enjoyable time, and said it honestly. Bennet acted surprisingly pleasant, and although he did not talk incessantly, he talked enough that neither Brother nor Sister Collins would have guessed there was any variance between father and son. He played his part well, and for once Annie thanked God that Bennet was a good pretender.

"And now it's your turn to come to our house for a meal," Annie said before they left.

"Thanks, Mother," Delores said, "but let's not keep track of turns. You just come back whenever you can. You must come again soon because Lowell didn't get to come along today, and Virginia doesn't have to work Sundays, does she?"

"No."

"Then all four of you come for Sunday dinner when they can come along. This was too short, anyway. May we count on you?"

"Whatever Bennet says," was Annie's answer.

Bennet cleared his throat nervously and ran his hand around his hat brim twice and said, "Whatever Annie says." What else should he say? What else could he say? His brain went into a whirl and he could not think of an excuse.

"And Joseph," said Brother Collins, stepping close to him and placing a hand on the younger man's shoulder, "come to see us. I mean it seriously, not just to be nice because you've so graciously entertained us. If the time ever comes that you want to buy a farm of your own, remember there are some nice farms out our way, and our little church could use a young man like you. May the Lord's will be done in your life, and good-by, Joseph."

That same kind of feeling like the sudden shock that he felt when Grissley Steward stood at his bedside went through Joseph's entire body, distinct and real, challenging him again to be true to that ever-present force that controlled his life. There was no use trying to discount that feeling, or shake it off. He had tried and failed. But at times like this it gripped him afresh.

"Did you take any academy work?"

Brother Collins was on the last step now, and Joseph's father was walking toward the gate.

"No, I didn't get to go."

"But he studies almost every night, Brother Collins," Delores said.

"That's fine, Joseph."

"Why did he say that?" asked Delores as the two entered the house.

"I guess he thinks I need it," Joseph said musingly.

Bennet Armstrong had a sick headache on Sunday. He did not go to church. Annie called and said they could not come to dinner.

Bennet had difficulty in getting hired help. It was impossible for him to do the work in the vineyard alone; Lowell was too young, and had he been older, there was plenty to keep him busy on the farm. Besides that, he had another year of school. The grapes were ready for market, but for some reason Bennet could not find a man to help. The circumstance he found himself in worked on his nerves. The possibility of losing money put him in a very disagreeable situation, to say the least. He told Annie it was as bad as being in a strange city without friends or money. He could not eat, and neither could he sleep.

While Annie was alone in the house, she called Joseph on the phone.

"Father is almost beside himself with the work in the vineyard," she said. "The grapes should go to market immediately, and he cannot find help. One man helped him half a day and quit."

"That's strange. Did he try Earnie?"

"Yes, but he couldn't get him."

"Did he try?"

"Joseph, he's tried three times, I'm sure. I've never known him to be so nervous and unstrung. Could you possibly see your way clear to help him out a day or so?"

"If I'd get up at two-thirty or three and do my work here, maybe I could come over and help take a load or two to town for a few days, and work overtime here."

"That would be too hard on you, Joseph. You couldn't stand that very long."

"But I'll do it for a while, Mama. I'm glad you called. I'll see if I can borrow or rent John's team and wagon and come over and help Father tomorrow."

That is exactly what Joseph did. He passed his father on the road going toward the vineyard with a borrowed team and wagon; Bennet going toward town with a load of grapes. Joseph spoke, but his father looked straight ahead and never batted an eye. By the time Joseph had his wagon loaded, Bennet was over half way home. They passed each other at the foot of the hill. Joseph spoke again, but Bennet looked straight ahead, his steely face set and cold. Four times Joseph spoke, and four times Bennet refused to answer.

"This is heartbreaking," cried Joseph that evening. "He saw me every time; I know he did!"

"Well, you'll get your reward anyway, Joseph," Delores said.

"I'm not doing it for a reward. I'm doing it to try to prove to him I've got nothing against him; and I want to make it easier for Mother. I suppose he's almost impossible around home."

"Are you going again tomorrow?"

"Yes, I'll go again tomorrow."

"Even if he doesn't appreciate it?"

"Yes, I'll go again tomorrow."

And Joseph did. He went back the next day, and the next, and the next; and not until the last day did Bennet Armstrong give his son a nod of recognition. By that time Joseph was in tears when he came to the supper table. Tired to the point of exhaustion from loss of sleep and overwork, he dropped his head on the table and burst out with sobs.

"There's no use trying to be nice to Father, and I'm just about ready to—to move clear away from here where he won't see me. He acts like he hates me worse than ever, and God knows I've tried to help him. Today he nodded only slightly and made a grunt."

"Maybe he thinks you're trying to heap coals of fire on his head, and he can't stand that."

"I can't help what he thinks. Before God I've done this out of love and because he couldn't get help, and because he's my father, Delores, my own father!"

"Don't cry, Joseph. It hurts me as bad as it does you.'

"It couldn't."

"But it does, Joseph. Aren't we one in everything? What hurts you, hurts me. Didn't I promise to stand by you in joy or sorrow as long as I live?"

"Yes, dear, you did." Joseph raised his tear-stained face and drew Delores close to him. "And do you wonder now why I wanted to pray that evening before we went to get married?"

"I didn't understand it so well then, Joseph, but I do now."

"And you'll stand by me no matter how Father acts?"

"Why, Joseph Armstrong! You know I will!" And both her arms tightened around his neck.

"Would you be interested in going west to look for a farm?"

"Now?"

"As soon as we can."

"If that's what you think we should do, Joseph."

CHAPTER LVIII

In Joseph's book of sweet memories was one Sunday afternoon at home with his mother and Lowell and Virginia.

"You're coming along home with me today," Annie said. "Father is gone."

"Gone! Gone where?" asked Joseph.

"He's gone on a trip west somewhere."

"For what?"

"He has some money to invest."

"He has?" Joseph's eyes opened wide with surprise. But why should he be surprised? Of course Father had money to invest.

"He said before someone wants to borrow it, he'll buy a farm to rent out."

"Wish Father had enough confidence in me to rent me a farm." Joseph said it sadly, almost sarcastically, and as soon as he had said it he felt like biting his tongue.

"I think," answered Annie softly, "when it comes right down to it, maybe Father has more confidence in you than he lets on."

"But he'd never rent me a farm. I met Squire McCracken in town yesterday, and I had a long talk with him—but this is Sunday. Let's go. I shouldn't be thinking of such things today."

"You'll be over then?"

"Yes, we'll be there."

What strange emotions filled Joseph's breast as he hung his hat behind the kitchen stove and walked through the house—his father's house! A blooming begonia on the window sill in the living room took him back to something that happened almost twenty years before—but there was no yellow cat beside it, and the window wasn't a bay window. This wasn't the same house, but there was

403

a rocking chair much like the one on which his mother used to sit when she held him on her lap and told him stories. He'd never forget the sweet, clean smell of the starch in her apron. There was a new roll-top desk and a sectional bookcase he had never seen before, and a safe. He had never seen the rug on the bedroom floor, or the glass-doored corner cupboard in the dining room. Although nothing was expensive, the furnishings were good, and the home had a comfortable appearance that Joseph appreciated. If only the head of the house had a husbandly, comforting atmosphere! That influence was absent, and the absence was remarkably evident. Joseph and Delores enjoyed an agreeable, delightful afternoon, free from all strain of speech or conduct.

*   *   *

Bennet was gone ten days. He brought home the news that he had purchased a one hundred and sixty-acre farm six miles north of Admore and had rented it for a year to the man who was living on it. When Annie told Joseph, something within him sank for a moment, but he soon conquered that feeling of defeat. Hadn't he and Delores both prayed earnestly that God would overrule every move they made in life? Hadn't they asked God every night and every morning to lead them step by step in every undertaking? Would God be God now and let them stick, or fall, or stumble? No! Joseph would not acknowledge that he even cared.

The year rolled around. Joseph worked as he had never worked, earning, and figuring, and saving, with an end in view—a comfortable home for his little family which now numbered three. Danny Gene was born just the week before the unexpected happened. All alone Annie drove over to see her first grandchild.

"He's as sweet as he can be, Delores," she said, holding back the blue blanket from his tiny round face. "And do you know what Father said this morning?"

"I couldn't guess."

"Indeed you couldn't. He said he'd rent the farm to Joseph; and if he wants it, to say so right away."

"Really?" gasped Delores in surprise. "Did you tell him we wanted it?"

"I told him a long time ago I thought you might be interested. Farms around here are so high, and he knows that."

"And what did he say then?"

"He just looked at me in astonishment, or I couldn't tell you exactly how. He said practically nothing until this morning. I think the year is about up, and he only promised it to that party for a year."

"I'll tell Joseph when he gets home."

"Where is he now?"

"He went to town with the milk. He'll likely be back in an hour. Can you stay?"

"Hardly that long, Delores. It will be dinnertime till I get back. Bennet still says every move of his must count, and I'm to help him make them count, so I'll have to go back. I'm baking bread today. Are you getting along all right?"

"Yes, Mother. Mrs. Hawkers comes in every now and then to see what I want. She's been so good to us."

"You dear little Danny!" Annie Armstrong touched his soft, soft cheek and went back home. She couldn't help seeing a likeness between this little boy and the one she had cuddled and cried over more than twenty years ago. But with the similarity she thanked God that there was a vast difference in this—her son's father resented his coming; but Danny Gene was wanted. She knew Joseph would be a real father to him—a loving, gentle, understanding father. Danny Gene would not be harshly spoken to or beaten unjustly. For every sorrow and disappointment, for every aching void of bygone days, Joseph would try to bring satisfaction to his own soul by lavishing love on his son. And so, with such thoughts in her mind, Annie felt like humming a little as she drove along. She really didn't often feel like it, although she sometimes hummed to chase away sad thoughts. God had been good and kind to her. He had heard her prayer, and extended her life to see Joseph saved and happily married. And now he was a happy father. Wasn't it worth the hardness of life to have that one glance at Danny Gene? Annie thought so. She pulled the lap robe up around her waist and faced the cold wind; but around her heart she had a warm, happy feeling that her life hadn't been in vain altogether.

Joseph talked to his father on the telephone. Bennet's words were few and to the point; but the point was understood perfectly, and Bennet agreed to rent the farm to his son for a year, rent payable in advance.

"Delores, we'll go in about a month."

"Really, Joseph? Do you think we'll like it out there?"

"I think we will. It will be altogether different, but—"

"We'll have each other," she said sweetly. Her face was radiant.

"That's right, Delores. We'll have each other, and Danny Gene, and a good pastor, Brother Collins. You'll like him and Evalena, I know."

"I wonder what the folks will say?"

"I wonder too. Do you suppose they'll object?"

Delores shrugged her shoulders a little and put Danny in his basket. "They may hate the idea of us going so far away, but they'll understand."

*   *   *

Joseph's first summer on his rented farm was a great disappointment. He experienced almost a complete crop failure. With what cash he had when he came he had purchased four horses, a plow, a wagon, a cow, and a secondhand automobile. By fall he was out of both feed and money. After much thinking and discussing the problem with Delores, he decided to write his father a letter.

"Dear Father,

"Due to lack of rain, the crops this summer amounted to practically nothing. I am entirely out of feed, and the garden yielded very little. Delores had nothing to can for the winter. We like it fine here, however, and if we have more rain next year, I think we can make it. I hate to ask you, but I hardly know what else to do, Father. I'm wondering if you would loan me $100.00 for six months? This leaves us all well, and I trust you are in the best of health. Danny is doing fine.

"Your son,
"Joseph."

When the answer came a week later, Joseph ran— almost bounded into the house. He held the letter up to the light and tore it open. "Joseph," he read. "Just as I said once, you'd be coming back some day—" Joseph's hands trembled. He caught his breath—"begging for a crust of bread if you didn't take . . ." Joseph reeled for an instant and staggered to the nearest chair. The words on the paper got blurred, and his head began to swim with a sickening sensation.

"Joseph!" cried Delores. "What is it? Read it out loud. Is it from your father?"

"Yes."

Joseph's arms dropped like so much lead, and the paper fell to the floor. Delores caught it up and read, " 'Joseph,' " "Why—why," she choked, "he doesn't even say, dear Joseph. 'Just as I said once,' " she read, " 'you'd be coming back some day begging for a crust of bread if you didn't take my advice.' When did he say that, Joseph?" choked Delores.

"Oh, one night when I was going with you."

"Why did he say that?"

"Read on and I'll tell you."

" 'I warned you plenty,' " she read. " 'Why don't you write to Jeddie Bays for money, or have you already, and he hasn't got it? Likely not. I haven't money to loan out either.

" 'J. Bennet Armstrong.' "

"Oh, Joseph!" And when Delores spoke, her voice was a stifled scream. Tears blinded both her eyes, and she leaned hard against the wall. "When did he say that about begging for a crust?"

Joseph got to his feet and paced back and forth across the kitchen.

"One night—one night I've tried for years to forget," he cried. "He tried to make me promise I'd never go with you again, just because your father wasn't wealthy. Money—money—money. He loves it, and he's got plenty. I know it! And he refuses to help me out. I won't ask your father for it. I won't—I won't if I have to eat grass—I won't ask your father for help!"

"Then I will, Joseph."

"No, you won't! I'll write to—"

"To who?"

"I'll try Art Olterham. I'll write to him and tell him to keep it to himself, and I know he will. Father! My own father! McCracken would loan me if I only asked him for it. I know he would, but I'd sooner borrow from someone in the church. Father! Take that letter and put it in the stove so I can't ever see it again!"

"Don't be angry, Joseph," said Delores a little reprimandingly.

"I'm not, Delores." Joseph gathered his wife in his arms and held her close.

"No, dear," he whispered. "I won't be angry. Only I wish now I hadn't asked him for it."

"And just think, he never offered to pay you for the work you did for him that first fall we were married."

"Oh, well, he didn't need to. I guess he thought if I was fool enough to come over and work without being hired that I didn't have enough to do to keep me busy at John's. I'd like to forget that too."

"You mean that you were fool enough to help him?"

"No, I mean the way he refused to speak to me. As for helping him, I'd do it again for nothing, to please Mother. But he saw me on the road. He saw me. I know he did."

"Don't let it hurt you, Joseph."

A letter from Art Olterham had arrived with a check inside. The letter read,

"Dear Joseph,

"I'm more than glad to be able to help you out. However, I've got only $85.00 to loan you just now. Maybe I can send you the other $15.00 in 30 days. My prayer is that God will prosper you and reward you for what you've meant to me. I'll always be thankful for the day when you asked me to become a Christian. If you hadn't I don't know where I'd be today. I hope you are helping other poor lost sinners like I was.

"Sincerely, your brother in Christ,
"Art Olterham."

That same feeling like a sudden electric shock went through Joseph's entire body when he read that last sentence. Slowly he folded the letter and put it in his Bible on the table.

"Delores," Joseph said, "I'm going to promise God from this day on that I'll give Him a tenth of all I make."

"You are?"

"Yes, I am. I've felt I should for some time, and I'm going to make it a promise now, right now."

Joseph borrowed several hundred dollars from the Admore bank, and before many months had passed his tithe for the Lord was nearly equal to the amount he had borrowed. From the very day he made the promise to God his efforts were blessed; his crops brought back two-fold—fourfold—tenfold—fortyfold. Joseph almost gasped when he read the figures.

The next day he mailed his mother a box. In it was a piece of gray silk material for a Sunday dress and a piece of blue for Virginia.

CHAPTER LIX

"We may forget her melting prayer
While leaping pulses madly fly,
But in the still unbroken air
Her gentle tones come stealing by;
And years—and sin—and manhood flee,
And leave us at our mother's knee."

Annie's arms got stiff and she felt cold all over. She had experienced many a severe disappointment in life, but none equal to this. She was struck numb! She was appalled! She was terrified! She couldn't recall any harsh word from Bennet that had affected her like this. She gripped the letter in both trembling hands and swayed for a moment with acute anguish of soul. For fear she misread a single word she read the letter again.

"Dearest Mother,

"My weekly letter to you will be several days late, but I've been pretty badly upset. I feel like giving up."

Annie's head went round and round, then the entire house started moving, and she staggered to the nearest chair. It was some time before she could see to read on.

"The cruelest words I ever had to listen to were given to me last week by a man who is supposed to be a good brother in the church here. It nearly knocked me flat, for I thought I was doing the will of the Lord when I got the rebuke. It has taken me all my life to reason away the shame and truth that I've been an unwanted son. All my life I've had to battle against self—doubts— and that inferior feeling, because of Father. I'm happily married, Mother. Delores is wonderful. I know that it was God who brought us together and has prospered us financially to the extent that we're able now to buy a farm of our

411

own; but why I've had to get such a knock out here, is more than I can understand. I am really discouraged, to be honest, and Delores is homesick. For the last few days I haven't been able to pray right. You pray for me, Mother."

Annie Armstrong burst into sobs that shook her entire body. What subtle change had come over her boy Joseph? What cruel words had the brother spoken to him? The letter was dismaying to say the least, and incomplete. It didn't sound at all like Joseph. He had never written like this before. Could it be true? Was it really from Joseph? Yes, it was his handwriting! And with what eagerness she had opened the letter while all alone in the house and no one to disturb! She had expected a precious missive from her beloved son Joseph who had overcome each new obstacle in life and grown to useful manhood and fatherhood, and was now prospering financially, but instead had received such a discouraging one. What was wrong?

Oh! Annie wanted to take the next train to Admore. But how could she ever do it? If Bennet read the letter, he would only hoot and laugh, and say, "that wonderful boy you've pampered and spoiled!" She had no money. Annie never had money. How could she go to her boy without a ticket, and without saying why? Oh, if ever in her life Annie wished she were a bird and could fly (as David the psalmist put it) to yon mountain, she wished it now.

Dropping suddenly on her knees, she covered her tear-stained face with two slender hands and prayed out loud. "Oh, God!" she cried, "Wherever Joseph is right now, right now, O God, wrest him in his way and make him think seriously on Thee. My God, don't let him go! Don't let him give up! Hold fast to him! I don't know what the dreadful thing is that has caused him to be so

iscouraged; but if ever you heard the cry of a heart-
roken mother, hear mine today. He's my boy. I dedi-
ated him to You years ago. He's the boy You raised as
t were from dead, and he said, O, Lord Jesus, he said,"
he could scarcely pray for crying, "he heard Your voice
alling him outside the barn—and—and how often I've
rayed that he would be a fruitful bough. And now, oh,
God, (and here Annie shook again with sobs uncon-
rolled) if the archers have sorely grieved him, and shot
it him, or even hated him, make his arms and hands
strong again by the hands of the mighty God of Jacob.
Dear Lord, I can't believe anything else but that You'll
wrest him right now—today—wherever he may be, or
at whatever he may be doing. Help him feel his mother's
praying for him. Make him know—make him see some
blessing through this trial—make him remember his
promise on bended knees—make him feel Your hand of
love upon him. Oh, my God, make him see Your tender
face, and hear Your gentle voice above those cruel words.
I cannot believe he's going to give up. I will not believe
he's going to turn back when You've found him, and called
him, and saved him, and led him all these years. Maybe
I've not been so faithful as I should have been in my
prayers. Maybe I've sinned in taking for granted he
was strong and firmly established. Maybe I've been too
proud of him; O God, for Christ's sake, forgive me if I
have. If Joseph goes wrong and I'm to blame, how can
I ever appreciate Heaven? I am smitten to the depths
of my soul. If it should be conviction he is fighting—"
Annie heard horses' hoofs on the road. "Lord, if he is
in dark despair, send him light right now!"

A sudden change passed over Annie Armstrong's tear-
stained face, altering it with a faint peacefulness, and
she stretched herself upon the cot beside the dining-room
window. She folded the letter and tucked it in her apron

pocket, and when Bennet came in, he thought she wa
sleeping.

* * *

In the field beyond the barn a lone pine tree lifted hi
head high into the evening sky that was fast growing dar
with a threatening storm. Joseph was sitting on th
edge of the porch with his feet on the ground, reading ou
loud from the newspaper. He was reading out loud s
Delores, who was preparing supper in the kitchen, coul
hear. He did not see the man approaching. When Josepl
looked up, he was less than ten feet from him.

"With a voice like you've got," the man said, "you
surely ought to be a preacher."

Joseph jumped as though he'd been shot. He was no
frightened but he tingled all over.

"A-a-what?" The newspaper dropped. A bird flew
by.

"I said a preacher, sir. You've got a voice that carries
well. You pronounce your words clearly and with unusua
emphasis. I heard you distinctly way down the road."

"A-uh," Joseph was struck speechless. He didn't know
what to say. In stiff silence he stared at the man, then
he said in a quick, curious voice, "My name is Armstrong,
and what's yours?"

"My name is Henry Hews. I live back three miles
past Green Top. I've been by before. Nice place you
have here. Renting, I suppose?"

"Renting—yes, sir, but we'll be moving on our own
place by spring."

"That's nice. Well, I'll be moving on. I'm on my way
to town."

"Walking?"

"Yes, walking this time. I had my old truck over-
hauled, and I'm going in after it."

"You may get wet," Joseph said.

"Wouldn't care. We need a rain."

*   *   *

There it was again—that same sensation like an electric shock surged through his body. Conviction like a mighty hand took hold of Joseph's heart and body. It gripped him tenaciously. It would not let go. The top branches of that tall pine tree swished and twisted this way and that in the wind. Alone it stood in the field; but the trunk remained firm. The wind could not move it. Then there came a stillness in the air. A sudden lull, and the tree branches hung motionless.

"What are you looking at?" Delores stepped to the open door.

So deep was Joseph in thought that he did not hear her.

"He found him in a desert land," he was saying to himself, "and in the waste howling wilderness"; he held his breath, "he led him about, he instructed him, he kept him as the apple of his—"

"Joseph!"

Joseph jumped, "Yes." He turned.

"What are you looking at?"

"Nothing in particular, I guess."

"I heard what the man said to you." Joseph didn't answer. He rubbed one hand over his one eyebrow, and then over the other.

"Don't you think he might be right, Joseph?"

"Delores!" Joseph gathered up the newspaper.

*   *   *

Annie Armstrong was dusting around Bennet's desk when she noticed something white on the floor behind it. Just a scrap of paper. Annie stooped to pick it up. With a little difficulty she pulled it out. It was a letter addressed to Bennet Armstrong, and the name was printed in a strange backhand. She looked at it curiously. The postmark was Chicago, and the date showed it was mailed Oct. 12, four years before. Annie pulled out the letter. On a single white sheet were only a few words, "Meet me at the La Seg-117, 10:30 Fri. S. M."

Annie put the sheet back into the envelope, and laid it on top of the desk. She finished dusting the room, then picked up the envelope once more and looked at it. A perplexed expression crossed her face.

Every night of the week Bennet unlocked his desk and hovered over his books and figures. Always on Saturday nights he studied his Sunday school lesson. He did that as religiously as some folks count their rosary.

He walked briskly across the room and pulled out his key ring and found the key he wanted. He stopped abruptly. He caught his breath and held it awkwardly. His eyes were riveted on the letter on top of his desk. He snatched it and held it before him a moment. He hurried to the bedroom where Annie was preparing to retire early, for she was tired; and she wanted to spend some extra time in prayer tonight.

"What were you doing in my desk?" demanded Bennet angrily.

"I was not in your desk, Bennet."

"You were. Where did this letter come from if you weren't?" he shouted.

"I found it on the floor this morning when I was dusting," Annie said.

"I can't believe that," Bennet panted. "You unlocked my desk."

"How could I without a key?"

"You used a screw driver, or a hair pin, or some other key."

"No, indeed, Bennet," Annie said wearily. "I've never unlocked your desk. Not once. I don't even know where

ou keep the key. And anyway, why are you so upset
hen one of your letters fell out in some way?"

"Where was it?" he demanded.

"Come in here, and I'll show you right where it was,"
nd Annie stooped down and showed him exactly. She
ut her finger on the very spot where she had found it.

"And how many others have you found like that?" he
napped.

"None," said Annie. "That's the first and only one.
3ut why are you so upset, Bennet? Who is S. M.?"

"S.M?" shouted Bennet. He sniffed for a little, and
aid with a forced, sheepish grin, "S. M. stands for Squire
McCracken, of course. Who else could it stand for?"

A tense pause followed.

"Who do you suppose it stands for?" Bennet laughed
ut loud now. "Thought you had something on me now,
lidn't you?" And he tore the letter in bits and threw it
nto the waste-paper basket.

After Annie walked away, she heard Bennet unlock his
lesk, and half an hour later she thought she heard him
pen the stove, and she thought she heard him light a
natch.

*   *   *

A mother's love is one of the strongest forces in the
vorld; but a mother's prayers are stronger yet. Before
:he letter came, Joseph knew he had grieved the heart of
:he most priceless human influence of his life. It came on
Saturday. His mind roiled with excitement, a heavy
veight lodged in his breast, and sweat trickled down his
iandsome face as he unfolded the tear-stained sheets.

"My dear, dear Joseph." With an odd, fascinated
look in his eyes he gazed lingeringly on those four words.
She had never before used two dears.

"Read it out loud, Joseph," Delores said softly. There
was blank astonishment in her soft eyes, for never before

had Joseph hesitated to read his letters out loud to her?
What held him?

"Maybe—I'd better read it to myself first," he said
in a voice that was shockingly tense for Joseph.

"Why, Joseph!" Her voice was almost inaudible, and
a dazed, unbelieving expression crossed her pretty face.
He had never kept anything from her. Never. They had
promised to tell each other everything. Delores knew
Joseph had been hurt by an unkind remark from a brother
in the church; but it wasn't Brother Collins. She had
reminded Joseph over and over of that. She knew Joseph
had written to his mother; but she hadn't read the letter
over. She seldom did, but always and always they read
to each other letters from home. What was wrong?
What held him? Her eyes widened. She took a step
toward him. He dare not ignore her.

"Why, Joseph!" she repeated in a low, hurt tone.
"You're not keeping something from me I ought to know,
are you?"

A queer, almost ironical smile crossed Joseph's face.
He had never smiled like that before.

"You won't keep something from me, dear?" she said,
cleverly probing him.

"I couldn't if I tried, Delores," he answered at length.
"Here, you read it to me. It's from Mother."

"My dear, dear Joseph," Delores read. "Your letter
was shocking. It cannot be—it dare not be that you
would give up."

"Why, Joseph!" Delores shifted her glance from the
paper to her husband, who was nervously biting his lip.

"Go on," he said.

"Give up?" gasped Delores. "You mean, give up the
Lord? You didn't write that to your mother, did you,
Joseph?"

"Go on," he said huskily.

"But Joseph! Your poor mother. Think how that must have made her feel. You surely didn't mean it!"

"Go on, Delores," he repeated.

She began where she left off.

"Think of all you've already endured from little up. Why would you allow anyone to discourage you now after the Lord has been so good to you? It will kill me, Joseph, if you turn aside now. It was true in Joseph's day that his hardest trials and severest temptations came through his own brethren. Remember the way you talked to me at the top of the stairs the night Father told you to—"

Joseph's head dropped in his hands, for he was crying. "Stop!" he choked. "Stop! I can't bear the rest now. Oh, God," he sobbed, "forgive me—forgive me."

"Joseph," cried Delores, hurrying to him. She put an arm around his neck. "I won't be homesick any more if you get over this being discouraged. You must have told your mother all—"

"I told her too much," he said remorsefully, "but then I guess it's what I had to do to help me over this. She knows me better than anyone else. Someone is knocking. Delores, you go to the door. I'll have to wash my face."

"Is Mr. Armstrong at home?" A tall, thin man stood outside.

"Yes, he is, Mr. Cornstalk. Come in. Take a chair. He'll be in soon."

CHAPTER LX

Joseph heard the name, and it sent a slightly unpleasant sensation through him. Had he come now to rebuke him further?

"Good evening, Joseph," spoke Mr. Cornstalk, almost pleasantly. "Here's a receipt for your tithe offering."

"But you didn't need to come over just for this," Joseph said.

"I was going by anyway. We decided to send $100.00 to South American Missions, $100.00 to the Indian Orphanage, $75.00 for Colportage work, and $75.00 to the Bladford Home for the Aged. Is this satisfactory with you?"

"I told you your committee could decide what to do with it. It belongs to the Lord, and I gave it for the Lord's work."

Mr. Cornstalk scratched his head and put on his hat. "Never heard tell of such—but good night. Nice evening outside, nice evening," he said as he walked away.

Joseph waited until the brother was out of sight, then closed the door slowly.

"Where's Mama's letter, Delores?" he asked. "I want to read the rest of it."

"Don't you think, Joseph, that he came to sorta apologize for what he said the other night?"

"Did you think he was apologizing?"

"Well, not exactly, but maybe he wanted to and just couldn't, or didn't know how."

"Maybe so, but he don't need to. I—I got a blessing out of keeping my promise, and I doubt if he's ever had that blessing. I must write Mother another letter tonight."

Joseph sat with his elbows on the table and the letter before him. Every now and then as Delores moved

420

about at her work, she heard Joseph blowing his nose; and when she came into the room his head was on the table buried in his right arm.

"Don't cry, Joseph," she said, softly brushing her hand over his hair.

"I guess that's what I ought to do," he said at length. 'I ought to stick my head in a hole. Put the letter away. If I'm ever tempted again to give up over something George Cornstalk says, I'll get it out and read it."

It was late when Joseph sealed the letter to his mother. There were pages and pages.

The following week, Joseph was informed that he was appointed teacher of the older men's class in Sunday school.

Then the telegram came.

"Mother passed away early this morning. Funeral Friday.

"J. B. Armstrong."

Joseph stood speechless and stunned. His heart seemed to pound violently with every tick of the clock. After a prolonged silence he folded Delores in his arms, and hot tears rolled down his sun-tanned cheeks and fell on her thick blond hair.

"How glad I am—how glad I am I wrote her that last letter," he cried brokenly.

"Yes—yes," whispered Delores, "so am I."

*　　*　　*

It seemed the train would never get them there.

"Will we go straight to your home, or mine, Joseph?"

"Father has never yet invited us to come there."

"But the telegram surely meant come, don't you think?"

"I suppose so. I'll call Father when we get there."

But it was not necessary. Jeddie Bays was at the depot waiting.

"How did you know we'd be on this train?" Delore
asked.

"I just figured you'd be. Since it's so late and you'
tired you'll go home with me for the night. I talked t
your father this morning, Joseph, and he said it woul
be quite all right. Let me take Danny. No? You won
come to Grandpa? Don't know me at all? My, how he'
changed. A big boy already! Won't come to Grandp;
Bays? Well, well. I'll get you tomorrow. Yes, I will!'
and Jeddie Bays' voice sounded a wee bit hurt.

"Can you tell us how Mother died?" Joseph inquired
anxiously. He could scarcely speak for the lump in hi
throat.

"I guess her heart just wore out, Joseph," Jeddie saic
feelingly, as he put a strong hand on Joseph's shoulder

"Well, was she down sick in bed?"

"I don't think so, Joseph. She was in church Sunday
morning; but she must have been feeling bad then, fo;
Mary said she noticed several times she sorta gaspec
for breath."

The next morning right after breakfast Joseph anc
Delores went over.

"Father." Bennet himself opened the door. Joseph held
out his hand and his father shook it awkwardly. There
was Aunt Hepsi sitting stiffly in a rocking chair, a gray
fringed shawl pinned around her shoulders, long full
skirts hanging to the floor; the same Aunt Hepsi, but
her streaked gray hair was now white. Virginia and
Lowell kissed Joseph, and each cried on his strong
shoulder; then Aunt Sara came in. In the next room
was Uncle Tom Bradly, Lottie Ashelford, Mrs. Lanyard,
Katy Bantum, Bessie Wiggers, Uncle Timothy, and
Lois Doane. Somehow the sight of these good friends
had a strengthening effect on Joseph. He had dreaded

ɔming home if Mother wouldn't be there to greet him.
˙he thought made him sick and weak all over.

"You want to see your mother," whispered Aunt Sara,
nd she led the way into the living room.

Joseph did not cry outright, but through his silent,
ɔlinding tears he looked at the peaceful, smiling face of
is mother. She had on a soft gray silk dress he had never
:en her wear.

"She looks like an angel," he whispered, and he placed
is big warm hand over her slender cold ones.

"Yes, she does," Delores whispered. "An angel
ɔuldn't look sweeter. How happy she must be!"

After everyone else had gone out, Joseph stood by
he casket a long time. He could not quit looking at her
appy face. Just what all he said no one knows but God
nd the angels, but it almost seemed that when he walked
way and came back again, the smile on her lips was a
ttle more marked.

Hundreds of people who had learned to love Annie
tokes Armstrong were waiting in the church in the vale
ɔ pay their last respects. A holy hush filled the audito-
ium. The aged Brother Grissley Steward, though white-
aired and feeble, quoted from memory the entire 116th
'salm, slowly, distinctly, impressively; and so quiet was
he audience that every one in the house heard him. At
he fifteenth verse he hesitated and repeated it over,
"Precious in the sight of the Lord is the death of his
aints," and he looked down at the coffin below him.
Γhen Herbert Lanyard preached, not loud, not dramatic,
ɔut with a tranquil fervency Joseph would never forget.
Near the close of his message he read a poem:

Mother Has Fallen Asleep

"Mother was tired and weary,
　　Weary with toil and pain;
Put by her glasses and rocker,
　　She will not need them again.
Into Heaven's mansions she's entered,
　　Never to sigh or to weep;
After long years with life's struggles,
　　Mother has fallen asleep."

Joseph covered his face with his handkerchief. Benne looked straight ahead.

"Near other loved ones we'll lay her,
　　Low in the churchyard to lie,
And though our hearts are near broken,
　　Yet we would not question, 'Why?'
She will not rest 'neath the grasses,
　　'Though o'er her dear grave they'll creep;
She has gone into the Kingdom,
　　Mother has fallen asleep."

Joseph was shaking with sobs. Bennet folded hi arms and bowed his head slightly.

"Rest the tired feet now forever;
　　Dear wrinkled hands are so still.
Blast of the earth shall no longer
　　Throw o'er our loved one a chill.
Angels through Heaven will guide her;
　　Jesus will still bless and keep.
Not for the world would we wake her,
　　Mother has fallen asleep."

"No! Not for the world!" said Joseph, amid his tears.

"Beautiful rest for the weary,
    Well-deserved rest for the true,
When our life's journey is ended
    We shall again be with you.
This helps to quiet our weeping,
    Hark! Angel music so sweet!
He giveth to His beloved,
    Beautiful, beautiful sleep."

Bennet raised his head and looked straight forward. He drew a long, deep breath. Soon it would be over.

Hundreds — actually hundreds of people shook Joseph's hand and Delores's, and extended their sympathy, and reminded Joseph that his mother was a wonderful little woman. He appreciated their sympathy, and in most cases he felt certain it was heartfelt and genuine, but he did not need to be reminded of the fact that his mother was a good woman. He knew it. Never before was he so sure of it as now. Every caress, every kind word, every sacrifice, every prayer, every smile she had ever given him loomed before him as a magnetic spiritual force which had helped him grow into the Christian man he was. Her lips were closed in death, her hands stiff and cold; but her gentle words rang in his ears like sweet music, and her letters of motherly concern and admonition were at home put away in safe-keeping where he could read them again and again. If only he had just one such letter from Father.

Brother Lanyard stood waiting to speak to him. "You'll be staying over Sunday, I suppose?"

"Yes."

"I'd like you to give a talk after the Sunday-school hour on Sunday morning if you feel you—"

"Brother Lanyard—it's not that I wouldn't be glad to if I could control myself."

"I understand, Joseph. That's all right. I buried a mother, too, one day and I know just how you feel. I only thought if you could talk you would have some wonderful things to tell us how the Lord has been dealing with you."

"Why, have you heard?" Joseph took a step backward. Had his mother told Brother Lanyard? Horror struck him to the heart. Delores caught his hand and pressed it.

"I haven't heard anything in particular, but I just know, 'For whom the Lord loveth, he chasteneth; and scourgeth every son whom he receiveth,' and 'He will try us as gold is tried'; and again He says that we are to rejoice when we are partakers of Christ's sufferings, that when His glory shall be revealed we may be glad with exceeding joy. Those who can stand such things are His beloved—His chosen, and you're one of those He's called, aren't you, Joseph?"

A terrible obstruction came into Joseph's breast and extended up into his throat. It would choke him. It would suffocate him. He could not speak, but Brother Lanyard was holding his hand and waiting for an answer. Tears trickled down Joseph's hot cheeks, and he covered his face with his handkerchief. Why did Brother Lanyard say that?

"You need not answer, Joseph," he said warmly. "We'd like to have you folks come to our place for dinner Sunday. We've already invited your father and Virginia and Lowell."

"They're coming?"

"Yes, they said they would. This has been hard on Virginia. We want to do what we can to make it easier for her."

"That's kind of you. It is all right with you, Delores?"

"Your folks are invited too," Brother Lanyard said.

"Oh, then I'll be so glad to come. Thanks. Mother thinks our stay at home will be too short."

"I suppose everybody would like you to come, but I now how you feel."

* * *

Monday came. They would soon start their long trip back home. Joseph tossed almost all of the night. His father, as always, was cold and unapproachable, even on the day of the funeral. He talked to others, but not to Joseph. He spoke only when he had to. What could Joseph do to break down this awful barrier between them. He must do something! He could not go back without at least trying to be reconciled. If it was anyone else but his own father, maybe it would be easier. If he could only put his finger on the day when this wall between them started. But he couldn't! As far back as he could remember it had been growing higher, wider, and less destructible. Today it seemed insurmountable. It loomed up before him like a wall whose foundation went to the beginning of time.

Sometime before dawn Joseph got out of bed and dropped on his knees by the window, the window above the strawberry patch. Delores and Danny Gene were both sound sleep. The clock downstairs struck four. Somehow that clock always had a stimulating effect on Joseph. Every sound and every smell about Jeddie Bays's home effected him that way. It always had. It was here he had found love; true, satisfying, enduring love that he had craved for. He hadn't been disappointed in Delores, nor in his father-in-law. If Father wouldn't warm up to him, at least he had Jeddie's confidence and respect. Father had scarcely noticed dear little bright-eyed Danny, though everyone else had.

Joseph did not wear his feelings on his coat sleeve either, but his Father's ignoring attitude touched him.

Of course it did. Delores shed a few tears over the fact but she dried them when she thought of Joseph's prayer before they went to the marriage altar. She had married Joseph in pure, undefiled, unadulterated, unalterable love, and in patient hope that Bennet would someday be won. She had seldom complained. She had never grumbled. She had never flung it in his face. Delores had been a true wife in every sense of the word. More than that, she had exceeded his expectations. The only time she had disagreed with him was when he got discouraged over what George Cornstalk had said so bluntly. Even though she agreed it was both unkind and unjust, she still insisted that the injury wasn't sufficient to cause Joseph to feel so discouraged. How she talked to Joseph that night! How straight from the shoulder she talked to him. Dear, faithful, honest Delores! As Joseph knelt by the window above the strawberry patch, he thanked God first of all for her.

He met his father in the morning at the yard gate.

"Father," he said, "I'd like to talk to you a little if you're not too busy?"

"Too busy?" scowled Bennet. "I'm always a busy man. Have you ever seen me idle?"

"No, Father, never."

"What is it? If it's money you need, I haven't got it. This funeral—"

"No, I didn't come to ask for money," answered Joseph, trying to stay calm. "I came to try to make reconciliation with you before we go back."

Bennet shifted from one foot to the other, and blinked.

"Reconciliation?" he asked perversely, squinting both eyes. "I don't know what you're talking about. That sounds bad. That sounds like we've been a couple of children and had a quarrel. I don't know of anything I've quarreled over with you."

"But, Father," continued Joseph seriously, "there isn't the love and harmony between us there ought to be."

Bennet looked up sharply. He coughed. He rubbed his large Roman nose. He seemed to be fumbling for words.

"Well," he said at length, "things might be different if you had taken my advice. You married against my wishes."

"I know that, Father, but I'll never say I'm sorry for that. I married the one I loved, and I married in the will of the Lord. Delores is a wonderful wife. You're not reconciled to that yet, even if I'm satisfied?"

"How can I be reconciled to something I'm not satisfied with?" asked Bennet resentfully.

"But I'm the one who lives with her, Father. Aren't you glad that I'm happy with her?"

Bennet did not answer.

"Anyway, Father, before I ever went with Delores, you were cold and distant toward me for some reason."

"Cold and distant?" shouted Bennet. "Why bring up the past? Did you expect me to fondle over you like your mother always did? That isn't what fathers are for. They're to show their boys how to work; and if you're making good today, in spite of the fact that you've married one of Jeddie Bays's girls, you ought to thank God I taught you how to work."

"I do," Joseph said. The lump in his throat got bigger and harder. A sickening, sickening thought that his father would never be different, overwhelmed him with a crushing grief. Disappointment surely was his portion to suffer.

"Well, I just came to tell you, Father," Joseph said sadly, "that I hold nothing against you."

"That's fine," hacked Bennet.

"And before we go back I wish I could know you've got nothing against me. If I've wronged you in any way, I ask your forgiveness."

Joseph waited, but his father did not answer. He bent over and pulled up a blade of grass and tore it in pieces.

Joseph waited.

"I wish you'd write to us sometimes now since Mama's gone."

"I'm no hand at writing letters. Never was. Virginia can write."

"But that's not you, Father."

Bennet laughed.

"No," he said, "Virginia's not me, and I doubt if she ever will be."

"Mama was a wonderful woman," Joseph said reverently.

"I've heard nothing else since the day she passed away," his father said peevishly. "Just as though I didn't know that when I married her. Why are people forever telling me that? Of course she was a good woman, and the good Lord took her where such good women belong."

"We'll be leaving tomorrow. Good-by, Father." Joseph held out his hand. "Come to see us sometime if you can."

Bennet took Joseph by the hand and shook it very, very moderately. "I doubt if I'll have a chance to get away much now. Better go in and say good-by to Virginia and your Aunt Hepsi. She's leaving today."

"I will." And with a heavy heart Joseph went toward the house. When he came out, his father was not in sight.

CHAPTER LXI

"Many men owe the grandeur of their lives to their tremendous difficulties."—Spurgeon.

Joseph found real joy in teaching that class of men. One day he overheard someone say, "That Joseph Armstrong would really make a preacher, if he only had an education."

Again Joseph was struck to the heart.

The second baby boy came. When Sherman cried for an early morning feeding, Joseph got up and studied until breakfast. He bought a Bible dictionary, an encyclopedia, a concordance, a topical text book, a harmony of the Gospels, and studied his Bible diligently, devotedly. That hunger for knowledge had never been satisfied. The more he learned, the more he wanted to learn of the truths and deep mysteries of that Book of books his mother had taught him to believe and trust in, if all else failed.

Delores leafed through his Bible one day and noticed it was full of marks and underlinings. The gilt was worn off the pages, and on the fly leaf she noticed, in line beside two dates, two Scripture references, Genesis 49:22 and Deuteronomy 32:10-12. She observed a steadily growing stability and deep joy in Joseph, that even showed on his face. His devotion to God seemed deep-rooted and firm. How happy she was!

The next year Joseph got votes for teacher from every class in the Sunday school. The teen-ager boys wanted Joseph Armstrong for their teacher. The young fathers voted for Joseph Armstrong; the young mothers, the old men, the grandmothers, the high-school pupils. After a long discussion by the superintendent and pastor, it was decided that Joseph Armstrong should be appointed

substitute teacher for the entire Sunday school. Tha
meant that before the year was over, he had taught ever
class in the school, from the first class in the primar
department to the grandfather class upstairs. The nex
year he was elected assistant superintendent, and alsc
substituted frequently as teacher. He was a busy man.

*   *   *

In the mail that came one day in August was a marriag
announcement of Freddie Stokes to Lillian Bond; anc
in the envelope was a note which read, "If we take ou
trip west, we may drop in to see you."

"I hope they do," said Delores.

"I hope, too, they do," added Joseph.

That same week Delores had a letter from her mother
which bore the sad news that Brother Grissley Steward
had died; the glad news that Art Olterham was keeping
company with Martha Denlinger; and the shocking news
that Bennet Armstrong had his farm up for sale, and had
told someone he would probably retire and buy a property
in town. "I suppose it is best," the letter said, "since
Virginia wants to go back to her place, and Lowell is of
age now."

Joseph sat in deep thought. Father must have decided
this very recently, for the last letter from Virginia made
no mention of the fact.

Yet another surprise came to Joseph that week in
August, when Brother and Sister Collins called on them
one evening.

"At the conference we just came from," Brother Collins said, "we were granted permission to ordain an
assistant pastor for our congregation."

Joseph's hands fell limp at his sides, and a fear clutched
at his throat. He had never before, not even in his boyhood days, felt a fear equal to it, not even in the dark.

It was not just a timidity or dread, but actual panic that seized him. The color left his face, and he stared at the wall past Brother Collins in both wonder and consternation.

"I don't know whether you know it or not, Joseph," continued Brother Collins, not seeming to notice (and yet he did), "but a number of brethren in the congregation have already expressed themselves to me that you have the qualifications for such an office."

Joseph gasped. He sat up very straight, and looked Brother Collins straight in the eyes.

"That's where they are all wrong, Brother Collins," he said emphatically. "I am not qualified."

"You should know, Joseph," the other said, "but would you mind telling me why you say that?"

"You surely know I have no education, Brother Collins. No one would want to listen to a man preach who can't even speak good English, and who's never gone to high school. Nowadays people want to hear a man who has something to tell, and how can he tell it unless he knows it?"

Joseph's face turned red. It felt hot. His heart was pounding madly in his breast, and yet above it all, he could hear that tender voice calling him by name outside the barn. Oh, if he could only forget it like one does a dream. It was real—as real as life itself, and he had heard it when he was awake. He had gone to the house that night—that very hour, and told his mother. "And was it about five o'clock?" his mother had asked him. Oh, that memorable night—that remarkable, unforgettable night when his mother had said, "Someday, Joseph, I believe it will be revealed to you."

There are men who would give their right arm for such an experience to bring into memory. There are thousands who would be glad to give a small fortune to hear the voice of God calling them by name just once, and now Joseph felt like withstanding, even openly resisting it.

"I did not come here tonight to distress or disturb you in any way, Joseph," spoke Brother Collins, "I only came to find out whether or not you've had any personal convictions to preach."

Joseph wanted to scream. He got up and walked across the room. He came back and stood behind his chair.

"The Lord calls men through the church, but before we would allow your name, or any other name, to come before the body as a candidate to be voted on, or before we'd expect a man to enter the lot, we'd first expect to get an expression from him. If you can honestly say you've never had any convictions to preach, of course we'll drop the matter with you. But, if you say—" Brother Collins stopped abruptly, and left the sentence hanging. Once before Joseph had a feeling as if he was being suspended between Heaven and earth, and must light any second. He couldn't hang up there long.

Joseph drew a long, deep breath, and sat down. His body never felt so tired and heavy. His arms and feet felt like lead. His back ached, his head hurt; he felt as if he'd been flogged and pounded from head to foot.

"Well," he said, "I—I," he picked at the corner of the table cloth. "I can't be honest, Brother Collins, and—" his eyes got misty, "and say I've never had a call, but—"

"But what, Joseph?"

"There are those who'd never believe me."

"What makes you say that?"

"One brother in the church evidently thought—" Joseph bit his lip.

"Thought what, Joseph?"

"Thought I was trying to make an impression when I turned in my tithe. God knows, Brother Collins, I didn't do it for that. If I had to buy my way into the favor of the church just to be made a preacher, I hope God puts me down where I belong."

"Why, Joseph—why, Joseph Armstrong, I'm surprised! I knew nothing of this feeling on the part of anyone. Are you sure?" Brother Milton Collins stood up.

"I'm sure. There is no mistake. I was rebuked to my face; but it's past now and I've forgiven the brother, only it had an awful effect on me. For a while I felt confused—whipped, and afraid to face the future."

"Why, Joseph!" gasped Brother Collins. "Why didn't you come and tell me?"

"I couldn't. I thought maybe you knew it."

"A lot of things can happen in a congregation that the pastor doesn't find out about."

"I'm—I'm thoroughly ashamed," Joseph said sadly, still looking down, "but at a rash moment I even wrote and told my mother I felt like giving up."

"What?" shouted Brother Collins. "You surely didn't mean it, did you?"

Joseph's face burned, and his soul burned within him.

"No," he said, "at my best moments, how could I mean such a thing? I've asked God to forgive me, and I made it right with Mother. I—I shouldn't have mentioned it, I know, but all my life, Brother Collins, from my earliest childhood, I've had opposition from—my—father."

"Yes."

"You know?" Joseph bent forward in his chair.

"I wasn't altogether blind when you lived here."

"You saw?"

Brother Collins laughed very, very softly. It was a sympathetic, understanding laugh, however.

"I never told," Joseph said. "Mama never told. How could you tell?"

"Reading character comes by experience, I guess," Brother Collins said; then he added shortly, "You say you've felt a call from God?"

That heavy feeling in Joseph's breast was suddenly lifted.

"Long ago," he said in almost a whisper.

"Then don't try to discredit it, my boy. You had a wonderful, godly mother who, I'm sure, spent hours in prayer for her children."

Joseph was crying now.

"And anyway, Joseph, it's true the greatest preachers that have ever lived are those who have gone through extreme difficulties, and suffered trials and disappointments in life. Don't you know, the preacher who can shed a genuine, sympathizing tear helps more souls than the one who can only titter and joke? Did you ever think of that, Joseph?"

"No, I never did exactly."

"But you believe it, don't you?"

"I have to," answered Joseph.

* * *

On a table in front of the church were three books exactly alike. The song was ended, and the prayer had been offered. A warm sun was shining on the mountains in the distance, but no soft rain was falling that Sunday morning. A few clouds dotted the sky. Three young men sat on the front seat waiting. Each felt his own pulse beating fast, and each looked straight ahead in holy wonder as Bro. Collins nodded to Joseph Armstrong first to come forward and choose a book. The second went forward, and then the third. All three opened their books at the same time, and in the front of the one book was a slip of paper. It was in Joseph Armstrong's book! The lot had fallen on Joseph, he was to be the minister.

The battle in his soul was not over yet. The fact that

he had no education stared him in the face like a hideous monster which told him with fire-flaming eyes, and hissing lips, he'd make a failure as a preacher before he ever tried. "Most of the people will laugh at you," it said. "Some will get up and walk out before you've said a dozen words; and those who stay will stay to criticize and condemn. Why didn't you take the middle book and avoid all this? You had a feeling that that paper was in that book, didn't you?"

What Brother Collins said next, Joseph didn't know. That terrible monster had him panting with terror. All he knew was that the services were over and people were shaking hands with him, and some were saying, "God bless you"; and one old lady said, "I'll stand by you, Brother Joseph"—some kind-voiced grandma who knew his first name, but he was too dazed to know who it was. Then he heard little Sherman cry at the front of the church; and when he looked up, Delores was waiting patiently by the door, Sherman in her arms, and Danny Gene at her side. He noticed a strange, sweet, serious expression on his wife's face that reminded him of the look he had often seen on his mother's face.

"She's making a good mother for my little boys," he said to himself.

"Are you ready to go, Daddy?" she asked looking up at Joseph trustingly.

"Yes. Let me carry Sherman to the car."

"We're almost the last ones out," she said. "We'll have a late dinner today."

"I don't feel as if I can eat a bit of dinner," Joseph said, as they started down the road.

"Why, Joseph?"

"This has upset me."

"Why? I thought you felt God's leading?"

"I did, Delores. It's not that."

"What then?"

"The people. No one will have any confidence in me. Who am I but a poor stick who's never had a chance to go—"

"Joseph! Daddy! Don't talk like that. I have confidence in you. Don't you trust God that He can help you?"

"He'll not only have to help me; He'll have to do it all, Delores. I'm telling you the truth," and Joseph stepped on the brakes and brought his car to a dead stop. He put his arms up over the steering wheel, and a bewildered, startled look crossed his face. "Unless God helps me out of this, I can't even drive home. I feel just as if I'm down in a deep, dark pit, and I can't pull myself out of it. I'm afraid of the people. I—who am I to be an assistant pastor, when there beside me sat two men, both better qualified than I? Delores, this is —I—I—"

Suddenly in the eastern sky the clouds parted, and a blinding light, dazzling white, reached from Heaven to earth right in front of the car, and a glory that few saints have ever experienced, rested for a moment on Joseph's face, and seemed to reach out over all his future days, giving him the assurance that the Father who called him would help him in his work. So marvelous was this heavenly manifestation, that it was to Joseph like the Shekinah glory from the mercy seat, reflecting from the overshadowing cherubims; and when the light had disappeared, the very presence of God filled his heart with great joy; and that Spirit bore witness with his own spirit that his conscience was clear, and his purpose in life pure.

CHAPTER LXII

Joseph drew a deep, deep breath and his arms dropped from the steering wheel.

"What—was—that—Joseph!" Delores asked under her breath and as she spoke she clutched his arm. Terror and sudden confusion painted her face white.

"Did—did you see it?" he whispered.

"It wasn't lightning, was it?" she choked.

Joseph shook his head. For a few seconds he sat gazing up into the sky at the place where the clouds had parted. The translation of that strange sign language was instantaneous and correct. He stepped on the starter. He shifted gears. The car moved on down the road.

Above the storm of his own self will, his strong deep personal feelings, his violent fear of people, the clamor and outcries of public opinions, the church's demands— above all these the spirit of the beautiful, blessed, submissive Christ was expressed in every line on his face. Clear and strong he seemed to hear words from the Master's own lips meeting his every and ever-present need. His comforter had come. He knew He was with him. He knew He was for him, and in him. He drove home a different person than he had ever been before.

Two weeks passed. Joseph opened his gilt-edged Bible, and, taking his place behind the sacred desk in the chancel, he preached his first sermon. A holy smile lit up his serious face, with the peculiar contentment that comes after the complete commitment of one's life to God through Christ. His leadings had been definite and unmistakable.

For a text he read from the book of Ecclesiastes the twelfth chapter, that ancient Old Testament exhortation to "Remember now thy Creator in the days of thy youth." Though his legs trembled, no one knew it but himself. With a distinct appeal to the young people present that

morning, he spoke in a sincere and impressive manner,
for thirty minutes, using only a few notes besides his
Bible. His message pleaded for the dedication of growing lives in the freshness and vigor of youth, for the
surrender of those lives to God's will, then for courage to
go on in spite of trials and discouragements or even opposition. Every eye was riveted on Joseph Armstrong. No
one sneered. No one laughed. Brother Collins sat with
his lips slightly parted in mute astonishment. He had
had fond hopes for Joseph, but the message far exceeded
his highest expectations. For months he had felt a deep
heart-yearning for ministerial help in his growing congregation. He had dreamed of a young brother to assist
him, but even in his most intimate and personal petitions
he had not prayed for a helper that could speak in so
challenging and forceful a manner as this. He would
have to work to keep ahead of this young assistant. He
was quite taken aback. Joseph's first sermon was splendid,
and penetratingly spiritual. Brother Collins felt tears
creeping down his cheeks. Joseph was saying things that
stirred his finest emotions. He was expressing old ideas
in such a new and different way. He spoke in common,
simple sentences, yet in such an abundant, graceful, illu-
minating way as though he knew from experience.

"And now friends," Joseph said, closing his Bible
and looking straight into the eyes of the congregation,
"Paul's letter to the church at Corinth comes to a conclu-
sion by saying, that we are to be on the watch, to stand
firm in our faith; act like men; be strong; do everything
with love. To those of you who have already given your
hearts to God, this passage should very fittingly follow
the one in Ecclesiastes I have quoted. Now, while heads
are bowed will you listen to the words of this poem which
has become a part of my own life in the very recent past."
Strong and distinct, in a rich, deep voice, Joseph read the
poem from a green-backed hymnbook.

O Jesus, I have promised
  To serve Thee to the end;
Be Thou forever near me,
  My Master and my Friend:
I shall not fear the battle
  If Thou art by my side,
Nor wander from the pathway
  If Thou wilt be my Guide.

O let me feel Thee near me;
  The world is ever near;
I see the sights that dazzle,
  The tempting sounds I hear;
My foes are ever near me,
  Around me and within;
But, Jesus, draw Thou nearer,
  And shield my soul from sin.

O let me hear Thee speaking
  In accents clear and still,
Above the storms of passion,
  The murmurs of self-will:
O speak to reassure me,
  To hasten or control.
O speak, and make me listen,
  Thou Guardian of my soul.

O Jesus, Thou hast promised
  To all who follow Thee,
That where Thou art in glory
  There shall Thy servant be;
And, Jesus, I have promised
  To serve Thee to the end;
O give me grace to follow
  My Master and my Friend.

Let us sing the song together, and then Brother Collins
will close the meeting as he sees fit."

A number of people (not many) shook hands with Joseph, and commented on his sermon. He did not tarry long.

At the dinner table he was very reserved, and took sparingly of his favorite dishes.

"Are you not feeling well?" Delores asked anxiously.

"I'm not exactly sick," Joseph answered after a brief pause."

"What then, Daddy?" she asked, reaching over and touching his hand lightly. She waited. She searched his face thoughtfully.

"I must give myself more to prayer before I ever try it again," came Joseph's answer. He shook his head. He cleared his throat. "I dare not think of the way I preached today." His face colored and he lowered his head into his hand.

"Preached?" cried Delores somewhat stunned.

"It was so far from what I wanted it to be. I wonder if I can ever get up there again." Joseph took out his handkerchief and wiped his entire face.

"It was good, Joseph," Delores pulled his hand away from his face and looked straight into his deep blue eyes.

"How can you say that?" he asked huskily.

"I mean it, Joseph. For the first sermon, I wasn't disappointed."

"I was. And I'm afraid maybe God was too," he said quietly. "I must give myself to more prayer. Since I haven't the education I need, I must get a double preparation in that then. And remember, Delores, I miss Mother's prayers for me." Joseph swallowed hard twice.

"I believe that, Joseph," Delores answered softly, "but while you were making your vows, I made some too."

"You did?" Both of Joseph's hands dropped, and he looked full into her honest, open face.

"I did, Joseph, and by God's help I mean to keep every one of them."

"I presume from what you've been saying, this is not like playing church then?" He put his handkerchief into his pocket.

"Like playing church! Why Joseph Armstrong! What makes you say such a thing?"

"I was—I mean, I'm trying to tell you, Delores, how I appreciate your attitude. I do." Joseph said it seriously and without reserve.

"Am I surprising you then?" Her voice was on the verge of faltering. Neither was eating. "Look, Danny is falling asleep in his chair. Take him in to his bed, Daddy."

"Delores," Joseph said in a deep voice impressively, "you are always surprising me. I mean, dear," and he gathered Danny Gene in his strong arms tenderly, "if it's true that a man will never rise any higher than his wife will let him—it won't be your fault if I don't make good." He walked toward the bedroom door, and her eyes followed him all the way.

"I hope you will pray for me every day," he added when he returned. He brushed her shoulder with his hand as he passed.

"Did you throw the cover over him, Daddy?"

"Yes. Did you say you had a mince pie warming in the oven, Delores?"

"Oh, Joseph! I forgot all about it. I didn't even smell it. Do you want a piece? It's awfully hot now."

"Give me a piece. I'll wait until it's cooled. So you really don't feel I made a complete failure today?"

"Why, Daddy! Why, Joseph! No. No one thought that, I'm sure."

"Well, I know I must pray more, and study, to be any good at winning of hearts to God. If I can somehow have the spirit of Brother Grissley and Uncle Tom, and the wisdom of both, and the patience of Brother Lanyard, and the kindness of Brother Collins—"

"And the understanding of your mother," Delores added; "well then, Joseph, you'll be a great preacher some day."

The art of preaching is not learned in a day, and it takes years to become an artist in any of the fine arts. The secret of Joseph Armstrong's radiant personality was not found by following a formula in a preacher's manual. The light on his face, the buoyancy of his spirit, were an inspiration to everyone. His counsel and advice were sought by many. All those who listened to his sermons were refreshed and strengthened, and by the end of the first year several dozen had publicly confessed Christ under his preaching. He showed an unusual touch of personal interest in the young people of the congregation, and his sympathy and love gave them both hope and courage for service. He visited the sick and aged, always lingering at their bedside or chair to offer a fitting prayer. He learned the names of all the children in every family in the congregation, and took special pains to notice each one. He went where there was sorrow, trouble, sickness, and misfortune without being told to go. He had a way of making the old folks feel they were essential, and the children they were necessary, too. He was not only a leader with young and old, but also a good supporter to others in their plans for church activities.

The day came when Joseph got a call to hold a series of evangelistic meetings in a small church about two hundred miles from Admore.

"Are you going to go?" asked Delores.

"Shall I?" Joseph folded the letter and put it on the table.

"When do they want you to come?"

"The first of October."

"Could you get away then?"

"I'm going to ask you to tell me that."

"Why me, Joseph?"

"I want you to tell me whether or not you could get along without me. As for the farm and stock—well, I've promised to put the Lord's work first."

"And you must put Him before me, too, Joseph. If God tells you to go, I want you to go."

"Delores, why do you talk to me like this?" He stood close to her now.

"Because when you were ordained, Joseph, I made a consecration myself. And I meant it. I still mean it. I want you to be just what God wants you to be, nothing more and nothing less. It will be hard to see you go, of course, but if you can lead one soul to Christ, I will feel well repaid for the sacrifice, if I could call it that."

"Then I'll tell them I will come? But Delores, this will be a new experience for me, and a hard one. Why they ever asked me, I can't imagine."

"You don't need to know, do you, Joseph?"

That was the first, but not the only revival Joseph Armstrong held.

*   *   *

J. Bennet read feverishly in the church papers about his son's success and growing popularity throughout the church. The subject was introduced into many a conversation where he was in the group. Bennet made himself conspicuous for what he did not say. Some would have thought him extremely humble about his son's usefulness, which soon would reach from coast to coast.

The very thing he feared came to pass. The church where Joseph was born, and saved, and baptized, decided to ask him to come back home to conduct a three-weeks' revival. The vote was practically unanimous. Of course no one would have expected Bennet to vote for his own boy. But how could he endure it? How could he possibly undergo three weeks of such agony of soul? Joseph was too young, too inexperienced, too incapable of such a task. The church was unwise and thoughtless in making such a decision. What the church needed was an evangelist with some gray hairs, and one who had proved his loyalty to the doctrines for many years. Delores and the children would likely have to come along, and then folks would be inviting him out here and there for meals with them.

Bennet was nervous and ill at ease. He had worked hard all his life and had never taken special care of his health. At his age one needed, and deserved, a change. He had known plenty of drudgery, plenty! Virginia would be married in a few weeks, and Lowell had already married a sweet-faced little girl of a woman, with big brown eyes, and sealskin hair, whom Bennet didn't like much more than he liked Delores Bays. After all his pleadings and ambitions he had for his children, they insisted on marrying just common clay. Bennet was mortified and vexed. And the fact that Lowell and Virginia were moving out of the state did not make him any happier. Was it Joseph who gave them the fever? Or what? There he was alone in a big house. So why should he stay? What was there to hold Bennet? He was foot-loose now. The property in town could be sold or rented, furnished. Either would be possible and neither would be a money-losing deal.

Before the date of the opening night of the revival, J. B. Armstrong bought a railroad ticket for Toronto and other points north—a vacation to build up his nerves.

CHAPTER LXIII

"We'd better not go along, Joseph."

"But your folks will expect you, I'm sure."

"But listen, Joseph."

"I'm listening," Joseph smiled. Delores seemed so unconsciously serious.

"You can put your whole self into those meetings better if we stay at home."

"I don't know why, Delores."

"If we're along you know we'll sit up and talk every night when you could be praying, or studying, or resting, or talking to someone else in spiritual need. If we go along, the boys will be crawling all over you. And it will cost money if we go."

"But your folks are expecting you. Everyone in the congregation will be asking me about you, and Danny Gene, and Sherman. Here comes the mailman." Joseph hurried to the box and returned with a letter from Jeddie Bays. Neither was completely surprised when it contained a check for Delores to come along and bring the boys. They must come.

Joseph found the hunger of hearts a common condition. He preached with fervor and unusual liberty. The Spirit gave him unfailing utterance, for on the way he received a new anointing for the task. He received it because he asked for it. He felt his nothingness with sharp reality.

Each night his sermon was inspirational, true to the Word of God, and with a deep spiritual background that was not only constructive, but also refining.

Men and women, young and old, felt the touch of conviction that was irresistible. People from far and near packed the building to capacity. Every night Joseph felt the breath of his mother's prayers, and the very atmosphere seemed light and fragrant with the memory of

447

her sweet words and love for him. They permeated all
the space around and above him, and as he unfolded the
Scriptures she had taught him from childhood to love
and believe, he was more and more determined to hold
out faithful to the end, by God's help. The very fact
that once he was tempted to give up made him plunge
more prayerfully and persistently into this soul-saving
achievement. Delores, too, kept herself as much as possible in prayer. Joseph lavished his affections on God.
It made him supremely happy, and her too. That is
what his mother would have wanted him to do, he was
sure. He'd light his candle and let it burn down to the
socket to prove he had truly repented. In the multitude
of faces there was none to mar the freedom with which
he preached. More than once Joseph referred to his
mother's life while tears of sincerity filled his meaningful
eyes. How he longed to meet her someday in that land
of God's tomorrow.

Joseph tried not to act surprised at his father's absence.
He was determined not to let it hurt him. His absence
was much easier to take than his presence would have
been with disregardings and slightings and inconsidera-
tions. Only on very rare occasions did Joseph ever hear
directly from his father. What he heard came through
Virginia, or Lowell, or Uncle Timothy. Joseph knew
nothing of his father's plans or dealings.

Increasingly Joseph's influence grew. His intimacy
with the Master endeared him to many who delighted in
his Christian fellowship. Joseph Armstrong grew
stronger in his ministry because of his constant fellowship
with the Saviour. He loved the lost, the discouraged, the
mistreated, and the needy with a growing, deepening
affection that people felt. He pictured the suffering and
loving Christ as beautiful and chaste as Heaven itself.
Who could resist his invitation? Who could say no to

the measureless height and depth of that wealth of love he preached about?

* * *

"God bless you!" Joseph Armstrong stepped from the platform to meet him, and throwing his arms around the man's neck cried with tears of joy streaming down his warm cheeks.

"Earnie, Earnie, God bless you! Please take a seat right here, and I want to have a talk with you and pray with you after we dismiss."

There is joy in Heaven over one sinner that repenteth, but while Heaven and all the angels rejoice, the servant of God rightfully rejoices also. There is no other joy of the human heart so deep, so sweet, so blessedly satisfying as that.

* * *

The week after Thanksgiving the message came. Joseph was about ready to retire when the phone rang. "What!" Joseph cleared his throat and his hand clutched the receiver. "Will you please repeat, sir."

" 'Bennet Armstrong found dead in Westmore depot. Waiting family instructions. Signed Frederick Victoria, undertaker.' Did you get that, Mr. Armstrong?" asked the telegraph operator.

"I—yes, sir, I got it. When did he die?"

"It doesn't say, Mr. Armstrong."

"Delores."

"What is it, Joseph?" Delores came, half running, "Who died?"

"Father."

"My—father!" cried Delores, "Oh, Joseph! My father!"

"My father," Joseph said huskily. He backed to the wall, and stood leaning hard against it. For a moment he swayed with a sickness of soul he had never known before. He did not feel like crying, as he did when the telegram came that his mother had passed away. He stared at the pattern on the wall until the flowers all began to move toward him.

"Was he sick, Joseph?" Delores broke the silence.

"I don't know."

"Who sent the telegram?"

"I don't know."

"Don't know?"

"I forget—I mean—I'll have to call back. He didn't die at home."

"Where then? I thought Mama said she saw him in church on Sunday."

"He evidently went away again or else—this is—a mistake. There maybe could be another Bennet Armstrong, you know. I think I'll call Uncle Timothy—or your father—and check. Maybe you'd better go on to bed, Delores, or you'll catch a cold. I may be using the phone well up into the night."

There was no mistake. It was Joseph's father who lay cold in death, a handsome, only slightly gray, well-dressed figure in a walnut casket.

* * *

Brother Lanyard preached the funeral sermon. Little did he know of the inner life of the deceased. What did it matter? He preached to the living anyway. All the good things he said fitted someone who had gone on before.

And what was that he was saying, "Death is just a swinging door to push us through to the other side—into another world. There is no escape, for some day we shall be caught in that swinging door, as those in the past thousands of years. And we are now at this moment reminded that another faithful brother has passed through, and will not return. We will miss his face, but it must have pleased the Father to remove him to that better world. So—

"Why be afraid of death as though your life were breath?
Death but anoints your eyes with clay. Oh, glad surprise!

"Why should you be forlorn? Death only husks the corn.
Why should you fear to meet the thresher of the
wheat?

"The dear ones left behind? Oh, foolish one and blind,
A day and you will meet; a night and you will greet."

Brother Lanyard offered prayer, and then they passed
out to the cemetery.

After everything was over, Joseph called Lowell and
Virginia aside and they talked alone, the three of them,
for each had a gnawing pain that they all understood.

"Do you really think?" here Joseph's voice broke, but
with great effort he brought himself under control. "Do
you think," he repeated, "that I really did my duty toward
Father?"

"As far as I know you did, Joseph," Virginia said. "I
offered him a home, but I knew before I mentioned it
that he wouldn't consider it."

"I never asked him to come live with us, but I did
beg him to write and come to visit us, but—" Joseph
shrugged his shoulders.

"I think I did my duty," Lowell said. "Father never
was friendly to Hilda. Joseph, you said you'd never
marry for money, and I didn't either. We're happy, and
I never could make myself tell Hilda everything. What's
the use?"

"What's the use?" added Virginia.

"That's what I wanted to talk to you about in particular, while we're all here together," Joseph said sadly.
"Delores, of course, knows how it went before we were
married, and afterwards. But if Mother could keep her
sorrows to herself, why shouldn't we?"

"Well, I don't ever intend to tell anyone just for the sake of telling," Virginia said in subdued tones. "It wouldn't help any of us, would it?"

"You're right, Virginia," said Joseph. "I simply cannot let myself dwell on the subject, for the kindest words my father ever spoke to me—were said—while I was partly unconscious, and I wouldn't have known for certain he said those—but—Mother told me he did." Joseph could hold himself in no longer. He shook now with sobs uncontrolled. He buried his face in both his hands and covered it with his handkerchief. "You two can't imagine how I feel when I get up into the pulpit—to preach. I can refer to a—mother's love—but never—a —father's. Whenever I see a father playing ball with his boys I—I—could cry—till my heart breaks.

"Well, I've decided long ago," Lowell said, "that if God blesses us with children, I'm going to try—to give them—everything we wanted—and didn't get."

"Father was faithful in going to church," Joseph said. "That is one good thing we can say about him."

"Maybe we'd better go now," Lowell said, looking toward Hilda waiting beside Delores. "I wonder if Father had a will?"

"It doesn't really matter to me," said Joseph frankly. "I'm willing to work for all I get of this world's goods. Mother left us all something worth far more than money."

"That's right," Virginia said, as Heaven's light that had lit Annie Armstrong's sweet face, rested on each of her children's faces, dispelling their gloom. And the Christ she served led them into measureless depths of His love. He made her firstborn, her son Joseph, a mighty man of God, a fruitful bough leading hundreds and hundreds to see that same light.